**Praise for *New York Times* bestselling author
Maya Banks**

"More stories like this will make me a very happy
reader indeed."
—*SmartBitchesTrashyBooks.com* on *The Bride*

"Banks' story has it all: wit, charm, mystery and
sparkling chemistry between the characters."
—*RT Book Reviews* on *Billionaire's Contract Engagement*

"Banks has a top-of-the-line story with opposites
making their way toward a new middle road together."
—*RT Book Reviews* on *Tempted by Her Innocent Kiss*

**Praise for *USA TODAY* bestselling author
Carol Marinelli**

"[Marinelli's] unforgettable characters will compel
readers and pull at their heartstrings."
—*RT Book Reviews* on *An Indecent Proposition*

"Marinelli's *In the Rich Man's World* is a fast-paced read
with exciting characters and some intense emotional
scenes. This page-turner is a great…read."
—*RT Book Reviews*

MAYA BANKS

has loved romance novels from a very (very) early age, and almost from the start, she dreamed of writing them, as well. In her teens she filled countless notebooks with overdramatic stories of love and passion. Today her stories are only slightly less dramatic, but no less romantic.

She lives in Texas with her husband and three children and wouldn't contemplate living anywhere other than the South. When she's not writing, she's usually hunting, fishing or playing poker. She loves to hear from her readers, and she can be found on Facebook, or you can follow her on Twitter (@maya_banks). Her website, www.mayabanks.com, is where you can find up-to-date information on all of Maya's current and upcoming releases.

CAROL MARINELLI

Originally from England, Carol now lives in Melbourne, Australia. She adores going back to the U.K. for a visit—actually, she adores going anywhere for a visit—and constantly (expensively) strives to overcome her fear of flying. She has three gorgeous children who are growing up so fast (too fast—they've just worked out that she lies about her age!) and keep her busy with a never-ending round of homework, sports and friends coming over.

A nurse and an author, Carol writes for the Harlequin Presents and Harlequin Medical Romance lines and is passionate about both. She loves the fast-paced, busy setting of a modern hospital, but every now and then admits it's bliss to escape to the glamorous, alluring world of her Presents heroes and heroines. A bit like her real life actually!

For more on Carol and her latest releases, visit her website, www.carolmarinelli.com.

New York Times Bestselling Author

MAYA BANKS

The Bride

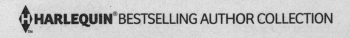
HARLEQUIN® BESTSELLING AUTHOR COLLECTION

Recycling programs
for this product may
not exist in your area.

ISBN-13: 978-0-373-18069-1

THE BRIDE
Copyright © 2013 by Harlequin Books S.A.

The publisher acknowledges the copyright
holders of the individual works as follows:

THE TYCOON'S REBEL BRIDE
Copyright © 2009 by Sharon Long

IN THE RICH MAN'S WORLD
First North American Publication 2005
Copyright © 2005 by The SAL Marinelli Family Trust

This edition published by arrangement with Harlequin Books S.A.

For questions and comments about the quality of this book, please contact us at CustomerService@Harlequin.com.

Printed in U.S.A.

CONTENTS

Dear Reader,

I'm so excited that one of my favorite Harlequin Desire books, *The Tycoon's Rebel Bride*, is being reissued so that readers can revisit beloved characters and that new readers have a chance to meet them for the first time.

Bella has long been one of my favorite heroines that I've ever written. She's smart and sassy but most important, she's determined when it comes to landing the man she loves. It's so much fun to watch how befuddled Theron is by the gorgeous package of dynamite that explodes into his life and completely upends it.

I hope that you'll enjoy reacquainting yourselves with Bella and Theron, and if it's your first encounter with them, I hope you'll enjoy their love story every bit as much as I have.

xoxo

Maya Banks

THE BRIDE

New York Times Bestselling Author

Maya Banks

To Fatin and Lillie, two terrific ladies
I am very privileged to know and call friends

Chapter 1

Theron Anetakis sifted through the mountain of paperwork his secretary had left on his desk for him to read, muttering expletives as he tossed letters left and right. Occasionally one would garner more than a brief glance and then he'd shove it to a separate pile of things requiring his attention. Others, he consigned to the trash can by his feet.

His takeover of the New York offices of Anetakis International hadn't been without its pitfalls. After the discovery that one of the staff members had been selling Anetakis hotel plans to a competitor, Theron and his brothers had cleaned house, hiring new staff. The culprit, Chrysander's former personal assistant, was behind bars after a plea bargain. They had been leery of replacing her and allowing another employee unfettered access to sensitive company information, but in the end, Theron had opted to bring in his secretary from the London office. She was older, stable and most importantly, loyal. Though after the debacle with Roslyn, none of the Anetakis brothers were keen to trust another employee implicitly.

Theron's arrival from London had been met by a pile of documents, contracts, messages and e-mails. Two days later, he was still trying to make sense of the mess. And to think his secretary had already weeded out the majority of the clutter.

He paused over one letter addressed to Chrysander and almost tossed it as junk mail, but yanked it back into his line of vision when he saw what it said. His brow furrowed deeper as he scanned the page, and stretched out his other hand for the phone.

Uncaring of the time difference, or that he would probably wake Chrysander, he punched in the number and waited impatiently for the call to go through. He spared a brief moment of guilt that he would also be disturbing Marley, Chrysander's wife, but hopefully he would pick up the phone before it wakened her.

"This better be damn good," Chrysander growled in a sleepy voice.

Theron didn't waste time with pleasantries. "Who the hell is Isabella?" he demanded.

"Isabella?" There was no doubt as to the confusion in Chrysander's voice. "You're calling me at this hour to ask me about a woman?"

"Tell me…" Theron shook his head. No, Chrysander wouldn't be unfaithful to Marley. Whatever this woman was to Chrysander, it must have been before he met Marley. "Just tell me what I need to know in order to get rid of her," Theron said impatiently. "I've a letter here informing you of her progress, whatever the hell that means, and that she's graduated successfully." Theron's lips thinned in disgust. "*Theos,* Chrysander. Isn't she a bit young for you to have been involved with?"

Chrysander exploded in a torrent of Greek, and Theron held the phone from his ear until the storm calmed.

"I do not like your implication, little brother," Chrysander said in an icy voice. "I am married. Of course I am not involved with this Isabella." And then Theron heard Chrysander's sharp intake of breath. "*Bella.* Of course," he murmured. "I'm not thinking clearly at this hour of the night."

"And I repeat, who is this Bella?" Theron asked, his patience running out.

"Caplan. Isabella Caplan. Surely you remember, Theron."

"Little Isabella?" Theron asked in surprise. He hadn't remembered her at all until Chrysander mentioned her last name. An image of a gangly, preteen girl with ponytails and braces shot to mind. He'd seen her a few times since, but he honestly couldn't conjure an image. He remembered her being shy and unassuming, always trying to fade into the background. She'd been at his parents' funeral, but he'd been too consumed with grief to pay attention to the young woman. How old would she have been then?

Chrysander chuckled. "She's not so little anymore. She will have just graduated. Was doing quite well. Intelligent girl."

"But why are you getting a report on her?" Theron asked. "For God's sake, I thought she might be a former mistress, and the last thing I wanted was her causing trouble for Marley."

"While your devotion to my wife is commendable, it's hardly necessary," Chrysander said dryly. Then he sighed. "Our obligation to Bella had temporarily slipped my mind. My focus of late has been on Marley and our child."

"What obligation?" Theron asked sharply. "And why haven't I heard of this before?"

"Our fathers were longtime friends and business partners. Her father extracted a promise from our father that if anything should ever happen to him that Isabella would be looked after. Our father preceded her father in death, so I assumed responsibility for her welfare when her father also passed away."

"Then you should know that, according to this letter, she's arriving in New York two days from now," Theron said.

Chrysander cursed. "I can't leave Marley right now."

"Of course you can't," Theron said impatiently. "I'll take care of it. But I need details. The last thing you need right now is to be saddled with another concern. New York is my responsibility. I'll count this as yet another problem I've inherited when we traded offices."

"Bella won't be any problem. She's a sweet girl. All you need to do is help her settle her affairs and make sure her needs are provided for. She doesn't gain full control of her inheritance until she's twenty-five or she marries, whichever happens first, so in the meantime Anetakis International acts as the trustee. As you are now the New York representative of Anetakis, that makes you her guardian of sorts."

Theron groaned. "I knew I should have bloody well made Piers take over the New York office."

Chrysander laughed. "This will be a piece of cake, little brother. It shouldn't take you long at all to make sure she's settled and has everything she needs."

* * *

Isabella Caplan had no sooner made it past the airport security checkpoint when she saw a man in a chauffeur's uniform holding a sign with her name on it.

She held up a hand in a wave and made her way over. To her surprise, two other men stepped forward to flank her. Her confusion must have showed because the chauffeur smiled and said, "Welcome to New York, Ms. Caplan. I'm Henry, your driver for today, and these gentlemen are from Mr. Anetakis's security detail."

"Uh, hi," she said.

"I've arranged for someone to collect your luggage from baggage claim," Henry said as he herded her toward the exit. "It will be delivered to the hotel shortly."

Outside, one of the security men held the limousine door open for her then got in after her, while the second climbed into the front seat with Henry. Privacy wasn't in the cards, and what she really wanted to do was wilt all over her seat.

Isabella leaned back as the limousine pulled away from the passenger pickup area en route to Imperial Park, the hotel owned by the Anetakis brothers. Chrysander had arranged a suite anytime she visited New York, not that it had occurred often.

This trip had been planned as nothing more than a brief stopover on her way to Europe, a fact she'd apprised Chrysander of in her correspondence. All of that had changed the minute she'd received a terse missive from Theron Anetakis informing her that he was now overseeing her affairs, and he would meet briefly with her in New York to make sure she had everything she needed for her trip abroad.

He didn't know it yet, but her trip was a thing of the past. She was going to stay in New York…indefinitely.

The limousine pulled up in front of the hotel and ground smoothly to a halt. Her door opened, and the security guard who'd ridden in front extended his hand to assist her out. Once inside the lobby, she was ushered immediately to her suite, bypassing the front desk altogether.

Within ten minutes, her luggage was delivered to her room along with a bouquet of flowers and a basket filled with an assortment of snacks and fruits.

If that wasn't enough, just as she settled onto the couch to kick off her shoes and catch her breath, another knock sounded. Grumbling under her breath, she went to open the door and found another hotel employee standing there. He extended a smooth, cream-colored envelope.

"A message from Mr. Anetakis."

She raised an eyebrow. "Which Mr. Anetakis?"

The young man looked discomfited. "Theron."

She smiled, thanked him and then closed the door. She turned the envelope over and lightly ran her finger over the inscription on the front. Isabella Caplan. Had he written it himself?

Experiencing a moment of silliness, she brought the paper to her nose, hoping to catch his smell. There. Light but undeniably his scent. She remembered it as though it were yesterday. He obviously still wore the same cologne.

She broke open the seal and pulled the card from the envelope. In a distinctly masculine scrawl, he'd written his instructions for her to come to his office the next morning.

An amused smile curved her lips. As arrogant as she remembered. Summoning her like a wayward child. At least Chrysander had dropped by her suite to check in on her. But then she'd been a mere eighteen, and he'd also provided a veritable nanny to chaperone her for her visit to the city.

She'd be more than happy to meet Theron on his terms. It would make it that more satisfying to rock him back on his heels. The basis for her big trip to Europe had been solely because that was where Theron lived. Or had lived. When Chrysander married, he and his wife moved to his Greek island on a permanent basis. Which meant that Theron had moved a lot closer to Isabella. Finally.

The trip to Europe was off. Her seduction of Theron was on.

She sank onto the couch and put her feet up on the coffee table. Vibrant red toenail polish flashed in front of her as she wiggled her toes. The delicate ankle brace-let flashed and shimmered with the movement of her foot.

Theron had only gotten more gorgeous over the last few years. He'd lost the youthful handsomeness and re-placed it with raw masculinity. While she'd been wait-ing to grow up so she could stake her claim, he'd only become more desirable. More irresistible. And she'd only fallen more in love with him.

It wouldn't be easy. She didn't imagine he'd fall read-ily into her arms. The Anetakis brothers were hard. They could have any woman they wanted. They were ruthless in business, but they were also loyal, and honor was everything.

The phone rang, and she sighed in aggravation. The phone was across the room, and she was quite comfort-able on the couch. Shoving herself up, she stumbled over to answer it.

"Hello?"

There was a brief silence.

"Ms. Caplan—Isabella."

She recognized the accented English, and a thrill skirted down her spine. It wasn't Chrysander, and given that Piers was out of the country and had never so much as had a conversation with Isabella, it could only be Theron.

"Yes," she said huskily, hoping her nervousness wasn't betrayed.

"This is Theron Anetakis. I was calling to make sure you made it in okay and are settling in with no difficulty."

"Thank you. Everything is fine."

"Is the suite to your liking?"

"Yes, of course. It was kind of you to reserve it for me."

"I didn't reserve it," he said impatiently. "It's my private suite."

She looked around with renewed interest. Knowing that she was staying where Theron spent a lot of his time gave her a decadent thrill.

"Then where are you staying?" she asked curiously. "Why would you give up your suite?"

"The hotel is undergoing renovations. The only available suite was…mine. I'm temporarily taking a different room."

She laughed. "I could have taken other accommodations. There was no need for you to move out for me."

"A few days won't make a difference," he said. "You should be comfortable before your trip to Europe."

She swallowed back the denial that she would be going to Europe. No sense in putting him on guard as soon as she arrived. There'd be plenty of time to apprise him of her change in plans. Mainly when he had no chance of talking her out of it.

A mischievous smile curved her lips. "I received your summons."

He made a sound of startled exclamation that sounded suspiciously like an oath. "Surely I didn't sound so autocratic, Ms. Caplan."

"Please, call me Isabella. Or Bella. Surely you remember when we weren't so formal? Granted it's been a few years, but I haven't forgotten a single thing about you."

There was an uncomfortable silence. And then, "All right, Isabella."

"Bella, please."

"All right…Bella," he conceded.

He made an exasperated sound in her ear and then said, "Now what was it we were discussing again?"

He sounded distracted, and though he was unfailingly polite, she knew he wanted rid of her as soon as possible. She grinned. If he only knew…

"We were discussing your autocratic demand for me to appear at your office tomorrow."

"It was a request, Bella," he said patiently.

"And of course I will honor it. Shall we say ten in the morning then? I'm a bit tired, and I'd like to sleep in."

"Of course. Don't overtax yourself. Order in room service tonight for dinner. Your expenses are being taken care of."

Of course. She hadn't expected anything less and knew better than to argue. The Anetakis brothers were thorough if nothing else. And very serious about their perceived obligations.

"I'll see you tomorrow then," she said.

He uttered an appropriate goodbye, and she hung

up the phone. A smile popped her lips upward as she hugged her midsection in delight. Oh, she'd planned to pay him a visit the next day, all right.

Chapter 2

Theron sat back in his chair and surveyed the skyline of the city from his window. After a busy morning of meetings and phone calls, he actually had a few minutes to breathe. He glanced at his watch and grimaced as he remembered that Isabella Caplan was due in a few minutes.

He felt like a revolving door. Isabella was in, and then she'd depart for Europe, while Alannis would be arriving in a week's time from Greece. Thankfully he'd be rid of his obligation to Isabella in short order. He'd make sure she was adequately provided for, arrange for someone from Anetakis International to meet her in London and have a security team see to her safety for the duration of her stay.

Alannis, on the other hand… He smiled ruefully. She was his own doing. He and Alannis had what could only be considered a close friendship. Perhaps an understanding was a better term, though he was open to the relationship growing into more. He knew he needed to settle down now that he was taking over the New York office. It was something he'd discussed candidly with Alannis a few weeks before.

They'd make a good couple. They understood each other. She was from a solid Greek family, old friends of his father's. Her own father owned a shipping company. They were well matched, and so it stood to reason that they'd gravitate toward each other.

She'd give him friendship and children. He'd give her security, protection.

Yes, it was time to settle down. His move to New York was in all likelihood permanent, as Marley had no desire to move from the island where she and Chrysander had made their home. And if he was going to be living here on a permanent basis, it seemed the best course to find a wife and start his family.

His thoughts were interrupted by a knock on his door. He frowned and looked up as he uttered the command to enter.

"Sir, Ms. Caplan is here to see you," Madeline, his secretary, said as she poked her head in the door.

"Send her in," he said brusquely.

As he waited, he straightened in his seat and drummed his fingers idly on the desk. He tried to draw on his vague memories of the girl but all he could picture was a very young Isabella with big eyes, gangly legs and braces. He wasn't even sure how old she was now, only that she'd graduated. Wouldn't that make her somewhere around twenty-two?

He summoned a gentle smile as the door swung open. No need to scare her to death. He was on his feet and walking forward to greet her when he pulled up short, all the breath knocked squarely from his chest.

Before him stood not a girl, but a stunningly beautiful woman. An invisible hand seized his throat, squeezing until he twisted his neck to alleviate the discomfort.

She smiled tentatively at him, and he felt the gesture to his toes. For a long moment, all he could do was gawk like a pimply-faced teenager experiencing his first surge of hormones.

Isabella was dressed in formfitting jeans that slung low on her hips. Her top, if you could call it an actual top, hugged her generous curves as snugly as a man's hands. The hem fell to just above her navel, and that, coupled with the low-slung jeans, bared her navel to his view.

His gaze was drawn to it and the glimmer of silver in the shallow indention. He frowned. She had a belly ring?

He looked up, embarrassed to be caught staring, but then he locked eyes with hers. Long, dark hair fell in layers beyond her shoulders. Long lashes fringed sparkling green eyes. A hint of a smile curved plump, generous lips and white teeth flashed in his vision. Two dimples appeared in her cheeks as her smile broadened.

This was not a woman who could ever escape notice. The past several years had wrought big changes. To think he'd remembered her as someone who faded into the background wherever she was. A man would have to be blind, deaf and dumb to overlook her in a room.

"What the hell are you wearing?" he demanded before he could think better of it.

She raised one dark brow, amusement twinkling in her eyes. Then she glanced down as she smoothed her hands over her hips.

"I believe they're called clothes," she said huskily.

He frowned harder at the playfulness he heard in her voice. "Is this the sort of thing Chrysander allowed you to run around in?"

She chuckled, and the sound skittered across his nape, raising hairs in its wake. It was warm and vibrant, and he derived so much pleasure from it that he wanted her to laugh again.

"Chrysander has no say in what I wear."

"He is—was your guardian," Theron said. "As I am now."

"Not legally," she countered. "You're doing a favor for my father, and you're the executor of his estate as it pertains to me until I marry, but you're hardly my guardian. I've managed quite well on my own with minimal interference from Chrysander."

Theron leaned back against his desk as he studied the young woman standing so confidently in front of him. "Marry? The terms of your father's will is that you gain control of your inheritance when you turn twenty-five."

"Or I marry," she gently corrected. "I plan to be married before then."

Alarm took hold of Theron as he contemplated all sorts of nasty scenarios.

"Who is he?" he demanded. "I'll want to have him fully investigated. You can't be too careful in your position. Your inheritance will draw a host of unwanted suitors who only want you for your money."

Another smile quirked at the corner of her mouth. "It's nice to see you again, too, Theron. My trip was fine. The suite is lovely. It's been awhile since I last saw you, but I'd recognize you anywhere."

Her reproach irritated him because she was exactly right. He was being rude. He hadn't even properly greeted her.

"My apologies, Isabella," he said as he moved forward. He grasped her shoulders and leaned in to kiss her on either cheek. "I'm glad to hear your trip was satisfactory and that the suite is to your liking. May I get you something to drink while we discuss your travel arrangements?"

She smiled and shook her head, and then moved past him toward the window. Her hips swayed, and her bottom, cupped by the too-tight denim, bobbed enticingly. He sent his gaze upward so that he wasn't ogling her inappropriately.

It was then that a flash of color at her waist stopped him. He blinked and looked again, certain he had to be mistaken. As she stopped at the window, the hem of her shirt moved so that a tiny portion of what looked to be a tattoo peeked from between her jeans and her shirt.

His gaze was riveted as he strained to see what the design was. Then he scowled. A tattoo? Obviously Chrysander had failed miserably in his role as her guardian. What the hell kind of trouble had she gotten herself into? Tattoos? Talk of marriage?

He closed his eyes and pinched the bridge of his nose as he felt the beginnings of a headache.

"You have a wonderful view," she said as she turned from the window to look at him.

He cleared his throat and sent his gaze to her face. Anywhere but at the breasts hugged tight by the thin T-shirt. *Theos,* but the woman was a walking time bomb.

"Have you already made all the arrangements for your trip to Europe or would you prefer for me to see to them?" he asked politely.

She shoved her fingers into her jeans pockets, a feat he wasn't certain how she managed, and leaned against the window.

"I'm not going to Europe."

He blinked. "Pardon?"

She smiled again, the dimples deepening. "I've decided not to travel to Europe for the summer."

He put a hand to his forehead and massaged the tension. Damn Chrysander for getting a life and saddling him with Isabella Caplan.

"Does this have anything to do with your sudden desire for marriage?" he asked tiredly. "You still haven't answered my question about the intended groom."

"That's because there isn't one yet," she said mischievously. "I never said that I had a man lined out yet, just that I intended to be married before I turned twenty-five. As that gives me three more years, there certainly isn't a need to start ordering background checks."

"Then why aren't you going to Europe? It was your plan at least a week ago according to the letter you sent to Chrysander."

"I sent Chrysander no such thing," she protested lightly. "The man Chrysander hired to oversee my education and my living arrangements informed Chrysander of my trip to Europe. I simply changed my mind."

His hand slipped to the back of his neck as a full-blown migraine threatened to bloom.

"So what do you intend to do then?" He was almost afraid to hear the answer.

She smiled broadly, her entire face lighting up. "I'm getting an apartment here in the city."

Theron choked. Then he closed his eyes as he felt the cinch draw tighter around his neck. If she stayed here, then he would be stuck overseeing her affairs, checking up on her constantly.

Suddenly her impending marriage didn't strike such

a chord of irritation. She was twenty-two. True, it was young to marry these days, but certainly not outside the realm of possibility. Perhaps the best thing he could do for her was to introduce her to a man well equipped to provide security and stability for her.

The thought was already turning in his head, gaining momentum, when she spoke again.

"I'm sorry?" he said when he realized he had no idea what she'd said to him.

"Oh, I only said now that we've gotten my arrangements out of the way, I need to be going. I have an apartment to find."

Alarm bells rang at the idea of Isabella traipsing around a city she wasn't intimately familiar with, alone and vulnerable. Hell, she could wind up in an entirely unsuitable neighborhood. And then there was the matter of her security. Now that she was going to be here and not in Europe, he'd have to scramble to get a team in place. The last thing he needed was for her to be abducted as Marley had been.

"I don't think this is something you should do alone," he said firmly.

Her expression brightened. "That's so sweet of you to offer to go apartment hunting with me. I admit, I wasn't looking forward to it on my own, and your knowledge of the city is so much better than mine."

He opened his mouth to refute the idea that he'd volunteered anything, but the genuine appreciation on her face made him snap his lips shut. He let out a sigh, knowing he was well and truly screwed.

"Of course I'll accompany you. I won't have you staying just anywhere. I'll have my secretary come up with a few suitable places for you to view and then we'll go. Perhaps tomorrow morning? You're welcome to stay in the suite for as long as you need it."

She frowned. "But I hate to put you out."

He shook his head. "It's no bother. Chrysander still has a penthouse here that I can use. I need to be looking for a place as well now that I've permanently relocated here."

Her eyes sparked briefly, but then her expression faded to one of neutrality.

"In that case, I appreciate the offer, and I'd love to go apartment hunting with you tomorrow. Shall we do lunch as well?" she asked innocently.

"Of course I'll feed you," he said with a grunt. Why did he feel as though he'd been run over by a steamroller? The idea that this mere slip of a girl had run so roughshod over him left him irritated and feeling like he'd been manipulated, but there was nothing but genuine appreciation and relief in her expression.

She hurried over and threw her arms around him. She landed against his chest, and he had to brace himself to keep from stumbling back.

"Thank you," she said against his ear as she squeezed him for all she was worth.

He allowed his arms to fold around her as he returned her hug. Her body melted against his, and he felt every one of those generous curves he'd noticed earlier. His hand skimmed over the small portion of flesh on her back that was bared by her shirt, and he wondered again over the tattoo he'd seen there. It was driving him crazy not to know what it was.

He shook his head and gently extricated himself from her grasp. "Let me call for the driver so he can return you to the hotel."

She kissed him on the cheek and then turned toward

the door. "Thank you, Theron, and I'll see you first thing tomorrow."

He was left rubbing his cheek where her lips had brushed just seconds before. Then he cursed and strode around to the back of his desk again. He'd been so ready to condemn Chrysander for being involved with someone so young, and here he stood lusting over the same girl. Pathetic. It had obviously been way too long since he'd been with a woman.

He buzzed his secretary and quickly gave her instructions to find three or four possible apartments. If all else failed, he could give her Chrysander's penthouse to use.

After talking with Madeline, he then picked up the phone to arrange for a security detail for Isabella.

As he hung up, he remembered that Alannis would be arriving in a week, and he groaned. He'd counted on not having Isabella to contend with when his future fiancée arrived. One woman was always more than enough, and splitting attentions between more than one was a recipe for disaster.

But maybe Alannis would have ideas where Isabella was concerned. Together they could introduce Isabella to a few eligible men—men who'd passed muster with Theron, of course.

Deciding that this was another task suited for Madeline, he buzzed her and asked her to compile a list of eligible bachelors complete with background checks and a checklist of pros and cons. She sounded amused by his request but didn't question him.

Theron sat back in his chair and folded his hands behind his head. This wouldn't take long at all. He'd find her an apartment, find her a husband, and then he would turn his attentions to his own impending nuptials.

* * *

"Isabella!" Sadie cried as she threw open the door to her apartment.

Isabella found herself enveloped in her friend's arms, and she returned the hug just as fiercely.

"Come in, come in. It's so good to see you again," Sadie exclaimed as she ushered Isabella inside.

The girls sat down in the small living room, and then Sadie pounced. "So? Did you see him?"

Isabella smiled. "Just came from his office."

"And?"

Isabella shrugged. "I told him I wasn't going to Europe and that I was going to look for an apartment here. He's going to help me," she added with a small smile.

"So he took it well?"

Sadie flipped her long, red hair over her shoulder, drawing attention to her pretty features. A year older than Isabella, she had graduated the term before and moved to New York to pursue a career on Broadway.

"I wouldn't say well," Isabella said in amusement. "I think it was more a matter of him wondering what on earth he was going to do with me. The Anetakis brothers take their responsibilities very seriously. They're Greek, after all. And I am one huge responsibility Theron needs to be rid of. I'm sure he was looking forward to herding me onto a plane for Europe as soon as possible."

"Okay, so spill," Sadie said eagerly. "What's your plan?"

Isabella grimaced. "I'm not altogether sure. I had planned to go to Europe and be an all-around nuisance to him there. Now all of a sudden he's here in New York so I'm having to scramble with the change of plans. The good news is we're having lunch tomorrow when we go apartment hunting. I guess I'll see where things go from there."

"How did he react when he saw you?" Sadie asked. "It's been what, four years since he got a good look at you?"

"Ugh. Yes. Thank goodness I've finally blossomed."

"So? Did he appreciate your womanly charms?" Sadie asked with a wide grin.

"I'm sure he noticed, but I think it was a cross between interest and being appalled. You have to understand that Theron is very, um, traditional." She sighed and leaned back against the couch. "But if I had shown up dressed like a good, modest Greek girl, he wouldn't have given me a second glance. I would have been relegated to little sister status, just as Chrysander has done, and there would be no changing it."

"Ah, so better to throw out the challenge from the outset," Sadie acknowledged.

"Exactly," Isabella murmured. "If he never sees me as a nonthreatening entity, then it will be damn hard for him to turn a blind eye to me."

Sadie laughed and clasped Isabella's hands in hers. "I'm so glad to see you again, Bella. It has been too long and I've missed you."

"Yes, it has. Now enough about me. I want to hear all about you and your Broadway career. Tell me, have you landed any roles?"

Sadie twisted her lips into a rueful expression. "I'm afraid the parts have been few and far between, but I haven't given up. I have an audition next week as a matter of fact."

Isabella frowned. "Are you making it okay, Sadie?"

"I have a job. Not many hours. Just a couple of nights a week. The money is fantastic and I get to look drop-dead gorgeous," Sadie said cheekily. "It'll do until I get my big break."

Isabella viewed her friend with suspicion. "What is this job?"

Sadie grinned slyly, her eyes bright with mischief. "It's a gentleman's club. Very posh and exclusive."

Isabella's mouth dropped open. "You're working as a stripper?"

"I don't always strip," Sadie said dryly. "It's not required per se. But I get better tips when I do," she added with a bigger grin.

Isabella stared for a long moment and then burst out laughing. "Maybe I should take lessons from you. Theron would have to notice me if I did a striptease in front of him."

Sadie joined in her laughter until the two of them were wiping tears. "If he didn't notice you, hon, then the man is dead."

Impulsively, Isabella leaned up and hugged Sadie. "I'm so glad I'm here. I've missed you. I have such a good feeling about being here in New York. Like maybe this will actually work and I can make Theron fall in love with me."

Sadie returned Isabella's hug and then pulled away, a gentle smile on her face. "I have every faith that Theron will fall hopelessly in love with you. But if he doesn't? You're young and beautiful, Bella. You could have your choice of men."

"I only want Theron," she said softly. "I've loved him for so long."

"Well then, we need to think of a way to catch him, don't we?" Sadie said with a grin.

Chapter 3

"Alannis," Theron greeted her smoothly. "I trust things are well with you?"

He listened as she uttered a polite greeting, somewhat distant and reserved, but then he expected nothing less. Alannis was steeped in propriety and would never offer a more effusive greeting. It simply wasn't her style.

"I've made arrangements for the Anetakis jet to fly you from Greece to New York a week from now. Will your mother be traveling with you?"

It was a senseless question, meant to be more polite than inquisitive since he knew well that Alannis's family would never allow her to travel to see an unmarried man unchaperoned.

"I'll look forward to your arrival then," he continued. "I've arranged for a night at the opera shortly after you arrive." If all went well, he'd request a moment alone to propose and then the two families could go ahead with the wedding plans.

Of course now he needed to apprise his brothers of his intentions.

He hung up the phone and stared at it for a long moment. He had no doubt Chrysander would, in his new-found loving bliss, be reluctant to encourage Theron to enter into a loveless marriage. Piers on the other hand would shrug and say it was Theron's life and if he wanted to mess it up, that was his prerogative.

In time he could grow to like Alannis very well. He liked her already and respected her, which was more than he could say for a lot of the women of his acquaintance. He knew better than to expect a woman to love him as deeply as Marley loved his brother. But he'd like to think he could be friends with his future wife and enjoy her companionship in and out of bed.

He frowned when he thought of Alannis naked and in his bed, beneath his body. He glanced down at his groin as if expecting a response. If he was, he was disappointed.

Alannis…she came across as cold and extremely stiff. He supposed he couldn't blame her for that. She was most assuredly a virgin, and it would be up to him to coax the passion from her. It was his duty as her husband.

With a sigh, he checked his watch, and to his irritation noticed that Isabella was late. He drummed his fingers impatiently on his desk. Madeline had provided three possible apartments, all in good areas and in close proximity to the Imperial Park Hotel. She hadn't as of yet provided a list of eligible men.

No matter. The first order of business was to see her settled. The sooner, the better. Then he'd worry about marrying her off.

When he heard his door open, he looked up, startled.

Then he frowned when he saw Isabella stride inside. On cue, his intercom buzzed, and Madeline's voice announced somewhat dryly that Isabella was on her way in.

"Good morning," Isabella sang out as she stopped in front of his desk.

He swallowed and then his gaze narrowed as he took in her attire. It wasn't exactly immodest, and as such he couldn't offer a complaint. It covered her. Sort of.

His mouth went dry when she put her hands on his desk and leaned forward. Her breasts spilled precariously close to the neckline of her T-shirt, and he could see the lacy cups of her bra as they pushed the soft mounds upward.

He cursed under his breath and directed his gaze upward. "Good morning, Isabella."

"Bella, please, unless you have an aversion to the name?"

He didn't, though it somehow seemed more intimate, particularly when he took the meaning of the Italian form of her name. *Beautiful.* That she was. Stunningly so. Different from the usual sophisticated type of women he gravitated toward, but beautiful nonetheless. There was something wild and unrestrained about her.

He ground his teeth together and shifted his position. Where his groin had remained stoic when thinking of Alannis, it had flared to life, painfully so, as soon as Isabella had walked into his office.

He was her guardian, someone to look after her welfare, and here he sat fantasizing about her. Disgust filled him. Not only was it disrespectful to Isabella but it was disrespectful to Alannis. No woman should have to put up with her soon-to-be fiancé lusting after another woman.

"Bella," he echoed, taking her invitation to use her nickname. It suited her. Light and beautiful.

He rose from his seat and walked around the front of his desk. She eyed him curiously, and he found himself asking her why.

She laughed. "You're dressed so casually today. I'm so used to seeing you in nothing but suits and ties."

"When have you seen me?" he asked in surprise. He thought back to the times when she would have seen him, and while he probably was wearing a suit, it was hardly a basis for her supposition.

She flushed, and he watched in fascination as color stained her cheeks. She ducked away, her hair sliding over her shoulder.

"Pictures," she mumbled. "There are always pictures of you in the papers."

"And you get these papers all the way out in California?" he asked.

"Yes. I like to keep up with the people looking after my financial well-being," she said evenly.

"As you should," he said approvingly. "Are you ready to go? I have a list of potential apartments. I took the liberty of scaling down the possibilities to a few more suitable to a young woman living alone."

And then he realized he'd made a huge assumption. There was certainly no reason to believe that a woman as beautiful and vibrant as Isabella would be living alone. He refused to retract the statement or ask her if she was currently involved with anyone. But he'd need to know because if she was involved, seriously, then he could forego the whole process of introducing her to prospective husbands.

"I'm ready if you are," she said as she smiled warmly at him.

As they walked from the building that housed the Anetakis headquarters, Theron put his hand to the small of Isabella's back. She felt the touch through her shirt. It seared her skin, and she was sure that if she could look, there would be a visible print from his fingers, burned into her flesh.

After loving him from afar for so many years, she'd been prepared for disappointment, that maybe the man he'd become wouldn't live up to the dream. She'd been so far removed from the truth that reality overwhelmed her. He was more, so much more than she could have imagined. Her feelings hadn't gone away when she'd seen him again. They'd cemented.

She sat next to him in the back of the limousine. In addition to the driver, Henry, there was one additional member of his security detail that rode up front. When they pulled up in front of the first apartment building, she noticed that another smaller car pulled in behind them, and two men got out and cautiously scanned the area.

"I don't remember the security being this tight the last time I visited," she murmured as they walked toward the entrance.

Theron stiffened. "It's a necessary evil."

She waited for him to say more but he didn't volunteer further information.

Three hours later, they'd toured the apartments on his list with him vetoing the first two before she could even offer an opinion. He was tight-lipped about the third but offered her the choice between it and the last on their list.

She stifled her laughter and solemnly informed him that she liked the fourth. He nodded his approval and set about securing it for her.

"Will you have your things shipped to the apartment?" he asked as they walked back to the limousine.

She shook her head. "I plan to shop for everything I need here and have it delivered. It will be quite fun!"

He growled something under his breath but when she turned to him in question, he pressed his lips together.

"I'll arrange for someone to take you shopping," he said grudgingly.

She raised an eyebrow. "I assure you, I have no need of a babysitter, Theron. Chrysander saddled me with one four years ago, and I had no more need of it then than I do now."

"You will not roam all over the city by yourself," he said resolutely.

She shrugged and offered a faint smile. "You could always go with me."

He gave her a startled look.

"No? You seem the logical choice given I don't know anyone else here." She purposely kept silent about Sadie. There was no reason for Theron to know about her, and he wouldn't approve if he knew she worked in a strip club. And find out he would, because the instant she let him know of someone she was spending time with, he'd perform an extensive background check and then forbid her to associate with Sadie any longer.

Not that she'd listen, but she intended for their relationship to get off to the best possible start. Lust was fine for now, but she wanted to make him fall in love with her. She wanted him to need her.

"You're right, of course," he said with a grimace. "I forget you've lived in California and have only been here to visit."

She slid into the limousine and smiled over at him

as he got in on the other side. "Does that mean you'll go shopping with me?"

He grunted, and she couldn't hold the laughter in any longer. His eyes widened, and he stared openly at her as though he found the sound of her laughter enchanting.

All the breath left her as she saw for just one moment a look of wanting in his eyes. Just as soon as it flashed, he blinked and recovered.

"I'll see if my schedule permits such a trip," he said tightly.

"Where are you taking me for lunch?" she asked, more to remind him of their date than any real curiosity over their destination. She didn't care where or what they ate. She just wanted the time with him.

"We have an excellent restaurant at the hotel," he said. "My table is always available to me. I thought we could eat there and then you could retire to your suite to rest."

She resisted the urge to roll her eyes. He was smooth. Plotting the easiest way to get rid of her. She couldn't blame him. She was an unexpected burden, and he was a busy man. She chewed her bottom lip and looked out the window at the passing traffic as she contemplated how to get him to see beyond the inconvenience to the woman who loved him and wanted him so badly.

"Is something the matter, Bella?"

She turned to see him staring at her in concern. She smiled and shook her head. "Just a little tired. And excited."

He frowned. "Maybe you should allow me to see to the furnishing of your apartment. If you would mark down your preferences, I could have a designer work with you so that you didn't have to go out shopping for all the things you need."

"Oh, no, that wouldn't be near as much fun. I can't wait to pick out everything for the apartment. It's such a gorgeous place."

"What are your plans, Bella?" he asked.

She blinked in surprise. "Plans?"

"Yes. Plans. Now that you've graduated, what are your career plans?"

"Oh. Well, I planned to take the summer off," she hedged. "I'll focus on the future this fall."

He didn't say anything, but she could tell such an approach bothered him. She smiled to herself. It probably gave him hives. He and his brothers all were intensely driven with a *take no prisoners* approach when it came to business. They weren't the world's wealthiest hotel family for nothing.

When they arrived at the hotel, Theron ushered her inside as his security team flanked them on all sides. It was odd and a bit surreal, almost like they were royalty.

A few minutes later, they were escorted to Theron's table at the restaurant. It was situated in a quiet corner, almost completely cut off from the rest of the diners.

He settled her into her chair and then circled around to sit across from her. He dropped his long, lean body into his seat and stared lazily at her.

"What would you like to eat, *pethi mou?*"

Isabella cringed at the endearment. He'd called her the same thing when she was thirteen. *Little one.* It set her teeth on edge. Hardly something that evoked images of the two of them in bed, limbs entwined.

"What do you suggest?" she asked.

She studied his lips, the hard, sensual curve to his mouth and the dark shadow already forming on his jaw. She was tempted, so very tempted to reach across and run the tip of her finger along the roughness and then to the softness of his lips.

What would it be like to kiss him? She'd kissed several boys in college. She said *boys* because next to Theron, that's all they were. Some were very good, others awkward and "pleasant."

But Theron. Kissing him would be like chasing a storm. Hot, exciting and breathless. Her pulse jumped wildly as she imagined the warm brush of his tongue.

"Bella?"

She blinked and shook her head as she realized Theron had been calling her name for a few seconds.

"Sorry," she murmured. "Lost in my thoughts."

"I was suggesting you try the salmon," he said dryly.

She nodded jerkily and tilted her head toward the waiter who was standing beside the table waiting for their order.

"I'll have what he suggests," she said huskily.

Theron placed their order in succinct tones, and the waiter hurried away shortly afterward.

"Now, Bella," Theron said, as he sat back in his chair. He looked comfortable, at ease as he raked his gaze over her features, setting fire to every nerve receptor. "Perhaps we should talk about your future."

A nervous scuttle began in her stomach. "My future?" She laughed lightly to allay the pounding of her heart. If she had any say, her future would be inexorably linked to his.

"Indeed. Your future. Surely you've given it *some* thought?"

He sounded slightly scornful, impatient with someone who didn't have an airtight plan. If he only knew. She'd done nothing else for the past years but plan for her future. With him.

"I've given it a lot of thought," she said evenly.

"You mentioned marriage. Are you truly considering being married before you turn twenty-five?"

"I count on it."

He nodded as if he approved. She almost laughed. Would he be so approving if he knew he was her intended groom? A sigh escaped her. She felt so evil, like she was plotting an assassination rather than a seduction.

"This is good," he said almost to himself. "I've taken the liberty of forming a list of possible candidates."

Her brow crinkled as she stared at him in puzzlement. "Candidates? For what?"

"Marriage, Bella. I intend to help you find a husband."

Chapter 4

Isabella eyed Theron suspiciously, wondering if he'd suddenly developed a sense of humor.

"You intend to do *what?*" she asked.

"You want a husband. After my initial misgivings, I've decided it's a sound idea. A woman in your position can't be too careful," he continued, obviously warming to his subject. "So I've taken the liberty of drawing up a list of suitable candidates."

She burst out laughing. She couldn't help herself. As absurdities went, this might well take the cake.

He blinked in surprise then frowned as she continued to chuckle. "What do you find so amusing?"

She shook her head, the smile not dropping from her lips. "I'm in the city all of two days, and already you're planning to marry me off. And tell me, what do you mean by *a woman in my position can't be too careful?*"

"You're wealthy, young and beautiful," he said

bluntly. "You'll have every man between the ages of twenty and eighty plotting to wed and bed you, not necessarily in that order."

She sat back in mock surprise. "Wow. And not a word about my intelligence, wit or charm. I'm glad to know I don't plan to wed for superficial reasons."

Theron sobered then reached over and took her hand. Warmth spread up her arm as his fingers stroked her palm. "This is precisely why I felt I should be involved in your search for a husband. Men will try to take advantage of you by pretending they're something they're not. Fortune hunters will pretend they know nothing of your wealth. They'll be swept away by your *kindness* and *generosity*. It's important that any man we allow close to you be carefully vetted by myself."

Her lips twitched, but she dare not laugh. He was utterly serious, and she had to admit that his concern was endearing. It would be quite sweet if he weren't so intent on marrying her off to another man.

"Don't be disheartened, *pethi mou,*" he soothed. "There are many men who would give you the world. It's a matter of finding the right one."

It was all she could do not to cringe. If that wasn't a painful lecture, she'd never heard one.

"You're right, of course," she murmured.

Because what else was she going to say? What she really wanted to do was lean over and ask him if he could be that man. But she already knew the answer to that. He couldn't be that man. At least not yet. Not until he had time to get used to the idea.

Theron smiled his approval and slipped his fingers from hers as he leaned back in his chair. She glanced down at her open hand, regretting the loss of his touch.

"So tell me, what are your requirements in a husband?" he asked indulgently.

She gazed thoughtfully at him, her mind assembling all the things she loved most about him. Then she started ticking items off on her fingers.

"Let's see. I'd like him to be tall, dark and handsome."

Theron rolled his eyes. "You've described the wishes of half the female population."

"I also want him to be kind and have a sense of responsibility. As I'd prefer not to have children right away, his agreement on that matter would also be important."

"You don't want children?" he asked. He seemed surprised, but then he likely thought all women aspired to pop out a veritable brood as soon as they got a ring on their finger.

"I didn't say I didn't want them," she replied calmly. "Let me guess, you'd want them immediately?"

He arched one brow. "We aren't discussing me, but yes, I see no reason to wait."

"That's because you aren't the one having them," she said dryly.

For a moment it looked as though he would laugh, but then he waved his hand and urged her to continue with her wish list.

She pretended to consider for a moment. "I want him to be wealthier than I am so that my money is a nonissue."

Theron nodded his agreement.

Then she let her voice drop, and she leaned forward. "I want him to burn for me, to not be able to go a day without touching me, holding me, caressing me. He'll be an excellent lover. I want a man who knows how to please me," she finished in a husky, longing-filled voice.

He stared at her, his eyes sharp. For a moment she imagined that there was answering passion in his eyes as they flickered over her exposed skin.

"Do you not agree that these are things I should expect?" she asked softly as she studied him.

He cleared his throat and looked briefly away. Was she affecting him at all or was he completely immune? No, there was something in his eyes. His entire body emanated sexual awareness. She might be young, but she wasn't naive, and she certainly wasn't stupid when it came to men. She'd had her share of interested parties. She could read harmless, flirty interest, and then there was the dark, brooding intensity of a man whose passions ran deep and powerful.

Never before had she felt the intense magnetism that existed between her and Theron. She'd spent years searching for something that even came close to the budding awareness that had begun in her teenage years.

She'd experimented with dates. Kisses, the clumsy groping that had inevitably led to her showing the guy the door. There was only one who ever came close to coaxing her to give him everything. In the end, it had been him who'd called a stop to their lovemaking. At the time, she'd been embarrassed and certain that she'd made some mistake. He'd kissed her gently, told her that he was greatly honored by the fact that he would be her first, but that perhaps she should save her gift for a man who held a special place in her heart.

Then, she'd seen it as a cop-out, a man running hard and fast from a woman who obviously equated sex with commitment or at least a deeper relationship. Now, she was just grateful that she hadn't blithely given away her innocence. Travis was right. Her virginity was special, and she'd only give it to a special man.

She blinked again when she realized Theron was talking to her.

"I think you are wise to place emphasis on…these qualities," he said uncomfortably. "You wouldn't want a man who'd mistreat you in any way, and of course you'll want someone who shares your vision of marriage and a family."

"But you don't think I should want a good lover?" she asked with one raised eyebrow.

His eyes gleamed in the flickering lamp situated in the middle of the table. Her breath caught and hung in her chest, painful as her throat tightened. She swallowed at the raw power radiating from him in a low, sensual hum.

"It would indeed be a shame if a man had no idea what to do with a woman such as yourself, Bella."

He looked up in relief when the waiter came bearing the tray with their food. Isabella, on the other hand, cursed the timing.

Theron surprised her, however, when after the waiter retreated, he caught her eye and murmured in his sexy, accented voice, "Your mother died early in your childhood, did she not? Has there been no one else to speak to you about…men?"

She gaped at him in astonishment. Did he honestly think she'd reached the ripe old age of twenty-two without ever hearing the birds and the bees talk? She wasn't sure who was more horrified, her or Theron. He looked uncomfortable, and hell, so was she.

Picking up her fork, she cut into her fish and speared a perfectly cooked piece. It hit her tongue, and she nearly sighed in appreciation. It was good, and she was starving.

Theron was clearly waiting on her to answer his question. His really ridiculous question aimed more at a fourteen-year-old, pimply faced girl than a twenty-two-year-old woman.

"If I say no, are you volunteering to head my education?" she asked with a flash of a grin.

He shot an exasperated grimace in her direction. "I'll take that as a yes that someone has spoken to you of such matters."

"Next you'll be offering to buy my feminine products," she muttered.

He choked on the sip of wine he'd just taken and hurriedly set the glass back down on the table. "You imp. It's not polite to make someone laugh as they're taking a drink."

"I'll remind you that you started this conversation," she said dryly.

She watched him take a bite and then wipe his mouth with his napkin. He had really gorgeous lips. Perfect for kissing.

"So I did," he said with a shrug. "I merely wondered if you'd spoken to another woman about men and husbands and of course which men make the best husbands."

"And lovers," she added.

"Yes, of course," he said in resignation.

She sat back in her seat and stared at him in challenge. "You don't want the woman you marry to be a good lover?"

He gave her what she could only classify as a look of horror. "No, I damn well do not expect my wife to be a good lover. It's my duty to…" He broke off in a strangled voice. "We're not discussing my future wife," he said gruffly.

But her curiosity had been well and truly piqued. She sat forward, and placed her chin in one palm, her food forgotten. "It's your duty to what?"

"This is not a conversation that is appropriate for us to have," he said stiffly.

She sighed and nearly rolled her eyes. He sure didn't mind playing the guardian card when it suited him, and the last thing she wanted was to plant any sort of parent role into his brain. But she desperately wanted to hear just what he considered his duty to be to the woman who'd share his bed.

"You're my guardian, Theron. Who else can I talk to about such matters?"

He let out a long-suffering sigh and took another sip of his wine. "I don't expect my wife to be sexually experienced when she comes to my bed. It's my duty to awaken her passion and teach her everything she needs to know about…lovemaking."

Isabella wrinkled her nose. "That sounds so medieval. Have you ever considered that she might teach you a thing or two?"

He set the glass down again, a look of astonished outrage on his face. Clearly the thought had never occurred to him that any woman could teach him anything when it came to sex. So he fancied himself a good lover then. She had to fight off a full-body shiver. She wanted his hands on her body so badly. She'd be more than willing to be an eager pupil under his tutelage.

"I assure you, there is little a woman could teach me that I am not already well acquainted with," he said with a thread of arrogance.

"That experienced, huh?"

He grimaced. "I don't know how our conversation deteriorated to this, but it's hardly an appropriate conversation between a guardian and his ward."

And up went the cement wall again. At least he was struggling to put her back on a nonthreatening level which meant he considered her just that. A threat.

She dug cheerfully into the remainder of her meal, content to let silence settle over the table. Theron watched her, and she let him, making sure not to look up and catch his stare. There was curiosity in his gaze but there was also interest, and not the platonic kind. He might fight it tooth and nail, but his eyes didn't lie.

When they were finished eating, Theron queried her on her next course of action.

"I'll need furniture, of course. Not to mention food and staple items."

"Make a list of food items and any other household things you need. I'll have it delivered so that you don't have to go out shopping," Theron said. "If you can stand a few more days in the hotel suite, I'll see if I can fit in a furniture shopping trip later in the week."

"Oh, I need everything," she said cheerfully. "Towels, curtains, dishes, bed linens—"

He held up his hand and smiled. "Make a detailed list. I'll see that it is taken care of."

He tossed his table napkin down and motioned for the waiter. Then he glanced at Isabella. "Are you ready to return to your suite?"

Isabella wasn't, but she also knew that she'd monopolized Theron's entire morning, and he was a busy man. She nodded and rose from her seat. They met around the table, and he put his hand to the small of her back as they headed for the exit.

"I'll see you up," Theron said when they walked into the lobby.

The elevator slid open and the two stepped inside. Even before it fully closed, Isabella turned to Theron. He was so close. His warmth radiated from him, enveloping her. She could smell the crispness of his cologne.

"Thank you for today," she murmured.

She reached automatically for his hands and knew that he was going to lean in to kiss her on either cheek. The elevator neared the top floor.

"You're quite welcome, *pethi mou*. I'll have my secretary call you about your apartment and also about our shopping trip."

As she thought, when the elevator stopped, he leaned down, his intention to kiss her quickly. She stepped into his arms, her body molding to his chest. Before he could react, she circled her arms around his neck and as his lips brushed against her cheek, she turned her face so that their lips met.

The air exploded around them. Their mouths fused and electricity whipped between them like bolts of lightning. At first he went completely still as she boldly kissed him. And then a low growl worked from his throat and he took control.

He yanked her to him until there was no space between them. His arms wrapped around her body, and his hand slid down her spine, to the small of her back and then to cup her behind through her tight jeans.

She was intensely aware of his every touch. His fingers felt like branding irons against her skin, burning through the denim of her pants. His other hand tangled roughly in her hair, glancing over her scalp before twisting and catching in the thick strands.

It wasn't a simple kiss, no loving caress between two

people acquainting themselves. It was the kiss of two lovers who were starved for each other.

No hesitancy or permission seeking. It was like they'd been separated for a long period and were coming back together, two people who knew each other intimately.

The warm brush of his tongue coaxed her mouth further open and then he was inside, licking at the edge of her teeth and then laving over her tongue, inviting her to respond equally.

She went willingly, tasting him and testing the contours of his lips.

His hand moved from the curve of her bottom up underneath her shirt and to the small of her back where his large hand splayed out possessively as he crushed her to his hard body.

Her breath caught, and she gasped when his hand made that first contact with her bare skin. Her breasts swelled and throbbed against his chest.

She dare not say a word or make a sound, because if she did, the moment would be lost. He would remember who he was kissing. Instead she focused her energy on making it last as long as she could.

When his lips left hers and stuttered across her jaw and to her neck, she moaned, unable to remain silent. She shivered and quaked, her senses awakening after a long winter.

Never had she felt anything like his lips, whisper soft, across the delicate skin beneath her ear.

Her knees buckled, and she clutched frantically at him. Suddenly his mouth left her, and he cursed. She closed her eyes, knowing the moment was over.

He yanked her away, his hands tight around her arms. His eyes blazed, equal parts anger, self-condemnation and…hunger. She stared helplessly back at him, unable to say anything.

He cursed again in Greek and then shook his head before shoving her out of the elevator. He ushered her to the door where he jammed the card into the lock.

He held the door open with one hand, and she slowly entered. When she turned around to say something, he was already letting the door close. Before it clicked shut, she heard his footsteps hurrying away.

Turning until her back rested against the door, she closed her eyes and hugged her body as she relived those precious moments in Theron's arms.

Their passion had been immediate. The chemistry between them was positively combustible. The last unknown was unveiled. In every other aspect, Theron had proved himself to be her perfect match. All she hadn't known is if they were sexually compatible, not that she'd harbored any doubts, and now in the space of a few heated moments in the elevator, the last piece had fallen neatly into place.

Now all she had to do was make him see it.

Chapter 5

Theron pinched the bridge of his nose between his fingers and cursed long and hard. His head felt like someone had taken a hammer to it, he was tired, and he hadn't slept more than an hour the entire night.

Madeline kept staring at him throughout the morning as though he'd lost his mind, and maybe he had. He'd forgotten two meetings and had waved off three phone calls, one of which was from his brother Piers.

All that occupied his thoughts was a dark-haired minx with sultry green eyes. *Theos mou,* but he couldn't forget her kiss, the feel of her mouth on his, her body molded to his as though she were made for him.

He was her guardian. He was responsible for her well-being, and yet he'd damn near hauled her into the bedroom of her suite and made love to her. His body still ached to do just that.

He shook his head for what seemed like the hundredth time since he'd gotten to his office this morning. No matter what he did, though, he couldn't rid himself of her image. Her scent. She was destined to drive him crazy.

Impatient and more than a little agitated, he slapped the intercom. Madeline's calm voice filtered through as she asked what he needed.

"Do you have that list drawn up for me yet?"

"Which list would that be?"

"The list of eligible men I asked for. The men I intend to introduce Bella to."

"Ah, that one. Yes, I have it."

"Bring it in then," he demanded.

A few moments later, Madeline walked through his door holding a piece of paper.

He motioned for her to sit down in front of his desk. "Read them off to me," he said as he leaned back in his chair.

"Did you sleep at all last night?" Madeline asked, her eyes narrowing perceptively.

He grunted and closed his eyes as he waited for her to give up and do as he asked.

"Reginald Hollister."

Theron shook his head immediately. "He's an immature little twerp. Spoiled endlessly by his parents. Bella needs someone…more independent."

Madeline made a show of scratching him off. "Okay then, what about Charles McFadden?"

Theron scowled. "There's rumor that he abused his first wife."

"Bradley Covington?"

"He's an ass," Theron said.

Madeline sighed and quickly crossed him off.

"Tad Whitley."

"Not wealthy enough."

"Garth Moser?"

"I don't like him."

"Paul Hedgeworth."

Theron frowned as he tried to think of a reason why he shouldn't consider Paul.

"Aha," Madeline said when nothing was forthcoming. She drew a large circle around his name. "Shall I invite him to your cocktail party Thursday night?"

"He's too handsome and charming," Theron muttered.

Madeline smiled. "Good, then Isabella should be well pleased."

She glanced down her list then looked back up at Theron. "I think we should include Marcus Atwater and Colby Danforth, as well. They're both single, very good-looking and aren't currently in a relationship."

Theron waved his hand in a gesture of surrender. This was probably best left to Madeline anyway. She'd know better what Isabella would like than he would.

They were interrupted when the door burst open and Isabella hurried in, a bright smile on her face.

"Sorry to just barge in," she said in an out-of-breath voice. "I didn't see Madeline…oh, there you are," she said when she caught sight of his secretary.

Madeline rose and smiled in Isabella's direction. "Quite all right, my dear. I was just on my way out. I'm sure Mr. Anetakis has time for you. He appears to have canceled all his morning meetings."

He scowled at Madeline, not that she seemed particularly intimidated. She patted Isabella on the arm as she passed and then she turned as she reached the door. "I'll hold your calls and take messages."

"That won't be—"

But Madeline was gone, and he was left with Isabella. His gaze drifted over her to see that she was wearing shorts. Really short shorts that bared her long, tan legs.

A dainty ankle bracelet hung loosely at her foot. She wore sandals that showed off bright pink toenails. As his gaze drifted upward again, he saw that the T-shirt she wore was cut off so as to bare her midriff, and the belly ring she wore, and it molded to her breasts like she was planning to enter a wet T-shirt contest.

He wasn't going to survive this.

He cleared his throat and gestured toward the seat that Madeline had vacated. "I'm glad you're here, Bella. We need to talk."

She turned for a moment, and he caught a glimpse of the tattoo on her back. It sparkled almost. It was either a fairy or a butterfly. He couldn't tell and it was making him nuts. He wanted to go over and shove her shorts down so that he could see it.

A tattoo. He caught himself just short of shaking his head again. What had she been thinking? If she was his, she would have never done something so foolish. There was no reason to take such a risk with her body.

Theos, now he was sitting here considering what he would and wouldn't allow her to do if she was his. She wasn't his. Would never be his. He mustn't even entertain such a thought.

She settled into the seat in front of him which put her breasts right in his line of vision. He certainly couldn't accuse her of baring too much cleavage. The shirt covered her very well, but the shirt clung to the globes, outlining every curve and swell. It was far more enticing than the lowest cut neckline.

"What did you want to talk about?" she asked.

By now he was hanging on to his temper and control by a thread. And yet she stared calmly at him as though they were about to discuss the weather. He wanted to beat his head on the desk.

He rubbed his hand tiredly over his face and then focused his attention on the matter at hand.

"About last night…" he began.

She held up her hand, startling him into silence.

"Don't ruin it, Theron," she said huskily.

He blinked in surprise. "Ruin what?"

"The kiss. Don't ruin it by apologizing."

"It shouldn't have happened," he said tightly.

She sighed. "You're ruining it. I asked you not to."

He stared at her openmouthed. How the hell was he supposed to hand her the lecture he'd carefully planned when she looked positively disgruntled over the fact that he'd brought it up?

"If you positively must regret it, I'd appreciate it if you did so quietly," she said before he could offer anything further. "You're allowed to forget it ever happened, you're allowed to regret it, you're allowed to swear on all that's holy that it'll never happen again. Just don't expect me to do the same, and I'd appreciate it if you didn't patronize me by making light of it. As kisses go, I thought it was damn near perfect. You saying differently doesn't make it any less in my mind."

He was speechless. A first for him. He who always had something to say. He was the diplomat in the family, always the levelheaded one, and yet he'd been reduced to a mindless, gaping idiot by this infuriating woman.

She crossed one leg over the other and pressed her hands together in her lap. "Now, if that's all you had on your mind, I thought we could finalize the arrangements for the apartment and plan our shopping trip? I arranged for the papers I need to sign for the apartment to be faxed here since I was sure you'd want to look over everything first."

That was it? She could so easily shove what happened the night before out of her mind when he'd been consumed the entire morning? The memory didn't just consume him, it tortured him endlessly.

Even now he looked at her lips and remembered the lush fullness against his mouth. He could remember her taste and scent. The throb in his groin intensified as he imagined how she'd look, spread naked on the bed as he moved over her.

He cursed again and ripped his mind to present matters.

"Check with Madeline and see if she has the agreement. I'll have my lawyer look it over if you like. As for shopping, Madeline will know my appointments for the week. Stop on your way out and have her schedule a few hours for us to pick out your furniture."

She flashed him a smile that warmed parts of his body that didn't bear mentioning. With a toss of her long hair, she rose gracefully from the chair. She gave him a small wave bye then turned and walked to the door.

A fairy. Her tattoo was a fairy with a sprinkling of glittery dust and sparkles radiating from the design.

It suited her.

But it brought up another very intriguing thought. Did she have any other tattoos? Maybe one or two that could only be seen when she wore no clothing? It made him twitchy as he imagined going on a hunt with her body as the map.

Isabella left Theron's office, biting her lip to keep from smiling. He'd certainly been prepared to give her an endless lecture on how they could never again do what they'd done the night before. It wasn't anything she hadn't expected which was why she'd been prepared to head it off before he ever got started.

She mentally patted herself on the back at the expert way she'd diffused the situation. He was probably still off balance and trying to figure out just what had happened.

She approached Madeline's desk and politely asked if Madeline had received a fax for her.

Madeline tapped a stack of papers at the edge of her desk and then smiled up at Isabella.

"Did he tell you about the party?" Madeline asked.

Isabella picked up the rental agreement and frowned. "No, he didn't mention it."

Just then Theron stuck his head out the door. "Bella, I forgot to tell you that I have a cocktail party planned this Thursday that I'd like you to attend. Seven p.m. at my penthouse. Madeline will arrange for a car to pick you up at the hotel."

Before she could respond, he withdrew into his office again and closed the door.

"Well, there you have it," Madeline said in amusement. "I don't suppose he's also told you the occasion?"

Isabella turned back to the older woman, her frown deepening. "Why do I get the idea that I'm being royally set up?"

"Because you are?" Madeline said cheerfully.

Isabella flopped down in the chair beside Madeline's desk. "Tell me."

Madeline pulled out a sheet of paper and thrust it toward Isabella. "I wasn't told to keep this secret so I'm not violating anyone's confidence, and I figure if I was invited to a party where my future husband was in attendance, I'd at least want the opportunity to buy a gorgeous dress for the occasion."

Isabella snatched the paper and stared back at Madeline in astonishment. "Husband?"

Madeline's eyebrows went up. "He didn't tell you that he was searching for a husband for you? I'd have to think that came up in conversation at least once."

"Well it did, briefly I mean. Just yesterday. He's already found someone?"

Isabella tried to keep the horror from her voice, but she wasn't entirely certain she'd been successful judging by the sympathy she saw in Madeline's eyes. She'd gone along with it because she hadn't really thought that Theron was serious, and even if he was, she figured she had plenty of time.

"Maybe he's in a hurry so that he can concentrate on his own upcoming wedding," Madeline said in a soothing voice.

"What?" Isabella croaked.

"He didn't tell you that, either?" Madeline asked cautiously. "Well then, you didn't hear that from me."

Isabella leaned forward. "Tell me," she said fiercely. "Is he really getting married? Is he engaged?"

Madeline looked stunned for a moment and then understanding softened her expression. "Oh dear," she breathed.

She got up and walked around to where Isabella sat stiffly, her hands gripped tightly in her lap. "Why don't we go into the conference room," Madeline said quietly.

Isabella let Madeline lead her into the other room where Madeline shut and locked the door. "Have a seat," she directed Isabella.

Numbly Isabella complied and Madeline took the seat next to her.

"Now, how long have you had this crush on Theron?"

"Crush?" Isabella asked in a mixture of amusement and devastation. "A crush is a passing fancy. I've been in love with Theron ever since I was a young girl. Back then it might have been considered a crush, but now?"

Madeline shook her head and patted Isabella's hand. "He has the right idea to introduce you to potential husbands then. He has an arrangement with the Gianopolous family to marry their daughter Alannis. She and her mother arrive in New York in less than a week's time. I'd hate to see you…hurt. Perhaps the best thing to do would be to focus on the men Theron has in mind for you. This fascination with Theron can only end in disappointment."

Isabella knew that Madeline was nothing but well-intentioned, but she also had no idea of the depth of Isabella's feelings and her determination.

Still, the thought of Theron already being engaged, of having a commitment to another woman… She closed her eyes against the sudden stab of pain. No wonder he was so put off by the kiss they'd shared the night before.

"When do they marry?" she asked in a soft voice.

"Well, he has to propose first, but from what I understand that's a mere formality. He didn't want a long engagement, so I imagine it will be this fall sometime."

"So he hasn't even proposed yet?"

Relief filled Isabella. If he hadn't asked, then there was time to make sure he didn't.

Madeline frowned. "I don't like the look you're giving me."

Isabella leaned forward and grabbed Madeline's hands. "You have to help me, Madeline. He's making a huge mistake. I need to make him see that."

Madeline shook her head vehemently. "Oh, no. I'm

not getting involved in this. Theron has made his choice, and I make it a point never to get involved in my employer's personal life. You're on your own."

Isabella dropped Madeline's hands with a sigh. "You'll thank me for this when he's a much happier man."

Madeline stood and regarded Isabella with reservation. "Don't make a fool of yourself, Isabella. No man is worth losing your self-respect over. If your mother was alive, she'd probably tell you the same thing."

"My mother loved my father very much," Isabella said softly. "He loved her, too. They'd both want me to be happy. They'd want me to marry the man I loved."

"Then I'll wish you luck."

Isabella smiled, though it was completely forced. "Thank you, Madeline."

They left the conference room, and Isabella quickly signed the rental agreement before handing it over to Madeline. "Let him read over it and if he has no objections, fax it back for me, please."

"And your shopping trip? When would you like to schedule that?"

Isabella shook her head. "I'll go by myself. When is the cocktail party again?"

"Thursday night. Seven."

Isabella slowly nodded. "Okay, I'll be there."

She turned to walk out of the office, her mind reeling from the unexpected shock of Theron's upcoming proposal. She flipped open her cell phone and dialed Sadie's number.

"Sadie? It's me, Isabella," she said when Sadie answered the phone. "Are you busy? I need to come over. It's urgent."

Chapter 6

"This is a disaster," Isabella groaned as she flopped onto Sadie's couch.

Sadie sat next to her, concern creasing her pretty features. "Surely you aren't giving up. He hasn't even proposed to her yet."

"*Yet.* That's the problem," Isabella said glumly. "*Yet* means he fully intends to, so for all practical purposes, he's engaged."

"She might not say yes," Sadie pointed out.

Isabella gazed balefully at her. "Would you say no to Theron Anetakis?"

"Well, no...."

"Neither will she," Isabella said with a sigh. She stared up at the ceiling as she raced to come up with a plan. "She's no doubt a good Greek girl from a good Greek family. She'll have impeccable breeding, of course. Her father probably has loads of money, and she would probably drink battery acid before ever going against her parents' wishes."

"That exciting of a girl, huh?"

Isabella laughed as she looked back at Sadie. "I'm not being very charitable. I'm sure she's lovely."

"Now you make her sound like a poodle," Sadie said in amusement.

Isabella covered her face with her hands and tried not to let panic overtake her. Or despair.

"Oh, honey," Sadie said as she wrapped her arms around Isabella. "This doesn't change anything. Truly. You still have to do the same thing as always. Get him to see you. The real you. He won't be able to resist you once he spends time with you."

Isabella let herself be embraced by her friend. At the moment she'd take what comfort she could get. Being alone had never really bothered her, but now she was faced with the possibility of not being with the one person she wanted.

"We kissed last night," she said when Sadie finally drew away.

"See? I told you," Sadie exclaimed.

"Don't celebrate yet," Isabella said glumly. "He gave me the lecture this morning, or at least he tried."

Sadie's eyebrow went up. "The lecture?"

"Oh, you know, the whole *this can never happen again, it was a mistake* lecture."

"Ah, that one."

"At least now I know why."

"Okay, so it won't be as easy as you thought it might be," Sadie said. "That doesn't mean you won't be successful. From what you've said, it hardly sounds like a love match."

Isabella sighed again. "So what do I do, Sadie?"

Sadie squeezed her hand and smiled. "You make him fall in love with *you*."

"Which requires me to make him see past this whole guardian-ward thing. The kiss was..." She took a deep breath and smiled dreamily. "It was hot. I need him to see me like he did in that moment."

"If I can make this all about me for a moment, I might have a somewhat devious method for getting him to see you sorta naked."

Isabella reared her head back in surprise. "You certainly have my attention now."

Sadie grimaced. "I'd planned to ask you this anyway, and it sounds awfully self-serving, but it *could* work. Maybe."

"So, tell me," Isabella said impatiently.

"I have an audition Saturday night. Well, it's not exactly an audition but it could turn into one if I play my cards right."

"Will you just get on with it?" Isabella said. "The suspense is killing me."

Sadie grinned. "I have to work this Saturday. It's a pretty big deal. A group of rich out-of-towners who only come through once a year. Well this weekend is it and they've rented out the entire club for the night. All of the dancers are expected to be there, no excuses. Only I have this party I was invited to. Howard Griffin is going to be there and Leslie is going to introduce me."

"Who is Howard? And who is Leslie?" Isabella asked.

"Howard is producing a new Broadway musical. And, he's opening auditions next week. They're by invitation only. People would kill to get an invite from him. Including me. Leslie has an invite but then she's all over Broadway right now. Everyone wants her. I met her a couple of weeks ago, and we became friendly. She's doing me such a huge favor by basically recommending me to Howard. I can't miss that party."

"Okay, so what does that have to do with me?"

Sadie gave her an imploring look. "If I don't show up for work, I'll lose my job, and until I land enough steady roles—big roles—I can't afford to lose the kind of money I make at the club. So I thought you could fill in for me just for a few hours Saturday night."

Isabella burst into laughter. "You want me to pose as you in a strip club? Sadie, we look nothing alike. I'm a terrible dancer. I'd get you fired in two seconds."

Sadie shook her head vigorously. "First of all, I wear a blond wig. We're of similar height and with the right makeup, no one would be able to tell the difference if you wear the same clothes. No one looks at your face in that place anyway," she added dryly.

"And how does this have anything to do with Theron? He'd have heart failure if he knew I even went into a strip club, much less worked there for a night."

Sadie's eyes twinkled in amusement. "Just think about it. If he knew where you were, he'd blow a gasket, and he'd no doubt go haul you out by your hair which would of course force him to see you half-naked."

"How does this not get you fired?" Isabella asked pointedly.

A frown creased Sadie's forehead. "Damn," she muttered. "I hadn't thought of that."

Isabella instantly took pity on her friend. "How about I cover for you without Theron knowing, and I'll figure out another way to get his attention."

"Are you sure?" Sadie asked anxiously.

"I'll give his security team the slip. Apparently he's

hired a team to follow me around New York. If you ask me, he's taking this guardian thing a bit far."

Sadie's mouth gaped open. "You have a security team?"

"Yeah, I know, ridiculous isn't it? I'm to report to his office bright and early in the morning to meet them, and then, according to Theron, I'm to go nowhere without them."

A mischievous smile curved Isabella's lips.

"Why do I get the impression you'll see this security as a challenge?" Sadie asked.

Isabella's grin broadened. "It'll make Theron crazy. See, I can give them the slip to cover for you at the club. Word will get back to Theron. He'll never know where I went, but it'll give him another chance to lecture me. I'll think of some way to get his attention. If the lecture gets too bad, I'll just kiss him again."

"You know, I hope he's worth all this trouble you're going to," Sadie said. "My first thought is that no man is worth all this effort."

"He's worth it," Isabella said softly.

Isabella climbed out of the taxi in front of Theron's office building and walked briskly toward the entrance. She took the elevator up to his floor, and when she entered his suite of offices, she saw a pile of luggage in the hallway.

She walked into Madeline's office to ask what was going on, but saw that the area was full of people. She approached Madeline's desk and leaned over to whisper.

"What's going on?"

Madeline cleared her throat. "Alannis and her mother arrived early. That is your security team," she said, pointing in the direction of three intimidating-looking men. "And the others are this morning's appointments which are waiting because Alannis and company are in his office."

Frowning, Isabella straightened and glanced toward Theron's closed door. Without another word, she headed for his office, ignoring Madeline's calls.

Part of her wanted to run as fast and as far away as she could, but another part of her wanted to see for herself the woman that Theron wanted to marry.

She threw open the door and walked in. Theron, who was standing in front of his desk, looked up and frowned when he saw her. Not good. An older woman also turned, and her frown was much larger. The last, who had to be Alannis, picked up her head and stared curiously at Isabella.

Of course she wouldn't be homely, because that would be asking far too much. Alannis and her mother both were extremely beautiful in a classy, elegant way. While her mother wore her hair upswept in a neat chignon, Alannis's hair fell to her shoulders in a dark wave. Her brown eyes were warm and friendly, and she smiled tentatively in Isabella's direction.

"Bella," Theron said gruffly. "Did Madeline not tell you I was occupied?"

The reproach was clear in his voice, but Isabella ignored it. She was too busy trying to find fault with Alannis. Unfortunately for her, unless Alannis's voice was grating, the woman was darn near perfect. She and Theron even looked fabulous together.

"She might have mentioned that you were busy," Isabella murmured.

"Who is this?" Alannis's mother asked imperiously.

Theron turned and smiled reassuringly. "This is the girl I told you about, Sophia." Then he looked back at

Isabella. "Isabella, I'd like you to meet Alannis Giano-polous and her mother, Sophia. Ladies, this is Isabella Caplan, my ward."

Sophia immediately lost her guarded look and smiled warmly at Isabella. To Isabella's further surprise, the older woman approached her, holding her hands out.

"It's a pleasure to meet you, Isabella. Theron has told us so much about you. I think it's wonderful that he's taking the time to introduce you to potential husbands."

Sophia kissed her on either cheek while Isabella murmured her stunned thanks.

"I'm very happy to meet you, Isabella," Alannis offered with a shy smile.

"Likewise," Isabella said weakly. Her gaze found Theron's again. She looked for any sign that he was miserable, but his expression was unreadable.

"Was there something you needed?" Theron prompted.

She made a show of checking her watch. "You told me to be here this morning. Well, here I am."

He frowned for a moment and then remembrance sparked in his eyes. "Ah, yes, of course. You'll have to forgive me." He flashed a smile in Alannis's direction. "In the excitement of Alannis's arrival, I completely forgot about your security team. They're waiting out front. I've briefed them on my expectations. Madeline can go over the rest with you."

He walked over to his intercom and proceeded to tell Madeline that he was sending Isabella out to meet her security force.

And just like that, she was dismissed.

Sophia hugged her warmly while Alannis gave her a friendly smile. A moment later, Isabella found herself all but shoved from the office.

Numbly she made her way back to Madeline's desk. Madeline gave her a quick look of sympathy before getting up and circling her desk.

"Come with me," she directed as she all but dragged Isabella after her.

Isabella allowed herself to be led into the same conference room as the day before. Madeline shut the doors behind them and then turned on Isabella.

"I've changed my mind. I've decided to help you."

Isabella looked at her in surprise. "What do you mean?"

Madeline sighed. "Alannis is a lovely girl."

"Now you're making her sound like a poodle," Isabella pointed out, remembering that Sadie had told her the same.

"She's truly lovely, but she's all wrong for Theron. I knew it the moment I met her and her forceful mama. Alannis is a mouse while Theron is more of a lion."

"Maybe he wants a mouse," Isabella murmured.

"Have you given up then?" Madeline asked as she tapped her foot impatiently.

Isabella gave her an unhappy frown.

Madeline shook her head in exasperation. "This marriage would be a disaster. You know it and I know it. Theron has to know it somewhere behind that thick skull of his."

"I thought you had a strict policy against interfering in your employer's personal life?" Isabella said.

Madeline snorted. "I'm not going to interfere. You are."

Isabella raised her eyebrows.

"He plans to propose this Friday night after the opera. He has the tickets, the ring, the entire evening planned. I've given you the information. What you do with it is up to you," she said with a shrug.

"So soon?" Isabella whispered.

"Yep, which means you have to move fast," Madeline said cheerfully.

Isabella slowly nodded. Her mind was already racing a mile a minute.

"While you're pondering, let me introduce you to your security team," Madeline said as she herded Isabella back toward the office where the men waited. "They have strict instructions to accompany you wherever you go." She turned to Isabella and grinned. "Should make things interesting for you."

Isabella only half heard the introductions. She had to crane her neck to look up to the three really large men. They certainly fit the part of security, though she couldn't imagine that subtlety was their strong point. But then subtlety wasn't one of Theron's strong points, either.

As Madeline introduced the last man, Theron's door opened and he and Alannis and her mother came out. Alannis's arm was linked with Theron's, and his head was bent low as he listened to something she said.

Isabella stared unhappily at them until Madeline elbowed her in the ribs.

"You're being far too obvious, my girl," Madeline whispered. "Smile. You don't want mama bear to be suspicious. I get the impression she can be a barracuda when it comes to her daughter."

Isabella forced a smile to her lips just as the three approached.

"I trust you found your security team to your liking?" Theron asked politely.

Isabella nodded and smiled more broadly. Then in

an even bigger effort to kill them all with kindness, she turned her attention to Alannis. "How was your trip? Everything went well, I hope."

Alannis's smile lit up her entire face. "It did," she said in only slightly accented English. "I'm very happy to be here." She glanced up at Theron, and Isabella flinched at the open adoration in her expression.

"We look forward to seeing you again Thursday evening," Sophia said.

"Thursday?" Isabella parroted. She glanced at Theron in confusion.

"The cocktail party," Theron said smoothly. "I, of course, extended an invitation to them, as well."

"Of course," Isabella said faintly.

Though his almost fiancée stood at his side, clinging to his arm like seaweed, Theron's gaze was on Isabella, his dark eyes probing. His eyes traveled a path of awareness over her skin.

Did he love Alannis? Did he feel a certain affection for her? She was older than Isabella, but not by much. Maybe a few years? There was youthful innocence in Alannis's eyes that made Isabella feel older and more jaded.

Isabella swallowed the rising knot in her throat and she turned brightly to Sophia. "I too look forward to seeing you again. Perhaps you can tell me all about Greece. I've heard it's such a lovely place to visit. Maybe I can honeymoon there after I marry."

Sophia beamed at her while Theron's face darkened.

"We should go now," Theron said to Sophia. "You and Alannis have had a long trip. I'll have your luggage delivered to the hotel at once."

He nodded in Isabella's direction as he and the other

women walked past. "Let me know if you have any problems, Bella."

She nodded, unable to speak past the lump in her throat that she couldn't quite make go away.

Chapter 7

He couldn't stop thinking about her. Theron rubbed his face in annoyance as he focused on what Alannis and Sophia were talking about. He'd taken them to lunch after they'd settled into their suite, but he was only reminded of having eaten with Isabella at this same table just before kissing her senseless in the elevator.

Sophia was overjoyed with his plan to propose to Alannis after the opera. He'd planned the evening meticulously, buying tickets for Alannis's favorite performance with a plan to end the evening with an after-party at his hotel.

So why wasn't *he* more enthused?

Alannis was obviously excited. Theron was sure Sophia had hinted broadly of his plan to ask Alannis to marry him, although he'd asked Sophia to keep the details secret.

It seemed everyone was thrilled except him.

"Have you found suitable candidates for Isabella?" Sophia asked.

"Pardon?" Theron asked as he shook himself from his thoughts.

"You mentioned that you were trying to find her a husband," Sophia said patiently. "I wondered if you'd found a suitable match yet."

"Oh. Yes, of course. I plan to introduce her to a few carefully screened men at the cocktail party Thursday night."

Sophia nodded approvingly. "She's a beautiful young girl. She seems lonely, though. I doubt she'll have any problem in finding a husband."

Theron frowned. No, she wouldn't have any trouble in that area. Men would line up for a chance to be her husband.

Sophia leaned forward, excitement lighting her eyes. "You know, Theron, I'd love to sponsor Isabella myself. She could return to Greece with me. Myron would be more than happy to introduce her to any number of fine young men from good families."

"That's a wonderful idea, Mama," Alannis said.

"I'll bring it up to her when I speak to her next," Theron said. He wasn't sure why, but the idea of her leaving the country and marrying someone so far away left a very bad taste in his mouth.

Not that her marrying closer made him feel any better.

He listened as Alannis recounted the details of her trip and her excitement over visiting New York for the first time. But his mind simply wasn't on the present. His thoughts were occupied by a vibrant, dark-haired temptress with a smile that would melt a man at twenty feet.

As if he'd conjured her, he glanced up and saw her across the room. She was walking beside the host as he directed her to a table by the window.

Remembering Sophia's assertion that she seemed lonely, he took the opportunity to study her. Sophia was right. Isabella did look lonely. Even a little sad.

She was dressed in jeans and a plain T-shirt. Her hair was drawn into a ponytail, and the smile that he'd just pondered over was absent.

She was seated by herself, and then she smiled up at the waiter as he attended her. But her smile didn't quite reach her eyes.

For the first time he reflected on her circumstances. How difficult it must be for her to be alone in an unfamiliar city. No family, and if she had friends, he hadn't been made aware of them. Guilt crept over him as he remembered his eagerness to rid himself of her.

Now he was glad he'd planned the cocktail party for Thursday night. Maybe instead of making it a bland gathering at his penthouse with polite conversation, he could turn it into a party at the hotel welcoming Isabella to New York. He could still introduce her to the men on Madeline's list, but at least she would have some fun if he livened things up a bit. A girl her age would be bored silly at the kind of gathering he'd first envisioned.

Feeling marginally better, he refocused his attention on Alannis and reminded himself that in a few days' time, he'd be asking her to be his wife. She'd be his lover and the mother of his children. She was the woman he'd spend the rest of his life with.

Cold panic swept over him until sweat beaded his forehead. Instead of infusing comfort and contentment, the idea of making such a commitment filled him with dread.

Why was he reacting so badly now when a week ago he looked forward to a life with Alannis? It didn't make any sense.

Again his gaze wandered to where Isabella sat. She stared out the window, a pensive expression on her face. Her fingers twined in a strand of her hair as she twirled it absently. She sipped at a glass of water, her gaze never breaking.

Theron reached into his pocket and pulled out his BlackBerry. He thumbed a quick message to Madeline asking her when his shopping trip was scheduled with Isabella. After all, he didn't want to commit to an appointment with Alannis at the same time.

After a moment, Madeline returned his message. He frowned when he read it and then glanced up at Isabella again. She was going alone? She didn't want him to go with her?

Still frowning, he keyed in his response to Madeline.

Find out when she's going. Clear my schedule.

As soon as Isabella left her suite, a man fell into step beside her. She still hadn't gotten used to this whole security team thing, and it made her nervous to have men dogging her heels everywhere she went.

He got onto the elevator with her and stood in the back as they rode down. When they got to the lobby, they were joined by the other members. Trying to pay them no mind, she headed out the front where the taxis waited.

Before she got two steps toward the first in line, one of the men stepped in front of her, barring her path. She drew up short and sighed in exasperation.

"Look…what is your name?" They had been introduced to her yesterday, but she'd been reeling from the news of Theron's upcoming engagement. "Or should I just call you Huey, Louie and Dewey?"

The man in front of her flashed white teeth as he grinned. So they did have another expression besides the stone statue look.

"You can call me Reynolds." He gestured to the two men on either side of her. How had they gotten there anyway? "The one on your left is Davison and the other guy is Maxwell."

"Okay, Reynolds," she said patiently. She addressed him because he seemed to be in charge, and he was the one blocking her way to the taxi. "I need to get into that taxi. I'm going shopping. There isn't any need for you guys to follow me on a girly trip. You could wait here at the restaurant."

He smiled again. "I'm afraid I can't do that, Ms. Caplan. Our orders are to go everywhere you go."

She muttered an expletive under her breath and watched as amusement crossed his face again. "Even to the bathroom?" she asked sweetly.

"If necessary," he said, wiping the smile right off her face.

"Well, hell," she grumbled. And then she pointed out the obvious. "There's no way we'll all fit in that cab." She smiled as she waited for him to agree.

He looked sternly at her. "We have strict instructions that when you go anywhere, you're to take the car that Mr. Anetakis provided for you. This morning, however, you're to wait here for Mr. Anetakis to arrive."

She frowned and then stared at Davison and Maxwell. If she expected confirmation or denial from them, she was sorely disappointed. They simply stood, their gazes constantly moving around and beyond her as though looking for potential danger.

"You must be mistaken," she said to Reynolds. "I'm not meeting Theron today. I'm going shopping for my apartment."

Reynolds checked his watch and then looked up as a sleek, silver Mercedes vehicle pulled up and stopped just a few feet from where they stood.

To her never-ending surprise, Theron stepped from the car and strode in her direction. As he drew abreast of her, he pulled his sunglasses off and slipped them into the pocket of his polo shirt.

He reached for her hand, his fingers curling firmly around hers. Then he turned to Reynolds. "Is there a problem?" he asked with a frown.

Reynolds gave a quick shake of his head. "Ms. Caplan was about to leave in a cab. I was in the process of explaining to her why she couldn't."

Theron nodded his approval and then turned back to look at Isabella. "It's important that you heed my instructions, *pethi mou*. The arrangements I have made are for your well-being and safety."

"Of course," she murmured. "I won't keep you. I'm sure you're here to see Alannis." She glanced over at Reynolds. "Will you call for the car since I'm not allowed in a taxi?"

Theron raised one eyebrow. "A few days ago, you wanted me to accompany you. Have you changed your mind?"

Confusion crowded her mind, and she scrunched up her brow as she stared up at him. "I assumed that since you have guests here, that you wouldn't have time to go with me."

"Ah, but you're my guest, too," he said as he pulled

her hand. He guided her toward the still-waiting Mercedes and gestured for her to get into the back. Then he spoke to Reynolds over the door. "You're excused until we return. My team will handle her security."

Isabella scooted over and settled into the comfortable leather seat. Theron ducked in and sat down next to her. As the driver pulled away, Isabella shook her head and smiled ruefully.

"When was the last time you didn't get your way about something?"

He gave her a puzzled look.

"And why all the security?" she asked in exasperation. "It seems a little pretentious."

His face immediately darkened. "Before they were married, Chrysander's wife was abducted and held for ransom. She was pregnant at the time. Her kidnappers have never been apprehended. I take no chances with the safety of those under my care."

"How are Chrysander and his wife?" she asked softly.

"They are well. Marley prefers the island so they stay there. Chrysander occasionally leaves for business purposes but he doesn't leave Marley or their son very often."

"I can't imagine Chrysander so in love," she said with a laugh. "He seems so intimidating."

"You obviously don't feel the same about me," Theron said dryly.

She let her gaze wander slowly up his body until she stared into his eyes. "The way I feel about you in no way compares to how I feel around Chrysander."

There was a surge in his expression, an awareness that he fought. Such conflicting emotions shooting across his face. Before he could respond to her enigmatic statement, she turned to look out the window.

"So what made you come along this morning?" she asked cheerfully.

Though she was no longer facing him, she could feel his every move. She could feel him breathe, so tuned into his body was she.

"I would have thought you'd be far too busy with work and entertaining your…guests."

"I'm not too busy to renege on a promise I made," he said. "I told you I'd go shopping with you and here I am."

She turned then and smiled. "I'm glad. Thank you."

They spent the morning going down the list of items she wanted for her apartment. Theron seemed appreciative of the fact that she didn't take forever making her selections. But the fact was, she didn't really labor over furniture styles because if things went the way she wanted, then she wouldn't be staying in the apartment long term. And if they didn't go her way, she wasn't going to stick around New York City only to watch Theron with another woman.

By two in the afternoon, she was tired and hungry and told Theron so. He suggested they eat at the hotel again. She was thrilled that he didn't seem intent on rushing back to Alannis as soon as the shopping was done.

When they got back to the hotel, they were met by Reynolds who told Theron he and the others would stand by in the restaurant while they ate. Already, she was growing used to the small entourage of people who followed Theron wherever he went.

If he was this protective over someone he deemed

"under his care," then how much more so would he be when it came to someone he loved?

She smiled dreamily as they were escorted to Theron's table. She could handle his overprotective tendencies if it meant he loved her.

"You look well pleased with yourself, *pethi mou.*"

Theron's voice broke through her thoughts.

"Are you happy with your purchases?"

She nodded and smiled. "Thank you for going with me."

"It was my pleasure. You shouldn't be alone in such an unfamiliar place."

After placing their orders, Theron sat back in his seat, glass of wine in hand and stared over the table at her.

"So tell me, Bella. Why New York? Did you not have friends in California you preferred to stay close to? And have you given more thought to what you will do now that you've graduated from university?"

She smiled patiently. "My indecision must drive someone such as yourself insane, but I really do have a well-thought-out plan for my future."

"Such as myself?" he asked. "Dare I ask what that's supposed to mean?"

"Just that I imagine your life is planned out to the nth degree and that you have no patience for people who aren't as organized as you. Am I right?" she asked mischievously.

He struggled with a scowl before finally relaxing into a smile. "There's nothing wrong with having one's path planned out in advance."

"No, there isn't," she agreed. "I have mine quite mapped out, however, things don't always go according to plan. The real test is how you manage when your plans fall apart."

"Very wise words coming from someone so young."

She wrinkled her nose and rolled her eyes. "Do you keep reminding yourself of my age so that you aren't tempted to do something outrageous like kiss me again?"

He blinked at her, his mouth falling open. Then he snapped it closed and his jaw tightened. "I thought we agreed to forget that ever happened."

"I agreed to do no such thing," she said lightly. "You can do as you like, however."

He was saved from making his response when the waiter returned bearing their food. Isabella watched Theron all through the meal. His agitation was evident in his short, jerky motions as he dug into his food and ate. Several times he looked up and their gazes connected. There was such fire in his eyes. He wasn't immune to her. Not by a long shot. If she had to guess, he was very affected.

She'd already shoved her plate aside when she heard Theron's name called from a few tables away. She glanced over to see a handsome man approach their table. He was well dressed, he screamed wealth and refinement, and he looked at her with undisguised interest even though it was Theron's name he spoke.

Theron looked less than pleased by the interruption, but it didn't seem to bother the man who now stood at their table.

"Theron, it's good to see you. I was happy to receive your invitation for Thursday night."

He glanced over at Isabella as he spoke and she stared back, wondering if this was one of the men on

Theron's infamous potential husband list. She cocked her eyebrow in question but Theron ignored her.

"Are you coming?" Isabella spoke up, offering the man a bright smile. "I have it on good authority that Theron is using Thursday's little soiree to find me a husband."

She grinned at the man's look of surprise. Then he laughed while Theron scowled even harder.

"You must be Isabella Caplan. I'm Marcus Atwater, and yes, I'll be attending. Now that I know my attendance puts me in the running, I wouldn't miss it for the world."

Isabella smiled and extended her hand. "Please, call me Bella."

Marcus took her hand but instead of shaking it, he raised it to his lips and kissed it.

"All right, Bella. A beautiful name for an equally beautiful woman."

"Is there something you wanted, Marcus?" Theron asked pointedly.

His glare could melt steel, but Marcus didn't seem to be too bothered—or intimidated.

Isabella sat back. Maybe Theron seeing another man openly flirt with her would bring out those protective instincts. Maybe, just maybe if he suddenly had a little competition…

"Nothing at all," Marcus said congenially. "I saw you with a beautiful woman, and I merely wanted to make her acquaintance and see for myself if this was the mysterious Isabella Caplan, the same woman you were throwing the party for. I'm glad now that I came over." He glanced back at Isabella again. "Save me a dance Thursday night?"

She smiled and nodded. "Of course."

She watched him walk away before turning back to Theron. "So tell me, how did he rate among the other men you considered for my husband?"

Theron gave her a disgruntled look. "He's toward the top," he mumbled.

"Oh good, then you won't mind if we spend time together at your cocktail party."

"No," he said through gritted teeth. "He would be a good choice. He's successful, doesn't have any debt, he's never been married before, and he's healthy."

"Good God, tell me you didn't hack into his medical records," she said in disbelief.

"Of course I did. I wouldn't suggest you marry a man who was in ill health or had defects that could be passed on to your children."

He seemed affronted that she'd ask such a question.

She stifled her laughter and tried to look serious and appreciative. "So can I assume that any man at your party has been carefully screened and has your stamp of approval then?"

He nodded slowly but he didn't look happy about the fact.

"Well then, this should be fun," she said brightly. "A room full of wealthy, good-looking men to choose from." She leaned forward and pretended to whisper conspiratorially. "Did you also find out if they were good in bed?"

Theron choked on his drink. He set it down and growled in a low voice, "Of course I didn't question their sexual prowess."

"Pity. I suppose I'll have to find out myself before settling on one man in particular."

"You'll do no such thing," Theron snarled.

Her eyes widened innocently as she viewed his obvious irritation. He looked near to bursting a blood vessel.

His phone rang, and he looked relieved as he fumbled for it. After a few clipped sentences, he rang off and looked over at her.

"You'll have to excuse me, but I have to go. I have an important meeting I can't miss."

She shrugged nonchalantly. "Don't mind me. I was going up to my suite anyway."

Theron motioned for Reynolds and then rose from his chair.

"Your security detail will see you up to your suite. And Bella, don't try to go anywhere without them."

Chapter 8

Theron's admonishment still rang in Isabella's ears the next morning as she plotted her path past her security team. It wasn't that she minded them going shopping with her. They might even be able to offer a male perspective on which dress looked best on her. She wanted to look good for the cocktail party, and not because of the men Theron had invited with her in mind.

As soon as she stepped out of her room, Reynolds fell into step behind her.

"Good morning," she offered sweetly.

"Good morning," he offered in return. "Where would you like to go this morning?" He pulled out his cell phone to call for the car.

"I want to do a little sightseeing," she said. "I don't know my way around the city very well, so I'll have to rely on you."

"What interests you?" he asked politely.

She pretended to think. "Museums, art galleries, oh, and I'd like to see the Statue of Liberty."

He nodded even as he relayed her wishes to the driver.

The elevator opened into the lobby where they were joined by Davison and Maxwell. She halted in front of them, took one look and shook her head.

"Is there a problem?" Reynolds asked.

"Look, if you guys are going to shadow me, I'd prefer you didn't look like something out of a mafia movie. Not to mention, I'd rather not broadcast the fact that I'm going around with three bodyguards. That will only make me more conspicuous."

"What do you suggest then?" Maxwell muttered. He didn't look entirely pleased with her assessment.

"Well, you could lose the shades. They make you look like Secret Service wannabes."

Maxwell and Davison both removed the sunglasses, and Davison glared at her. She grinned in return.

"Now get rid of the tie and the jacket."

All three men shook their heads. "The jackets stay." Davison spoke up for the first time. To get his point across, he pulled the lapel, opening the jacket enough that she could see the pistol secured by a shoulder holster.

Her mouth fell open. She wasn't a screaming ninny about guns. She well understood the need for them. She just hadn't realized that Theron was that concerned over her safety. For a moment she wavered. Maybe breaking away wasn't such a great idea. But then in her mind, having three hulking men made her much more noticeable than if she zipped to the department store and back for her dress.

"Okay, definitely leave the jackets," she muttered.

They walked outside where the car had pulled around. Davison got into the front while Maxwell walked around to the opposite passenger door and climbed in. Reynolds opened the passenger door closest to her and waited for her to get in.

She faked exasperation and slapped her forehead with her open palm. "Wait right here. I forgot my purse," she said.

"I'll get it for you. You get in," Reynolds said.

But she was already striding toward the hotel entrance. She turned back holding up a finger. "I won't be a minute."

Reynolds started after her, but she quickly rounded the corner and ducked into the men's bathroom. He'd most definitely search the women's room when he figured out she'd disappeared, but hopefully he wouldn't think to look in the men's.

She cracked the door just enough that she could look out. Reynolds hurried by and then he barked into a small receiver that hung from his shirt.

Seconds later, Maxwell and Davison ran by the bathroom, their faces grim. She slipped out with no hesitation and ran for the hotel entrance, hoping they didn't look back in the time it took her to get to a taxi.

She slid into the cab at the front of the line and offered the driver double his fee if he got the hell out fast. Only too happy to comply, he peeled out of the entryway and rocketed in front of two other cars. Horns sounded and angry shouts filled the air but the driver shook his fist and then grinned.

"Where you going, miss?"

She glanced up to see him staring at her in the rearview mirror.

"I'm not completely sure," she admitted. "I need a

dress. A really gorgeous dress that'll make a man drool at a hundred yards."

"I know just the place," he said, nodding his head.

Not completely willing to forego any precautionary measures, she asked if he'd wait while she shopped, meter running of course.

He dropped her off in front of the upscale department store then gave her his cell number.

"Give me a ring when you're checking out, and I'll pull up and pick you up here," he said.

"Thank you," she said as she climbed out.

Making sure to keep in a clump of people, she entered the store. She wasn't a complete idiot when it came to safety. She avoided corners, anything off the beaten path and stayed in plain sight of the security cameras. When it was time for her to try on her dresses, she had the extremely helpful saleslady accompany her to the dressing room. After all she needed an opinion.

After trying on six dresses, she found the one. It slipped over her body, hugging every curve like a second skin. The genius of the dress was in its simplicity. There weren't any ruffles or frills, nothing to take away from the shape of her body. It was sheer with spaghetti straps, and it fell two inches above her knee. With a pair of killer heels, she'd have the men eating out of her hand.

She frowned as she realized it didn't really matter what the other men did. Theron was the only one who mattered, and it was anyone's guess how he would react.

She stepped out of the dressing room to show the saleslady. Her entire face lit up.

"It's perfect, Ms. Caplan. Just perfect. With the right shoes, you'll be a knockout."

Isabella smiled. "Would you happen to have a pair

of black shoes in a three-inch heel that would go well with this dress?"

The saleslady smiled. "I'll be right back."

A few minutes later, Isabella twirled and glanced down her legs at the shoes. The heels were basically toothpicks, but they did look gorgeous on her.

Not content to sell her an outrageously expensive dress—the shoes were nearly as expensive—the saleslady also insisted she accessorize with just the right jewelry— and handbag of course.

Two hours after she'd ditched her security team, Isa-bella settled into her cab and headed back to the hotel. When they pulled up, she collected her bags and leaned up to pay the driver.

"Thank you so much. I truly appreciate you wait-ing for me."

"It was no problem, miss. Good luck at your party tonight. I'm sure you'll knock their socks off."

She smiled and got out then waved as he drove away. With a smile, she entered the hotel and headed for the elevator. The absence of her security team gave her pause, and then guilt crept in. She'd been so caught up in her shopping that she hadn't even considered phon-ing Reynolds to assure him that she was okay, and she hadn't ever provided him or Theron *her* cell number, so it wasn't as if they could have called her.

With a sigh, she pulled out her cell as she inserted the key to her hotel room. She entered, punching Reynold's number. Then she looked up and saw four very angry men staring at her from inside her room.

Theron rose from where he was sitting on the couch, his eyes sparking. He motioned to the other three men. "Leave us," he said shortly.

Isabella let the bags slide from her fingertips as the

three men filed by. Reynolds shot her a disapproving look, and she smiled tentatively.

When they were gone, she glanced over at Theron who had closed the distance between them. He glowered menacingly, his face a veritable storm cloud.

"You didn't fire them, did you?" she asked uneasily.

"Rest assured I know exactly where the blame lies," he gritted out.

She bent down to collect her bags and walked around him toward the couch.

"Taking off from your security team was a foolish thing to do, Bella. Did I not impress upon you the need for them? What were you thinking?"

She turned and regarded him thoughtfully. "I had my reasons," she said simply.

He threw up his hands in exasperation. "What reasons?" he demanded.

She smiled. "Nothing you would approve of. I didn't stay long, and I took precautions. The very nice cab-driver looked out for me quite well, and the saleslady never left my side. Well, except when she went to get me shoes."

Theron's face went gray. "Cabdriver? You entrusted your well-being to a cabdriver?"

"Relax," she said with a grin. "He was a perfect gentleman. He drove me to the department store and waited for me until I was through."

Theron swallowed and looked as though he was fighting to keep his temper in check. Hmm. Theron losing his cool. That might be worth the price of admission.

"Why did you leave without your security team? What was so important that you would risk yourself in this manner?"

She held up her shopping bag. "I needed a dress for the party tonight."

He drew in a deep breath, closed his eyes and then reopened them. He strode over to where she stood and gripped her shoulders. "A dress? You gave me the fright of my life for a dress?"

He shook her as he spoke and she gripped his waist to keep her balance.

"It wasn't just any dress," she murmured as she tried to keep the smile from her face. She probably shouldn't bait him as she was, but making him lose his composure had suddenly become her mission. "I could hardly meet my future husband in anything but a truly spectacular dress."

"You are the most infuriating, frustrating woman I've ever had the misfortune to meet," he growled.

And then he crushed her to him, slanting his lips over hers in a forceful kiss that took her breath away. She moaned as his hands gripped her arms then slid over her back like bands of steel.

He tasted her hungrily, like a man starving, as though he couldn't get enough. Tingling awareness snaked up her spine. Her breasts throbbed, and her nipples became taut points, pushing at his chest.

The sounds of their kiss, hot and breathless, filled the room. One of his hands slipped to the waist of her jeans, and he yanked at her shirt until it came free. Then he slid his fingers over the bare skin of her lower back, right where her tattoo rested. He traced patterns over the small of her back as though he was aware of what was there.

Eager to taste him, she traced his lip with her tongue until he reached out to duel delicately with his own.

Warm. So masculine, he tasted of strength, of heady power.

She lost herself in his arms, melted against his mouth. Her pulse sped up and bounced erratically. How she craved him.

His hand crept higher until it collided with her bra strap. He fumbled over the clasp and then he froze.

With a muffled curse, he broke away, his breaths coming hard and ragged. His eyes blazed like an out-of-control fire, and then he dropped his hands from her body like she'd burned him.

He swore again, a mixture of Greek and English and then ran a hand through his hair.

"*Theos mou!* We can't…not again. This mustn't happen again. I'm sorry, Bella."

He held up his hands and then backed away. He paused at the door, his motions haphazard, like he was drunk. Then he turned to stare at her, his eyes still burning with unresolved desire.

"Your security team goes *everywhere* with you. Are we understood? From now on, they even go to the bathroom with you."

She nodded, unable to do anything more. She was shaking too badly. As he left her hotel room, she gripped her arms and rubbed up and down to make the chill bumps go away.

"You can deny it all you want," she whispered to the empty room. "You want me every bit as much as I want you."

Chapter 9

Theron rubbed the back of his neck in an effort to relieve the enormous tension that gripped him. Isabella still hadn't arrived, and he felt equal parts relief and disappointment.

He glanced around the ballroom of the Imperial Park Hotel, taking in the guests milling around, talking and laughing as a jazz band played softly from an elevated platform.

Alannis stood at his side, her hand resting on his arm. Sophia stood on Alannis's other side, her pride in her daughter evident.

He ducked his head to hear what Alannis was trying to tell him and nodded appropriately though his concentration was shot. When he stood to his full height again, his gaze went to the doorway, and his breath caught in his throat.

She was here.

Isabella stood as she gazed nervously over the room. Theron swallowed when he took in her attire. The term *little black dress* could have been coined for this occasion.

The material molded to her every curve and settled a few inches above her knees. She wore her hair up, drawing attention to the shape of her neck. Stray tendrils escaped the elegant knot and whispered against her skin.

His fingers itched to let her hair down and watch it fall to her shoulders. He wanted to run his hands through the silken mass, feel it twine around his knuckles.

"Oh, look, there's Isabella," Sophia exclaimed.

As if he wouldn't be aware the moment she stepped into the room.

"Excuse me," he murmured to Alannis.

She let him go with a smile, and he made his way to where Isabella stood.

There wasn't an easy way to address the awareness between them, so he chose to ignore it—and the fact that he'd kissed her just hours before.

"Bella," he greeted as he stopped in front of her.

She gazed up at him with wide green eyes, her mouth curving into a smile of welcome.

"Sorry I'm late," she said in a breathy voice. "I don't suppose you saved me a dance?"

He nearly groaned. The thought of having her pressed that close to his body was torture.

"The dancing hasn't begun yet," he said as he turned to look at the band. "Perhaps we can kick it off together, and then I'll introduce you around."

He motioned to the pianist who nodded in return. A slow, sultry melody started, and Theron offered his hand to Isabella. Her fingers trembled slightly in his grip, and he squeezed to reassure her.

When they reached the middle of the area that was the designated dance floor, he turned, and she went willingly into his arms. The moment she melted against him, he went completely rigid.

Her scent surrounded him as the warmth from her touch invaded his body. There wasn't a single inch that wasn't aware of her feminine form. He glanced down as they made a slow turn and swallowed hard. She wasn't wearing a bra and the lush mounds were pressed tightly against his chest, thrusting upward, straining against the neckline of her dress.

It was all he could do not to haul her out of the room so that no one else could see her.

He blew out his breath as inconspicuously as possible and reminded himself that she wasn't his, and he had no right to be possessive.

It still didn't help the rise of irritation when he saw how many men were staring avidly at Isabella. No, she wouldn't have any shortage of suitors after tonight. He should have been relieved, but he was anything but.

It was all he could do to keep the scowl from his face.

"The party is lovely," Isabella said with a smile as she gazed over his shoulder. "Thank you for putting it on."

"You're quite welcome, *pethi mou*. I want you to enjoy yourself."

"How are your guests settling in?" she asked innocently.

His eyes narrowed. Did she know of his plans for Alannis? It wasn't as if she wouldn't know in a short time, but for some reason he was reluctant to tell her of his impending engagement. Or maybe he was a first-class slimeball who'd kissed another woman within days of asking another woman to marry him.

"They're settling in quite well," he muttered as he swung her around so that she wasn't facing Alannis and her mother.

Guilt filled him. What kind of a man took advantage of a young woman when he had an agreement with another? Even Piers, who was never without a woman, would frown on seducing his ward when he had a soon-to-be fiancée waiting in the wings.

Chrysander wouldn't hesitate to kick his ass all the way back to Greece for pulling this kind of stunt with Isabella.

"So which ones are my potential husbands?" she asked as she craned to see around him.

She wore a mischievous smile that only made her sparkle all the brighter.

"I'll introduce you as soon as our dance is over," he said.

For this moment, she was his, in his arms, and he wasn't in any hurry to relinquish her to her waiting suitors. They'd gathered around the perimeter of the dance area like a bunch of vultures.

For the first time, he regretted his hasty decision to assist Isabella in her search for a husband. She was too young to think of marriage. She should be out having fun, not thinking of making a lifelong commitment.

And yet he was poised to do just that. Panic scuttled up his spine. Then he firmly tamped it down. Before Isabella came bursting into his life, he was more than content over the idea of marrying Alannis and settling down to have children. Isabella was a temporary distraction, nothing more. As soon as things were settled between him and Alannis, and he had Isabella on her path to security and stability, he was confident that he'd embrace his future without hesitation.

When the song died, Theron dropped his hands and then enfolded Isabella's in his. "Come, *pethi mou*. Your party awaits."

Isabella donned her best smile and allowed Theron to lead her through the assembled guests to where the band was set up. Theron held a hand out, and the music stopped. Then he turned to face the guests.

"I appreciate you coming for the occasion to welcome Isabella Caplan to our city," Theron said in a congenial tone.

A waiter approached and handed Isabella a glass of champagne then turned to offer Theron one. He held it at waist level as he continued to address the crowd.

"We're here to enjoy an evening of entertainment, dancing and conversation. You're welcome to stay as long as you want, or until the booze runs out," he added with a smile.

Laughter rang out.

He turned to Isabella and held out his glass. "A toast to Isabella."

"To Isabella," the guests echoed.

Theron touched his glass to hers and their gazes locked. For a long moment they simply stared. And then Theron broke away and took a long swallow.

Though she had no desire to wade through the eligible men assembled at Theron's request—it reminded her of choosing steaks at a butcher shop—she knew she'd have to play the part, particularly if she had any hope of making Theron jealous. It was a long shot, because he'd have to feel more for her than simple lust, but at the moment, it was her only hope.

The toast seemed to have signaled a return to normal activities. The band struck up a song, and people swirled onto the dance floor.

"Come with me, Bella. It's time to introduce you around."

"You mean it's time for me to meet the men you've assembled for me," she said dryly.

He glanced questioningly at her. "Would you prefer not to meet them? There's nothing to say you have to."

He sounded almost hopeful, a little too eager, which was strange considering the time he had to have spent putting together his group of bachelors. The background checks alone would have been an enormous undertaking. And he wouldn't have left a single stone unturned.

She nearly grinned at the thought.

"No, let's do it. My future awaits and all that," she said lightly.

She curled her hand around his arm and allowed him to lead her into the crowd. Unsure of what she could expect, and maybe she'd thought there would be a stampede, she was pleasantly surprised by how civilized the whole process was.

Theron took her around from group to group, introducing her to business acquaintances and friends. It was easy to immerse herself in the fantasy that she and Theron were together, and he was acting as her escort and not a man bent on marrying her off. It was also easy to forget that just a few feet away, Alannis and her mother stood, observing the goings-on.

Still, Isabella wasn't ready to let reality intrude, and she clung to Theron's arm all the while offering a smile or a laugh as she engaged in conversation. After awhile she found herself relaxing and genuinely enjoying the festive gathering.

She glanced up as an attractive man made his way

in her direction, a determined look on his face. She recognized him as Marcus Atwater, the man who'd introduced himself in the restaurant the day before.

"Isabella, my apologies for my late arrival," he said as he approached. He flashed her a charming smile that she couldn't help but respond to. "I was unexpectedly tied up with a client."

He took her hand, and as he'd done in the restaurant, he lifted it to his lips. Then he cast a questioning look in Theron's direction—Theron who stood there looking as though a black cloud had parked itself right over his head.

"I'd like to borrow Isabella. I promise to keep her safe, and you can return to your own date, who, if you don't mind me saying, looks very much like she'd like to dance."

Theron scowled, and Isabella glanced over to see Alannis eyeing the dancing couples with what could only be construed as a wistful glance. Isabella didn't want to feel pity. She wanted to dislike Alannis. If she was a complete ogre it would be so much simpler, but the fact was that both mother and daughter had been extremely nice to her.

"Are you borrowing me for a dance or for some other purpose?" she asked teasingly as she slipped her hand into Marcus's.

"How about we dance first and we can discuss other purposes later," he said with a teasing glint in his eye.

Theron's expression was glacial. She released his arm to go with Marcus, but he caught her free hand, pulling her between the two men.

She stared at him for a moment, waiting for him to speak, but he seemed to be at a loss for words, or maybe he hadn't intended to pull her back.

"Was there something you wanted?" she asked.

He released her hand and shook his head even as he glanced in Alannis's direction. "No. Have fun, *pethi mou*. This is your night."

With one last look in his direction, she turned and let Marcus lead her back to the dance floor. He spun her in an expert move, and she landed against his chest. Laughing blue eyes shone down at her, and she smiled in return.

"Are you still husband hunting or have I arrived too late for consideration?" he asked with mock seriousness.

"Aren't men supposed to run in the other direction when marriage is mentioned?"

"Not if he doesn't mind being caught by the woman in question."

"You're a total flirt," she said with a laugh. "I can't possibly take such a charming man seriously."

He grinned but didn't refute her claim. They danced among the crowd of couples, and every chance she got, she snuck a peek Theron's way.

He and Alannis were dancing on the far side. She stared laughing up into his eyes, and it didn't take a genius to see how starstruck she was by Theron. Isabella knew that feeling well.

"So," Marcus said casually as he spun her around. "Are you going to let him get away?"

She yanked her gaze guiltily away from Theron to meet Marcus's amused smile. When she realized she hadn't a hope of playing ignorant, she sighed.

"Am I that obvious?" she asked in resignation.

"Only to another man who's scouting the territory for competition."

Her shoulders slumped downward. "I knew I shouldn't have agreed to this farce. This was Theron's idea in case you haven't guessed. He's decided that it's his duty to marry me off with all possible haste."

Marcus touched her chin and gently tugged upward until she looked him in the eye. "Have you told him how you feel?"

She glanced back over at Theron then shook her head. "It's complicated."

"Tell you what. Why don't we head to that corner over there. I'll get us a drink and you can tell me all about it."

Theron's gaze found Isabella again as he listened politely to Alannis and Sophia and the small group of people who stood in the loosely formed circle to the side of the dance floor. He ground his teeth together as Marcus leaned in close to Isabella, his lips hovering precariously close to her ear as he murmured to her.

She laughed and the seductive sound rose over the clink of glasses and the murmur of conversation. Marcus's fingers drifted over her bare shoulder, lingering there much longer than Theron thought appropriate.

He had to swallow the sound of anger that bubbled up in his throat when Marcus trailed one finger down her cheek and then seductively down the side of her neck and around to the hollow of her throat.

Isabella leaned toward Marcus as if seeking his touch, and then he angled in and pressed his lips very softly to the expanse of skin just below her ear.

"Theos mou," Theron growled. "Enough is enough."

"Theron, is something wrong?" Alannis asked.

She touched his arm and he turned to see concern reflected in her eyes.

"It's nothing," he said shortly.

Alannis glanced at Isabella and then back to him. "She seems to be having a good time."

"Yes." His gaze drifted back, his annoyance growing as Marcus grew bolder in his advances. "Excuse me a moment, will you, Alannis?"

He nodded to Sophia and walked as calmly as he was able over to where Marcus was standing with Isabella. He all but had her trapped in the corner, his body moving in like a predator closing in on a kill.

Just as Theron started to speak up, Marcus lowered his head to nuzzle Isabella's neck. Rage exploded over Theron. He closed the remaining distance and grabbed the other man by the shoulder, tearing him away from Isabella.

"What the…" Marcus began but broke off midsentence. "Theron, is there a problem?"

"Come here, Isabella," Theron bit out. He held his hand out as Isabella stared at him agape.

"What on earth is wrong?" she asked even as she slid her hand into his.

He pulled until she was against his side then he focused the full force of his glare at Marcus.

"Keep your hands off her," he snarled. "You aren't to touch her. You aren't to so much as think about her. Understand?"

Marcus surprised him by grinning and then backing away, hands up. "Whatever you say." Then he winked at Isabella. "I guess I'll go. Something tells me I've overstayed my welcome."

"Oh, no, Marcus, stay." She glanced back up at Theron with a puzzled expression. "I'm sure Theron has no objections."

"I have plenty of objections. He was mauling you in plain view of a roomful of people." Then he turned again to Marcus, as he pulled Isabella even closer. He dropped his voice low enough not to be overheard. "If I find you near her again, I'll take you apart. Are we clear?"

He ignored Isabella's stunned gasp. Marcus merely smiled and continued to back away, his expression smug.

"I'll see you another time, Bella."

"Goodbye," she said softly.

"Come on," Theron said, half dragging her along with him. "You're not to leave my side for the rest of the night."

To his surprise, she didn't offer any argument. Halfway back to where Alannis and her mother still stood, Isabella stumbled, and he turned back quickly to catch her.

"Slow down," she said. "I can't walk that fast in these shoes."

"Sorry," he said gruffly as he righted her. He held her arms until he was sure she had her footing. "Better?"

She nodded and they started back again.

"Isabella, are you all right?" Sophia asked in concern when they walked up.

Isabella offered a smile. "Yes, Mrs. Gianopolous. I'm fine. Thank you for asking."

"Please, do call me Sophia." Sophia reached out and took Isabella's hand from Theron's. "Can I get you something to drink? Have you had anything to eat since you arrived?" She turned to Alannis. "Will you excuse us for a minute, dear? You stay here with Theron while I take Isabella over to grab a bite to eat."

Theron held up his hand to stop the endless stream of chatter. His head was pounding, and what he really wanted was to go pound on Marcus for touching Isabella, for putting his lips on her.

"Just stay here. I'll have a waiter bring around a tray. I'd prefer that Isabella remain with me for the remainder of the evening," he said brusquely.

The older woman's eyes widened in surprise. Alannis moved closer to Isabella and touched her arm. "Are you sure you're all right, Isabella?" she asked softly.

Isabella's smile seemed strained when she looked back at Alannis. "I'm absolutely fine. Theron overreacted." She shot him a challenging look. "I'm not sure how he expects me to find a husband when he flips his lid the moment a man pays attention to me."

Theron took a deep breath. "I don't think what he was doing could be classified as paying attention to you. *Theos!* He was making love to you for all to see."

She raised her eyebrows and a slow smile formed on her lips. "Is that what they call kissing these days?" she taunted.

His nostrils flared at the reminder of the kisses they'd shared. He was well and truly caught in a trap of his own making.

"His actions were inappropriate," he gritted out. "You are under my protection. You'll heed my instructions."

She turned cheekily to Sophia and Alannis. "I suppose he'll mark that one off the list of potential husbands now." Then she sighed dramatically and dropped her hands helplessly to her side. "I didn't even get to dance again."

"Theron will dance with you," Alannis urged. "He's a marvelous dancer as I'm sure you determined earlier."

"Yes, do go on," Sophia said. "I'll make sure there is food when you return."

Theron's mouth went dry. He wouldn't survive another dance with her lush body molded to his. One torture session was enough for the night.

But then the alternative was letting her dance with the circling pack of men. Men he'd hand-selected.

Over his dead body.

Without another word, he snared Isabella's hand and dragged her toward the dance floor.

"You're hell on these shoes," she murmured as he pulled her into his arms.

For the first time since Marcus had arrived, Theron relaxed as Isabella's soft body molded so sweetly to his. There was an innate sense of rightness. He loved touching her. It was difficult to keep his hands from roaming up and down her soft curves.

"You feel it, too," she said softly as she gazed up at him. "You don't want to. You fight it, but you feel it every bit as much as I do. It's why you've kissed me." She laughed softly. "You can't help but kiss me, just as I'm unable to resist. I don't want to resist."

He shook his head even as his body hummed agreement.

She smiled and put a finger over his lips as they swayed with the music. Then turning, so that his back was to Alannis, she let her hands run down his chest. Her eyes narrowed to half slits, and she parted her lips in a hungry gesture.

He groaned. "We mustn't, Bella. You make me so crazy. You have to stop with the teasing."

"Who says I'm teasing," she asked as she arched one eyebrow.

He took her hands and pulled them away from his body before turning her around again so that they were sideways to Alannis.

"You see her? Alannis. I'm going to ask her to marry me, Isabella."

She greeted his announcement with calm. No visible reaction. Had she already known?

"This must stop between us," he pressed on. "We're going to marry different people."

"And yet you keep kissing me," she said with a slight smile.

"I won't do so again," he vowed.

Instead of deterring her, a sparkle lit her eyes. "If I have anything to say about it you will."

Before he could respond, she pulled away. "I'm starving." Then suddenly she leaned close and murmured so only he could hear. "You say you don't want me, yet you don't want another man to have me. Pretty strange wouldn't you say?"

She turned and walked away, her hips swaying gently as she navigated her way back to where Sophia waited with a plate of food.

Chapter 10

"He still plans to propose tonight?" Isabella asked in dismay. She held the phone tightly to her ear as she listened to Madeline.

Somehow she'd hoped that after last night Theron would have realized he felt *something* for her. Maybe not love. Not yet, but she'd thought he'd wake up to the attraction between them.

Okay, maybe he wasn't completely unaware, but he certainly seemed determined to ignore it.

She closed her eyes as she listened to Madeline confirm that according to Theron, the proposal was still on.

"Thanks, Madeline," she said slowly.

She hung up the phone and sunk lower into the bed. Theron with Alannis. She just couldn't imagine it. Theron needed…someone to shake him up, someone who wouldn't let him get too serious and organized.

He needed someone like her.

Alannis wouldn't challenge him. There was no spark of chemistry between them. Alannis may as well be his daughter for all the attraction that existed.

Maybe Theron wanted a comfortable, dull marriage.

She shook her head. No, she wouldn't believe that, because if she did, then she'd have to give up, and she wasn't ready to do that yet.

Reaching for the phone again, she dialed the number that Marcus had given her the night before.

"Marcus, hi, it's Isabella," she said when he answered.

"Isabella, how are you?" he greeted.

She sighed. "Word is the proposal is still on."

"Sorry to hear that. I was certain he was ready to beat me into a pulp after our little act last night."

"He frustrates me," she said glumly. "I can't figure the man out. He's so controlled in all things except when he's alone with me."

Marcus laughed. "I can't say I blame the man. I have a feeling you'd try the patience of a saint and the vows of a priest."

"I don't suppose you could get tickets to the opera tonight? I hate to ask, but I'm desperate. He and Alannis are going to the opera and then to an after-party at the hotel where he plans to pop the question."

"I'm sure I could arrange it, but how do you plan to stop him from proposing?"

Isabella sucked in a deep breath. "I'm not sure," she said softly. "But I'll think of something."

"I don't suppose now would be a good time to admit that I hate the opera," Marcus said with a laugh.

She smiled faintly. "I'm not much of a fan myself, but apparently, it's Alannis's favorite performance."

"Then might I suggest an alternative?"

Her brow puckered, and she sat up in bed, the covers gathering at her waist. "What did you have in mind?"

"How about a date? You inform that security team of yours of your plans for the evening, that you'll be out with me. I have no doubt that they report to Theron regularly." Amusement threaded through Marcus's voice. "It'll drive him crazy that he's stuck at the opera with Alannis, and he'll have no idea what we're up to, whereas if we're both at the opera, he'll be able to see us."

"But what about the party and his plans to propose?"

"I'll have you to the party before Theron arrives. Maybe by then you'll have come up with a plan."

"I don't know," she said slowly.

"Come on," he cajoled. "We'll have a nice dinner. It'll drive Theron crazy. Then you show up at the party. He'll be putty in your hands."

"All right," she conceded.

"Great. I'll pick you up at seven then. I'll call right before I arrive so you can come down."

They rang off, and Isabella swung her legs over the edge of the bed. Once again, she was in need of the perfect dress. Something gorgeous. She wasn't sure they sold dresses for the occasion of preventing a marriage proposal.

She had a sudden, alarming thought. Did this make her the other woman? Was she a femme fatale breaking up a relationship? The thought was an uncomfortable one, and it didn't give her a good feeling. But on the other hand, she knew that she and Theron were right for each other. Even if he didn't know it yet.

Besides, nothing was settled yet. Alannis wasn't wearing a ring, and no commitment had been made. Until that happened, all was fair in love and war.

She almost groaned at the cheesy cliché. Clearly she needed to come up with something more worthy.

Pushing herself up, she headed for the shower. She only had until tonight to figure out how she was going to prevent Theron from making a huge mistake. And to prevent her own heartbreak.

Theron picked up the phone as Madeline called back to say that Reynolds was on the phone to give his daily report. He listened as Isabella's head of security listed the morning's activities which consisted of shopping and lunch alone at the hotel.

His hand tightened around the receiver when Reynolds got to her plans for the evening. An outing with Marcus Atwater.

He swore in Greek and then quickly recovered. What was she thinking? Surely she couldn't be attracted to a man such as Marcus. He was smooth, too smooth, and he'd been all over her at the party.

Not to mention he had a different woman on his arm every week.

"You are to keep a close watch on her," Theron ordered. "I don't trust this man she's going out with. Under no circumstances are they to be left alone."

"Yes, sir," Reynolds replied.

Theron hung up the phone, his lips compressed into a tight line. Was she just trying to drive him insane? She had to know he wouldn't approve of her spending time with Marcus after what had happened the previous night.

And maybe she could care less what he approved of. She hadn't exactly paid him any heed in any other area.

He leaned back in his chair and opened his desk drawer, reaching for the small black box that nestled in the corner. His fingers touched it, and then he picked it up and opened it.

The diamond ring sparkled in the light as he studied it. Tonight he'd put it on Alannis's finger. So why wasn't he more enthused? Why wasn't he looking forward to his future?

This time next year he could even have a child, a family. He'd be settled. And yet he felt decidedly unsettled about her—about everything.

His intercom buzzed again, and Madeline announced that he had another important call. She cut the connection before he could ask who. Shaking his head, he picked up the phone.

"Have you lost your damn mind?" Piers's demand made Theron frown.

"Give him a chance," Chrysander said dryly. "Then we'll ascertain whether he's lost his sanity."

"You told Madeline not to tell me it was you two calling, didn't you?" Theron accused.

"Damn right," Piers said. "You wouldn't have answered if you'd known. Coward."

"There's nothing to say I won't hang up," Theron said idly.

"Your sister-in-law wants to know why you didn't tell her you were thinking of getting married," Chrysander said.

Theron winced. "It's not fair of you to use Marley to make me feel guilty, and you know it."

"What are you doing?" Piers asked impatiently, cutting through the banter. "What could you possibly be thinking?"

"What our brother is trying to say is that we were caught by surprise, and we'd like to offer you our congratulations, just as soon as we understand why we're only just now finding out," Chrysander said diplomatically.

Piers made a rude noise. "Not me. If he tells me he's really doing this, I can only offer my condolences."

"What's wrong with me getting married?" Theron asked, surprised by Piers's reaction.

"Besides the fact that I think anyone willingly entering the institution of matrimony has a few screws loose, there is the fact that you're marrying Alannis Gianopolous. She's so wrong for you," Piers said bluntly.

Theron frowned. "Alannis is a perfectly acceptable choice."

There was a long silence, and then Chrysander cleared his throat. "*Acceptable choice?* That's an odd way of putting it."

"I'm more interested as to why you believe she's so wrong for me," Theron said, ignoring Chrysander's remark.

"Hell, Theron, apart from the fact that her father has been angling for her to marry one of us for years, she's…she's…"

"She's what?" Theron cut in.

"Just tell us why the sudden urge to get married," Chrysander said calmly. "And why you felt the need to include such momentous news in an e-mail."

"Probably because of the reaction I'm getting now," Theron said pointedly.

"Since when did you become so worried about what we thought?" Piers asked.

"Does anyone find it ironic that not so long ago, it was me and Piers having this talk with Chrysander about Marley? We were wrong about her, and you two are wrong about Alannis."

Chrysander sighed, and Theron knew he had him.

What could he say when it was the truth? Theron and Piers had been quite vocal in their opposition of Marley. They'd also been dead wrong.

"Just be sure this is what you want," Chrysander said in resignation. "And keep us apprised of your plans. Marley will want to make it for the wedding."

Piers wasn't quite so ready to throw in the towel. "Think about what you're doing, Theron. This is the rest of your life you're talking about here."

"I appreciate your concern," Theron said dryly. "I am capable of making my own decisions."

"Tell me how things are going with Isabella," Chrysander broke in, an obvious attempt to change the subject. "Did you get her off to Europe?"

Again, there was a long silence. Theron wiped a hand through his hair wishing he'd pressed Madeline harder about who was on the phone.

"She didn't go to Europe," he said.

"Who is Isabella?" Piers demanded. "Are we talking about little Isabella Caplan?"

"I'll fill you in later," Chrysander said. "Why didn't she go to Europe? Where is she then?"

"She's here. She's decided to stay in New York," Theron said. "And she's not so little anymore," he added, though he was unsure why he felt the need to make that point.

Chrysander chuckled. "Poor Theron. Saddled with women on all sides. I imagine you're cursing me about now."

If he only knew.

"I've seen to Isabella's needs, and gotten her settled in. Everything is fine. *I'm* fine. You two can get off my back now."

"He sounds a little defensive, does he not?" Piers

said smugly. "I smell something here. Something rotten. I only wish I was in New York to see for myself."

"You just stay the hell where you are," Theron muttered. "You have a hotel to build."

Piers's laughter flooded the line.

"I'm hanging up now," Theron said before lowering the receiver.

Now he knew how Chrysander had felt when he and Piers had given him such a hard time about Marley. Well-meaning relatives were always the worst.

Chapter 11

"Have any idea what you're going to say yet?" Marcus asked Isabella as he picked up his wineglass and brought it to his lips.

Reluctantly she shook her head and stared down at her barely eaten entrée. "I don't want to make an ass of myself, but at the same time I have to make him see that I'm not teasing. I'm not playing some silly game nor is he a passing infatuation."

When she looked up, she saw sympathy in Marcus's dark eyes.

"Put yourself in his shoes," she murmured. "You're about to ask a woman to marry you. You've kissed another woman twice, and you're fighting the attraction hard. What could this other woman say to you to convince you not to marry someone else?"

Marcus set his glass down, leaned back and blew out his breath. "Boy, you don't ask the hard ones, do you? I guess it would depend on whether I truly loved the woman I was about to marry, but then I wouldn't propose unless I was certain of that. And if I was certain, and I intended to propose, then nothing would sway me."

"I was afraid you'd say that," Isabella muttered.

"All you can do is try," he said gently. "Nothing ventured, nothing gained, and all that jazz."

A smile cracked through her lips. "Between you and me, we have all the trite clichés wrapped up."

He reached over and took her hand. "Are you sure this is what you truly want, Bella? I hate to see you hurt or disappointed."

"You're sweet," she began.

"Lord, but a man hates to hear those words from a woman's lips," he said with a groan. "It's as bad as hearing *you're just like a brother to me.*"

She laughed and relaxed her shoulders. Tension had crept into her muscles until her entire body had gone stiff with it. Marcus was right about one thing. All she could do was try. Whatever happened afterward was out of her control.

"You look fantastic tonight," he said as he relinquished her hands.

"Thank you. You really *are* too sweet."

She glanced down at the royal-blue evening gown she'd chosen on her whirlwind shopping trip she'd dragged her bodyguards on earlier that day. She was dressed to kill, or to do battle at the very least. Without false modesty, she knew she looked her best.

High-class, posh, a far cry from her preferred jeans and flip-flops and brightly polished toes. Tonight, she fit into Theron's world. Her world too, for that matter, just one that she'd never fully embraced. She had the money and pedigree, just not the desire to fit in.

"What time should we leave?" she asked anxiously.

She couldn't help the surge in her pulse when she imagined making it to the party too late. It made her want to break into a cold sweat that she'd arrive only to see the happy couple already engaged.

Marcus smiled reassuringly. "The opera has only just begun. We have quite awhile yet. Not to worry, I'll have you there in plenty of time. Try to relax and enjoy your dinner. It would be a terrible thing if you got to the party and promptly fainted at Theron's feet from hunger."

"Then again, it might be just the thing to stop the show," she said mischievously.

He chuckled and shook his head. "I'm almost sorry I agreed to help you, Bella. I would have rather pursued you myself."

"And if my heart weren't already lost to Theron, I would most gladly lead you on a very merry chase," she said with a grin.

"Then let me say this, and I won't broach the subject again," he said. "Should things not go the way you'd like…I ask only that you remember me."

She reached over to take his hand this time. "Thank you, Marcus. You've been a wonderful friend in the short time of our acquaintance. I hope you'll remain my friend no matter what. This is a lonely city when you know no one."

"I'd be honored. Now eat. I insist. They have the most wonderful desserts here."

Theron sat broodingly in his chair as the performance yawned on before him. Beside him, Alannis watched the stage with rapt attention, her face aglow with delight. Sophia was less enthused, but she still focused her attention forward.

Just before the performance had begun, Reynolds had reported that Isabella was meeting Marcus Atwater for dinner after a day of shopping. There wasn't a whole lot Theron could do at that point given that he was firmly entrenched in his evening. In the end, he gave Reynolds strict instructions to stick to Isabella like glue and make damn sure that Atwater didn't take advantage of her.

He was tempted to send a message to Reynolds from his BlackBerry, but he wasn't sure that Alannis was so ensconced in the performance that she wouldn't notice, and he'd promised that no business would interfere tonight.

Still, he'd requested periodic updates from Isabella's security team, and he'd find a way to check his messages even if it meant a trip to the bathroom.

For the entire next hour, he fidgeted, ready to be done. It irritated him that on a night he should be relaxed, that he was forced to think about Isabella's well-being. She was seeping into his life in a manner that didn't sit well with him. What did it say when he couldn't enjoy an evening with his future wife for thinking about Isabella Caplan?

Alannis touched his arm, and he was jerked from his thoughts.

"Theron, it's over," she whispered.

He glanced quickly to see the curtain drawn. Had he missed the encore entirely? Another nudge from Alannis had him rising to his feet. He offered her his arm and filed out of his box, Sophia and two of his security team following behind.

"And how did you enjoy the show?" he asked as they made their way to the waiting limousine.

"It was wonderful," Alannis gushed. "I do so love the opera. There was a time…"

She ducked her head, but not before he saw a bright blush form on her cheeks.

"There was a time, what?" he prompted.

"Oh, there was a time that I wanted to be an opera singer," she said self-consciously.

"And why didn't you pursue it?"

She smiled and shook her head. "I wasn't good enough. Besides, Father wouldn't have had it. He thinks it's a vulgar career."

Theron raised an eyebrow. "I wouldn't have thought such talent could be considered vulgar."

"Oh, he thinks any career that lands you on stage is inappropriate for a young girl. He'd much prefer that I marry well and give him grandbabies."

Something flashed in her eyes before it quickly vanished into blandness.

"And what do you want?" Theron asked curiously.

"I like children," she said simply before turning to her mother.

Theron ushered them into the car and settled in himself as they started for the hotel. His hands were clammy, and he shook his head in disgust over his apparent nervousness. He prided himself on his control and his calm. Nothing about this situation should cause him any anxiety. He had his future mapped out, and everything was proceeding exactly as planned.

After that reminder, he relaxed in his seat. He felt in his pocket for the ring then let his hand fall when he reassured himself that it was there.

Traffic moved quickly, and a half hour later, they

arrived at the hotel. Alannis yawned as Theron helped her out of the car.

He smiled and took her hand. "I hope you aren't too tired for the party."

"What party?" she asked in surprise.

Sophia smiled and tucked her arm in Alannis's. "He's planned a party in your honor, dear. It's a very special night." She winked at Theron behind Alannis's back, and Theron felt his unease increase.

"A party for me? It sounds so exciting," Alannis said, her eyes sparkling in delight.

She really was quite lovely, in a quiet, understated way. For some reason, however, he couldn't chase the image of another woman from his mind when he looked at her.

He glanced away, his jaw tight as they walked through the lobby toward the ballroom. When they entered, the band struck up and confetti fell from the ceiling.

Alannis looked up, her eyes rapt. She held her fingers up to catch the flurries as they spiraled down like crazy, neon snow.

"Oh, it's wonderful, Theron," she breathed.

He nudged her forward again, his heart pounding with each step they took. His hand drifted into his pocket as they neared the center of the room. The edges of the box scraped against his fingers, and he fumbled with it, coaxing the velvet box inside free.

Would she be as excited when he asked her to be his wife? Would he? Or was he about to make the biggest mistake of his life?

"Alannis…" he began, cursing the fact that his voice was so shaky.

She turned and looked up at him, eyes shining and a smile curving her lips. Lips that he had no desire to kiss. "Yes, Theron?"

Isabella sat forward in her seat, straining to see out the front window. "What's the holdup?" she asked desperately. "Why aren't we moving?"

Marcus took hold of her shoulder. "It's a wreck, Bella. Calm down, sit back. We'll get there. He won't propose as soon as the party starts."

She stared out the window at the sea of cars all at a dead stop. They'd never get out of this in time.

In a burst of frustration, she reached for the door handle and yanked the door open.

"Bella, what are you doing? Get back in the car. You can't go running through the streets of New York City," Marcus exclaimed as she clambered out.

She turned and bent to stare back into the car where he sat. "I have to go, Marcus. We'll never make it in time and you know it. I have to get there before he proposes. I can't..." She swallowed and looked away for a moment. When she looked back, tears clouded her vision. "I have to go. Thank you for everything."

She closed the door, picked up the long skirt of her dress in her hands and ran through the traffic, ignoring the honks as she cut in front of cars trying to inch forward. She heard the shouts of Reynolds and glanced back to see that he was hotfooting it down the street after her. Turning, she kept on running. She didn't have time to stop and explain.

Unsure of where she was going, she kept to the sidewalk, paralleling the traffic. When she saw an unoccupied taxi, she ran to the window and tapped.

The cabbie gave her a disgruntled look and rolled

down his window. "Look, lady, no one's going anywhere in this mess."

She held up a hand. "Please, can you tell me how to get to Imperial Park Hotel? How far am I?"

His eyes narrowed as he stared back at her. "As the crow flies, not far. If you cut over from this street a block then up two, you'll be six or so blocks from the hotel. Just head straight for five blocks, turn left and you'll see it as soon as you round the corner."

With a murmured thanks, she gathered her dress, shed her shoes and took off running as fast as she could go.

"Hey, lady, you left your shoes!" the man shouted from behind her.

By the time she'd gone three blocks, it had started to rain lightly. Not that it mattered. She already looked a fright, and her hopes of looking like a million dollars when she burst into Theron's engagement party were doomed.

When she rounded the corner of the last block, the heavens opened and it began to pour. Blinking the water from her eyes, she dashed toward the hotel, avoiding the puddles that were already forming beneath her feet.

Please, oh please, let me be on time.

Her hair was plastered to her face by the time she made it under the awning. Water dripped from her body and from the sodden mass of her ruined dress. Her feet ached, and she was sure she'd cut her right foot on something.

Ignoring the inquisitive looks thrown her way, she rushed past several people who were trying to hurry inside. Skidding on the polished floor, she righted herself and ran as fast as she could with a wet dress wrapped around her legs.

As she neared the ballroom, she heard cheers from inside and then mad clapping. *No.* She couldn't be too late, she couldn't.

She thrust herself inside the door, her gaze wildly searching the crowd gathered. There, in the middle, stood Theron and Alannis. Alannis was beaming from head to toe as she gazed lovingly up at Theron who was smiling down at her. Around them people clapped and then they brought their glasses up in a toast.

The words were lost to Isabella. She heard nothing except the buzz in her ears. She saw nothing but how radiant Alannis looked. It was a stark contrast to how dead Isabella felt in that moment.

Slowly, every part of her aching, she turned, tears swimming in her eyes, and walked slowly back out of the ballroom. She nearly ran into Reynolds as he hurried up to her. Keeping her head down, she continued on, ignoring his demands to know if she was all right.

All right? Nothing would ever be all right again.

Gradually the sounds of laughter and happiness diminished, and she was left with only the murmur of the people milling about the lobby.

A tear slipped down her cheek, and she made no move to wipe it. Who would notice? It would look like she was caught in the rain as she had been.

As she neared the entrance, Marcus ran in and stopped abruptly in front of her.

"Isabella, are you all right?" he demanded. "That was a foolish thing you did."

He caught her shoulders and spun her so that she looked at him. And then he must have seen the misery in her eyes because his tirade ceased, and gentle understanding shone in his eyes.

"You were too late?" he asked needlessly.

She nodded and squeezed her eyes shut as more hot tears escaped.

He gathered her in his arms. "I'm so sorry, Bella. I promised I would have you here on time."

"It wasn't your fault," she whispered.

"Come on, let me get you up to your room," he urged as he turned her toward the elevator. "You're soaked through." He nodded tersely at Reynolds. "I'll take her up."

Numbly, she let him escort her into the elevator. As they rode up, images of Alannis and Theron filtered through her mind. They'd looked so happy.

Happy.

Almost like…they were in love.

She closed her eyes again. Why couldn't he love her?

Marcus took the key from her shaking fingers and unlocked her door. Cool air immediately washed over her, eliciting a chill.

"You're soaked, too," she said as she became aware of his wet shirt and slacks.

He gave her a wry smile. "I took off after you and got caught in the downpour."

She tried to smile and failed miserably. "Sorry."

He sighed. "Why don't you go take a hot bath? I'll order up room service and see if they can't also get me some dry clothing brought up from the boutique."

She nodded and shuffled toward the bathroom.

Theron slipped his hand in the inside pocket of his suit and pulled out his BlackBerry. He frowned when he saw his last message had gone unanswered.

Excusing himself from Alannis with a smile, he nodded to the other guests assembled around them and backed away. He walked out of the ballroom and headed to the men's room just two doors down. As he was about to enter, he looked down the hallway and saw Reynolds standing next to his men. He was soaking wet.

With a frown, Theron stalked toward the three men. Reynolds glanced up as he heard Theron approach.

"Where's Isabella?" Theron demanded.

"In her room with Atwater," Reynolds replied.

Sure he had heard wrong, Theron's eyes narrowed. "With who?"

"She went up a few minutes ago with Atwater," Reynolds said calmly. "They were both soaked."

Theron's pulse pounded against his temple. It was all he could do not to charge up to her room and drag Marcus out. Then he'd beat the hell out of him.

With a muttered curse, he spun around and headed for the elevator. Anger rushed like lava through his veins. What the hell was Marcus thinking? Theron knew damn well what he was thinking, and what he was thinking with.

When he finally reached Isabella's door, he rapped sharply. A few seconds later, the door opened to a smiling Marcus who wore just a bathrobe.

He looked startled to see Theron standing there, and then his eyes narrowed to slits. "Sorry, I thought you were room service," Marcus said. Then he turned his head toward the bathroom. "Stay in the tub a little longer, sweetheart. Food's not here yet."

Turning back to Theron, Marcus did a slow up and down perusal, and then he asked in a bored voice, "Now, what can I do for you?"

"You arrogant…" Theron said in a menacing voice.

"You broke away from your engagement party to come up here and call me names?" Marcus asked in amusement.

A sound down the hallway had Theron looking to see the room service cart being wheeled toward Isabella's door. Marcus pressed forward and stared as well.

"Ah, there's the food now. If you'll excuse me. Or was there something you wanted?" Marcus asked pointedly.

Theron backed away, unsettled and feeling like he'd just gone a round in the boxing ring. Without a word, he turned and stalked away, his fists clenched into balls at his sides.

His gut churned as he got back onto the elevator. Why did it matter? He'd set Marcus up to be a choice in Isabella's hunt for a husband. Why then did he feel absolutely sickened by the prospect that Isabella had made her choice?

Chapter 12

Isabella was wakened by a loud knock at her door. She opened her eyes, wincing at how scratchy and dry they felt. Her hands went to wipe the swollen lids, and she remembered that she'd cried herself to sleep the night before.

Theron had proposed to Alannis. She'd been too late. And they'd looked so *happy*.

Fitting that she was completely miserable.

A knock sounded again, prompting her to slide her legs from the covers and push herself from the bed. Gathering her robe that lay over the chair a few feet away, she pulled it on and tied it as she walked to the door.

When she stared through the peephole, she saw Sadie standing outside, or at least someone who resembled Sadie. It was hard to tell with the platinum-blond wig adorning her head. She opened the door, and Sadie brushed by talking a mile a minute.

"Thank goodness you're here," Sadie said. "For a minute I thought you'd forgotten about tonight."

Isabella closed the door and turned to look at Sadie.

"I've got everything in my bag, and we have plenty of time to prepare," Sadie chattered on. "It'll be a snap."

Then Sadie stopped as she got a good look at Isabella. Her brow creased in confusion, and her lips parted.

"Bella, what's wrong? Have you been crying?"

To Isabella's dismay, she felt the sting of more tears. Irritated, she blinked them away, determined not to shed a single one.

Sadie closed the distance between them and slung an arm around her friend, guiding her toward the couch. Isabella found herself seated, and then Sadie plopped down beside her.

"What happened?" she asked. "Is it Theron?"

Isabella closed her eyes and nodded.

"Oh, honey, I'm sorry." Sadie enfolded her in her arms. "Did he propose to Alannis? Is that it?"

Isabella nodded against Sadie's shoulder. Sadie pulled away and brushed the hair from Isabella's face.

"Let's forget all about tonight. We'll order in some really good takeout and binge on desserts that have a gazillion calories."

Isabella smiled. "You can't miss your party, Sadie. It's too important. Just because my life is in shambles isn't a reason for you to lose your job and your chance at Broadway."

Sadie looked doubtfully at her. "I'm not sure you're up for this, Bella."

Bella forced a broader smile to her lips. "How bad can it be? I'll dress like you, dance some and attract male attention. It won't last long, and you'll keep your job."

"Are you sure?"

Isabella nodded. "Let's order something to eat. I'm starved. Then you can teach me the moves I need to know." She glanced at the bright wig Sadie was wearing. "Is that what I'm wearing out of here tonight?"

Sadie grinned. "It's the perfect way past your security guys. I made sure they saw me come in, and honestly, who could miss this?" she said as she slid her hands suggestively down the curves of her body.

Isabella cracked up. "No false modesty for you."

Sadie winked at her then continued on. "We'll dress you like me and you'll sashay out of here. No one will know that I'm still up here. I'll give you a good head start and then I'll get ready for the party and leave, looking nothing like the blonde bombshell who arrived earlier."

"Well, what's the worst that can happen?" Isabella asked with a shrug. "We get caught and Reynolds throws another fit. I'm sure Theron is too busy with his new fiancée to give a damn about my whereabouts."

"That's the spirit," Sadie crowed. "Let's do it!"

She was certifiably insane to have agreed to this. Isabella took a deep breath as the elevator stopped at the lobby level, flipped a long lock of the blond hair over her shoulder and waited for the doors to open.

The getup that Sadie had poured her into was many things. Modest wasn't one of them. And while Isabella didn't mind displaying her assets to her best advantage, this bordered on obscene.

The heels of her thigh-high boots clicked on the marble floor as she hurried for the exit. Her shorts were a slightly more expensive version of a denim Daisy Duke style, and they dipped low in front, showing her navel and more skin.

And her top. Not even a Dallas Cowboys cheerleader showed more cleavage.

But as Sadie said, no one would bother looking at her face. Not when so much else of her was on display.

She wobbled her way toward a waiting taxi and got in. As he pulled away, she supplied the address that Sadie had provided her. He didn't even blink an eye, and who could blame him with the way she was dressed? It amused her to think he might have assumed she was at the hotel for "business" purposes.

Nervousness tickled her stomach as they maneuvered through traffic. By the time the cab pulled up to the back entrance of the club, sweat beaded her forehead.

She sat for a moment staring out her window until the driver cleared his throat.

"Sorry," she muttered. She shoved the appropriate money over the seat and then got out. "Well, here we go," she said, as she tentatively walked to the door.

The hallway just inside the door was cloaked in darkness. A good thing. Even though Sadie had assured her that no one would notice the slight differences in the girls, this charade still made Isabella extremely nervous.

She was wearing so much makeup, that even her overbearing security team hadn't been able to tell it was her.

When she got to the door simply marked "girls," she eased inside. There was a flurry of activity, and no one paid her any mind. Another girl bumped into her as she walked past, and Isabella shied away, afraid of getting too close.

"Hey, Sadie," another girl called. "We weren't sure

you were coming. You're up after Angel, so you better hurry and get ready."

Isabella's stomach dropped, and she swallowed back her panic. She could do this. No one knew it was her. While she wasn't the expert that Sadie was, she could still move well, and Sadie had spent the afternoon teaching her the necessary act.

She smiled and nodded in the girl's direction and took a spot at Sadie's dressing station to check her makeup and to make sure her wig was securely in place.

When she caught her reflection in the mirror, all that she could think was how sad her eyes looked. No matter how made-up her face was, how perfect the hair, the eyes told the story. And the story was that she'd lost the one man she'd hoped to spend the rest of her life with.

More to have something to do than any real need to repair her makeup, she slowly applied more lipstick, watching as her lips glistened bloodred. Mechanically she brushed the mascara wand over her eyelashes, elongating her already dark lashes.

But still, her green eyes stared lifelessly back at her.

"Sadie, you're up in five," a male voice barked from the door. "Get a move on."

Isabella pushed herself jerkily from her chair and spared one last glance in the mirror. She looked scared to death.

Sucking in a deep, steadying breath, she adjusted her clothing, plumped up her breasts and headed for the door.

Theron stared out the window of Chrysander's penthouse, his mostly forgotten drink still in hand. Dusk was falling, and the lights of the city were coming alive, popping on the horizon.

He still wasn't sure his decision had been the correct one. He'd questioned himself repeatedly through the day, and yet, he could find no fault with the path he'd taken.

But now he had no idea what to do about Isabella.

He turned in irritation when his BlackBerry rang. It was sitting on the coffee table several feet away where he'd tossed it earlier. With a resigned sigh he walked over to pick it up

Seeing Reynolds's name on the LCD immediately put him on edge. He hit the answer button and put the phone to his ear.

"Anetakis," he said shortly.

"Mr. Anetakis, this is Reynolds. We have a situation, sir."

Theron put his drink down with a thud. "What situation?" he demanded.

"Earlier this evening, Ms. Caplan gave us the slip. Again."

"What? And you allowed her to do this again?"

"I'm afraid it's worse, sir. I'll be happy to fill you in on the details later, but at the moment we're on our way to La Belle Femmes." He paused for a moment. "Are you familiar with it, sir?"

Theron's brow furrowed in concentration as he absorbed the information. "Isn't that a gentleman's club? And why the hell are you going there?"

"Because that's where Ms. Caplan went," Reynolds said calmly. "I assumed you'd want to know."

"Damn right I want to know!" Theron exploded. "I'm on my way now, and don't think I won't want to know exactly how this went down."

He hurried toward the door, his finger on the button

to call for his driver. By the time he made it to the lobby, the car was waiting in front of the building.

What in God's name was Isabella doing in a gentleman's club? What was she thinking? Was Marcus somehow responsible for this? Theron was going to kill him.

When his driver screeched up to the club entrance, Theron got out and saw Reynolds along with his two men hurrying toward him.

"Is she here?" Theron demanded.

"We just arrived," Reynolds explained. "We were about to go in to see."

Theron strode ahead of them to the door and was stopped by a large man wearing dark glasses.

"Your name, sir?" the man politely inquired.

"Theron Anetakis," he said impatiently. "Someone I know is in there. Someone who shouldn't be here."

"Unless you have a membership, I can't allow you inside."

Theron seethed with impatience and then he turned to Reynolds. "Take care of this. Pay the man whatever is necessary for membership and then rejoin me inside. I'm going in after Isabella."

"But sir, membership is not instant…."

Theron heard no more as he pushed by the man and went inside. He trusted that Reynolds and the others would be able to overcome whatever objections the club's security guard had to his presence.

The club was different than Theron was expecting. From the moment a gentleman's club was mentioned, it conjured images of a seedy, back-alley environment where prostitution and drug use ran rampant. Here, though, it seemed the establishment catered to an upscale clientele.

The interior was clean, lavish even, reminding Theron

of many high-roller areas of casinos. The waitresses, through scantily clad, weren't cheap-looking-tart material. The patrons were well-dressed, smoking expensive imported cigars and sipping only the finest brandy.

It was a place Isabella shouldn't even know existed.

Theron weaved around the tables, sharp-eyed, his brow creased in concentration as he took in every single woman. Toward the front of the room, more men were assembled in front of a curtained platform. Evidently a show was imminent.

He dismissed the men when he saw no women among them. Where the hell was Isabella and had Reynolds gotten his information correct?

He glanced toward the entrance and saw Reynolds and the two other security men rush in. Theron gestured curtly at them, and Reynolds wove his way through the tables to where Theron stood.

"Why do you think Isabella is here?" he demanded.

"I have it on good authority she is," Reynolds said grimly. "You're looking in the wrong—"

He was cut off when music began blaring behind Theron. He winced and turned around only to see the curtain rise and stage smoke slither sensuously up the long legs of a woman.

She wore thigh-high boots that only accentuated her slim legs and drew attention to her shapely behind. She began rocking in rhythm to the music, her hips swaying as her arms fell gracefully to her sides.

As the smoke cleared, she raised her arms and gripped the pole in front of her. But Theron's gaze was drawn to the tattoo in the small of her back.

He knew that tattoo. Knew it damn well. He should; he'd spent plenty of time fantasizing about it.

And then she turned, whirling around in a mass of

blond hair—fake blond hair. He saw her eyes before she saw him. He saw the fear in her gaze, the wild panic as she surveyed the room full of men all eyeing her like a tasty treat.

Theron's blood boiled.

She looked up and locked gazes with him, her fear turning to utter shock as recognition flickered in her eyes.

Chapter 13

Isabella blanched when she saw Theron, who was clearly furious, standing beyond the group of men all crowding the stage. He vibrated with rage, and his eyes flashed as he stared her down.

She had the sudden urge to cross her arms over her breasts and run for cover.

Before she could seriously contemplate doing just that, Theron stalked forward, closing in on the stage like a predator on the hunt.

He didn't stop at the edge, didn't call out to her to come down. He jumped onto the platform, and in one swift motion hauled her into his arms and threw her over his shoulder.

She gave a startled cry just as the music stopped and the place erupted in chaos. She raised her head to see Reynolds, Maxwell and Davison fend off the security guards trying to come to her aid.

Customers rose from their seats and viewed Theron with gaping mouths, but were too civilized to embroil themselves in the situation. It would probably ruin their thousand-dollar suits anyway.

The floor spun crazily as Theron leaped down. The force drove the breath from her, and she wiggled trying to get him to ease his grip.

He merely tightened his arm over the back of her legs as he strode for the exit. Then she heard him snarl, "Back off, she's mine."

And surprisingly, he walked through the door and into the night.

Still stunned, Isabella made no effort to free herself from his grasp, not that it would have done any good. His arm was like a steel band around her body, and he walked effortlessly, bearing her weight as if it were nothing.

He stopped at his car, and leaned down to thrust her through the opening into the interior. Immediately, he climbed in beside her and slammed the door.

"Imperial Park," he said curtly.

Lying at an odd angle on the seat, she attempted to straighten herself, but her legs bumped into him, and she pulled them hastily away which only made her position more precarious.

Damn the boots. She felt gawky and ungainly. A glance down made her gasp in dismay when she saw that her cleavage was precariously close to spilling from the suggestive top. She folded her arms over her chest and scooted back until her back hit the other door.

She opened her mouth to speak, but he silenced her with a glare.

"Not a word, Bella. Not one damn word," he said menacingly. Anger vibrated off him in waves. "I'll have a full explanation when we return to the hotel. Until then I don't want you to say anything."

She swallowed then gulped as she stared wordlessly at him. Never had she seen him so…angry! He was usually so unbothered. Cool and collected. He was the epitome of order and calm.

The Theron she knew would never haul someone out of a public place nor would he snarl at a security guard twice his size.

She looked away, wrapping her arms a little tighter around herself.

"Here," he said gruffly as he shrugged out of his suit coat.

He held it out with one hand and pulled her forward as he settled it around her shoulders. She tugged at the lapels to bring it tighter around her, grateful that it at least covered her.

Several long minutes later, they pulled up to the hotel. Theron gave her a look that suggested she stay put, and she complied. He got out and walked around to her side and opened the door.

To her surprise, he reached in, drew his coat together so that not an inch of her flesh was displayed and then he simply plucked her out of the seat.

"Theron, I can walk," she protested.

"Silence," he ordered as he strode in the doors, ignoring the curious stares of passersby.

She frowned but settled wearily against his chest. He got into the elevator and stabbed at the button for her floor. Okay, she got that he was mad. Furious even. But he seemed to be taking it personally. Why wasn't he off somewhere with his new fiancée?

A fresh stab of pain soared through, taking her breath with it. She closed her eyes against the single truth that prevented her from having the man she loved. He belonged to someone else.

"Bella?"

His voice had changed, softened, and it reflected uncertainty. She pried open her eyes to see him regarding her with concern.

"Are you all right? Did something happen?" he demanded. "Did someone hurt you or threaten you?"

She shook her head, unable to speak past the lump in her throat. For a moment she could immerse herself in the fantasy that she did belong to him, that he cared about her in a deeper capacity than as a guardian, someone tasked to see to her welfare.

But it was a lie. It was all a lie.

"Then why?" he muttered.

The elevator opened, and with a shake of his head, he strode off and down to her room. Neither of them had a key, but then he didn't waste time trying to find one. He simply kicked loudly, instead of putting her down to knock. But who would open it? No one was there.

To her eternal surprise, and there had been many tonight, the door opened and a man who had security detail written all over him opened the door to admit Theron.

The surprises didn't end there. As soon as Theron walked in, a cry sounded from across the room.

"Bella! Are you all right?"

Isabella yanked her head left to see Sadie running across the room. Finally Theron let her down, and Sadie threw her arms around her.

"What are you doing here?" Isabella whispered. "Your party, Sadie. You weren't supposed to miss your party."

Sadie flushed guiltily. "The party doesn't matter. I should have never let you do this for me, Bella."

"In this we agree," Theron said stiffly. "It was irresponsible and dangerous. It's not a place that either of you should ever go into."

"But you missed your chance," Isabella said softly, ignoring Theron's outburst.

Sadie smiled sadly. "There'll be others. Besides, it wasn't worth the risk you took. I'm sorry."

"What happened?" Isabella asked in confusion. "Why are you still here and," she said, turning to face Theron, "how did he know where to find me?"

"Your security detail phoned me, as they should have," Theron said darkly.

Isabella turned back to Sadie. "How did they know?"

Sadie looked down and sighed. "When I left your room for the party, one of your guys immediately stopped me. They'd obviously seen you, posing as me, leave earlier and as we planned, never assumed it was you. However, they knew the real me hadn't entered your room, so they were suspicious. I had to tell them everything," she said uncomfortably. "They made me remain here while they went to get you." She glanced angrily at the man who was still standing by the door. "I had to endure a lecture from him the entire time you were gone."

"It's good that someone tried to talk sense into you," Theron bit out. He nodded toward the security man. "See that she gets home safely, and remain on watch to see that she doesn't go back to that club."

"But I work there!" Sadie exclaimed.

"Not any longer," Theron said with a growl. "I won't have Bella traipsing through some strip club because her friend works there."

"But—" Sadie sputtered even as she was escorted away by the security detail.

When the door closed behind them, Theron turned to glare at Isabella. He stepped forward, and she stepped back uneasily. His scowl became more ferocious as he reached to detain her.

"Now, Bella, I'll deal with you," he said in a soft, dangerous voice.

Theron's hands curled around her shoulders as he yanked Isabella to him. The coat she'd held so tightly around her fell to the floor, and her breasts thrust obscenely into his chest.

She couldn't bring herself to meet his gaze. If she did, he'd know. He'd immediately see everything she now wanted to hide. Things he hadn't been able to see before.

"Go get cleaned up," he said in a gruff voice. "I'll wait for you here."

Only too grateful to flee, she turned and headed for the bathroom. She grimaced when she caught a glimpse of herself in the mirror. Tawdry was a word that came to mind. Garish.

Sad.

She washed the heavy makeup from her face and tore the wig from her head. Then she unpinned her own hair and ran her fingers through it to tame it. A long, hot bath was extremely tempting, but not when Theron waited outside, likely growing more impatient by the moment.

She stripped out of the boots and clothes, tossing them aside. Then she realized she hadn't brought in something to change into. With a shrug, she made a grab for the bathrobe hanging on the back of the door and wrapped it securely around her.

Then she padded back out to the sitting room in bare

feet, hands thrust into the pockets of the robe. Theron waited, standing by the window that overlooked the avenue below.

When he heard her, he turned, his eyes still flashing with unsettled intensity.

"Why are you here, Theron?" she asked, finally regaining her composure.

He closed the distance between them, once again curling his fingers over her shoulders. "You dare to ask that as if I have no right? As if you didn't just do something incredibly stupid? Do you have any idea what I thought when I heard where you'd gone? The fear I felt? Or the shock upon seeing you on that stage, half naked for all those men to leer at? Tell me, Bella, what would you have done if someone other than me had rushed that stage? What if he had put his hands on you? Forced you to go with him?"

She blinked at his ferocity and the absolute anger tightening his features. Any number of explanations circled her frazzled mind, but she didn't think he'd be interested in any of them. So she kept quiet.

Theron ran a hand through his hair in a gesture of frustration before locking gazes with her once more.

"Did Marcus know you were doing this?"

Isabella bobbed her head backward in surprise. "Marcus? Why would he need to know anything I was doing?"

"I would hope he was more protective of what was his—or what he had staked claim on anyway," Theron growled.

She blinked in confusion. "You're not making any sense. Marcus has nothing to do with anything. He's a friend. I don't feel the need to apprise him of my comings and goings."

Theron snorted. "*A friend?* Is that what they're calling them these days?" he asked, throwing her mocking words about kissing back at her.

"What are you insinuating, Theron?" she asked as she folded her arms over her chest.

"I was here, Bella. Last night. I came up…to see about you," he added uncomfortably.

"So?"

"And Marcus answered your door in only a bathrobe," he snapped.

Isabella's mouth fell open. "And from this, you assume I'm sleeping with him?"

"Are you saying you did not?" Theron challenged.

"I'm saying it's none of your damn business," she huffed.

A long silence fell between them as they stared at one another. Oh, she would have loved to have told him yes, that she'd slept with Marcus, but really, what was the point? He was engaged to Alannis, and she had no desire to make herself look promiscuous. He did still have control over her inheritance until she married someone else.

"I didn't sleep with him," she said tightly. "We were caught in the rain and he came up so that dry clothing could be brought to him. He changed into a robe, and I stayed in the tub until he was dressed. We ate room service and then he left."

There was a flicker of relief in Theron's eyes. Why? What could it possibly matter to him? And then he shook his head.

"Why do you insist on driving me utterly crazy?" he murmured. "Is it not enough that I spend my time thinking of you? Remembering the feel of your mouth beneath mine?"

He moved in closer, his breath hot against her face. Unconsciously, she licked her lips nervously as he moved and tilted his head in a dance around her mouth.

"You shouldn't...kiss me," she whispered.

"You've never had an objection before," he muttered just before his mouth closed hot over hers.

Chapter 14

Isabella's knees wobbled, and she clutched frantically at Theron's shoulders to keep from sliding down his body. He caught her tightly against him as his lips plundered hers.

This kiss...was different. She moaned softly, a sound of surrender? Honestly, she didn't care. Maybe it was a sound of need. Or want.

He took her. There was no other word for it. He took possession of her mouth as if he owned it, as if he had exclusive rights to her mouth and refused to share it. Ever.

Her body melted against his, and she loved the hardness of his chest, his thighs, shivered as his hands roamed up her body to her neck. He cupped her nape, holding her so that she couldn't escape him. As if she wanted to.

She was a willing captive. This...this was what she'd

dreamed about. Fantasized. Wanted so much. So desperately.

"I want to make love to you, Bella," he said with breathless urgency, his lips barely separating from hers. "I've fought it. *Theos,* but I've fought, but if I don't have you, I'm going to go mad."

"Yes," she whispered. "I want you so much, Theron."

His hands fumbled with the tie at her robe, his lips never leaving her mouth. It was as though he couldn't bear to stop kissing her. He devoured her even as he yanked her robe open.

And then his hands pressed against her naked skin, and she moaned and trembled, going completely weak against him.

"Soft, so soft and beautiful. Like silk," he murmured as his palms caressed her sides, moving up until he cupped her breasts.

Finally, he moved from her mouth, his lips brushing over her jaw and to her ear and then lower, down her neck. He nipped then sucked at the tender skin, eliciting shiver after shiver.

His mouth continued downward, and she caught her breath as he sank to his knees in front of her. He snaked his arms inside her robe and wrapped them around her waist, pulling her downward so that her knees bent.

His mouth was precariously close to her breasts, so much so that his breath beaded and puckered her nipples into tight knots. And then he slid his mouth over one, rolling his tongue gently over the peak.

Her robe fell to the floor at her feet, and she was naked in his arms. He sucked at her breast, his dark head flush against her body. How erotic it looked, this proud, strong man, on his knees, his arms wrapped tight around her—as though he'd never let go.

Before she allowed herself to become too entrenched in *that* fantasy, he released her nipple, and she groaned her protest.

He glanced up, his eyes glowing in the lamplight. "You're beautiful, Bella," he said in a low, husky voice that was passion-laced.

His grip loosened just enough that he could rise to his feet, his shirt scraping along her bare skin. She reached out with her fingers to snag at his buttons, wanting them gone and to feel his bare skin against hers.

But he collected her hands in his and held them tightly together. "Oh, no, Bella *mou*. This is my seduction. And I intend to seduce you thoroughly."

He swung her into his arms and walked slowly to the bedroom, his gaze locked with hers. She was afraid to speak. Afraid that he would hastily back away if the spell was broken.

He laid her on the bed then straightened to his full height over her. She felt strangely vulnerable beneath his intense gaze. Shy and a little uncertain.

Her hands crept upward in an attempt to shield herself.

"Do not hide such beauty from me," he whispered.

Emboldened by the obvious approval in his eyes, she let her hands fall away. Lust flared over his face as his hands went to the buttons of his shirt. Halfway down, he lost patience and ripped the remaining buttons. He shrugged out of the sleeves and then tore impatiently at his pants.

She sucked in her breath and held it when his boxers, with his pants, slipped down and his turgid manhood came into view. Then it stuttered out, a silent staccato in the quiet as he moved closer.

He spread her knees and fit his body to hers, settling

between her thighs as he came down onto the bed. Hot, silken and yet rough in a heady, masculine way, his skin clung to hers, burning her, making her move restlessly underneath him.

They kissed again, and she wrapped her arms around his neck, prolonging the mating of their tongues. Soft and wet, clinging and dueling, a precursor to the dance their bodies would yet perform.

"I've never felt so out of control," he admitted. "So restless and out of my skin. You make me crazy, Bella. I have to have you."

"Yes."

The softly whispered surrender slid from swollen lips. His mouth skated downward to her neck and then over the slope of her shoulder.

He moved, lowering his body so that his lips found her breasts. She stared up at the ceiling, the intricate painting blurring as pleasure overtook her. For several long seconds, he lazily tongued the rigid peaks, and then he blazed a wet trail with his tongue down her midline to her belly.

He toyed with her belly ring for the briefest of seconds before traveling even lower.

She tensed when his mouth found her soft femininity, the very essence and core of her womanhood. Helplessly she arched into him, seeking more of his bold tongue. He chuckled and gave her another soft nuzzle.

"Please, Theron," she begged. "Take me."

"I want you to be ready for me, Bella *mou*," he said as he trailed one finger over her damp flesh.

"Take me," she said again as she looked down and met his gaze. "I'm yours."

Her words seemed to push him beyond his control. He slid up her body, spreading her legs and fitting himself to her in one deft movement. One moment he was probing, the next he slid inside her, breaking through the slight resistance as though it were nothing.

For a moment she went rigid with shock, only a twinge of pain, but more than that a sense of such fullness that it overwhelmed her. Her eyes flew open, and her hands went reflexively to his shoulders to push him away.

Theron stared at her in confusion even as his hips moved, and he thrust forward again. She relaxed beneath him, letting her hands glide over his shoulders and to his neck. Pleasure, sweet and yearning, bloomed, spreading like fire in the wind.

His lips found hers again in a gesture of reassurance, molding sweetly to hers, suddenly gentle and tender.

"Move with me, *agape mou*," he urged. "Wrap your legs around me. Yes, that's it."

Her skin came alive, crawling and edgy with need. Theron planted his elbows on either side of her head and held his body off her enough that she didn't bear the full brunt of his weight as he moved between her legs.

Breathing became hard. She panted against his lips as their mouths met again.

"Come with me," he whispered.

Helpless to do anything but follow the winding pleasure building so earnestly, she cried out as he stiffened above her. He gathered her softly against him, crushing her to his hardness. Murmured words fell against her ears, some she understood, some slipping away.

And then he collapsed, pressing his warm body to hers. For several long seconds, their ragged breathing was the only sound that filled the room.

Then he raised his head to stare down at her. He

kissed her lightly then shifted, easing his body from hers. "I'll be right back."

She watched lazily from the bed while he strode nude to the bathroom and returned a moment later with a washcloth.

"Did I hurt you?" he asked in a low voice.

She sat up and reached for the cloth, but he held it out of her reach and then brushed it gently over her skin to clean her.

"No, you didn't hurt me," she returned quietly.

"Why didn't you tell me?"

There was no recrimination, no accusation in his voice.

"I wasn't entirely certain you'd believe me."

"And so you let me ravage you when you should have been handled gently? Made love to and cherished?"

There was genuine regret on his face. Not that he'd made love to her, if she had to guess, but for what he considered his rough treatment of her.

She reached out and touched his face, enjoying the feel of the slight stubble on his jaw. "You didn't hurt me, Theron. It was perfect."

He dropped the cloth on the floor and then framed her face in his hands. "No, it wasn't perfect, but I can make it that way."

He lowered his mouth to hers, kissing her with a tenderness that made her chest ache. Desire fluttered deep within, awakening and unfolding, reaching out.

He took his time, lavishing kisses and caresses over every inch of her body. He murmured endearments and praise, each one landing in a distant region of her heart that she'd reserved only for him.

She soaked up each touch, each word like parched earth starved for water.

And when he cupped her to him, sliding carefully into her wanting body, she knew she'd never loved him more than she did at this moment. For so long she'd waited to have him like this. Focused on her, seeing her, touching her and loving her as she loved him.

This time he urged her to completion before taking his own, and only when she quivered with the last vestiges of her orgasm did he sink deeply within her and hold himself so tightly that she could feel the tension rippling through his body.

He dropped his forehead to hers, their lips just an inch apart as he dragged in deep breaths. She tilted her chin upward so that her nose brushed against his, and then their lips met in a sweet kiss that she felt to her soul.

"Better?" he murmured.

She smiled. "Better."

Theron woke to a sweet female form wrapped tightly around his body. As he opened his eyes and blew a tendril of dark hair from across his lips, he realized that Isabella was more draped across him than wrapped exactly.

Her breasts were pressed to his chest, and one arm was thrown across his body possessively. Her limbs were tangled with his, and she slept soundly, her soft, even breathing filling his ears.

Reality was swift to come, and with it, the weight of what he'd done. It wasn't unexpected, this guilt and resignation. He could blame it on passion, lust—a whole host of things—but he knew the truth.

He'd wanted her and he'd taken her, and he'd certainly known what he was about in the heat of the moment. Not once in his thirty-two years had he ever lost all conscious thought when making love, and he wasn't likely to start now.

He hadn't even used a condom, and for the life of him he couldn't dredge up a plausible excuse for his stupidity. It wasn't even that he didn't have one on him at the time. He lived his life in a state of preparedness, and he always had not one, but two condoms in his wallet.

And yet he hadn't stopped to get one, hadn't protected her, and worse, it had been a conscious decision. There was no one to blame in this whole mess but himself, and he damn well knew it.

Carefully, he extricated himself from her warm body. He tensed when she gave a soft little sigh, but then she snuggled back into the covers and settled down once more.

He strode to the bathroom to shower, aware that there would be consequences for his choices. Already he was mentally preparing and making plans. Through it all, there was an odd sense of peace instead of pained resignation.

Still, he dreaded all he had to do. And say.

Wrapping a towel around his waist, he walked out of the bathroom and recovered the clothing he'd worn yesterday. Thankfully he always kept several changes of clothing at his office. That would be his first stop.

As he was pulling on his pants, Isabella stirred, her long hair sliding over her body as she turned and reached out her hand as though seeking him. His body tightened, and arousal hummed through his veins, a soft whisper that grew louder as he stared down at her.

She opened her eyes sleepily, blinking when she saw him. He reached down and touched her cheek, smoothing a stray strand of her hair from her skin.

"There are things I have to take care of, Bella. Important things."

He bent and kissed her softly on the hair, and then without another word, turned and walked out of the bedroom.

Isabella stood beside the bed, wrapped in just the sheet, the ends clutched tightly in her hands. She glanced down at the discarded washcloth, at the evidence of her lost virginity, and felt an odd stirring deep in her chest.

Where had Theron gone? And would he be back? Or was she just the temptation that finally became too much, and he was rushing back to Alannis to make amends?

She closed her eyes and let her chin fall to her chest. She didn't want to be the other woman. She didn't like how it felt, didn't want to be responsible for someone else's sorrow. But why should she place another's over her own?

Feeling quiet sadness settle into her heart, she went into the bathroom to draw a hot bath. Part of her ached—a delicious ache—and she couldn't help but close her eyes and remember every touch, every kiss and caress, the feel of his body sliding over hers.

She soaked until the water grew tepid, and finally, shivering, she rose from the tub and wrapped herself in a towel.

There was a listlessness to her she was unused to. There was too much unknown, unresolved, and she worried that it would remain so.

Growing disgusted with her lethargy, she forced herself to dress. She refused to sit in her hotel room holding her breath like a lovesick fool, waiting for a man who might never return.

First she'd eat and then she'd head to her apartment. Her new furniture had been delivered, and Theron had arranged someone to stock all the necessities. She would go over and make a list of anything else she needed, and then maybe it was time to start thinking about what she was going to do with the rest of her life.

When she opened the door, she immediately came face-to-face with an unsmiling Reynolds. She tried to smile, but failed miserably. Then she sighed. "You might as well come in so I can apologize properly. Then you can accompany me to the hotel restaurant, and then we can go to my new apartment."

Reynolds actually smiled in return as he stepped inside. "*Now,* Ms. Caplan, you're getting the hang of how things are supposed to be done. You make my job a lot easier when I know where you're going and you aren't running off at every turn."

She made a face. "I truly am sorry I've been so much trouble. I think you'll find me a lot more accommodating from now on."

His amusement vanished, and he sobered as he studied her with questioning eyes. "I hope nothing has happened to upset you."

For a moment she said nothing. And then with a half-hearted smile, she gestured toward the door. "Let's go eat. I'm starving."

Theron settled wearily into the chair behind his desk and picked up the phone. Yet again, it would be the middle of the night in Greece, but he needed to have this conversation with Chrysander now so that he could go forward with his plans.

"Nai," Chrysander barked in a sleepy tone.

"I've done a terrible thing," Theron said.

"Theron?" Chrysander asked in a more alert tone. "What the devil are you doing calling at this hour? Again. And what terrible thing are you talking about? Are you in jail?"

Theron had to laugh at that. "No, I'm not in jail."

"Then what is wrong?"

Theron rubbed his hand across his face. "I seduced Isabella."

There was a long pause. "I'm not sure I heard that correctly," Chrysander finally said. Then Theron heard him speak to Marley. "No, *agape mou,* nothing is wrong. Go back to sleep. It's just Theron." Then he came back to Theron. "Give me a moment to take this call in my office. Marley has been up all night with the baby."

Theron waited patiently as he heard shuffling in the background and even a sound like Chrysander kissing Marley. A few moments later, Chrysander's voice bled back over the line.

"Now tell me you didn't do what I think you said you did," Chrysander said dryly.

"I can't do that. It's worse, though."

"Worse than you seducing a young woman under your care? I fail to see how it can get any worse."

"She was a virgin, and I didn't use protection."

Theron cringed even as he said it. It was a conversation that made him sound sixteen years old confessing his sins to his father.

Chrysander cursed and blew out his breath. "Damn it, Theron, what in the world were you thinking? Okay, scratch that. You obviously weren't thinking. That much is established. But what about Alannis? Were you not just telling me and Piers that you were marrying her? What were you doing in bed with Isabella? And *Theos,* without protection. Are you stupid?"

"And you were so careful with Marley?" Theron said defensively.

"I was in a relationship with Marley," Chrysander growled. "I was not engaged to another woman, nor was she someone under my direct care. Theron, this goes beyond stupid."

"I'm not engaged to another woman," Theron said quietly. "I didn't ask her to marry me."

Another stunned silence ensued.

"You better back up and tell me the entire story," Chrysander said wearily. "It's obvious that you've got a huge mess on your hands. Start with the part where you didn't ask Alannis to marry you."

"I couldn't do it," Theron said with a sigh. "I arranged the night, had a party, the ring, the confetti—"

"Confetti? Who the hell has confetti for a marriage proposal?" Chrysander demanded, a thread of amusement in his voice.

"It added to the festive mood," Theron defended. "Everything was there. The moment was there…and I couldn't do it. I had my hand on the ring, the woman staring up at me, and then I let go of the box, and asked her to dance instead. We spent the evening celebrating her visit to New York instead of our impending nuptials."

"So how did this lead to you taking Isabella's virginity? Without protection," he added dryly.

"I've admitted my stupidity. There's no reason to keep beating me over the head with it," Theron said irritably. "It happened after I hauled her out of the strip club."

"You *what?*" Chrysander broke into laughter. "Theron, this is sounding more absurd all the time. Do I even want to know why someone you were supposed to be watching over was in a strip club?"

"It's not important. What's important is that afterward, I seduced Isabella. We slept together. Without protection. She was a virgin. That covers it."

"Yes, I'd say it does," Chrysander said.

There was another long silence and then Chrysander spoke again. "She was under our care. Our father agreed that the Anetakis family would always care for her should something happen to her father. You're going to have to marry her, Theron."

Adrenaline surged in Theron's veins. "I don't *have* to marry her, Chrysander. I'm *going* to marry her."

Chapter 15

Isabella shoved aside the heavy curtains draped over the large window facing the street. Her apartment was on the top floor, larger by half than the apartments on the lower levels, and it had a wonderful view of a small park across the street.

There was no shortage of joggers, people out walking dogs, and children supervised by their nannies or mothers. It was a small mecca in the middle of a crowded city where someone could go and enjoy a short escape.

Could she live here knowing the man she loved was close by, married to someone else? On the surface it sounded absurd. In a city this size, she could go an entire lifetime without running into Theron. Except...except he controlled her inheritance and contact would be inevitable.

She sighed. She really did like the apartment, but she wasn't sure she could remain here.

The sound of her door opening didn't alarm her. Reynolds had been left waiting when she'd only said she'd be a minute. He probably lost patience and was coming to collect her.

Footsteps sounded behind her, and yet she still couldn't tear her gaze away from the scene below. Maybe it was the normalcy of it all—the promise of an ordered existence where agonizing emotions such as love and jealousy or despair didn't dictate her every breath.

Firm hands took hold of her shoulders, skimming upward, eliciting a small gasp from her.

"Bella, *pethi mou,* are you all right? What are you doing here?"

She spun around in surprise and stared up at Theron's worried eyes.

"I went back to your suite and you were gone. I'm beginning to wonder if my life is going to be a study in never finding you where you're supposed to be."

There was a hint of amusement in his voice, but she was puzzled by his words. They made no sense.

"When I called Reynolds and he said you were here, I came right over. But, Bella, there is no need of your apartment any longer," he said calmly.

She held up a hand to his chest, almost afraid to touch him. Her head was spinning a mile a minute, but she needed to understand what he was saying, or what he wasn't saying.

"I came to see if it was ready for me to move in," she said simply.

He captured her hand in his and held it in place over his heart. "You won't be needing this apartment, *pethi mou.*"

With his other hand, he dipped into his pocket and

drew out a small square box. She stared suspiciously at it as he flipped the lid off and let it fall to the floor. Maneuvering still with the one hand, he turned it over and shook out the velvet jeweler's box. With a few more flips of his fingers, it came open, and a brilliant, sparkling diamond caught the light from the window and flashed in her eyes.

She watched in complete astonishment as he picked up her hand and slid the ring onto her third finger.

"We'll be married as soon as possible," he said matter-of-factly.

She shook her head, sure that she must still be in bed back in her suite—dreaming. "I don't understand," she stammered.

"We must marry," he said again, only this time the emphasis was on the *must*. "You were a virgin…and you could be pregnant," he finished softly. "I didn't think… that is I didn't use protection. For this I am sorry."

No, she wasn't dreaming. In her dreams, her marriage proposal had always been somewhat more romantic. But then she was getting precisely what she wanted. It was hard to argue with that, no matter the motivation behind the proposal.

"Okay," she said quietly.

Relief flashed in his eyes. Had he expected her to argue? Maybe play the martyr and give him a weeping, tragic refusal because he didn't love her?

He pulled her into his arms, but instead of kissing her, he hugged her tightly. "We should go back to your suite. We have arrangements to make. Unless you'd prefer my penthouse? I'm afraid I'm no more settled in this city than you are, but we'll remedy that. We can buy a house. Wherever you like."

She wedged an arm between them and levered herself away. "What about Alannis?"

There was quiet between them finally, and his expression sobered. "She and Sophia are flying back to Greece tomorrow."

Isabella tried to disguise the flinch. She didn't want to think of Alannis's heartbreak or her mother's disappointment. Neither woman had been anything but kind to her. And now she was the femme fatale. It wasn't a very good feeling.

She nodded, not wanting to delve too deeply into Alannis. She was a subject better left alone.

The sparkle of the diamond in the sun drew her gaze back to the gorgeous ring adorning her finger. And then she allowed some of the joy to shine on her like the sun beaming through the window.

With a tentative smile, she looked back up at Theron. "You really want to marry me? Okay, scratch that. Bad question. I'm sure you don't really want to marry me. But you don't have to. Just so you know. I mean the whole idea of putting a ring on my finger just because I was a virgin and we didn't use protection—well, it's archaic. Nobody does that anymore. I mean even if I turned out pregnant, there's nothing to say we'd have to be married—"

He silenced her with his mouth, pressing his lips to hers in a deep, lustful kiss. For several long seconds, all that she heard was the soft smooching sounds of their lips. She went positively boneless.

Finally he pulled away, his eyes glittering. He may not *want* to marry her, but she knew his eyes didn't lie. He wanted *her,* and he definitely desired her. It was a start.

"Now if we're through talking nonsense, let's return to the hotel," he said huskily.

He didn't look any different. Isabella watched Theron from across the sitting room of her suite as he went through a myriad of phone calls. First he'd talked to the person she'd rented the apartment from. Then a few business calls had interceded. Now he was back to talking to God knew who about flights and planes, and she wasn't sure what else. Her head was spinning.

Maybe she'd expected him to look…well, she didn't know. Engaged? But then he'd been engaged for several days. Just not to her.

A knock at the door interrupted her moody dissertation on Theron's phone calls. Reynolds, who had been going over plans with Theron, strode to the door and opened it.

Isabella couldn't see who it was with the way Reynolds held the door, but a moment after opening it, he stepped back and glanced over at her.

"Sadie Tilton to see you."

Isabella made a quick motion with her hand for him to let her in. Sadie popped her head around the door, her eyes filled with caution. They lightened as soon as she saw Isabella and she hurried over to where Isabella sat on the couch.

"What's going on?" Sadie hissed. "You sounded so weird when you called."

Isabella didn't say anything but she raised her hand so that Sadie could see. A quick glance around her told her that Theron wasn't paying either of them any attention, so involved was he on the phone.

"Oh my God!" Sadie exclaimed as she pounced on Isabella's hand. "He proposed?"

"Shh, he's on the phone," Isabella murmured. "And yes, well, sorta. He didn't exactly ask. He informed me we were getting married."

Sadie frowned. "Are you happy about it?"

Isabella smiled. "I will be. He's all I've ever wanted."

"What did he say then? And what about Alannis?"

"Not much. Just that he'd taken my virginity, I could be pregnant and we needed to marry."

Sadie winced. "Are you sure you want to marry a guy for those reasons? I mean what about love? Or at least a legitimate reason that doesn't predate this century."

Isabella looked at her friend and sighed. "I can't very well make him fall in love with me if we aren't together, Sadie. Yes, ideally he would love me now, and we'd marry for all the usual reasons, but I have to take what opportunities I'm given. He feels something for me. That much I know. Something that goes beyond simple lust. He just needs time. But if I don't marry him, he'll marry Alannis, and where does that get me?"

"You're right, you're right," Sadie said in a low voice. "I was just hoping for something more. You've dreamed about this for so long. I wanted it to be perfect for you."

Isabella squeezed Sadie's hand. "It will be perfect. Maybe not yet, but it will be. The day he says *I love you* will make everything leading up to it worth it."

Sadie smiled. "Now that that's all settled, I have to say thank you. You didn't have to do it, but at the same time, I'm so grateful."

Isabella looked at her in puzzlement. "What on earth are you talking about?"

"The apartment, the rent, the account. You know, so I don't have to go back to work at the club."

Isabella shook her head.

Sadie frowned. "You didn't arrange for my apartment to be paid up for the next year?"

"No-o-o...."

They both turned and looked at Theron at the same time.

"Then I don't suppose you also arranged my meeting with Howard," Sadie murmured.

"No, I had no idea," Isabella said softly.

"You've got yourself a good man, Bella. Not that I'm fooling myself by thinking he did it for any other reason than he didn't want you ever going into that place," she said with a grin.

"He is a good man," Isabella agreed as she stared across the room at Theron.

As if sensing her perusal, he lifted his gaze, the phone still held to his ear and looked back at her. His eyes smoldered with quiet intensity. Suddenly all Isabella wanted was for everyone to be gone from her room and for it to be only the two of them. In his arms, she could forget a lot. Including that she wasn't the one he would have chosen as his wife.

"How about I have Reynolds see you home?" Isabella murmured to Sadie.

For a moment Sadie looked startled but then she followed Isabella's gaze toward Theron and grinned. Sadie leaned forward and hugged Isabella tightly.

"Just don't leave town without letting me know what's going on, okay?"

Isabella hugged her back. "I won't."

Isabella got up and walked over to where Reynolds stood. "You'll see her home?" she asked, though it wasn't a request.

Reynolds looked quickly over at Theron, who evidently heard Isabella because he nodded at Reynolds and made a go gesture with his hand.

Moments later, Isabella closed the door, and for the first time since he'd put his ring on her finger, they were alone. Well, almost. There was still the phone.

Slowly, she walked over to where Theron sat at the desk in front of the window. He looked up, his eyes darkening when she placed her hands on his knees and then straddled him, sliding up against his chest.

He tensed and tried to ward her off as he continued talking, something about figures, finances, hotel plans, blah blah. None of that interested her as much as the possibility of getting Theron naked.

She took the hand he held between them and guided it to her chest, sliding it just inside the neckline of her shirt. He curled his fingers into a fist, as if denying her.

Isabella only smiled and began unbuttoning his shirt from the top down. His voice became noticeably more strained, and he even broke off twice as he seemed to lose his train of thought.

If she were a good fiancée, she'd leave him alone, become invisible while he conducted business and re-appear later, but she'd already proven she wasn't the best at suppressing her own wants. Not when it came to Theron.

As she parted the lapels, she leaned forward and pressed her lips to his bare chest. She felt his quick intake of breath, heard his strangled response to whoever it was he was talking to.

She'd give him two more minutes tops. If he resisted beyond then, she'd have to give him credit for being very strong indeed.

Ignoring his disapproving look, she slipped from his lap and went seeking lower, unfastening the button of his pants. Every muscle in his thighs locked and went rigid when her hand caressed his equally rigid erection.

One minute left. Hmm.

She lowered her head as she gently freed him from constraint. When her mouth touched him, she heard his garbled response to whatever the other person on the phone had asked, and then she heard the unmistakable sound of a phone meeting the wall.

She smiled even as he lurched upward, grabbing her under the arms and hauling her into his arms.

A torrent of Greek flew from his mouth as he strode for the bedroom.

"English, Theron," she said with a laugh.

"*Theos,* but what are you trying to do to me?" he demanded as he tossed her onto the bed. "I'll have to ban you from my offices if this is the sort of thing you'll do when I'm trying to conduct business."

She tried to suppress the grin as he tore off his shirt and pants and sent them flying.

"Undress," he said seductively.

She raised an eyebrow. "Isn't that your job?"

He fell forward, landing his hands on either side of her shoulders as he stared down at her. Then he reached for her hands and pulled them over her head, transferring her wrists into one hand so the other was free.

Then he began to unbutton her shirt. His movements were jerky and impatient as he ridded her of every stitch of clothing.

When he was finished, he let go of her hands. "Turn over," he said.

She looked up in confusion.

His fingers roamed down her nakedness even as he urged her over.

"Do as I say, *pethi mou.*"

She shivered at the authority in his voice. Maybe she had started this whole thing, but it seemed he intended to finish it.

Carefully she rolled until her belly pressed against the mattress. She tucked her hands high, just over her head as she felt Theron lean down once more.

His fingers danced across the small of her back, and then she realized he was tracing her tattoo. She smiled.

"Do you like it?" she murmured.

"It's driven me crazy since the first day you walked into my office," he muttered. "I've had the most insane urge to throw you down and trace it with my tongue."

"There's nothing stopping you," she said lazily.

"Indeed not."

She jumped and closed her eyes when his warm tongue made contact with her skin. He emblazoned a damp trail over the small of her back and then he pressed a kiss right over her spine.

"The fairy is misleading. You should have had a devil tattooed on you."

She smiled again and rolled over, meeting his smoldering gaze. "And where do you propose this devil go?"

His lips curled into a half smile before he dipped his head and kissed the area right above the soft curls at the juncture of her legs. "Here," he murmured. "Where only I can enjoy it."

"Don't tease me, Theron," she whispered. "I want you so much."

"Then take me, Bella." He spread her legs and covered her with his body. And suddenly he was inside her, deep and full. "Take all of me," he said hoarsely.

She wrapped arms and legs around him, holding him tight as he filled her again and again. His lips found hers, sweet and warm. She drank from him, took from him, and still she wanted more. She wanted everything he had to give.

This time they came together, an explosion she felt to her very depths. As his body settled comfortably over hers, she sighed in utter contentment.

After a moment he rolled to the side and gathered her in his arms.

"Where did you learn such wickedness, Bella *mou?*" he asked as she snuggled into the crook of his arm and he stroked his fingers over her shoulder.

She rose up, positioning her elbow underneath so she could look at him. "What do you mean?"

"You were a virgin and yet you seduced me as thoroughly as someone with much more experience."

She laughed. "Theron, tell me you aren't one of these men who thinks the presence of a hymen equals complete ignorance on the woman's part."

But then given his antiquated views on honor, and the fact that he was marrying her over that thing called a hymen, perhaps it wasn't such a stretch to believe he thought she should be ignorant of sex.

He looked uncomfortable as he grappled with his answer. "I suppose I thought it unlikely that someone with no experience would be so…"

"Good?" she asked cheekily.

He gave her a look that suggested he wasn't amused by her teasing.

"I never said I wasn't experienced," she said lightly.

He tensed and raised his head to stare at her. "What do you mean by this? Who do you have experience with?"

She laid a hand on his chest. "Now, Theron, stop with the testosterone surge. You're the only man I've ever made love with. Experience can be gained without participation you know."

"As long as you don't ever decide to participate with another man," he said gruffly. "I will teach you everything you need to know."

She grinned. "And maybe as we've previously discussed, there are things I'll teach you, as well."

He yanked her to him, and she landed with a soft thud, her lips a breath away from his.

"Is this so? Well then, Bella *mou,* by all means teach me. I think you'll find me a willing pupil."

Chapter 16

Theron reached across the seat and buckled Isabella's belt. She roused sleepily and looked questioningly at him.

"We'll be landing soon," he said. "Then we'll take a helicopter to the island."

She yawned and nodded, trying to knock some of the sleep fog from her mind. "I'm looking forward to meeting Piers, well officially. I've seen him but just once and we didn't speak," she said as she shifted in her seat. "Though it's been so long since I've seen Chrysander, it will be like meeting him for the first time all over again. What's he like?" she asked.

He raised one eyebrow. "What's who like, *pethi mou?*"

"Piers," she said a little grumpily. "You know, the one I just said I hadn't met."

He smiled. "You're not at your best when you first awaken."

She yawned again and just frowned.

"To answer your question, Piers is…well, he's Piers," Theron said with a shrug. "He travels the most of any of us now that Chrysander has settled on the island. He's flying in from Rio de Janeiro right now where he's overseeing the building of our new hotel."

"Married or otherwise attached?"

Theron laughed. "Not Piers. He has an aversion to becoming entangled with any female for more than the length of a casual affair."

"Did your mother mistreat him?" Isabella asked dryly.

Theron shook his head. "You, Bella *mou,* have quite a smart wit about you. I'm going to have to think of ways to keep that mouth of yours occupied."

"And Marley?" she asked as the plane began its descent. Already she could see tiny twinkling lights from the ground. "What's she like? I admit, I find it hard to imagine a woman who could so easily subdue a man like Chrysander. He always seemed so…hard."

"It wasn't easy," Theron said, his expression growing serious. "They went through a lot together. Chrysander is lucky to have her."

"So you like her?" Isabella prompted.

Theron nodded. "I like her very much. She's good for him. Softens him just enough."

"She sounds…nice."

"You have nothing to worry about," he soothed. "You'll like them, and they'll like you."

She managed a stiff smile. What she really wanted to ask is whether they'd liked Alannis more. How would they feel about the fact he was marrying someone else? She didn't know how it worked in Theron's family, but would they have expected him to marry Alannis for business reasons?

Theron's hand found hers just a moment before the plane touched down. She was content to let her fingers remain entwined with his as they taxied. A few minutes later, they were disembarking the plane, and Theron was urging her toward a waiting helicopter.

"If I had thought, I would have arranged for us to stay on the mainland overnight so that you could see the beauty of the island from the air in daytime," Theron said as they boarded.

"I'll see it on the way back, right?" she said with a smile as Theron settled beside her.

He nodded as the engines whirred too loudly for conversation any longer.

The ride across the inky darkness was a little disconcerting, and then Theron pointed to a flash of light in the distance. She strained forward, leaning over him as they drew closer to the source of the light.

A few moments later, the helicopter lowered onto the well-lit helipad, and the pilot gestured to Theron when it was safe to get out.

Theron opened the door and ducked out, then reached back to help Isabella from the seat. His hand over her back, urging her low, he hurried across the concrete landing area toward the lighted gardens leading to the house.

As they approached the entryway, a man stepped from the door. Even from a distance, Isabella recognized him as Chrysander. He smiled, and she relaxed, even managing a smile in return.

"Isabella, how you've grown, even since your graduation," he said as he enfolded her in a hug.

"Thanks for making me feel like a girl who just shed braces and training bras," she said dryly as she pulled away.

Chrysander stared at her in obvious surprise and then burst into laughter. "My apologies. You're far from that as Theron has no doubt found out."

She couldn't prevent the flush that worked its way up her cheeks.

"Why don't you stop trying to find things to say and let us through," Theron said balefully. "Before we have to extricate both feet from your mouth."

Chrysander chuckled and gestured for them to pass. "Marley is waiting in the living room. She's anxious to meet you, Isabella."

He moved past her and Theron to call out in Greek to the man collecting her and Theron's luggage from the helicopter.

Theron took her arm and they walked inside. The house was absolutely beautiful, and she couldn't wait to see it in full light. And the beach. She could smell the salt air and even hear the waves crashing in the distance, but she wanted to see it and dig her toes into the sand.

A small, dark-haired woman who was bouncing a blanket-wrapped bundle in her arms was standing in the living room next to the couch. Isabella offered a tentative smile when she looked up.

"Theron!" she exclaimed as she walked in their direction.

Theron smiled broadly and caught her and the baby up in his arms. "How are my favorite sister and my nephew?"

"I'm your only sister," she said.

"Marley, I'd like you to meet Isabella, my fiancée," he said as he turned to Isabella.

Marley smiled, her blue eyes flashing in welcome. "I'm very happy to meet you, Isabella."

"Please, call me Bella," she offered. "And I'm very glad to meet you, as well."

"Has Piers arrived?" Theron asked with a frown as he surveyed the room.

"He's coming," Marley said. "He left to go change when we heard the helicopter. We've held a late dinner for you and Isabella."

Just then a tall, dark-haired man entered the room. He was easily the tallest of the three brothers, a little slighter than Chrysander but a bit more broad in the shoulders than Theron. Where Theron and Chrysander had golden-brown eyes, Piers's were dark, nearly black. His skin tone was darker as well, as though he spent a great deal of time in the sun.

His expression was bland as he looked at Theron. "There you are." He glanced over at Isabella. "And this must be the bride-to-be?"

"One of the many it would appear," Isabella said, refusing to dodge the inevitable awkwardness of the situation.

Piers's eyebrows drew together at her bluntness then he cocked one and offered what Isabella suspected was as close to a smile as he got. "I like her, Theron. She has spirit."

Theron didn't look disquieted by her outburst, but then he seemed resigned to her mouth, as he'd put it.

Chrysander moved to his wife's side and put an arm around her. "Want me to put him down so that we can eat?"

"If he'll go down," Marley said wearily. "Colic," she said with a grimace as she handed the baby to Chrysander. "We've been up with him for the last two weeks. I just hope you can sleep through it."

Chrysander brushed his lips across her forehead. "Don't worry, *agape mou*. I'll sit with him until he settles. You go eat and then I want you to get some rest."

Isabella's heart melted at the look of love in Chrysander's eyes. She wanted that. Wanted it badly. It was all she could do not to sigh as Marley smiled back at him, her eyes glowing. The look of a woman who knew she was loved.

Then Marley looked at Isabella, and she cocked her head to the side as if studying her. Isabella quickly looked away, hoping she hadn't betrayed herself in that moment. It was bad enough that she knew the truth about her engagement. She had no wish for anyone else to know she had schemed her way into Theron's life.

"Come, let's go into the dining room," Marley said.

Dinner was laid-back with casual conversation. Marley asked general questions about Isabella, her likes and interests. Piers remained quiet, his eyes following the conversation as he ate, and more than once, Isabella found him staring at her as if he were peeling back the layers of her skin.

It was a relief when Chrysander rejoined them and the conversation shifted to business. Even Piers shed his reserve and entered the fray as they argued and debated.

Marley caught Isabella's gaze, rolled her eyes and then motioned for Isabella to follow her from the table. The men didn't even notice when both women slipped away.

"Would you like to take a walk down to the beach?" Marley asked. "It's so beautiful by moonlight, and it's been awhile since Dimitri has settled down before two in the morning."

Isabella smiled. "I'd love it. I can't wait to see everything in daylight. It's beautiful just from what I can see."

They stepped through the sliding glass doors, and Marley led her down a stone walkway. The sounds of the ocean grew louder and then the pathway gave way to sand. Marley stopped and shed her shoes and urged Isabella to do the same.

"Oh, it's gorgeous," Isabella breathed when they walked closer to the water.

The sky was clear and littered with stars, carelessly strewn across the sky like someone playing jacks. The moon was high overhead, shimmering and reflecting off the dark waters.

"This is my favorite place in the world," Marley said softly. "It's amazing, like my own little corner of paradise."

"I don't think I've ever seen anything so beautiful."

Isabella walked to the edge of the wet sand and waited for another wave to roll in. Then she stepped into the foaming surf, loving the tickle of water over her toes.

"I told you we would find them here," Chrysander said in an amused voice. "My wife is forever escaping to her beach."

Isabella turned to see Theron and Chrysander standing, hands stuffed into their pants as they watched the two women. She couldn't discern their expressions in the darkness.

"Come, Bella," Theron said. "Let's leave the two lovebirds. You must be tired from our long trip."

Marley smiled at Isabella as she walked past on her way to Theron. He held his hand out to her as she neared, and she slid her fingers into his.

He brought them to his lips and pressed a gentle kiss

against her knuckles. Isabella relaxed for the first time. It would be easy if Theron acted as though he wanted to marry her, almost as though he felt something beyond lust and desire. And maybe he did. Did he? Could he love her?

She let him pull her back onto the stone walkway toward the house.

"They seem so in love," she said when she and Theron stepped inside the door.

Theron nodded. "They have quite a story. I'll tell it to you sometime. Right now, however, I'm only wanting a bed and a soft pillow."

She laughed softly and ran her hand up his arm. "There are parts of my anatomy that make for a good pillow."

His lips firmed for just a moment, and he glanced up at her, his expression indecipherable. "I think it would be best if we kept separate bedrooms here."

She recoiled, her head drawing away in confusion. "I don't understand. Why wouldn't we share a bedroom? We're engaged."

He pulled her into his arms. "Yes, we are, *pethi mou.* And as such, I'd show you the respect you're due by not flaunting our sexual relationship in front of my brother and his wife. It's enough that he knows I took your virginity, but I won't draw anymore undue attention to you."

Hurt and humiliation hit her hard in the chest. "He knows? You told him?"

Theron blinked in surprise. "It is my shame to bear, Isabella. Not yours."

She closed her eyes and looked away. So Chrysander, and by default, Marley, did know that Theron was only marrying her out of some outdated sense of honor.

"I'll go up to my room then," she said quietly. "I assume my stuff will be there. I can find my way."

"Bella," he called as she started for the stairs.

She turned and stared bravely at him, determined not to show any emotion.

"I didn't do this to hurt you."

She smiled. A tremulous, hesitant smile, but she pulled it off. "I know, Theron. I know."

Then she turned and headed up the stairs in search of her room.

Chapter 17

Isabella stared up at the ceiling, her hands behind her head. Sleep had eluded her, as she'd slept for most of the flight over. She'd opened her window before going to bed, and the sounds of the waves lured her.

A look at the bedside clock told her she'd lain awake for hours. With a resigned sigh, she tossed aside the covers and swung her legs over the side of the bed. If she were quiet, she could walk down to the beach and watch the sun rise. It wasn't as if she was ever going to sleep. She was too tightly wound. Too restless.

The air was warm coming in the window, so she dressed in a pair of shorts and T-shirt. Not bothering with sandals, she slipped out of her room into the darkened hallway and crept down the stairs.

The house was quiet and cloaked in darkness as she made her way through the living room. She stepped onto the patio and breathed in the warm, salty air.

Briefly closing her eyes, she let the breeze blow her hair from her face, and then she stepped onto the stone path leading to the sand.

The skies were already starting to lighten to the east, the horizon going pale lavender as the morning star shone bright, a single diamond against velvet.

The water was calm, lapping gently onto the shore, spreading foam in its wake. She walked down the beach, letting the waves rush over her feet as the world went gold around her.

A distance from the house, she saw a large piece of driftwood. Marley's seat, Chrysander had called it laughingly. She settled gingerly on the aged wood and stared at the beautiful scene before her. Truly she'd never experienced anything like it.

Unsure of just how long she sat there, basking in the dawn, she picked herself up and headed back toward the house. Sand covered her feet and she paused at the entryway to the stone path cutting through the garden to clean it off.

Voices carried from a short distance away, and she smiled. Theron was up. She could hear his soft laughter. Marley too and apparently Chrysander.

She started up the staggered steps when she heard her name. A surge of excitement hit her. Were they discussing the wedding? She took another step forward but faltered with Theron's next words.

He sounded…resigned. What was it he said? She glanced quickly over the hedge lining the walkway to the stone retaining wall surrounding the patio. There was a lattice wall that afforded the patio privacy and was covered with leafy greenery.

She strained to hear the conversation and then making a quick decision, she hiked her leg over the hedge and hurried to the retaining wall where she hunkered just below the breakfast area where the others were gathered.

As she listened to Theron's low voice explain the entire story to his brother and Marley, she turned so her back pressed against stone and slowly she slid until she sat with knees hunched to her chest.

Hearing her teasing and blatant flirtation from the mouth of someone else made it sound harsher, less earnest than it had been. She listened as he outlined his confusion over his desire for her and his desire to make Alannis his wife.

She put her head down on her arms. She wanted to close her ears, but she couldn't. This was the hard truth, and she'd done all that he said. Her only comfort was that he made it seem as though she hadn't done it purposely, as if she hadn't planned to seduce him. No, he still blamed himself for that.

And then the statement that hit her square in the gut, stealing her breath—and her hope.

"I wanted…I wanted what you and Marley have found," Theron admitted to Chrysander. "I wanted a wife and children—a family, a life with a woman I cared about. I had it all mapped out. Marriage to Alannis, a comfortable life. It all flew out the window so fast that my head is still spinning."

No longer able to stand the pain his words caused, she vaulted up, staggering down the slight incline. She landed on one of the smaller walkways that circled the gardens and nearly ran headlong into Piers.

He gripped her arms to steady her and stared down with piercing eyes.

"I'm reminded of the saying that eavesdroppers rarely hear good of themselves," Piers said.

"No," she said in a small voice. "It would appear they don't."

Something that might have been compassion softened his expression. She turned pleading eyes up to meet his gaze. "Don't tell him I heard. You already know everything. Everyone knows. There's no reason to make Theron feel any worse."

"And you?" Piers asked. "What about you, Bella?"

"It would appear I have a lot to fix," she said quietly.

She shook herself from his hands and hurried through the garden around to the back entrance. She stopped at the door and stared for a long moment at the helipad. Then she walked inside, making sure she wasn't seen as she mounted the stairs.

When she got to her room, she closed the door and leaned heavily against it even as a tear slid down her cheek.

Theron didn't love her. He couldn't. Because he loved Alannis. And because of Isabella, his chance of finding the happiness he wanted was ruined. Taken away by her selfishness and single-minded pursuit of *her* wants and *her* needs.

She took a long, hard look at herself, and she didn't like what she saw very much.

Loving someone shouldn't hurt so much, shouldn't be so destructive. Was she nothing more than a spoiled rich girl unwilling to accept that she couldn't have what she most wanted?

And then in a moment of sudden clarity, of anguish and realization, she knew that she had to let Theron go. She wasn't what he wanted. Alannis was. Isabella didn't even want to know the hurt and disappointment that the other girl had endured. What had Theron told her? That he'd been unfaithful?

Theron was bearing the brunt of Isabella's actions—the dishonor. When the blame was solely hers.

He isn't yours to keep.

The single thought echoed and simmered through her mind. And she knew it was true, no matter how much it hurt, how much it made her heart ache and pulse.

She bowed her head, allowing the tears to slither down her cheeks, falling to the floor beneath her. For a moment she let herself cry and then she raised her head, determined to regain her composure. She had to figure a way out of this mess.

First of all, she couldn't let Theron know that she'd overheard his conversation. He would feel hugely guilty. He'd want to do the right thing—according to him.

But this time—this time *she* was going to do the right thing.

Wiping at her face with the back of her hand, she went to her bags and dug for her handbag. Sophia had given her a card with her address and telephone number, had invited her to visit her in Greece whenever she resumed her plans to travel to Europe. Never mind that those plans had revolved around Theron and had been abandoned when Theron had relocated to New York.

Next she needed to locate a helicopter service, preferably one that wasn't on Chrysander's payroll. Not exactly easy when she was on an island, in a country where she didn't speak the language.

Hopefully Chrysander had internet in his office, or a directory, or something....

And then she had to talk to Theron.

The worst part was that she had to pretend that she'd never heard what Theron said. She had to smile and act as if nothing was wrong. As if her heart weren't breaking.

* * *

Isabella checked her watch as Marley cleared the dishes away after the light lunch she'd served on the patio. Isabella deserved an Oscar award, surely, because she'd smiled and laughed, responded when appropriate. Even as she cracked and broke on the inside.

Piers had watched her, his gaze finding her often, probing and assessing. When the eating was finally finished, it was all Isabella could do not to sigh in relief. Now she had a little time to talk to Theron before the helicopter would arrive to pick her up.

"Theron," she said as he stood from the table. "Could I speak to you? Alone?" she added with an apologetic look in the others' direction.

Piers's brow furrowed, and he gave her an inquisitive look as he stood. She avoided his scrutiny.

"Of course, *pethi mou*. Why don't we go for a walk on the beach?" Theron suggested.

She avoided his hand when he extended it, and instead, she brushed past him and to the walkway. He followed her down to the water, and this time, the water failed to soothe her. It mocked her with its false serenity.

The sheer beauty of the brilliant blue, stretching outward seeking the distant skyline, taunted her. Below the surface, there were ugly things. Things that never saw the light, that never disturbed the pristine surface that sparkled in the sun.

When she stopped, her feet sinking into the sand, Theron's hands closed over her shoulders.

"What's the matter, Bella *mou*?" he asked in his deep timbre. "You seem sad today."

She turned in his arms, finally finding the courage to face him. "There are things I need to tell you, Theron."

His expression sobered. "What things?"

She broke away and took a step down the beach before turning again. "The whole reason I planned to travel to London this summer was because I thought you would be there."

Confusion clouded his eyes, and he started to open his mouth. She silenced him quickly with an outstretched hand. "Please, don't say anything. Let me finish. There's a lot I need to say, and I won't be able to finish if you start asking questions."

He hesitated and then nodded.

"When I arrived in New York and learned that you would be remaining there permanently, I changed my plans on the fly, opting to rent an apartment I didn't really want and invented a host of other reasons to throw me into contact with you."

Her hands closed over her arms, and she rubbed up and down despite the heat that prickled over her skin.

"I knew you planned to propose to Alannis. I knew you'd planned your life with another woman. I was determined to try and seduce you away from her."

He sucked in his breath and opened his mouth again, but she stared at him so hauntingly that he quieted again. Only the glitter in his eyes gave the impression of what he must be thinking.

"I pursued you relentlessly. I'd even planned to crash your engagement party but arrived too late. That was the reason that Marcus was in my room. He'd followed me home in the rain when I took off on foot to try and stop your proposal."

His lips thinned, and he turned his face away to stare at the ocean.

"I thought I'd lost you, but then you came to the strip club, and then we made love in my suite. The next day you told me we had to be married, and I knew that you felt you'd dishonored me. I knew you didn't love me, but I was determined to have the chance to make you love me, so I said yes. I let you say all those things. Because in the end I'd have the one thing I wanted most. You."

She found his gaze again even as tears glided down her cheeks. "You see, Theron, I've loved you since I was a little girl. I thought it was infatuation, that it would go away, but each time I saw you, my love grew until I knew I had to try. I couldn't just live my life standing on the outside of my dream, never giving us a chance."

She took in a deep steadying breath, her quiet sobs shaking her shoulders. "But I was wrong. And I'm sorry. I ruined things for you and Alannis."

Quiet lay between them. Theron stood stock-still, his hands shoved into his pockets.

"You don't love me," she said in a remarkably steady voice.

She hadn't intended it to be a question, but it felt like a plea from the depths of her soul. And then he turned to face her again and her hopes shriveled and died. There were a host of things reflected in those golden eyes. Confusion, anger, but not love. Never love.

Quickly, before he could react, she stepped forward and leaned up to kiss him on the cheek. "I hope someday you can forgive me."

She slid her ring off her finger then slipped her hand inside his. Without another word, she turned and ran back up the path to the house.

"Bella! Bella!" Theron shouted after her.

She brushed past Chrysander at the top of the pathway, ignoring his hands as they reached out to steady her.

"Isabella!" he called.

She swallowed the sob caught in her throat and ran

inside. The helicopter would be here soon. Her bag was where she left it, at the doorway leading out the back of the house, past the pool and to the helipad.

She grabbed it and after a look back at the house, she hurried out to wait on the helicopter.

Chapter 18

Theron stared at the ring resting in his palm then at Isabella's retreating back. He simply couldn't comprehend everything she'd admitted. It sounded too far-fetched.

Had she really loved him for so long? It didn't seem possible.

He watched as Chrysander slowly walked down the path toward him. He came to a stop a few feet in front of Theron.

"Trouble?" he asked.

"You could say that," Theron murmured, still trying to come to grips with all she'd told him.

"She seemed pretty upset," Chrysander said.

Theron closed his fist around the ring. "She gave me my ring back."

Chrysander arched an eyebrow in surprise. "Did she say why? It's easy for anyone with half a brain to see she's crazy about you."

Theron cocked his head then shook it. "She just told me the craziest story. I don't even know what to make of it."

"Care to share?"

Theron opened his hand to see the ring still lying there. It looked all wrong. It should be on Isabella's finger. She should be glowing with happiness, not staring at him with tearstained cheeks.

"She said she's been in love with me since she was a girl," Theron said slowly. "And that her trip to New York was because I was there." He looked up at his brother. "She said the entire reason she planned to go to London was because she thought I'd be there."

Chrysander smiled. "Sounds like a determined girl."

Theron nodded. "That's not all. She seduced *me*."

This time Chrysander laughed. "Now this I have to hear."

Theron quickly told Chrysander everything that had happened since the day Isabella had walked into his office, now armed with the knowledge of what she'd really been doing. It all seemed so much clearer now. The sultry teasing, the apartment hunting, the shopping.

Chrysander remained silent for a moment. "So, are you angry?" he finally asked.

Theron gave him a strange look. "Angry?"

"You wanted to marry Alannis. Isabella prevented that."

Theron shook his head. "Isabella didn't prevent that, Chrysander. I did. I didn't propose, and Isabella was nowhere near me when that happened."

"Okay, so what are you then?"

"Flattered? Overwhelmed? Completely and utterly gobsmacked?"

Chrysander grinned. "That about covers it."

"My God, Chrysander. She's so gorgeous. She lights up the entire room when she walks in. She makes me crazy. Absolutely and completely crazy. She could have any man she wanted. And she wants *me*."

"Enough to drive you to your knees, isn't it? Finding the love of a good woman. They can certainly tie you in knots."

"I love her," Theron whispered. "All this time, I've been so focused on wanting a wife and children, wanting to settle down with the picture-perfect family, and perfection has been staring me in the face all along."

Chrysander smiled. "Why are you telling me all this? It would seem you have a very upset young lady who seems determined to do what's best for you, whether you like it or not."

Theron frowned and clenched his fist around the ring. "Fool-headed, stubborn…" He shook his head and stalked up the pathway, Chrysander falling in behind him.

They were halfway to the house when Chrysander stopped. Theron turned around to see him frown.

"You hear that?" Chrysander asked.

Theron strained to hear. In the distance, he heard the unmistakable sound of an approaching helicopter. "Did you call for the helicopter?"

Chrysander shook his head. "One wasn't scheduled until Piers's departure tomorrow."

Both men hurried up the pathway then cut left to circle the gardens to take the shorter route to the helipad. Even before the helipad came into view, they saw the chopper descend.

"That's not one of ours," Chrysander said grimly.

Chrysander broke into a run, and Theron followed. If Chrysander was worried then so was Theron. But when they rounded the corner and he saw Isabella standing as the helicopter door opened, his blood froze.

"Isabella!" Theron shouted.

She didn't even turn around. She wouldn't have heard him over the roar of the blades.

Chrysander waved frantically to the pilot, and Theron raced ahead of him, trying to reach Isabella in time. He watched helplessly as the door closed behind her, and then, as he reached the edge of the concrete, the helicopter lifted off.

The draft blew his hair and clothing, but he stood, waving his arms in an effort to gain her attention. The helicopter rose higher and then headed in the direction of the mainland.

Chrysander cursed as Theron stood there frozen.

"I've got to find out where she's going," Theron said as he turned back to the house.

Ahead, Marley and Piers came out the back door, Marley in the protective arm of Piers.

"What's going on?" Piers shouted.

Theron strode past him and Marley while Chrysander hung back. He tore up the stairs and into Isabella's room only to find her things gone. There was no note, no hint of where she'd gone.

He ran back down, finding the others in the living room. Chrysander was on the phone trying to track down the pilot service and figure out a way to hold Isabella when she landed.

Piers approached him, a grim expression on his face.

"There's something you should know."

Theron looked sharply at him. "What?"

"This morning, Isabella was on the beach early. I found her on the other side of the patio, visibly upset by something she'd overheard in your conversation with

Chrysander and Marley. She begged me not to say anything. She said she didn't want you to feel any worse."

Theron closed his eyes as he remembered waxing on about what he wanted. When what he wanted had been in front of his nose all along.

"I'm a damn fool," he muttered.

"No arguments here," Piers said with a wry smile. "The question is, what are you going to do to get her back?"

Isabella hadn't considered the repercussions of landing a helicopter on the estate of what appeared to be an extremely wealthy Greek family. As soon as they settled on the ground, they were surrounded by a dozen security guards. All carrying guns.

So maybe this wasn't her best idea.

The door was wrenched open, and she found herself staring into the grim face of one of the gunmen. He barked out something in Greek, and Isabella stared helplessly back at him.

"I only speak English," she said.

"What do you want? Why are you here?" he asked in heavily accented English.

She took a deep breath and tried not to stare at the muzzle of the gun which was precariously close to her nose.

"I'm here to see Alannis Gianopolous. It's important."

"Your name," he demanded.

"Isabella Caplan."

He lifted a small wire and released a torrent of Greek into what she assumed was a microphone. A few moments later, he lowered the gun and took a step backward.

"This way please, Ms. Caplan."

He even reached a hand in to help her down. A few moments later, he escorted her inside the palatial estate that was situated on a cliff overlooking the ocean. In any other circumstance, she would have spared a moment of envy for such a gorgeous place.

"Isabella, my dear!" Sophia exclaimed as soon as Isabella was inside. She took hold of Isabella and kissed her on either cheek. "What on earth are you doing here? And where is Theron?"

Isabella looked down for a moment and then back up at the older woman. "I need to speak with Alannis. It's very important."

Sophia frowned slightly, concern filling her eyes. "Of course. Is everything all right?"

Isabella offered her a shaky smile. "No, but it will be."

"Wait here. I'll get Alannis for you," Sophia said.

Isabella walked to the huge glass window that overlooked the steep drop-off to the ocean. Alannis even lived in a perfect spot. Close to Chrysander and Marley. They could all be one big, happy family after Alannis married Theron.

"Isabella?" Alannis's soft voice filled the room.

Isabella turned to see the other girl staring at her, clear confusion written in her dark eyes.

"Mama said you wanted to see me."

Isabella gathered her courage and crossed the room to stand in front of Alannis.

"I came to apologize and to right a wrong."

Alannis frowned harder. "I don't understand."

Isabella took a deep breath. "I set out to break up you and Theron. I knew he wanted to marry you, but I've been in love with him forever, and I wanted him. I never stopped to think about what he wanted or that I was hurting two people in the process. You and him."

"But—" Alannis began.

"He wants to marry you," Isabella continued on, cutting her off. "You're who he wants. Go to him, Alannis. The helicopter is waiting to take you to the island. He'll be glad to see you. I've ended things with him. I gave him back his ring. Make sure he gives you a different one. You deserve a fresh start. One not tainted by me. Make him do it right, with all the romance and fuss you deserve."

Tears filled Isabella's eyes again. "I'm sorry I hurt you," she said. "I hope you'll be happy."

She turned to walk back out of the house.

"Isabella, wait," Alannis called. "You don't understand."

All Isabella understood is that if she didn't get out soon, she was going to come completely unraveled. She just prayed the taxi would be waiting as she'd arranged.

"Please show me out," she choked out to the security guard who'd escorted her inside. "I have a taxi waiting out front."

As soon as the guard opened the front door, Isabella hurried down the drive toward the wrought-iron gate. They opened automatically as she neared, and to her relief, a taxi waited outside on the street.

"The airport," she said as she climbed in. As she pulled away, she saw Alannis waving to her to stop. Isabella ignored her, turning away.

No one had ever told her doing the right thing would hurt so much.

"How long can it possibly take for the damn pilot to get out here?" Theron demanded as he ran his hand through his hair for the tenth time in an hour.

Frustration beat at him. He was stuck here on the island until Chrysander's pilot could come out. Now, finally, he was supposedly on his way.

Chrysander put down the phone and turned to Theron. "Isabella's pilot took her to the Gianopolous estate."

Theron stared at him in utter confusion. "Why on earth would she have gone to see Alannis? I had no idea she even knew where she lived."

"She's trying to make things right," Marley said softly. "First with you and now with Alannis."

He dug for his phone to retrieve Alannis's number. If he could reach Alannis before Isabella left then he could have her detained until he could go after her himself.

Chrysander handed Theron his phone, and Theron hastily punched in the numbers. A few seconds later, Sophia answered the phone.

"Sophia, thank goodness. Has Isabella been by there? What? She left in a taxi?" Sophia filled him in on where Bella was headed then he hung up and turned to Chrysander. "Now where is your damn pilot?"

It had been impossible for Isabella to purchase a ticket leaving the country anytime soon. All the outgoing flights for the next few hours were booked. In the end, she'd gone to the charter service counter, plunked down her credit card, which she hoped was as platinum as the name stated, and hired a private jet to fly her to London.

At least she was on board now, waiting as the jet was fueled and was placed in the queue for takeoff. Exhaustion seeped into her bones. Not sleeping the night before coupled with the emotionally draining day had taken it all out of her.

She leaned her head back against the seat and closed her eyes. She heard shuffling in the distance and assumed it was the pilot, but then warm lips pressed gently to hers, and her eyes flew open.

Theron drew away, cupping her face in his hands as she stared at him in astonishment. He looked…well, he looked bedraggled. His clothing was dusty and rumpled, his hair was in disarray, and his golden eyes burned with feverish intensity.

Before she could say anything, he kissed her again, this time foregoing the gentleness of before. He dragged her to him, kissing her until she was left completely and utterly breathless.

Then he pulled away and uttered a command in Greek directed at the cockpit. To her increasing shock, the plane began to move. With Theron in it.

"Theron, wait," she protested. "This plane is going to London. You can't just leave here. What about Alannis? And your family?"

He pulled her out of her seat, maneuvered to the couch, then pulled her down onto his lap.

"Shouldn't we be in our seat belts for takeoff?" she asked dumbly, still unable to comprehend that he was here.

"I'll catch you if there is any unexpected turbulence," he said silkily. "Now that you can't run anywhere and I have you all to myself, you'll have to listen to every word I'm about to say."

Her eyes rounded, and her mouth fell open. He traced her lips with his finger then pulled her down to replace his finger with his mouth.

"Foolish, impetuous, beautiful, frustrating woman," he murmured. "If you think you're going to get rid of me after you've hooked me and reeled me in, then you have another think coming, Bella *mou*."

Hope stuttered and made a soft pitter-patter in her chest. She stared at him unsure of what to say. So many things raced through her mind that she was absolutely speechless.

Then he rotated, sliding her off his lap and onto the seat next to him. He got to the floor on one knee and took her hand in his.

"I love you, my beautiful Isabella. I adore you. I can't imagine my life without you. Will you marry me and make me the happiest man alive?"

He slid the ring that she'd given him back on her finger. Then he leaned down and kissed her knuckle.

"This was never another woman's ring, *pethi mou*. I never gave Alannis a ring, and the one I intended for her was replaced by this one. I chose it for you. I never asked her to marry me. I was yours from the day you walked into my office. You turned my world upside down, and it's never been set to rights."

"You didn't propose?" she croaked around the swell of tears knotting her throat.

He looked back at her solemnly. "I would have never made love to you belonging to another woman. I intended to propose the night of the party. I had the ring. The moment was arranged. But all I could see was you. All I wanted was you. The morning after we made love, I went to see Alannis. I told her that I was going to marry you."

Isabella's face fell. Theron smiled and touched her cheek. "How tenderhearted you are, *agape mou*. Alannis isn't in love with me and is in fact, quite anxious for me to find you and put this ring back on your finger."

"She's not? You're not? In love with her, I mean?"

She closed her eyes and shook her head, sure she had to be dreaming.

"I'm in love with *you*," he said softly. "Only you."

"But I heard what you told Chrysander, about you wanting what he and Marley had, a family, a wife. I don't fit into that anywhere," she said bitterly.

"What I want is you," he said simply. "Everything that I ever wanted, what I was so restless for and hoping to find was staring me in the face. I think I knew it that first day you came into my office. I saw that tattoo and it drove me crazy. I wanted to strip every piece of your clothing off so I could see more of it. But I had already started things rolling with Alannis. I fought my attraction to you because I was supposed to be acting as your guardian, not trying to think of ways to get you out of your clothing."

She raised a shaking hand to his face and cupped her palm to his cheek. He closed his eyes and leaned into her touch. Then he turned so he could press his lips to her fingers.

"Marry me, Bella."

"You want to marry me even if I don't want children right away?" she challenged.

"I have a feeling you'll keep me far too busy to think of children anytime soon," he said with an amused smile. He leaned in and kissed her again, his lips melting warm and sweet over hers. "We have all the time in the world, my precious love. Just promise me that we'll have it together."

She was sure that her smile lit up the entire universe as she stared back at him in awe.

"I love you, too," she whispered. "So much."

He sobered for a moment as he cupped her face lovingly. His expression serious, he said in a quiet voice,

"You could already be pregnant. Will it upset you very much if you are?"

She grinned, her heart lightening with every breath. "I'm not pregnant."

"Oh, then you've already…it's that time of the…"

"No," she said with a slight laugh. "I'm on birth control."

His brows came together in confusion and then he glared at her, but there was no heat in his scowl. "You little minx."

"Are you angry that I didn't tell you when you informed me before that we were to be married?" she asked a little nervously.

"If you can forgive my dim-witted actions and the fact that I didn't give you the most romantic proposal before, then I can forgive you for effectively capturing me, hook, line and sinker."

"Yes," she said as she threw her arms around him.

He laughed. "Yes, what, *pethi mou?*"

"Yes, I'll marry you. I love you so much."

He stood and swept her into his arms. She blinked in surprise when she realized that she'd completely missed their takeoff.

"Now, if that's settled, why don't you and I go join the mile-high club," he said wickedly.

She smiled as he carried her into the small bedroom in the back of the plane, her heart overflowing with sweet, unending joy.

And as they came together in body and soul, they whispered their love again and again.

Epilogue

The bride—and the groom—showed up to their wedding barefooted. Theron stood on the beach of Anetakis Island waiting next to the priest as Chrysander escorted Isabella to him.

She was dressed in a bikini top, and a floral sarong floated delicately down her legs. Her toenails—which Theron had painted himself in a night full of decadence—shone a bright pink. An ankle bracelet caught the sun and shimmered above her foot, and Theron knew that it was his name engraved in the small silver band.

His gaze traveled upward to the diamond teardrop belly ring that he too had purchased and delighted in putting on her. But what took his breath away was her radiant smile. Just for him.

She was so beautiful she made his chest ache.

Piers stood to Theron's left, having flown in again

for the wedding. Alannis and Sophia both were standing on the bride's side next to Marley.

There was a festive air, and everyone wore broad smiles. He could even detect the glimmer of tears in the women's eyes.

And then he reached out and took Isabella's hand, pulling her to him. It didn't matter that the vows weren't spoken, or that the priest cleared his throat cautiously. He simply had to kiss her.

Their lips met in a heated rush, soft against hard, sweet against salt. When he finally pulled away to allow the priest to officiate, tears shone in Isabella's eyes.

There was an odd catch in Theron's throat as he recited his vows. The words carried on the breeze, firm and clear.

Finally they were pronounced man and wife, and she became his.

There was much dancing on the beach, and later they moved to the gardens. Sophia and Alannis took great delight in teaching both Marley and Isabella traditional Greek dances while the men looked on, their smiles indulgent.

Later the helicopter came and whisked Theron and Isabella away to the bridal suite he'd arranged, a cottage on a cliff overlooking the sea.

He carried her to bed, where she whispered she had one last wedding gift for him.

Intrigued, he reared back as she untied the sarong and pulled it from underneath her.

"Do you remember telling me I should get another tattoo?" she asked with a mischievous glint.

His brow furrowed. "You didn't. Bella, tell me you didn't go to some tattoo parlor alone and undergo pain to get another tattoo."

"I didn't go alone. Marley went with me."

"And does Chrysander know this?" Theron asked incredulously.

Isabella laughed. "He might have had a thing or two to say when he barged in after us."

Theron muttered in Greek as he shook his head.

She hooked her thumbs in her bikini bottom and slowly, sensuously worked it down. There just above the juncture of her legs, right in the center, a straight line down from her belly ring, was an angel holding a pitchfork.

Theron couldn't contain his chuckle. Then he leaned down and brushed his lips across the design. "My own little demon angel," he said as he worked downward with his mouth.

* * * * *

Dear Reader,

Vaughan Mason is my kind of hero—ruthless, beautiful, sexy and at the top of his game. It's no wonder he's in demand. I didn't blame my heroine, Amelia, in the least for jumping at the chance to spend a week with him. I laughed, though, at her determination that the week would *not* be spent in bed. I have to admit that it would take a stronger woman than me to resist Vaughan, but at least Amelia tried!

Vaughan is very used to women and delights in constant company, but he is completely unused to trusting another. I really enjoyed exploring what happened when it's the hero's trust that is shattered. I confess that Vaughan's reaction had me falling just a little further in love with him.

I hope you enjoy their story.

Happy reading,

Carol x

IN THE RICH MAN'S WORLD

USA TODAY Bestselling Author

Carol Marinelli

For Fiona McArthur
A wonderful friend and an
amazing writer.
Carol x

Prologue

Bed.

Alone.

Just the thought of how tempting those two words sounded brought a wry smile to Vaughan's lips.

Bed alone was almost a contradiction in terms for Vaughan Mason, at least according to the journalists who tagged his every move, sensationalising every aspect of his professional dealings while attempting an angle on his private life—much to Vaughan's slightly jaundiced amusement.

Taking a belt of impossibly strong black coffee, Vaughan screwed up his nose.

He'd barely slept in thirty-six hours, had crossed several time zones and ingested enough caffeine to raise the shares of coffee beans by several per cent. All he wanted was to close his eyes on this impossibly long day, yet instead he had to face them—the journalists, the one *true* love-hate relationship in his life.

A sharp rap on his door dragged him out of his introspection. He leaned back in his chair and yawned as Katy Vale, his personal assistant, waltzed in, smiling her pussycat smile and revealing just a touch too much cleavage and thigh for a Friday afternoon as she leant over his desk and handed him a list.

'It's your lucky day.'

'I wish you'd told me that thirty-six hours ago,' Vaughan retorted. His day had started at some ungodly hour in Japan and been followed by a meeting in Singapore, then several draining hours at Singapore Airport. Now, finally winding up in his office in Sydney, he felt like the sun creeping across the globe in reverse, his body clock completely kaput as jet lag finally caught up with him. The very last thing he felt like doing was being put on parade for some long-overdue interviews, but now, peering at the list, seeing the red pen slashed through the reporters' names, he almost managed a smile.

'There's an election in the air—at least that's the buzz going around,' Katy explained. 'All the big-gun reporters have cancelled their interviews with you and flown to Canberra, trying to get their scoop...'

'Which means I can finally go to bed.'

That he had been cancelled at such short notice didn't offend Vaughan in the least—in fact it came as an unexpected pleasurable moment of relief. The Prime Minister was one of the few people who could knock him out of the headlines of the business pages, and Vaughan was only too happy to step down. The pleasure was entirely his.

Snapping the lid on his pen, he stood up and stretched. But he changed it midway into a long drawn-out sigh as Katy shook her head. 'Not just yet, I'm afraid. The *Tribute* has sent a replacement journalist.'

Peering at the list, Vaughan frowned. 'Why on earth would Amelia Jacobs want to interview me?'

'You've heard of her?' Katy asked, the surprise evident in her voice. 'Somehow I can't quite picture you reading the women's pages.'

'She's good.' Vaughan shrugged, but Katy screwed up her nose.

'She's overrated, if you ask me.'

I didn't, Vaughan almost responded, but he held his tongue. Frankly, he was too tired to be drawn into a long conversation with Katy.

Long conversations with Katy were becoming rather too frequent of late. Given any excuse, she'd sit her neat little bottom on the chair opposite and cross her perfectly toned legs, only too happy to flash her glossy smile and talk.

And could that woman talk!

What had happened to the quietly efficient woman he had hired as his PA? Where had the diligent worker who managed his impossibly tight schedule with barely a murmur gone? The woman who had glowed with pride when he'd commented on her new engagement ring, blushed with pleasure when her fiancé had arrived to pick her up?

'I mean,' Katy droned on, not remotely perturbed by his pointed silence, 'despite all the hype that surrounds her, there's not a single thing that could be described as deep about her articles; it's not as if this Amelia ever digs up the dirt on all these celebrities she interviews—there's nothing that can't be picked up in the rags...'

Vaughan suppressed a tired smile, and this time it was easier to hold back. She simply didn't get it. If Katy couldn't read between the lines that Amelia Jacobs so skilfully crafted, then it wasn't up to him to point it out.

Amelia Jacobs was a master.

Or mistress.

Or whatever the politically correct term was these days.

Amelia Jacobs had, in the few months she'd been writing for the paper, developed something of a cult following—a group of loyal readers who read her articles with their tongues placed firmly in cheek, perhaps sharing a wry smile with a fellow devotee as they glimpsed over the top of their newspaper in some café or airport lounge.

Amelia Jacobs, in Vaughan's not so humble opinion, had her finger on the pulse, but wasn't afraid to remove it when needed, to stray from the usual run-of-the-mill questions and delve a little deeper, to somehow get her subjects to finally confirm or deny the rumours that plagued them. Her interviews were a strange mix of cynicism and compassion.

'Why does she want to interview me?' Vaughan asked again, then corrected himself. Every journalist this side of the equator seemed to want a piece of him, but the fact he had neither dreadlocks nor body piercings, actually managed to eat and keep down three meals a day, and didn't have a father who'd abused him, didn't put Vaughan in the usual category of Amelia Jacobs's subjects. 'Or rather, why do you think I'd want to be interviewed by her?'

'Because you are always in the news for all the wrong reasons,' Katy responded in a matter-of-fact voice. 'There was that supermodel, the actress...'

'Definitely no bishop, though,' Vaughan clipped

back, but even his dry humour didn't allow him to dodge the uncomfortable issue.

Uncomfortable because suddenly discussing his sex life with Katy seemed like a very bad idea indeed.

'That was all over ages ago,' he said finally, staring coolly back as Katy rearranged her crossed legs, smiling sweetly over at him as he protested his rather recent innocence.

'I know,' Katy soothed. 'But you know what the press can be like once they've got the bit between their teeth. And you don't need me to tell you that you haven't exactly been the blue-eyed boy...'

'I don't,' Vaughan said, with a slightly warning edge to his voice.

Katy cleared her throat again. 'It was agreed at the last directors' meeting that if the opportunity came then you should show the media that there's a softer side to you.'

'But there isn't.' Vaughan shrugged. 'What you see is what you get.'

'I don't agree.' Dropping her voice, she stared back at him, flicking her hair away from her pretty face with her left hand, and Vaughan felt his heart plummet—the absence of her engagement ring was vividly noticeable for the very first time. 'Look how nice you were to me when I broke up with Andy.'

'I didn't realise you had.' Vaughan gave a very on-off smile, watching in slightly bored horror as she smiled over at him, from under her lashes now. He felt a subtle shift in the room that most men would miss—but Vaughan read women as easily as a recipe book, and while he'd been away Katy had clearly lined up all her ingredients and was right now stirring the pot and about to offer him a taste!

'We broke up a couple of weeks ago. It hurt a lot at the time, but I guess I'm starting to move on.' Boldly she held his gaze. 'Why don't you come over for dinner tonight, Vaughan? I'm sure cooking is the last thing you want to do now, and you must have had your fill of restaurants.'

'Thanks, but no thanks.' Vaughan deflected her offer easily, quite sure he wasn't hungry—on either count! 'I just want to go to bed.'

God, she was bold. A tiny smile twitched on well-made-up lips at the mere mention of the word, and she was still holding his gaze. Vaughan knew exactly what was on the menu—knew that if he took her up on the offer they wouldn't be starting at the entrée, instead they'd be bypassing the main course and moving directly to dessert!

Watching her face drop as he firmly shook his head and picked up his pen, Vaughan consoled himself that he was doing her a favour really—if he slept with her he'd end up firing her!

'Send Miss Jacobs in as soon as she arrives—and,' he added firmly, 'once she gets here you might as well go home.'

'I don't mind waiting,' Katy persisted, but Vaughan was insistent.

'Go home, Katy.' He didn't soften his rejection with a smile, didn't even look up from his work. Mixed messages were clearly not what were needed here. 'I'll catch up with you in Melbourne next week.'

Chapter 1

Send.

Amelia's finger hovered over the computer key, then pulled back.

She made a quick dash into the bathroom, and inhaled the delicious scent of bergamot mixing perfectly with frankincense and just an undertone of lavender. Her Friday afternoon routine was written in stone:

Read her article as objectively as possible.

Clean the flat while all the time reciting paragraphs of article out loud, adding mental commas and meaningful exclamation marks.

Head into the high street while still mulling over article.

Drop off dry cleaning.

Stop for a café latté—extra-strength with full-cream milk and three sugars.

Head for home.

Finish article, adding said commas and exclamation marks.

Take phone off the hook and run bath.

Finally hit 'send' and, as her work drifted into cyberspace, dive into the awaiting aromatic bath, allowing the fragrance to soothe. Lavender was supposedly fabulous for stress headaches, and for the past six months, come Friday at four p.m., a stress headache was exactly what she'd had.

Okay, her article would still make the deadline if she sent it at five, but she needed that hour. Needed to lie in her fabulous bubbly bath as the blood, sweat and tears she'd shed over the past seven days wafted through cyberspace and into her editor Paul's in-box. Needed that hour wallowing in the bath forgetting the horrors she'd been through the past week.

Sure, interviewing celebrities, eating out at fabulous restaurants and actually being paid to write about it sounded like most people's dream job come true. But for Amelia it was merely a means to an end. Contracted on a freelance basis to cover a nine-month maternity leave position, Amelia had taken the job with the sole intention of making a name for herself, networking with the right people, and hopefully—*hopefully*—landing a more permanent position in the offices on the second floor, the hallowed ground of the business reporters. There she would be writing not about the rise and fall of celebrities' bustlines or their latest off-on romances, but about the far more intriguing effect of rises and falls on world stock markets, or the impact of the US dollar on trading in Australia, and hopefully one day she'd get an inside scoop on a major business deal which would surely seal her arrival as a heavyweight. And maybe would even win her father's approval!

But so far nothing had happened. Sure, her editor, Paul, had made all the right noises—insisted he was talking to people behind the scenes as he handed Amelia her latest task for the week. But still nothing had happened, and with Maria's maternity leave galloping into the final run Amelia was starting to feel more than a touch anxious. Not just because of the lack of movement in the business side of things, but because she'd grown rather used to having a regular wage in the fickle world of journalism. She also had to admit it was because she'd be leaving a job she'd started to love…

Closing her eyes, Amelia let out the breath she'd been inadvertently holding, half expecting that if she opened her eyes she'd see her father's appalled expression at the fact that the daughter of Grant Jacobs, esteemed political reporter, could possibly *like* writing such articles, could actually *enjoy* interviewing celebrities, confirming or denying salacious rumours and feeding the never-ending quest for insight into Australia's most beautiful.

He'd never call it news!

With the soapy water now licking the edges of her claw-foot bath, Amelia twisted off the taps, ran into the lounge, which tripled as a dining room and study, and turned on her favorite CD. She listened as the decadent, fabulous voice of Robbie told her that once he found her he'd never let her go, and finally she did relax.

The phone was off the hook—as it always was when she'd finished a piece—her horoscope was waiting to be read, and a glass of chilled white wine was by the bath.

Routine firmly in place, she took a deep breath and, with her hand over the send key, closed her eyes and pressed it. Then, as she did every Friday, she ran like the wind into her tiny cramped bathroom, stripped off in record time, and winced as she submerged herself into too-hot water. She waited for her body to acclimatize and her over-sized boobs to waft up onto the surface, waiting for their owner to pluck up the guts to sink fully into the water. She would massage that deep heated conditioner that promised miracles into her hair, then lie back and read her horoscope just as she always did.

A fabulous period supposedly lay ahead. Virgos should be ready to embrace changes, throw caution to the wind and take up crazy offers, arming themselves for opportunity, getting ready to expect the unexpected and let a little romance shine into their lives.

For once Louis the astrologer had got it wrong.

Turning to the front of the magazine, Amelia stared at the scowling face of Taylor Dean, every inch the popstar, walking out of a chic restaurant, the requisite beautiful woman firmly entrenched on his arm. She was scarcely able to comprehend that six months ago it had been she, Amelia, on that arm.

Perhaps Louis had misplaced his notes—accidentally repeated her July horoscope in the middle of January—because six months ago today a fabulous period really had lain ahead. The crazy offer of a date with Taylor had literally fallen into her lap, and she'd been foolish enough to accept—stupid and naive enough to throw caution to the wind and let a little romance into her life. Only where had it got her?

Staring into Taylor's brown eyes, Amelia felt as if she were choking on her own humiliation—remembering with total recall the shattered remains their whirlwind romance had left in its wake and the almost impossible task of rebuilding her professional reputation. Colleagues had been only too happy to believe that every scoop she got, every inside piece of information she was privy to, must somehow have been gleaned between the sheets.

But she'd learnt from her mistake.

For the following five months she'd been with the *Tribute* Amelia had been the epitome of professionalism. All her articles had been in before their deadline, she had researched her subjects carefully, and, though friendly and personable, she had maintained a respectable distance, despite a couple of rather surprising offers, determined that by the time Maria returned from her maternity leave Taylor Dean would be a vague memory.

At least in her editor Paul's eyes!

Tears she simply refused to shed were blinked firmly back and the magazine tossed onto the floor. Taylor's features blurred as a sympathetic puddle on the floor licked at the front page—only not quickly enough for Amelia. Taylor's cheating eyes were still staring out at her, the wounds he had inflicted on her once-trusting heart still too raw not to hurt when touched, and she gave up on her relaxing bath, pulled out the plug and padded into the living room.

'*No!*'

Her wail went unheard as, standing shivering in a towel, she saw her computer —despite frantic pressing of Control-Alt-Delete, remain frozen. Its only movement was a red sign appearing, warning of Trojan horses galloping towards her and worms poking their heads out of the woodwork at the most inopportune time.

'*No!*' she wailed again, dragging a chair over with her wrinkled bath-soaked foot and with chattering teeth trying to wrestle with the unforgiving screen of her computer.

It was twenty to five!

Thoughts of Paul's reaction were the only thing that ran through Amelia's mind as she rang her computer guru—only to be told that it was happening to everyone, that computers were crashing with more speed than a pile-up on a freeway.

If she missed the deadline...she'd be dead!

Not even bothering to replace the receiver, not even remembering to thank him, Amelia gulped in air, picturing the scenario. Okay, the piece she was filing so urgently today wouldn't actually appear until next week's colour supplement, but in the cut-throat world of journalism deadlines came second only to a pulse.

First, actually.

Without fulfilling one's deadlines, your pulse didn't even matter.

She could almost see Paul's raised eyebrow as she stammered her way through an apology. Could almost feel the breeze from his dismissive wave as he assured her it didn't matter a jot, that of course this was a one-off and they'd naturally take into consideration when deciding her fate that every other piece she'd filed had been delivered before deadline...

No problem, Amelia. He'd smile. *Don't worry about it, Amelia,* he'd say, waving away her stammering excuses. *These things happen to the best of us.*

Oh, he'd make all the right noises, insist that it didn't really matter, while simultaneously checking with Personnel just how long it would be till the impossibly efficient Maria came back.

A whimper of horror escaped Amelia's chattering lips as she pressed every last key on her computer, watching with mounting horror as each page she attempted to open froze on top of the other, as words dropped like autumn leaves from her screen, replaced instead with the horror of empty white squares on empty white squares, as the stupid, defunct, way-too-late virus warning alerted her of impending doom.

Doom!

Raking fingers through aromatic oiled hair that badly needed a rinse, she squeezed a breath into her lungs.

Back-up.

'Please...' Amelia whimpered, pushing the eject button on her computer and pulling out the disk. Thank God she'd remembered to press 'save'! If she got dressed now, forgot make-up and managed to hail a cab in record time, she'd be just ten minutes late.

Rummaging through her wardrobe, berating the fact that her usual boxy suits were all stacked in a pile at the dry cleaners, Amelia pulled on some weekend jeans and pushed her damp body into a sheer lilac top that, had time allowed, would definitely have benefited from a bra. But time was of the essence. Hailing a cab, she dragged a comb through her short, spiky blonde hair as she rattled around on the back seat, making vague conversation with the driver and attempting a slick of mascara as they swung into George Street.

She was ready to hand over her disk to Clara the receptionist with a quick smile and then beat a hasty retreat, absolutely determined not to be caught looking anything other than the smart, efficient businesswoman she always portrayed.

'Amelia!' Mumbling into the phone receiver she was holding, Clara blew her fringe skywards and gave a grateful smile. 'Thank goodness you're here.'

Never had Clara seemed so pleased to see her. More to the point, never had Clara even grunted a greeting—her efficient smile was reserved for *real* journalists, the ones whose stories actually mattered, not some two-bit freelancer who appeared in the Saturday colour supplement.

'I'm only ten minutes late,' Amelia mumbled, pushing the shiny silver disk across the desk and glancing at the clock above Clara's head, praying it was going faster than her watch. 'I'm normally on time—I'm usually early...'

'Don't worry about that,' Clara said, screwing up her nose as she picked up the disk and, to Amelia's horror, tossed it into a drawer. 'Didn't you hear the news?'

'News?' Amelia gave a bewildered blink, cursing herself that the one time in the week she turned off the radio, the one time she let the world disappear to concentrate on a piece, something had really happened.

'There might be an election! Friday afternoon's a lousy time to call for a press conference if you ask me, but that's what's happened.'

Another bewildered blink from Amelia before excitement started to mount. Images of serious pieces with her name on them drifted into her mind, but before they had even formed Clara easily doused them.

'Which means all the big names are tied up.'

'Amelia!' Paul, her editor, appeared at the lift doors. He handed her a file as he juggled a call on his mobile and his pager bleeped loudly. 'Carter has had to fly to Canberra...'

'I heard,' Amelia replied as Paul decided the call on his mobile was more important. She flicked open the folder he had pressed in her hand for something to do, then caught her breath—not for the first time today, but for an entirely different reason.

Vaughan Mason.

That inscrutable face was actually smiling at her

from a black and white photo, but even with the healing balm of a soft-focus lens the slightly cruel twist to his full mouth was still evident. The black eyes stared back unnervingly, a dark jet fringe flopping over one superbly carved eyebrow. His unshaven, heavily shadowed jaw would have been more in place in a sports calendar than on a business shoot, but apart from that his utter supremacy screamed from every pore. Even the glimpse of his suit in the head-and-shoulders shot reeked of abhorrent wealth, and suddenly her horoscope made sense. Suddenly Venus was aligning with Pluto—or was it Uranus?—and the heavenly changes Louis had faithfully promised, no, warned her to be prepared for were really happening.

'Carter had a fifteen-minute spot with him,' Paul mouthed as he covered the mouthpiece on his mobile.

'When?'

'In twenty minutes' time. You're the fill-in.'

'Me?'

Paul nodded and, possibly realising the urgency of the situation, put his caller on hold. 'You'll be great, Amelia, you always are. I don't know how you do it, but somehow you manage to reel them in, get them to show their true colours, just like you did with Taylor Dean....' Seeing her paling face, Paul changed tack. 'As good as Carter is, he'd never have even attempted your angle.'

'What sort of angle are you looking for?' Amelia asked, Paul's insensitive words having hit a very raw nerve.

'The man behind the millions—what makes his cold heart tick...'

'Nothing?' Amelia ventured, but Paul shook his head.

'We've got a big story about to break on him. You

could be the perfect lead-in. I'll suggest that we hold next Saturday's middle pages for it.'

'Middle pages…' Amelia repeated, her face paling. 'Of the paper, not the…?'

'The paper,' Paul confirmed. 'If you're sure you're up to it.'

'Oh, I'm up to it,' Amelia responded quickly, with way more confidence than she felt. 'What sort of story's about to break? Do you think he's going to pull off the motor deal?'

'Oh, it's bigger than the motor deal,' Paul responded, unable to stop a small boast, but changing his mind at the last moment. 'Trust me, Amelia. The less you know, the better—he's sharp enough to know if you're fishing for information. Just dazzle him the way you did Taylor…'

'I'll have to get changed,' Amelia broke in, determined not to go there. Glancing down at her jean-clad legs and bare arms, she knew she couldn't face Vaughan Mason dressed like this. But Paul was already frog-marching her through Reception

'There isn't time for all that.' Paul shook his head firmly. 'Vaughan Mason won't be kept waiting—you'll just have to go as you are.' His reassuring smile rapidly disappeared as for the first time he took in her dishevelled appearance, giving a rather noticeable frown as he eyed her jeans and sandals. 'Frankly, Amelia, I expected better from you. Maria would never have—'

'I had no idea I'd be doing an interview this afternoon,' Amelia attempted. 'I only came by to drop off my article.'

'You're supposed to expect the unexpected,' Paul countered, sounding like her wretched horoscope. 'That's what journalism is all about.'

And he was right, Amelia conceded through gritted teeth. If it had been any other hour of any other day she'd have been ready—more than ready for the challenge. If only she had listened to her horoscope! If she had she wouldn't be standing here totally unprepared for the biggest break in her career.

'I want you to come back to the office after the interview and let me know how it went. I've pulled this from Carter's desk.' He held out another very thin folder.

'I thought you said he had something on him?' Amelia rolled her eyes. 'Don't tell me—that's for Carter's eyes only. What's in here?'

'Facts and figures,' Paul admitted. 'Have a quick read on the way—but, Amelia, try not to focus too much on the business side. Work your magic on him, see if you can get him to open up a bit about his family, his personal life...'

'His women?' Amelia rolled her eyes again.

Vaughan Mason's reputation was legendary. Pages and pages of the glossies had been filled over the years with tear-streaked gorgeous faces, broken promises and shattered hearts—seemingly the price for a night in this man's company. But through all the scandals, through all the revelations, Vaughan had remained tight-lipped, repeatedly refusing to comment. And his lack of excuses, his utter refusal to be drawn or, heaven forbid, to apologise, had only served to make women want him more.

'I'm hardly likely to get him to open up in a fifteen-minute time slot...' Amelia started, but a warning look from Paul had her voice trailing off. There was no room for negativity in the cut-throat world of journalism. 'It will be great, Paul—just great. You're not going to regret this.'

'I hope not.' Paul's eyes narrowed a fraction. 'Maria's going to be devastated that she missed this opportunity.'

Maria.

The one name that said it all. The one word that reminded her of the very temporary nature of her position.

She had to get it right.

Had to do as her horoscope said and embrace the opportunity. Had to somehow get noticed. So that next time the sniff of an election was in the air she'd be heading to Canberra, not standing in a humid, muggy Sydney street, attempting to hail a taxi in the middle of Friday-night rush hour and trying to call around and find out Vaughan Mason's latest value on the stock market.

Meticulous research was Amelia's forte.

That was how she got celebrities to open up.

Flattery heaped on flattery—it worked every time.

Watching appalling films, reading even worse biographies, seducing stars with her insight! But how was she supposed to woo Vaughan when all her research was being done in the back of a taxi hurtling through the city at breakneck speed towards a subject she knew nothing about other than the undeniable ruthlessness of his business dealings that had been reported in the newspapers, coupled with regular romance scandals that found their way into the glossies?

Gulping in the stuffy air, Amelia skimmed the facts and figures neatly typed in the folder in her lap, silently appalled that one man could hold so much wealth and power.

From what she could ascertain not a single cent of his millions strayed from his path. Normally a list of charities appeared in bios, in an attempt to soften the figures and show that there was a warmer side to a ruthless personality. Normally a few family shots appeared, or a snippet of personal information—a small sideline on hobbies or interests—but, thanks to Carter, all the file on Vaughan Mason contained were cold, hard business facts. How he'd built his massive wealth from the ground upwards, how he'd saved flailing businesses over and over, forging a reputation on gut feeling and confidence alone!

She could hardly quote the glossies to him! How was she supposed to get a different angle when there wasn't one?

Paying the taxi driver, she stared upwards at the impressive tower before her, scarcely able to believe she was really here. Catching sight of her reflection in a glass window, Amelia let out a low moan—the humid Sydney air had done nothing to accelerate her hair-drying and, glancing down at her watch, she wished for the umpteenth time that she could dart into a boutique and buy something—anything other than what she was wearing. That she could greet this demi-god if not on his level at least in smart clothes.

Maybe it would work in her favour, Amelia consoled herself, flashing her ID at an immaculate, very suitably dressed woman who might have been Clara Mark Two and being shown to a lift out of sight of the main reception area. She showed her ID again, to a gentleman who had more muscles than your average body builder and didn't even attempt conversation, then her stomach was left on the ground as the lift soared to the heavens, towards the very man himself.

'Miss Jacobs?'

Yet another clone of Clara was greeting her, but this one introduced herself as Katy, rouged smile firmly in place. Even with a few mils of Botox injected into her forehead this one couldn't quite hide her surprise at the scruffy-looking woman who had appeared in the office.

'Mr Mason's ready for you. I'll just let him know that you're here.' Picking up the phone, she spoke in low soothing tones, clearly for Vaughan's ears only. 'Well, if you're sure,' she soothed, purring into the phone. 'In that case I'll see you in Melbourne next Friday. Have a safe flight.' She turned her gaze to Amelia. 'He said to go right in.'

'Thank you.' Amelia nodded crisply, attempting blasé, but nerves finally caught up. 'Could I just use the powder room first?'

'Of course.'

Even the powder room was gorgeous: white marble everywhere, pump-action soap that was actually full, expensive moisturiser, and a mirror that was way too large in Amelia's present state. Still, she turned on the hand dryer full-blast and attempted to dry her hair, but to no avail—the heavy waft of lavender as the dryer met her damp hair did nothing to soothe Amelia now! She'd just have to put on her best smile and hope for the best…

Walking back into Reception, Amelia nodded to Katy, who was slowly pulling on her jacket, clearly reluctant to leave her boss in anyone's hands but her own. Knocking on the door, Amelia swallowed hard, forced a bright confident smile and pushed back her shoulders—not quite as ready as she'd have liked for the biggest moment of her career, but excited all the same.

'Mr Mason? I'm Amelia Jacobs…' She strode confidently forward, just as she had rehearsed during the taxi ride, hand outstretched. Her eyes scanned the room in a nano-second, her voice trailing off as her footsteps did the same, staring in utter disbelief at the sight that greeted her.

Vaughan Mason—business tycoon, eternally vigilant man of stealth—lay asleep on the jade leather couch.

Asleep.

And what made it even more inappropriate was how completely stunning he looked.

Dark lashes fanned the even darker rims under his eyes; razor-sharp cheekbones emphasised the hollows of his face. His unshaven chin was for once not set in stone, and that cruel, full mouth was unfamiliar in its relaxed state, lips slightly parted. His tie was askew, shifted to one side, and the bottom of his very white Egyptian-cotton shirt was inching its way out of an expensively belted waistband.

She was assailed with the most inappropriate of feelings, given the circumstance, and felt an almost instinctive need to reach out and touch him, as one might a work of art finally witnessed first hand—to feel the scratch of his stubble beneath her fingers, the cool marble of his skin. His beauty truly daunted her. Not a blemish marred his skin. The only fault, if you could call it that, was the too severe, almost too dark, eyebrows—yet even they seemed fitting somehow, as if some pensive artist had added them, and was waiting in the wings with a charcoaled thumb poised ready to blend them in further the moment she left.

Amelia had the most inappropriate urge to lean over and press her mouth against his, to feel those full lips under hers, to sneak a kiss when no one was looking, climb over the imaginary thick red ropes that separated art from mortals, ignore the mental signs that said 'Do Not Touch'. And though she never would have dared, never in a million years, it was like standing on a cliff face and wanting to jump—knowing it was treacherous, knowing it would prove fatal, but filled with a yearning all the same to throw caution to the wind and follow natural instincts.

Shaking her head fiercely, pushing impossible thoughts away, she felt a moment of sheer panic.

Panic!

And it didn't compare to the computer virus, nor even to anything she'd ever experienced in her life to this point.

She didn't know what to do—literally didn't know what to do.

Shake him, perhaps? Or go out and knock more loudly this time, pretend she'd never even witnessed this magnate in an off-guard moment?

But why should she? Amelia thought with a flash of anger. Why should she make things more comfortable for him? Why was she standing here feeling embarrassed when it should be Vaughan Mason squirming with shame and embarrassment? Sure, he dealt with journalists all the time, and everyone knew he didn't stand on ceremony for them, but she'd bet her bottom dollar that if it had been Carter doing the interview instead of her then Vaughan Mason would have at least had the decency to stay awake.

This was the biggest moment in her career—literally make or break—and bloody Vaughan Mason had the audacity to sleep through her entrance, had the temerity to doze off before her questions had even started, and relegate her to the struggling novice she was without a single word!

'Mr Mason,' Amelia said loudly, burning with humiliation and anger, stupid, stupid tears pricking her eyes. 'Mr Mason!'

Navy eyes peeped open—navy eyes that stared directly at her, that ignited something she couldn't at that moment identify. But it spun her further into unfamiliar disorder—her pulse-rate accelerating, her anger fanning as he had the audacity to stretch and yawn, not even bothering to cover his mouth.

'Sorry about that,' he said, not sounding remotely so, in the deep voice she'd heard during numerous appearances on the news and radio. 'I must have dozed off.'

'Oh, you didn't "doze off",' Amelia retorted, scarcely able to believe the provocation behind her own response. The consummate professional, she usually smiled through everything—yet for reasons she couldn't even begin to fathom here she was answering back when she should stay quiet, letting her subject know exactly what she thought of his appalling behaviour when she should just let it go. 'You were asleep, Mr Mason. Sound asleep. Snoring, in fact, when we're supposed to be doing an interview.'

'I don't snore,' he said easily, throwing incredibly long legs over the edge of the couch and bringing himself to a stand, tucking in his shirt and then towering over her, somehow instantly regaining control. 'Had you arrived on time the interview would have been over with by now…' He glanced at his watch—or rather he didn't glance. Glances happened in a split second, whereas Vaughan positively stared, letting out a long held-in breath as the second hand ticked loudly on. Twisting his mouth into the cruel smile she knew so well, he said, 'And, had you arrived on time, Miss Jacobs, I can assure that you'd have found me awake.'

It was Amelia running her fingers through her own hair now, colour flaming in her pale cheeks as she felt the oily mass that greeted her fingers, felt the unspoken derision in the flicker of his gaze as he dragged his eyes the length of her body.

Her editor's gaze had been derisive, and she'd dealt with it, Amelia reminded herself, but her body burned with shame as she felt Vaughan slowly take in her brightly painted toenails, her naked feet slipped into silver sandals. The faded jeans that had seen better days merited a raised eyebrow that spoke volumes, and she felt a scorch of further humiliation as he languorously lifted his gaze and stopped, she was sure, at breasts that moved unhindered as her breathing quickened. Breasts that were still damp and heavy from her bath, straining at the leash under her softly ruched top. Way, way too big for an outing into this office without the firm support of a bra. Even Paul had told her to her face that she was inappropriately dressed, but though it had stung it hadn't really mattered. Nothing from Paul could begin to compare to the sting of Vaughan's disapproval as his eyes finally sought her face.

'Your appointment was for five.' Staring down again at his preposterously expensive watch, he frowned with concentration. 'It's now nearly twenty past.'

She should have apologised, Amelia knew—*knew* that was what she should do. Hell, it wasn't as if Vaughan Mason was the first of her subjects to behave atrociously. She'd been left stranded at restaurant tables more times than she could remember when her interviewee had failed to show, had waited patiently for celebrity 'naturally thin' new mothers to return from the powder room between each course more times than she could count. She'd even had subjects fall asleep midsentence, come to that!

So why was she overreacting now? Why wasn't she swallowing this bitter pill with the sweetest of smiles and attempting to redeem what was left of this awful situation? Why wasn't she attempting to implement some sort of rescue plan? But it was as if her foot was stuck on an emotional accelerator; she could almost smell the petrol fumes as her mouth opened and she revved up again.

'I'm well aware of the contempt in which you hold journalists, Mr Mason.' Holding up his bio with slightly shaking hands, she attempted to fix him with a firm stare of her own. 'And I'm more than aware that I'd be flattering myself to imagine that fifteen minutes in my company might cause you even the slightest twinge of anxiety. But this happens to be extremely important to me, and to walk in and find you sound asleep...' She struggled for eloquence, attempting to swallow the shrill ring that was rising in her voice, to finish her argument with some crushing words that would shame him into submission. But settled instead for the only two words that sprang to her dizzy, emotional mind. 'How *rude*!'

'I wasn't *sound* asleep,' he said, his cool, utterly controlled voice the antithesis of hers. 'But funny you should say that when I was thinking exactly the same thing myself.' His mouth twisted into that familiar cruel smile. 'I was just thinking how *rude* it was of the newspaper to cancel at such short notice, how *rude* it was of them to send a replacement journalist without having the courtesy to first run it by me...'

'Your PA approved it—' Amelia started, but her voice faded mid-sentence as Vaughan overrode her.

'Indeed she did,' Vaughan clipped. 'Though no doubt at the time she was expecting a rather more suitable replacement.'

'So, were you expecting one of the bigger names?' Amelia bristled, but Vaughan shook his head.

'Oh, no, Miss Jacobs. I was told it was you that would be doing the interview.'

'Then why…?' Confused, she blinked back at him. Her mouth opened to ask what he meant, but quickly she closed it again, shame coursing through her as realisation hit home and she braced herself for a dressing-down Mason style. And Vaughan took great pleasure in confirming his displeasure at her attitude and attire, nailing his answer with a brutality that was as savage as it was legendary.

'Rude!' He said the word slowly, rolled it slowly out of full lips, his face impassive.

Amelia's cheeks flamed, and she swallowed hard under his scrutiny, wishing he would just get it over with so she could get the hell out of there. Clearly this interview wasn't going to happen, but Vaughan wasn't rushing. Her allotted time-slot might be well and truly over, but Vaughan Mason wasn't in any hurry to finish, mentally circling her like a vulture over his prey as the single word resonated in the air.

'Impolite, uncouth, inappropriate…' His forehead frowned slowly. 'Did my lying on the couch while I awaited your arrival offend you that much, Miss Jacobs?' He didn't await her answer; she'd never really expected him to. 'We must have a different understanding of the word.' He flashed a tiny smile that didn't meet his eyes, in fact he barely moved his lips. *'Rude* is arriving in my office with wet hair and inappropriate clothes. *Rude* is barging in here completely unprepared…'

'How do you know that I'm unprepared? How do you know that I haven't got a list of pertinent—?' Amelia attempted, but Vaughan shot her down in an instant, picking up a newspaper from his desk and waving it at her.

'Had you read your own newspaper you'd know that I've been on the go non-stop for the last thirty-six hours. That before I went to Singapore I had a prolonged stopover in Japan, meeting with Mr Cheng and drinking endless cups of green tea while trying to broker a deal that will bring jobs and dollars to this country and hopefully save a flailing industry that most people have written off.'

'I know about the motor deal you're attempting,' Amelia responded. 'In fact I've been monitoring it closely. I know that in a few weeks' time you're hoping to...'

'I move quickly, Miss Jacobs. And, had you been more professional from the outset, you might have been the first to find out...' His voice trailed off and Amelia watched in something akin to disbelief as Vaughan appeared to flounder, giving a tiny shake of his head, as if he couldn't quite believe what he had just revealed.

'It's about to go through?' Her voice was an incredulous whisper, her green eyes widening as she processed this piece of front-page news; everyone had said it was an impossible feat, a war that quite simply couldn't be won even if the David that faced Goliath happened to be Vaughan Mason. 'You've actually managed to pull it off?'

But it wasn't only Amelia's mind that was working overtime. Amelia wasn't the only one reeling at the snippet of information he had so easily imparted.

Vaughan quite simply couldn't believe it himself. Already embarrassed at being caught asleep, he could scarcely believe he had mentally relaxed twice in a row. His defences were eternally up, yet one moment in this woman's company and he had felt them waver. Her sparkling green eyes had caught him completely off guard—eyes that seemed to stare not at him but through him, through to somewhere deep inside, where no one was permitted. He had given this woman, this stranger, this *journalist* an opening, a chance to destroy what he had spent months building, and Vaughan knew that he had to somehow retrieve it, had to somehow pull sharply back, get her the hell out of here just as fast as he could.

'Repeat what I just said and I'll sue.' Direct, threatening and straight to the point.

Vaughan felt himself retrieve the grip he had momentarily lost and watched her face pale before him, utter despair filling those expressive eyes as he snatched back the tidbit he had so readily thrown. 'I think you should leave now.'

Amelia opened her mouth to argue, then closed it again, perhaps realising it would be futile, and Vaughan let out a breath of relief as without further ado she headed for the door.

And that should have been it. If it had been anyone else he was sure this rather uncomfortable exchange would be over by now, so why did she have to go and turn around? Why couldn't she have just cut her losses and got the hell out?

'I'm sorry.'

For Amelia, the apology that had spilled from her mouth was as unexpected as it was genuine. She'd meant to just leave—had fully intended to slam the door on this insufferable man. But with a stab of cruel honesty she realised that her anger was misdirected, that the only person who'd blown her chance was herself. Tears that had no place if she wanted to escape with her last withering shred of dignity were held firmly back and she gave a small shake of her head in defeat.

'I *have* been rude, appallingly so, and the truth of

the matter is I've no idea why.' She gave a tiny shrug. 'You're right. I have just come out of the bath and I'm woefully inappropriately dressed. I had the phone off the hook because I was working on an important piece.' Amelia gave a dry laugh. 'Well, it seemed important at the time. Then my computer got a virus…'

Her voice trailed off. Vaughan Mason didn't need details. An apology was the only thing needed now.

'Had I had any idea prior to five p.m. that I'd be interviewing you, Mr Mason, then I'd have spent every available minute researching you and would have arrived in the smartest of suits. I had no right to barge in here all accusatory. I was just…'

Again, she struggled for eloquence but gave in, words literally failing her, unable to justify even to herself what had just taken place, secretly hoping he'd put her out of her misery, end the torture she'd started and let her go meekly on her way. But Vaughan had other ideas.

'Just what?'

'Overwhelmed.' Amelia chewed on her lip as she struggled to find the words. 'I'm usually incredibly ordered. OCD is my middle name…' He didn't even laugh at her rather feeble joke. 'Obsessive compulsive disorder…'

'I know what OCD is.'

'I pride myself on being prepared, and when I found out I was interviewing you I guess I just panicked. I've been trying to move into business reporting, and had I handled it better this really could have been a huge break for me.' Forcing a brave smile, she offered her hand. 'I've already taken up enough of your time. Once again, I really am sorry.'

As his expression softened a shade she almost dared

to hope that he'd refuse her hand and, with a nod of that immaculately cut hair, relent and gesture for her to come in. But that vague hope was doused before it had even formed: after only the briefest of hesitations Vaughan Mason's warm, dry hand closed around hers.

'What will you say? I mean, what will you write?'

'My notice, probably, when I return to the office empty-handed.' Amelia sighed, but emotional blackmail clearly didn't move Vaughan Mason an inch. He just stood there as Amelia turned and pulled the heavy door open. 'Congratulations, by the way.' She saw the flicker of confusion in his tired eyes, realised only then just how exhausted he must be if a billion-dollar deal could so easily be forgotten. 'On the contract.'

'Oh, that!' He gave a tight nod. 'Thanks. Although it's a touch premature. It's far from in the bag, and, as I said—'

'Off the record, or you'll sue?' Amelia second-guessed him and gave a wan smile. 'Don't worry; my next piece will be called "You heard it here *last*".'

She slipped out of his office and into the hallway. The elevator must have been expecting her, because it slid open before she even approached, killing stone-dead any lingering hope that he might change his mind, might pull open the door and call her back in.

As if.

As if Vaughan Mason would even give their altercation a second thought.

Stepping out onto the street, she ignored the taxi rank and decided instead to walk. What was the point of rushing to the gallows?

She could almost see Paul's thunderous face when she told him what had happened. Could imagine her bank balance sliding into the red as she struggled to find another gig.

The one major scoop of her life had practically been gift-wrapped and handed to her on a plate, and she'd somehow managed to mess it up.

But it wasn't just her lack of journalistic acumen causing Amelia's feet to drag. Glancing back over her shoulder, she stared up at the ostentatious high-rise building, squinting into the low, late-afternoon sun at the black-tinted windows, remembering Vaughan lying asleep on the couch… And she was suddenly assailed with regret of a rather more personal nature.

If only she'd dared kiss him!

Chapter 2

'Paul said you were to go straight through,' Clara greeted her. 'And by the way he's not in the sunniest of moods.'

Perhaps he already knew. Amelia sighed, picking her way through the practically empty office and knocking wearily on his door. Perhaps Vaughan had wasted no time picking up the telephone and complaining to her senior about the poor replacement he had sent.

Oh, well, if nothing else it would save her the indignity of repeating the debacle; living through it the first time had been bad enough

As usual Paul was on the telephone.

As usual he gestured for her to sit, with barely a glance, and sit Amelia did—nausea rising with every breath and the oppressive scent of a large bouquet of stunning orchids which adorned Paul's desk doing nothing to help.

'How did it go?' Paul finally asked, hanging up the telephone and scribbling down a few notes. 'Oh, and these came for you,' he added when Amelia didn't immediately answer, pushing the bouquet forward, watching her strained face as she fingered the pale pink waxy petals. 'Most women would die to be in your position, you know? Most women would give their right arm to have Taylor Dean constantly sending them flowers and begging for forgiveness.'

'No, Paul, they wouldn't,' Amelia sighed, wishing Taylor would just drop it, wishing his ego could finally admit that it was over and he'd realise that for once in his life he wasn't going to be forgiven his sins.

'What's he got to say for himself this time?'

Amelia didn't need to read the card to find out—no doubt it was another ream of excuses, another plea for forgiveness.

'So, how did it go with Mason?' Paul asked again, returning to his notes. And, given that it was the second time he'd asked, given that Paul didn't like to be kept waiting, Amelia knew that her tiny reprieve was over. The curtain was lifting and the final act was about to begin

'Not very well.' She watched the smile wiped from Paul's face, watched as his pen froze over the paper and he instantly reverted from colleague to boss.

'Which means exactly what?'

Amelia swallowed hard, peeling open the envelope from the bouquet for something to do. Taylor's pathetic excuses were preferable to Paul's harsh, direct stare.

'He wasn't really up to an interview. He was tired…'

'Vaughan Mason's never tired,' Paul hissed. 'Vaughan Mason isn't a mere mortal who needs six hours' sleep to function, like the rest of us…'

'He *was* tired,' Amelia insisted, pulling the card out of the envelope and glancing down at the writing—anything other than meeting her boss's eyes. 'He's just flown back from Asia...'

'Did you find out anything about the motor vehicle deal?'

For a second she wavered. For a second integrity seemed a poor buffer against the harsh reality of a world without work. But unfortunately it must have been indelibly implanted, because after only the briefest of pauses she shook her head.

'No.'

'So what exactly *did* you find out, Amelia?' Paul clipped, with no smile to follow, no small talk to pad it out—it was a direct question that needed a direct answer.

'That he looks beautiful asleep.' Her voice was a pale whisper and she screwed her eyes closed. 'You see, he was asleep when I got there...'

'So?' Paul thumped the desk. 'You make the guy a coffee, wake him with a bright smile...'

If only...

She couldn't look at him. Instead she stared at the card in her hand, listening as Paul took her on a virtual tour of a hundred ways to butter up a reluctant subject, his voice growing louder with each passing sentence. He was oblivious to the sudden shift in Amelia, totally unaware of the metamorphosis taking place before him, blind to the fact that the world had just tipped on its axis, that Christmas had come eleven months early, that Amelia was actually smiling—really smiling—back at him.

'What did you get from him, Amelia?' Paul's voice

was deadly serious, and at any other moment in time it would have had her shrinking in her seat.

'Nothing,' she said again, only more firmly this time, her smile still in place, enjoying for a luxurious moment the confusion in his eyes. 'He's picking me up here in an hour. We're going for dinner.'

'Vaughan Mason's taking you for dinner?' He didn't even attempt to hide the incredulity from his voice. 'Vaughan Mason?'

'At seven,' Amelia confirmed. 'As I said, he was too tired to do the interview.'

'Oh, my…' Paul was on his feet now, pacing the office floor, staring at Amelia with undisguised and unprecedented admiration. 'I told Clara you could pull it off.' He waved his finger at Amelia. 'She said you should have got changed before you went over, but I told her you'd win him over…'

'You did no such thing, Paul.'

Confidence suited her, Amelia realised, standing up and picking up the bouquet, burying her burning cheeks in the cool waxy petals and inhaling deeply. The scent that had been so oppressive was truly beautiful now. She was scarcely able to comprehend that Vaughan Mason had sent it to her—and in record time too—scarcely able to believe that these gorgeous, tropical flowers had somehow beaten her back to work and saved her in the very nick of time.

'I'd better get ready.'

'Good idea.' Paul jumped up. 'I'll ring one of the boutiques and ask them to stay open for you. And I can call Shelly the make-up artist to come and work her magic—'

'I've got an outfit in my locker,' Amelia interrupted, but Paul shook his head.

'This isn't one of your usual extended celebrity lunches; one of your little dark suits won't do here, Amelia. This is *dinner* with Vaughan Mason!'

Which did nothing to quell her nerves!

'I've actually got a gorgeous black dress in my locker,' Amelia said airily, not adding that she'd had it hanging there for six months now, draped in plastic, waiting for this moment—waiting for the big break to come—so she could dash like Wonder Woman into the office loo and change from efficient to gorgeous. 'But if Shelly's available that would be great.'

Poor Shelly. Amelia smiled as she sank back in a chair and closed her eyes—summoned from the bowels of the car park as she attempted to creep out to the pub on a Friday with the rest of the mob. Called back in to work her magic on someone who wasn't even famous—yet!

Gorgeous!

Okay, the dusty mirrors in the toilet had the same positive effect as a soft focus lens, but Shelly really was a genius. She'd been working on Amelia for forty full minutes, telling her sharply to stay still as Amelia had begged her to go lightly, sure she must look more like Coco the Clown from the amount of jars and tubes Shelly seemed to be opening. But now, staring back at her reflection, Amelia felt more than a flutter of excitement.

Cheekbones Amelia hadn't known existed made her look positively gaunt, and her mouth looked all sparkly and animated, courtesy of the very latest in 'stay put' lipglosses. But it was on her eyes where Shelly had really come into her own. A smudgy grey eyeshadow, that Amelia would never have attempted, made the green so much more vivid, like glittering emeralds, her eyelashes impossibly long, and yet somehow she'd made it look if not subtle then tasteful. And as she stood and admired her reflection Amelia was scarcely able to believe that the sophisticated, demure woman staring back was really her.

'Oh, my,' Paul said for the hundredth time, barely able to contain his excitement as he stood waiting with her in the lobby. 'You've got spare batteries for your Dictaphone? Remember to turn off your mobile. There can be no distractions—not even from me. But if you need to call…'

'I'll be fine, Paul,' Amelia snapped, wishing he would just be quiet, wishing he would stop acting like some over-protective parent on his daughter's first date. 'Might I remind you, this isn't the first celebrity I've interviewed? I've delivered an article every week for the last six months.'

'But not one like this, Amelia.' Paul gave her an extremely annoying nudge as a slick silver car pulled up beside the pavement. 'This has shades of Taylor Dean written all over it—and look how much the paper made on that one article! Didn't he wrap up the interview by asking you to dinner?'

'This is nothing like Taylor Dean,' Amelia bristled, managing to simultaneously smile and give a small wave as she hissed the words out of the side of her mouth.

'No,' Paul responded. 'Because Vaughan Mason's got style.'

It was Vaughan who stepped out of the car, not his chauffer. Vaughan who pulled open the rear door as

Paul walked down the concrete stairs with her and delivered his final below-the-belt remark.

'If you two aren't in bed by eleven, I want you to ring me at twelve.'

Amelia was used to heads turning as she made her way into restaurants, used to the nudges and murmurs working their way around the room like a game of Chinese Whispers as the patrons recognised her companion, and she was used to the best, most secluded table being somehow magically conjured up, whether or not a reservation had been made. But walking in with Vaughan she felt like a complete novice, a pit of nervousness in her stomach as his warm hand grazed the small of her back, guiding her through the white-clothed tables.

The glow on her cheeks was nothing to do with Shelly's generous rouge and everything to do with her delicious companion. Even her breathing wasn't involuntary as the waiter pulled out her chair and she took a grateful seat; every breath was a supreme effort as finally she faced him, as the moment it seemed she had been dreaming of all her life finally arrived.

'Why?'

It was the first real question that had spilled out of her lips, although they'd chatted politely in the back of his sleek car while his chauffer had driven them to this exclusive little French restaurant nestled in The Rocks.

Vaughan had declined an entrée, but, determined to wring the evening for every last drop, Amelia had ordered one. Even if it killed her she'd have dessert, and then port and cheese as well. She had the middle pages to fill!

Cracking the crust of her bread over her French onion

soup, avoiding his eyes, Amelia found the nerve to ask the question that had been plaguing her since Paul's last derogatory remark. Despite the sheer heady pleasure of a night in Vaughan's company, she was utterly determined to set the tone early—to ensure Vaughan Mason understood that this was a business dinner and nothing else. Even if she might be merely flattering herself, Amelia had to be sure he had asked her here tonight for professional rather than personal reasons.

'Why the flowers? Why…?'

'Because on a last-minute impulse I picked up a bunch of orchids at Singapore Airport with the intention to give them to Katy as thanks for all her hard work. She's my PA,' he added, when Amelia frowned at his response. 'Anyway, suffice to say things became rather complicated, about ten minutes before you arrived in my office, and I'm sure that had I given the bouquet to Katy my life would have then taken a turn from complicated to extremely messy.'

'I meant why did you ask me for dinner?' Amelia asked, sure he had deliberately misinterpreted her question, but equally determined to get her answer.

'You asked about the flowers,' Vaughan pointed out. 'It seemed a shame to waste them, so I asked Gary, my driver…' He relented with a devastating smile. Perfect white teeth lit up his dark features, brooding eyes holding hers over the table. 'I don't know why I asked you to dinner,' Vaughan admitted, taking a long sip of his whisky. 'I suppose I wanted to get to know you a bit better.'

'It's supposed to be the other way around, Mr Mason,' Amelia answered quickly.

His response was the last thing she needed, because it would be easy—so very frighteningly easy—to forget her promise to herself that she would never cross the professional line again! Even though there was no denying the attraction that sizzled between them, Amelia knew that if she weakened even for a moment, if she allowed herself to lapse for even a smidgen of time, Vaughan Mason would crush her in the palm of his manicured, experienced hand—use her and toss her aside, just as he had every woman who had come before her.

She had to stay in control.

'You couldn't get me out of your office quickly enough,' Amelia deliberately reminded him, 'so why the sudden change of heart?'

She watched him toying with the rim of his glass, stifling a yawn, but in a sharp contrast to their initial meeting his distraction didn't irritate her now. Something akin to compassion washed over her as she closely studied his face, took in the lines of exhaustion grooved around the edges of his eyes. The artist waiting in the wings must have left for an extended coffee break, because he'd forgotten to blend in those dark smudges beneath them. Vaughan was almost cross-eyed as he squinted across the table at her, and suddenly the hows and whys didn't matter any more; the fact she was here was quite simply enough.

'You're exhausted, aren't you?'

'Unfortunately, no.' He took another slug of his whisky. 'I was exhausted at five, and had you not burst into my office I suspect I'd still be lying on the sofa fast asleep. However...' he smiled at her darkening cheeks '...now I'm wide awake, and no doubt will remain that way until five a.m. tomorrow.'

'You're an insomniac.' Amelia groaned sympathetically. 'I used to be one too.'

'Don't.' He held up a beautifully manicured hand. 'Please don't try and engage me with your sympathy, telling me you understand exactly how I feel and then wiping the floor with me in the colour supplement.'

'You should try counting sheep.' A cheeky smile inched over her lips and she barely noticed the waiter delivering her sumptuous main course and tucking a massive white napkin around her. Amelia's eyes were only for her most intriguing subject.

'Which would no doubt be relaxing if I hadn't grown up on a massive sheep farm. I can still remember listening to thousands of them bleating as I tried to nod off.' He smiled at her open mouth. 'Don't you do *any* research, Miss Jacobs?'

'But nothing, *nothing* in your bio even hints that you grew up on a sheep farm. I thought that you went to an exclusive private school…'

'I did.'

'I specifically remember reading that your father is an accomplished businessman.'

'He is.'

Finally he relented.

'My father is an extremely successful sheep farmer.'

'Oh!' Pulling back, trying to quell the surprise in her voice, Amelia asked a more relevant question. 'Whereabouts?'

Vaughan immediately shook his head. 'That's hardly relevant.'

'I'm just interested,' Amelia responded, making a mental note to research it. But Vaughan was clearly a mind-reader.

'Don't even think about looking it up, Amelia. You can say what you like about me, but my family stays out of anything that you write.'

'I was hardly going to dig up dirt on him,' Amelia countered, but Vaughan remained unmoved.

'My family stays out of it,' he said again, very firmly and very clearly. 'The last thing I want is a picture of my father in his work gear, drinking his cup of tea out of the blessed tin mug he insists on using, and the papers bleating about how I keep them in rags. My father would be devastated. And before you say I'm overreacting, that you have no intention of writing such a piece, you might not, but some other journalist certainly will. You'd be amazed how things can get distorted.'

Amelia sighed. 'I wouldn't. Okay,' she conceded, 'family stays out of it—for the article at least. But can you tell me anyway?'

'Why do you want to know if you're not going to use it?'

Which was a good question, and one Amelia struggled for a short while to answer. Truth be known, she wanted to know only for herself—wanted to get to know the man behind the legend, dig just a little bit deeper for her own selfish reasons—but she could hardly tell him that. Instead she gave a small shrug.

'It just helps with my writing. The more I know about you, the more intimate the piece.'

'Oh, well, I'm all for intimate.' He gave a smile. 'My family has a large property in the Blue Mountains. So you see, counting sheep for me really isn't a relaxing option, given that come shearing time there are thirty thousand sheep to muster and shear over a four-week period. It's actually the stuff of nightmares, although I love doing it.'

'You still work the farm?'

'Absolutely. Like I said, there's only a small window of time to get the sheep sheared, and Dad's one rule is that we all head over there once a year for a fortnight to help out. I wouldn't miss it for the world.'

She was assailed with a vision of him in jeans and outdoor boots, that jet-black hair whipped up by the wind, a contrast to the sharp-suited immaculate man sitting before her. Amelia was having serious trouble deciding which one she'd prefer, knowing only one thing—she wanted to see them both.

'"We all"?'

'You don't miss a trick do you? My brother and I.'

'And does this brother of yours have a name?' She watched him stiffen, but chose to pursue. 'Does this brother of yours have a family of his own?'

He wanted to tell her.

The internal admission startled him.

He wanted to tell this talkative, nosy woman about his mother and father, about his brother and his wife, about the child they both adored—wanted to share with her the inspiring beauty of the Blue Mountains he still called home: the damp, muggy smell of the fog as dawn crept in, the sweet taste of tea around a campfire, how, after a day of mustering, using his body instead of his brain, sleep for once came easily…

'Does your brother have children?' Her persistence was her downfall. The intrusion of another question snapped him back to reality, reminding him that this was a journalist sitting opposite him, and the words that had been on the tip of his tongue were swallowed along with a hefty belt of whisky.

'Like I said.' Vaughan gave a tight shrug. 'Family stays out of it.'

'Okay.' Clearly used to closed subjects, Amelia admitted defeat, shifting the topic to what she hoped was safer ground. 'How about reading?'

'Reading?'

'In bed.' Amelia grinned, but it wobbled midway. She was sure that Vaughan usually had far better things to keep him occupied in the bedroom, but she recovered quickly, pushing her line of questioning in the frantic hope of getting this very difficult man to open up a touch. 'To help you sleep—what sort of books do you like?'

'Crime novels. But the trouble with them is that I've no patience. I have to find out the end, which means…'

'You're up all night trying to finish it?' Amelia groaned in sympathy. 'I'm the same. What about something lighter—romance?' she teased, unable to fathom the sight of Vaughan lying in bed reading a love story. But to her utter surprise he nodded solemnly.

'Same problem. I'm up all night making sure they get together in the end. I'm a hopeless case, I'm afraid. Okay, funtime over.' He flashed a devilish smile. 'Let's get this over with—ask whatever it is you have to.'

'I don't work like that.' Amelia shook her head. 'Not when I'm doing an in-depth piece.'

Vaughan shuddered. 'Why don't I like the sound of that?'

'I find out a lot more just by talking…'

'You're certainly very good at that.'

'If you'd let me finish—' Amelia grinned '—I was about to say by talking with my subject in a relaxed setting—getting to really know them, finding out what's going on in their lives, building up a picture in my mind. It allows for a far more intimate portrayal than shooting a list of questions at them; anyone can do that. So the fun can continue.'

'And in the meantime is your *subject* allowed to get to know you?'

Her spoon paused midway from her plate.

'Of course.' Amelia recovered quickly. 'It's hardly fair to expect someone to open up if I don't give a piece of me back.'

'So I can ask questions too?'

Amelia nodded, bypassing her champagne glass and reaching instead for a heavy glass of iced water. Her throat was impossibly dry all of a sudden, as she wondered what Vaughan Mason could possibly want to know about little old her.

'Did you tell your boss what I said about the motor deal?'

Not by a flicker did she express her disappointment; of course that was all he wanted to know—work was his bible, at least where a nosy journalist was concerned. As if he had been going to ask if she was single, Amelia mentally scolded herself. As if he were remotely interested in the woman sitting before him. And, more to the point, this was, at her insistence, strictly business.

'No.' Thankfully she was able to look him in the eye.

'Good.' Vaughan nodded. 'I don't believe in celebrating until I've got a signature on paper.' Watching her slender hands lift a fork that looked way too heavy to her mouth, Vaughan paused. Amelia's eyes closed in bliss as she sampled her food. 'Nice?'

'Fabulous.' Amelia sighed. 'Eating out is one of the serious perks of the job. I absolutely love my food.'

'Me too.' He smiled at her questioning eyebrow as she eyed the rather sparse plate the waiter was placing before him. The tomato salad with balsamic dressing he had ordered as a main course was clearly in sharp contradiction to his statement. 'Oh, no you don't. Before you label me as some temperamental bulimic...'

'I wasn't about to.' Amelia grinned.

'Oh, yes, you were. The fact is, I've had about ten meals today—a sumptuous breakfast in Japan followed by a large business lunch, then a three-course meal on the plane to Singapore, and to top that off another breakfast...'

'Okay, okay.' Amelia laughed, putting her hand up in mock defence. 'I get the message.'

'So you see there's a very good reason for a plain tomato salad...'

'You've got me all wrong.' Amelia was still laughing as she took a sip of her mineral water. 'I'm not interested in starting rumours, Mr Mason, just squashing them or confirming them. I'm as bored as most people with stories that have little foundation. I'm tired of "confirmed" pregnancies that never seem to get past the first trimester, or reading about an idyllic marriage only to turn on the news two weeks later and find out they're filing for divorce.'

Signalling the waiter, Vaughan sat back as Amelia's glass was refilled with the most expensive of champagnes and her slightly trembling hand toasted her most unexpected host.

'I like your work, Amelia.' It was the first time he'd called her by her first name, and it sounded more intimate than she'd ever heard it before. Vaughan Mason seemed to register that fact.

'Vaughan,' he affirmed, without suggestion. 'I think we're both adult enough to deal with first-name terms.'

'You've read my work?'

He nodded. 'Every week, Amelia. And I don't know how you do it, but I have to hand it to you—somehow you manage to get the most unlikely of people to open up. Somehow you manage to slip in the most salacious piece of gossip and make it sound like girly talk. I have to admit it's making me a touch nervous.'

'You don't look it,' Amelia said, knowing he didn't mean it, but embarrassed and pleased all the same.

'So, how do you do it?'

'Do what?'

'Get them to open up?'

'I talk to them,' Amelia said simply. 'And, as for salacious gossip, I don't touch anything that hasn't already been hinted at. I see it as my job to give people the opportunity to confirm or deny. Which, so far, they have.'

'I'll say,' Vaughan responded, and Amelia felt her toes curl in pleasure at the dash of admiration in his voice. But her pleasure faded as Vaughan brought up the one name she really didn't want to hear ever again. 'That piece you did a few months ago where you got that alcoholic popstar to admit he'd been in rehab— you know the one…' He snapped his fingers, trying to recall the name, frowning as Amelia rather reluctantly filled him in.

'Taylor Dean.'

'That's the one.' Vaughan nodded. 'You didn't just get him to admit to being an alcoholic, you actually had him talking about how he'd dried out. How hellish the twelve steps had been for him. How? How did you get *him* to talk?'

'I asked him about it.' Amelia shrugged. 'Most people respond to a direct question. Most people, if they can see you're genuinely interested, are only too pleased to talk about themselves… Unlike you,' she added with a swift baleful look that was met with a smile. 'And, for the record, Taylor's a *recovering* alcoholic. He hasn't touched a drop for two years—at least that was the case when I wrote the piece.'

Vaughan didn't look particularly convinced, but Amelia refused to be drawn, instead fiddling with her glass and willing this part of the conversation to be over.

Thankfully Vaughan must have sensed her reluctance, because he swiftly moved on. 'How about that actress then? Miranda? For years I've wondered if she's had surgery, for years people have died wondering if she's been under the knife, and then you come along and suddenly we find out she's had the lot...'

'You really have done your research on me,' Amelia remarked, unable to keep the surprise out of her voice and suffused with both embarrassment and pride that this man had actually read her work—not just read it, but apparently enjoyed it.

'You're looking at a guy who spends half his life in airport terminals, Amelia. I read you because I like you.'

Maybe he was merely playing her at her own game—plying her with flattery—but here and now Amelia didn't care. Because whatever Vaughan was up to, it felt good. His positive words were like a salve to her fragile ego, and she decided at that point to relish the moment instead of analysing it—there would be plenty of time for that when this magical night was over.

But Vaughan hadn't finished yet. He was pulling apart a bread roll and soaking up the last of his balsamic dressing—long fingers working the plate, a decadent flash of gold on his wrist. Even his hands were beautiful!

'As bitchy as your pieces are,' Vaughan carried on, his mouth full, but still looking impossibly sexy, 'they still come across as if you like your subjects.'

'Because I do like them—neuroses and all.' She smiled at his frown. 'I truly admire them.'

'Admire them?' Vaughan questioned. 'It hardly takes a degree in rocket science to croon into a microphone or to strut one's stuff on the catwalk. I've dated a few models in my time,' he added.

'I heard,' Amelia answered cheekily, before responding to his question. 'Okay, I admit at first I was a mixture of cynical and overawed. Yet the more I interview these people, the more I get to know them as individuals, and the more highly I think of them. Models deserve every last cent of their millions! Can you imagine sitting in a restaurant as divine as this and ordering a tomato salad with dressing on the side if you hadn't eaten ten courses today?' Her voice was truly appalled. 'Heaven knows—someone who can give birth and then get out of her hospital bed and do two hours of Pilates with only an egg-white omelette to look forward to is a woman who knows what she wants. I absolutely couldn't do it, and I tell them that.'

Her plate was being cleared away now. She ached to dash to the loo, to check that no remnants of food were between her teeth and that Shelly's make-up was living up to its reputation, but Vaughan was staring at her—staring across the table in a broody, pensive way. And if four years at uni had taught her anything it was that now was not the time to go, that if she left now, then a few minutes after returning so would he.

'My turn now,' Amelia said, and she took a deep breath, eternally grateful that she had a completely legitimate reason to ask the one question she really wanted answered; after all, not a woman in Australia would forgive her if she didn't find out his romantic status.

'Are you involved in a relationship?'

'I assume we're not talking about my family here? Because I am involved with them—very much so.'

'You assume correctly. So, are you involved with a woman?'

'Amelia!' Vaughan feigned surprise. 'I would have thought someone with your rather cosmopolitan job would phrase her questions more carefully—cast a wider net, perhaps. For all you know I could be gay.'

'Most gay men don't have your reputation with women, Vaughan,' Amelia answered with the sweetest of smiles.

'Ah, but how do you know that isn't just a smoke-screen?'

'Please!' Amelia scoffed, leaning back in her seat. And she would have laughed, was about to respond with some swift but witty retort, but both her laughter and her words died on her lips as she caught his eye. She stared at him for a full moment, meeting his gaze and holding it, and the background noise of the restaurant faded into silence. The moment dragged dangerously on, tipping her from uncharted to dangerous territory.

She didn't need to ask him. Not for a second had his being gay even entered her head—because Vaughan Mason, in the few hours since she'd known him, had made her feel more of a woman than she'd ever felt in her life.

'I think we both know that's not the case.' Her voice was amazingly even, given her accelerated heart-rate, but she wished he'd drop his gaze first—wished she could win this tiny unspoken battle. Whatever game they were playing, it didn't come with a rule book. His eyes were holding hers unblinkingly as she wrestled to come up with a response. 'However, I stand corrected.

If you don't mind, I'll rephrase my question— are you in a romantic relationship?'

'No.'

The heady relief that flooded her shocked even Amelia, but determinedly she kept her features impassive, staring back at him, terrified to blink, to break the decadent beat of the moment. But this was work, Amelia reminded herself sharply. This was her career, the break she'd been praying for, and succumbing to Vaughan Mason's undeniable charms wasn't going to get her article written.

With a blinding flash of clarity she realised he was playing her—playing her as he did every woman who had crossed his path for the last quarter of a century, playing her just as Taylor had.

These were men who had learnt to flirt from the cradle.

It was Amelia who dropped her eyes, Amelia who gave up on the game she could never win. Sitting up a notch and clearing her throat, she spoke in what she hoped was a more assertive tone than the rather more seductive one that seemed to have been waiting in the wings for the best part of the main course.

'You're thirty-four, Vaughan.'

'Thirty-five, actually.' He flashed a perfect white smile and Amelia was sure she could see a glint of triumph in his eye…

She knew that he knew that he'd moved her.

'Thirty-five,' Amelia corrected herself. 'Have you ever thought of settling down?'

'Settling down?' He frowned.

A tiny cough, a tiny reminder to herself that she was allowed to ask this type of question—it was her job to be nosy!

'Getting married?' Amelia responded through slightly gritted teeth, knowing he was merely stalling, dragging things out so he could prepare his answer.

'I've never understood that.' Vaughan frowned across the table. 'Why do people refer to marriage as "settling down"? One would assume that you'd love the person you marry, yes?'

'One would hope so.' Amelia flashed a tight smile.

'And one could also assume, then, that you'd find that person incredibly sexually attractive. I mean, to actually have committed to that person for life you'd surely be sexually compatible, barely able to keep your hands off each other…'

Lucky, lucky woman, Amelia thought reluctantly. Lucky the woman who was the sole object of Vaughan Mason's desire, who had a man as utterly sexy as Vaughan permanently unable to keep his hands off her.

Trying to keep her breathing even, to keep a vaguely detached stance, she gave what she hoped was a vague nod, as if the picture he was painting in her mind *wasn't* causing her toes to curl under the table.

'Which hardly equates to settling down. Personally I'd refer to it as things hotting up—and considerably so.' He flashed a slightly triumphant smile. 'Does that answer your question?'

'Not in the slightest,' Amelia retorted, cheeks flaming, dying of embarrassment, but determined to get an answer. 'You do have a reputation,' she pointed out, then softened it with a smile. 'It would be almost criminally negligent not to broach the subject; my readers would never forgive me. You've been playing the field for quite some time, Vaughan.'

'But I've been sitting on the bench for a while. I

have,' he insisted as Amelia's lips duly pursed. 'Leop-
ards can change their spots, Amelia.'

'Or they learn to be more discreet,' Amelia responded dryly. 'Come on, Vaughan. I've heard it all
before—same tune, different song...'

For a second his eyes narrowed, but then surprisingly he laughed. 'Where did a sweet thing like you
learn to be so cynical?'

'It comes with the job description.' Amelia smiled
back. 'I'm writing an article, not a fairy tale.'

'Taylor Dean changed,' Vaughan pointed out. 'You
just said so yourself!' He registered the tiny swallow
in her throat, the nervous dart of her eyes—read her
as he read every woman who sat before him. 'You say
the guy hasn't touched a drop in two years, yet every
time he snaps at a shop assistant, every time he rocks
up ten minutes late or cancels a gig because he has
laryngitis, we're led to believe by your mob that he's
back on the bottle. The guy can't cross the street without looking twice; the next thing he knows he's tomorrow's headlines...'

'Leave Taylor out of this.' Her voice was too shrill,
too urgent, and Amelia fought to correct it, wishing
somehow they could turn back the clock, revert to
what they'd almost shared just a matter of seconds ago.
'We're talking about you...'

'I'm merely drawing an analogy. Anyway...' he
frowned '...what happened between you two? How
come you're so defensive...?'

He watched her flinch as if she'd been slapped, saw
the colour literally drain out of her cheeks, her shaking
hands reaching for her water glass. Normally it would
have given him a kick, a tiny surge of thrill to have
nailed it, to have hit the Achilles' heel that every liv-

ing mortal had. Only this time it didn't. Watching her flounder, that effusive, expressive face struggling to remain bland, he instantly regretted the pain he'd inflicted, and took no pleasure in watching her flail. 'I'm sorry. That was way too personal.'

She forced a smile. 'If I can give it, I should be able to take it.'

'It's not always that easy, though, is it?' Vaughan suggested, gently now. 'We all make mistakes. Only most people don't have to get up in the morning and read about them. Most people can hide under the duvet for a few days and that's the end of it.'

Reaching in his pocket, he pulled out his mobile and frowned. 'I'd have thought Mr Cheng would have rung by now.'

Eternally grateful for the change of subject, she smiled more naturally.

'Maybe no news is good news?'

'Let's hope so.'

'When will you know for sure?'

'Next week. Mr Cheng is flying into Melbourne to check over a few last-minute details, and hopefully on Friday it will be in the bag. I should be able to announce it the following Monday. Thanks for not saying anything, by the way.'

'You said it was off the record.'

'Which normally means zilch.'

He watched her tongue bob out to lick her lips as the waiter placed her dessert in front of her. Integrity was seemingly ingrained in every one of her pores. Off the record for once meant just that.

'The Japanese company I am dealing with are shrewd businessmen. They're also incredibly well-mannered,' Vaughan explained, 'and more than a touch superstitious; blasting the story over the papers without Mr Cheng being informed would have been disastrous for progress. I'd have hated to face him on Monday if this had got out.'

Amelia nodded, sinking her spoon into the most delectable white chocolate and nougat mousse, knowing it was going to taste even better than it looked. The thought was confirmed as the sweet goo melted on her tongue.

'Nice?'

'Heaven,' Amelia sighed, taking another spoonful. 'I don't care how many meals you've eaten today, there's surely a pocket of space for this. You really don't know what you're missing.'

As innocent as a child, she held out the spoon for him to taste. Shaking his head, he stared into that elfin face. Her mascara had long since smudged, the lipgloss had been lost somewhere between the main course and dessert, and Vaughan couldn't have disagreed with her more—he knew *exactly* what he was missing.

'Come.'

If her teeth hadn't been bound by nougat Amelia would have said something stupid, like *Where?* But the chocolate gods were being kind, allowing a semblance of sophistication as she refilled her water glass and washed down her dessert, forcing Vaughan to elaborate.

'Come to Melbourne with me next week.'

'Why?'

Even after a suitable pause, it wasn't the most sophisticated of answers. A *real* journalist would have murmured *I'd love to*; a real journalist wouldn't make her subject justify handing over such a magnificent scoop. But half a glass of champagne and a couple of hours in this divine man's company had eroded every last shred of sensibility.

'Well, if you're going to do an in-depth piece on me you might as well get the full picture. Of course there will be a few exceptions—I can't guarantee all of my contacts will want a journalist in the boardroom, and I'd like to go to the pool unaccompanied in the morning, given that I can't swim and talk at the same time.'

'You swim?'

'I do.' Vaughan grinned. 'And, yes, you can use that. But, on a rather more serious note, one of the reasons I'm trusting you to do this piece is the unbelievable fact that I haven't got fifty calls in my message bank asking me to confirm the motor deal.'

'I passed, then?'

'I guess so.' Vaughan smiled. 'But these are a couple of ground rules. I don't mind you doing an in-depth piece on me, but my clients' names stay out of it.'

'Of course.' Amelia nodded.

'And, apart from my morning swim, I do have a personal life. Every now and then I will have to disappear.'

It came as no surprise to Amelia how much that piece of news depressed her, but she gave a solemn nod. And even if Paul might kill her, even if she was putting doubts into Vaughan's jet-lagged mind, Amelia couldn't refrain from pushing the point that she'd let go earlier.

'Why now, Vaughan? You've never given a personal interview, never allowed anyone to get close till now. What's caused the change of heart?'

'My advisors.' Vaughan rolled his eyes. 'Which sounds horribly affected, but no CEO worth his salt is without them these days and, given what I pay them, I guess I should try acting on some of the advice they so gleefully dish out. We both know that when—or rather at this stage *if* the motor deal's announced I'll be a hero. A hero next Friday but a villain by Monday.'

Sad, but true.

'Once the euphoria has worn off my rescue plan will be analysed and scrutinised...'

'And criticised,' Amelia offered, and Vaughan nodded.

'Jobs are going to go. The fact that without me within a year *every* job would have gone will be conveniently forgotten.'

'I thought you'd be used to being the bad guy by now.'

'I am,' Vaughan shrugged. 'But the fact of the matter is the press are going to go to town on this one.'

'I'm the press, Vaughan,' Amelia pointed out. 'Why do you think you'll get anything different from me?'

'I don't know,' Vaughan replied, but his confident expression belied the ambiguity of his words, and not for the first time Amelia had the feeling he was playing her.

'You can buy me all the white chocolate nougat I can stomach, tell me I'm the best journalist in Australia and massage my ego for hours, but I write the truth, Vaughan. You won't sway me for a moment.'

'I wouldn't dream of trying. And, no, I'm actually not asking you along to do a hearts-and-flowers piece on me. The truth would be refreshing enough!'

Amelia stared at him thoughtfully for a moment. His answer had almost convinced her, but there was one thing she needed to get out of the way—one thing she needed confirmed before she accepted the assignment. And if it sounded presumptuous, then so be it. There was no denying the sexual sparks cracking in the air around them, and to disregard them could only be to her detriment. By ignoring the sparks she could be fanning the flames, which was a dangerous game indeed—especially with such a skilful player as Vaughan.

'Would you have asked Carter?'

'Carter's after a different angle. His mind's stuck purely on business.'

'So is mine,' Amelia retorted sharply, but Vaughan just laughed.

'I was actually referring to the different section of the newspaper that Carter covers. But if that's what's worrying you...'

'I'm not *worried*, Vaughan. I just like to make things clear from the outset.'

'Which you have,' Vaughan replied easily, smothering a yawn before signalling for the bill. 'And if it makes you feel any more comfortable I *never* mix business with pleasure—well, not recently anyway. It's a definite new rule of mine. It makes things far too messy and complicated. Katy today is a prime example. Believe me, Amelia, if I want casual sex I can think of easier ways of getting it than having a journalist glued to my side for a week.'

And therein lay the problem. With two small words he'd affirmed what she'd guessed.

Casual sex.

Walking out onto the street, momentarily blinded by the flash of photographers, Amelia managed a wry smile at their wasted efforts. Curses would later fill the darkrooms of rival newspapers as her face came into focus alongside Vaughan's, when they realised that not only did Vaughan Mason not have a hot date tonight, but she, Amelia Jacobs, had landed a wonderful scoop.

Refusing his offer of a lift, Amelia hailed a taxi, firmed up a time to meet him at the airport, then climbed into the back seat, managing a small wave as the taxi pulled off. But all the time her heart was hammering, her cheeks flaming at his throwaway comment.

Casual sex was all a man like Vaughan wanted from women, and she mustn't forget it—not even for a moment.

Chapter 3

'No proglem getting away?' Vaughan greeted her, and Amelia gave a crisp smile.

'No problem,' she confirmed—which was the understatement of the year!

Paul had practically died on the spot in delight when she'd told him—in fact, she was surprised he wasn't here at the airport now, to wave her off, hiding behind a pot-plant and attempting to catch her alone so he could give her just one more piece of vital advice.

After she'd told her editor of Vaughan's invitation the whole weekend had been a blur of vital advice—the questions she should ask, the subjects she should avoid. The only time Paul had been silent was when Amelia had asked him about the big story the paper was due to break on Vaughan.

'Like I said, Amelia, it's best you don't know.'

'Best for who?' Amelia pushed. 'How can I do an

informed piece when my own paper's holding back on vital information? If there's something about to go down with the motor deal, surely I should be aware—'

'It's nothing to do with the motor deal,' Paul broke in.

'Personal, then?' Watching Paul's eyes dart away a fraction too soon, Amelia knew she'd hit the nail on the head. 'Is he about to get engaged? Has he got some love-child…?'

'Stop fishing, Amelia. Just do your work and I'll do mine. I want your copy by two p.m. on Friday and not a second later. We're going to use it this same weekend. Not,' he added, with an utterly wasted reassuring smile, 'that I want you to feel as if you're under pressure.'

'Just know that I am,' Amelia retorted, relishing the task ahead yet terrified all the same.

And now here she stood, in a boxy little suit, hair slicked back, and looking not too bad given she'd had approximately five minutes' sleep the entire weekend. Her luggage was checked in, the newspaper was under her arm, her boarding pass was in her hand, and Australia's most eligible bachelor was at her side.

Life was certainly looking up.

Better still if he whizzed her off to some scrummy first-class lounge for a decent cup of coffee to wake her up while they waited for their flight. But that hope was soon dashed when Vaughan told her that, given how she'd managed to get there on time, he'd checked them onto an earlier flight.

'I'm going to get something to read. Do you want anything?'

'No, thanks,' Amelia answered, tapping the newspaper under her arm.

'You're sure?' Vaughan checked, pulling a suitably bored face at her choice of in-flight entertainment.

'I like to keep abreast—anyway, you don't really have time to go to the newsagent's, Vaughan. The six-thirty's already boarding.'

'So?' he answered with annoying arrogance, striding off towards the newsagent's.

And because it was all business passengers, because there were no irate toddlers or wheelchairs to board, the line of red-eyed passengers filed in quickly—leaving Amelia standing alone, avoiding the eye of an irritated air stewardess, who was chatting into the wall phone and tapping on the computer, and wondering just what the hell was taking Vaughan so long.

'Miss Jackson?' the air stewardess called, replacing the phone's receiver. 'I'm going to have to ask you to board now, please. The door's about to close.'

'It's Miss *Jacobs*,' Amelia corrected, hoping she sounded assertive. 'I'm just waiting for my colleague. He shouldn't be too much longer.'

'Well, when he returns you can tell *your colleague* that he's just missed his flight,' the stewardess huffed, tapping into the computer with impossibly long nails. 'The gate has just closed. I'll see if there are any spaces on the seven a.m. What's your colleague's surname?'

'Mason,' Amelia answered, scanning the empty corridor, praying for him to appear, terrified the whole week ahead wasn't even going to get past the first hurdle. 'Vaughan Mason.'

It was like watching a soluble aspirin drop into a glass.

The pretty face, set in stone, suddenly fizzed into animated life. The impassive stance gave way and the air stewardess positively sparkled at the mere mention of his name. Gone was the bossy harridan tapping into the computer, instead she was actually moving—walking,

in fact—over to the seriously camp air steward who was
shooting daggers at Amelia as he appeared at the desk.

Make that two soluble aspirin, Amelia thought darkly
as the air steward caught sight of his wayward passenger, carrier bag bulging, thumbing through a glossy
magazine, not remotely in a hurry.

Vaughan made his way over.

'Mr Mason!' Amelia wasn't sure who said it first,
both steward and stewardess were talking in effusive
tones, practically carrying him along the carpeted walkway as Amelia padded behind. 'We didn't realise you
were travelling with us this morning—what a pleasure.'

'What's wrong?' Vaughan asked as Amelia sat, still
bristling, in her seat.

The plane taxied along the runway, and the sigh from
the passengers was audible when the captain announced
that they'd missed their slot and would have to wait another fifteen minutes before take-off.

'Nothing.' Amelia sniffed, and waited for him to
push, to ask if she were sure, but when Vaughan merely
dug into his carrier bag and pulled out another magazine Amelia chose to elaborate. 'If you'd been anyone
else, the flight would have gone.'

'Probably,' Vaughan conceded.

'Yet you expected it to wait,' Amelia went on, warming to her subject. 'You kept a whole planeload of people sitting here while you chose a pile of magazines…'
Anger mounting, she watched as he unwrapped a tof-
fee and popped it into his mouth. 'And a load of sweets.
Don't you think that's rather arrogant, Vaughan?'

'You clearly do!'

'Yes,' Amelia replied hotly, 'I really do. Now, I know

I'm here merely to observe, but, given that you've involved me, I think I have a right to say something here!'

'Go ahead,' Vaughan offered, but he sounded so bored Amelia half expected him to put on the eyepads located in the little goody bag they had been handed.

'You change our flights because we're early, and then, instead of boarding at the correct time, instead of being pleased we'd been accommodated earlier, you head off to the newsagent, leaving me standing like an idiot to make excuses for your thoughtless behaviour.'

'Thoughtless?'

'Yes, thoughtless.' Her hand flailed, gesturing to the window, to the grey of the airport buildings as the plane taxied slowly along. 'Just so that you had something to read, you've ensured that two hundred people's schedules are put out for the day. I'd say that's pretty thoughtless Vaughan.'

'I guess it is,' Vaughan sighed. 'I just felt sorry for her.'

'For who?' Amelia frowned.

'The girl at the newsagent. It was only her second day, and she'd run out of till paper. I said I didn't want a receipt, but she insisted—said that she'd get into trouble if she didn't give me one.'

'Oh!' Blinking back at him, Amelia almost apologised, even opened her mouth to do so. But the ghost of a smile twitching at the edge of his lips gave him away, and her mouth snapped closed as she almost swallowed his bare-faced lie.

'Guess I'm just an arrogant bastard!' He winked, with no trace of an apology, and turned back to his magazine, laughing out loud at the problem page and then wincing loudly, not even bothering to flick over the page, from a before and after shot of breast enlargement surgery.

The air steward hovered to *double check* that his seatbelt was done up, and Amelia struggled through the business section of her paper, reading the most boring article about gender balance in the workplace and longing to bury herself in one of Vaughan's glossies.

But she'd die before asking.

'Help yourself,' Vaughan offered, as Amelia's eyes wandered for the third time in two minutes to the magazine he was holding. He held it out to her. 'I'm keeping *abreast* myself—though I have to admit it looks like bloody agony. Why do women do it?'

'That's a rather in-depth topic for six forty-five in the morning,' Amelia bristled, and Vaughan rolled his eyes.

'Just making small talk. Look…' his voice lowered '…this could end up being a very long week if we don't set a few ground rules: you want to see me warts and all; I want an honest piece written.'

'Yes,' Amelia agreed.

'So get your own back at the end of the week. Toss in a spiteful, cutting line about how thoughtless I am, if it makes you feel better, but please, don't sit next to me smarting. File it and save it for later.'

The rest of the flight was spent in rather more companionable silence. Amelia nibbled on a warm chocolate muffin, leafing through one of Vaughan's magazines, as he in turn drank three impossibly strong coffees and read, with markedly more interest than Amelia, the business section of her newspaper, barely even glancing up as the plane made its descent.

The hotel was as impossibly decadent. Vaughan glided through check-in as silent bellboys whizzed away their luggage, and with one glimpse of the massive bed as she stepped into her king-size suite, Amelia wanted to peel off her stilettos there and then and climb right in.

'All right?' Vaughan checked, knocking sharply on her door and not even waiting for a reply before he let himself in. 'I asked for adjoining rooms. I figured it would be easier to meet up that way.'

'It's fine,' Amelia replied nonchalantly, while privately imagining Paul's reaction when she put in her expense-claim form. 'Oh, look!' Peeling back the sheer curtains, she stared at the magnificent view below—there was not a glint of summer sky in sight; the entire complex faced in on itself, and the courtyard below was filled with early-morning Melburnians, pulling apart croissants and reading newspapers.

'That's a nice place to eat,' Vaughan said, nodding downwards to where a massive grand piano was the focal point of the dining area. 'Though I normally choose to eat on the balcony.' He gestured to the four square feet of space adjoining hers.

'We can wave to each other,' Amelia suggested, then, taking a deep breath, figured it was time to set *her* ground rules. 'Look, Vaughan, the last thing I want to do is crowd you. I'm thrilled you've entrusted me to do this piece, but if at any time over the next few days you need your space, then just say so.'

'Likewise,' Vaughan agreed, a flicker of relief washing over his face.

'So…' Amelia grinned as still he stood there.

'So?' Vaughan questioned.

'I'd like to unpack, and get better acquainted with that divine shower…' Her voice trailed off as Vaughan shook his head and glanced at his watch. 'Later?'

'Later.' Vaughan nodded. 'Much, much later.'

* * *

His staying power was formidable.

Even the chauffer-driven car constantly on call didn't suffice for his impossible schedule. Half an hour negotiating traffic was a sheer waste of Vaughan Mason's time, and if a helicopter ride across the city meant an extra few minutes could be crammed into his schedule, then that was the means of transport.

Amelia held her breath as she saw the Melbourne skyline from an entirely different angle, then barely had time to drag her fingers through her chopper-tousled hair before breezing into meeting upon meeting. She was completely aware that these meetings had been scheduled weeks if not months in advance, that a slice of Vaughan Mason's acumen was an expensive commodity, but over and over he delivered—commanding the entire room, ramming home his points. Most surprisingly of all for Amelia, she was allowed in to each one.

If Vaughan had okayed it then apparently it was fine…

'She's doing a piece on me,' Vaughan would shrug arrogantly. 'Not you, Marcus.' Or Heath, or any other poor soul whose business was being put through the shredder.

And she watched—watched the nervous, sweating faces around the boardroom tables as Vaughan, utterly composed, completely unmoved, sliced through their reams of excuses, their reasons, their attempts to justify the mess that had led them to this point, as easily as a hot knife through butter, cutting directly to the chase, exposing raw truths, absolutely ruthless in his assessments.

'Some of these staff have been with us for years!' Marcus Bates visibly reeled at the brutal proposal

Vaughan had outlined, balking at the prospect of laying off so many staff. 'We can't just throw them onto the dole queue. Some of these people are in their fifties…'

'Which means they'll receive a decent pay-out,' Vaughan pointed out, his voice like ice, watching as Marcus took a shaky drink of the cup of coffee in front of him, staring him down, until Marcus finally admitted to his directors the absolute, unsavoury truth.

'We can't afford to pay anyone out,' he said, his voice a hollow whisper, his shirt drenched in perspiration and his face like white putty.

Amelia actually felt sorry for this man she had never till now even met, as she glimpsed the impossible weight of the truth he had been carrying for months, perhaps even years, and the silence seemed to go on for ever.

'Finally,' Vaughan said slowly, 'we're getting to the truth. The fact is you can't even afford the coffee beans in your expensive machine.'

He stared around the table, stared at each nervous person in turn, and despite the smell of fear in the room Amelia could almost taste the respect as each pair of eyes looked to Vaughan for an answer, looked to the legend for a last-minute reprieve.

'The staff we lay off *will* be paid out,' Vaughan responded finally, and an audible sigh of relief went around the room as Vaughan Mason took on the impossible and the *you* became *we* as he flicked through the mountain of papers in front of him, hurling a chosen few across the table. 'And if that means you have to forgo your extended lunches and bring in your own cheese sandwiches for the next twelve months then it's a small price to pay, given the direness of your situation—these expense claims are deplorable! I want every member of staff entitled to a company car driving the same model and vehicle, at least while I'm running this ship. Believe me, guys, I want every last teabag accounted for in this place...'

Despite the brand-new stilettos which had rubbed the skin off the backs of her heels, and despite the utter exhaustion of the whirlwind that had blitzed her life seventy-two hours ago, over and over he impressed. Over and over she pressed the button on her digital Dictaphone to record a genius at work, even while knowing it was useless. Unless you were there, unless you actually witnessed him at first hand, holding the floor, utterly commanding, then it would take more than a degree in journalism to capture his formidable presence—the might that was Vaughan Mason could never be confined to a single article.

Yet she ached to try, her fingers literally itching to pound her keypad, to somehow get down the jumble of thoughts in her mind, and she was infinitely grateful for that fact as, for maybe the twentieth time that day, she found herself in the confined space of a lift with him. Only this time it was gliding them back up to their hotel rooms.

The hum of the lift was a blissful contrast to the lively chatter of the Japanese restaurant Vaughan had chosen for Mr Cheng, and Amelia was infinitely grateful for the fact that she could force her mind to focus on the work ahead and push aside the nerve-racking yet vaguely delicious feeling of claustrophobia that had seemed to hit her at various moments through the day, and was now peaking with alarming ferocity as the evening gave way to night.

'Interesting evening?' Vaughan asked, restless eyes scanning the lift numbers as he smothered a yawn.

'Very.' Amelia nodded. 'Especially the dessert.'

'I was talking about—'

'I know you were.' Amelia grinned. 'Actually, I'm still reeling from the fact that they all let me in. You'd hardly think a journalist would be permitted in some of those buildings, let alone in the meeting rooms. Look at Noble and Bates—I mean, I know there's been a few whispers, but why would they take the risk of allowing me in? Obviously I'm not going to name names, but why on earth would they allow a journalist in to hear that their business's back is against the wall.'

'But it isn't,' Vaughan answered as the lift door pinged open and they walked along the thickly carpeted corridor to their adjoining rooms. 'At least not any more.'

'You heard the figures, Vaughan!' Amelia responded, hobbling along on heels that were seriously killing her now, not quite comfortable enough to slip them off in his presence!

'I'm sure they're far worse!' Vaughan answered easily. They were at his door now, and she watched as he swiped his access card, pushing the door open and holding it that way with his wide shoulders. 'Look, Amelia, today had nothing to do with trust or risk, at least not on Noble and Bates's part. You're right—there have been whispers, and they're getting louder by the day and the directors know it. Their quarterly figures are about to be released and there are going to be a lot of shareholders baying for answers. Now they've got one.'

'What?'

'Me,' Vaughan answered without a trace of modesty, and somehow it suited him. 'I don't take on no-hopers and everyone knows that.'

'But their figures are appalling,' Amelia answered,

genuinely confused. 'Do you really think they can recover?'

'My word, they're going to. Especially given the fact that for the next three years Noble and Bates will be paying me ten per cent of their profits—and, given that I intend to keep right on living well, I'm going to make damn sure they're healthy ones. My team and I will whip their sorry butts into shape, get rid of all the dead wool that's been holding them back, and everybody knows it.'

'Wood,' Amelia corrected. 'The dead wood.'

'Wool.' Vaughan gave a glimmer of a smile. 'Growing up on a sheep farm taught me a lot of things, and one of them is that underneath that tired-looking old sheep is a little lamb waiting to skip off—and I intend to expose it.'

And he would. Amelia didn't doubt it.

Confidence was contagious, and Vaughan Mason epitomised the word. The mere fact he was taking them on, the mere fact he was prepared to invest his time in the ailing company, would be more than enough to appease the shareholders.

He'd never been wrong.

Amelia's mind raced for one exception to the rule, but admitted defeat almost instantly.

'Lucky Noble and Bates, then.' Amelia smiled up at him, but it faded midway. Nothing, *nothing* in his stance had changed—his shoulder was still blocking the door, his face was exactly the same as the last time she had looked—yet *everything* had shifted. Business was clearly over; senses were trickling in. Shifting her weight on her tired, aching feet, self-conscious under his scrutiny, her voice was slightly croaky as she wrapped up what she was saying. 'Having you to rescue them...'

Again she shifted her weight, and Vaughan gave her the gift of another small smile.

'New shoes?'

Amelia grimaced. 'They're too small. They didn't come in my size.'

'Then why on earth did you buy them?' Vaughan asked, clearly completely bemused.

'I guess I fell in love.' Amelia gave a tiny shrug. 'It was either these or go without completely.'

'And was it worth the pain?'

Amelia thought of her bruised, raw, shredded feet, but without hesitation nodded. 'Absolutely.'

For a beat he hesitated too, and Amelia was sure that for that fraction of time he was thinking about asking her in, weighing up in that calculated mind of his the pros and cons of prolonging this long day. And she only knew that she couldn't do it—couldn't enter into that room and hope to retain a distant façade.

'I'd better get on,' she attempted, as still he stared down. 'Paul will be screaming for my word-count.'

'Shame,' Vaughan said softly, but didn't elaborate, walking into his room without a backward glance.

The door closed gently behind him, leaving Amelia standing, mouthing like a goldfish at the smart mahogany woodwork, a retraction on the tip of her tongue, bitterly regretful that she hadn't said yes to his offer.

Chapter 4

'Well?'

Somehow Paul managed to deliver twenty questions with a single word.

'I haven't actually written anything to send you yet,' Amelia started, thankful for the hands-free phone so she could pace the room, as she always did when she was nervous; talking to Paul always made her nervous. 'We've only just got in. But I've got lots of material.'

'Such as?'

'I'm not sure yet,' Amelia answered feebly. 'I'm still building a picture.'

'If I wanted photos I'd have sent a photographer along with you,' Paul retorted nastily. 'I want words, I want facts, and I want details…'

'Paul!' Halting his tirade, even Amelia was shocked at the force behind her own voice. 'This is my piece. *My* piece,' she added, more so she could affirm it to herself than to Paul—assertiveness not really her forte at the best of times. 'You'll get your words and I can assure you they'll be interesting—riveting in fact—but if you're hoping for me to do a hatchet job on Vaughan Mason then you're going to be sorely disappointed. If you want facts and details, then give me a permanent job in the business section of the paper instead of a painfully temporary freelance position in the colour supplement.'

'Do this right,' Paul responded, 'and you'll have your permanent job, Amelia. You know that as well as I do.'

Her lack of response spoke volumes.

'That *is* what you still want, I assume?'

Amelia didn't answer; she truly couldn't. She had suddenly realised that she didn't really know what she wanted any more—the dream she'd chased for so long was so close now she could almost reach out and touch it, so why was she stalling? Why was she closing her eyes and having second thoughts?

'Just deliver a good piece and then we'll talk about it,' Paul concluded. 'But in the meantime remember who's paying that over-inflated hotel bill.'

And she would, Amelia decided, pulling open her laptop and flicking it on. Now really wasn't the most convenient of times to be having a career crisis!

Locating the file she'd set aside for her article, Amelia fiddled with the margins for a full moment before attempting to start. Her fingers hovered over the keys for an inordinate amount of time, even though they'd been itching to get started before Paul's call had stifled them.

As good for her career as it might be, she didn't want to waste even a second of her word-count on Noble and Bates—there were hundreds of journalists who'd be only too willing to step in and do that when the time came. Instead she wanted—no, needed to somehow divulge to her readers the subject she was spending time with, to transport them on a bleary Saturday morning to an alien world, to let them glimpse the man that was Vaughan Mason, allow them to glimpse the real person behind the hype…

To keep on doing what she had been for six months…

Wanted or not, a career crisis was exactly what she was having!

Pulling open the French windows, she let the clatter of diners below fill the room, pleasantly masked by the skilful fingers of a pianist. Stepping out onto the balcony she stared down, closing her eyes and letting the music soothe her, trying to put Paul's words out of her mind and focus on what it was she really wanted to do with her life.

'Problem?'

His voice was so close she literally jumped, turning, startled, to the balcony beside hers, where Vaughan sat nursing a huge brandy, totally relaxed in a massive toweling robe. His black hair was even blacker from the shower, and Amelia's body shot into overdrive. Even an intravenous shot of hormones couldn't have delivered a more potent effect. The mere sight of Vaughan away from the boardroom and in a clearly relaxed frame of mind was literally intoxicating. All she could manage was a feeble shake of her head.

'If you don't mind my saying, you look a bit anxious.'

She *felt* a bit anxious, but right now it had nothing to do with Paul and everything to do with the man on the next balcony.

The strategic waist-high Perspex wall between balconies was at least a semblance of a barrier, and it gave Amelia enough room to move mentally, feign nonchalance and give a small shrug.

'It's just a work issue.'

'So, tell me,' Vaughan offered, holding up the bottle, 'and on this side of the fence, preferably. I don't fancy shouting over Frank.'

As Amelia gave him a slightly perplexed look he added, 'Sinatra.' And a smile broke on her pale lips as, sure enough, the pianist broke into a musical rendition of a very old favourite. 'I've been here enough to know the pianist's routine by now. Come over and talk about it.'

'I'd say you're the last person I should be discussing my work problems with,' Amelia refuted, but of course Vaughan had an answer.

'On the contrary. I'm probably the *first* person you should be discussing them with, given that no doubt I'm the root of the problem.'

'That's very presumptuous.'

'But accurate,' Vaughan responded, at her darkening cheeks. 'Now, given that for the first time in living memory I'm offering some free advice, and given that however presumptuous it sounds I'm extremely good at what I do, then I'd take it if I were you.'

'It is about you,' Amelia admitted. 'Well, sort of. So how can I possibly…?'

'I can be very objective,' Vaughan persisted.

'I really need to have a shower,' Amelia attempted as a last line of defence, but Vaughan dealt with that excuse just as easily.

'It's way before my bedtime.' He flashed a wicked grin. 'Go and have your shower and I'll pour you a drink.'

Which sounded simple.

Which should be simple, Amelia thought, turning the knob in the shower and getting drenched in freezing water by a shower head that was surely as big as a dinner plate. But even a shower of icy water couldn't douse the nerves that were jumping now. And why, Amelia wondered, was she shaving her legs when she'd only done them last night? Why was she squeezing every last drop out of the tiny bottle of moisturising lotion the hotel provided and rubbing it into every inch of her body?

What should she wear?

The never-ending question that bypassed men and perpetually plagued women was making itself heard. Her entire suitcase was filled with smart business suits and endless strappy little numbers which she had packed for formal occasions. Sophisticated chic had been very much the order of the day when she'd been packing; tête-à-têtes in Vaughan's hotel room had definitely not been on the agenda. The only exception to the rule was a very skimpy pair of boxer shorts and a crop top that were strictly for bed.

Alone!

Punching in Vaughan's room number, she made one of the most embarrassing phone calls of her life.

'Would you believe me if I told you I have nothing to wear?'

'It's midnight, Amelia,' Vaughan drawled. 'We'll be sitting on a balcony talking and drinking brandy. You hardly need to dress up for the occasion.'

'Exactly,' Amelia sighed. 'But according to my suitcase *dress up* is all I can manage. Had you been asking me to a ball I'd be appropriately dressed—stunning, actually. Coffee in Chapel Street—no problem at all. But casual…'

'Walk towards the bathroom, Amelia.' She could feel

his smile and it made her lips twitch too. 'Pull open the door and what do you see?'

'Deodorant, toothpaste…'

'Okay, close the door. Now what do you see?'

'A towelling robe,' Amelia wailed. 'But I can't come over dressed—'

'We'll be matching.' Vaughan grinned down the phone.

Even though she was draped from head to toe in inch-thick terry towelling fabric, even though not a glimpse of newly shaved, freshly moisturised flesh was on show, Amelia felt as naked and as exposed as if she were wearing only the bottom half of a bikini. Knocking on his door with a tentative hand, she wished she had her time over and had thought to rouge her cheeks or add a splash of lipgloss to her lips—even the dreadful jeans she had first greeted him in would be preferable to this!

Damn!

It was the only word that resounded in his mind as he opened the door.

Damn, damn, damn!

Straight back to Go, straight back to the beginning of the game, when she'd spun into his office, gamine, hair damp, large eyes glittering in her wary face. Straight back to where he'd completely dropped his guard.

Yet he'd seen more women dressed in exactly the same attire than he cared to remember, Vaughan reminded himself as he let her in. Had opened the door over and over to a terry towelling robe with a voluptuous woman inside—so why the panic now?

Because normally the heavy scent of perfume was the first thing to greet him, followed by tumbling hair and a well made-up face. Normally Vaughan knew exactly what was on the agenda, but the signs were completely unreadable here.

If Housekeeping had taken to installing buttons on the robes, then Amelia's were done up the neck. The lapels were pulled tightly, the belt firmly double-knotted around her waist, and she was even wearing the slippers the hotel provided, unpainted toes peeping out. If nothing else they were something for him to focus on as he beckoned her inside, trying to ignore the sweet scent of shampoo and toothpaste and completely nothing else. Her eyes were utterly devoid of make-up, her hair still wore the marks of the comb she must have raked through it, yet for all her complete lack of effort, for all her hidden womanly charms, she was, quite simply, the most delicious parcel of femininity he had ever seen.

As wary as a puppy being let inside for the first time, she stalked into the room, tail firmly between her legs, as if any moment now she expected to be shooed out. Yet despite the vulnerability and the absolute lack of warpaint, despite the almost child-like demeanour, Vaughan knew from the way his body responded that it was every inch a woman crossing his threshold tonight.

Amelia wasn't faring much better. Even though their rooms were identical, Vaughan had already stamped his identity on his— the lights were dimmer and the air, still damp from a no-doubt extended shower, was filled with his heavy cologne plus that unique masculine smell that had assailed her over and over in the lifts. Damp white towels littered the floor—Vaughan was clearly only too happy for someone else to pick them up—and his dresser was littered with his watch and heavy silver cufflinks, his wallet and mobile.

But far more intimidating than the dim lights and the heady scent of maleness was the wide-shouldered man walking in front of her towards the balcony. Even his back view was somehow effortlessly divine—superbly cut hair, for once wet and tousled, belt loosely knotted around snaky hips and a glimpse of toned muscular calves peeping out at the bottom.

She felt as if she were stepping inside somewhere decadent and forbidden, like a teenager entering a bar for the first time—painfully self-conscious, feeling as sophisticated as a gnat, almost waiting for a bouncer to appear, to tell her to leave, that she should never have been let in, that this was somewhere a woman like Amelia quite simply shouldn't be.

'Brandy?'

He hadn't poured it yet—they weren't even outside—but she could see a second glass waiting by the bottle on the balcony. Amelia shook her head, deciding her wits were firmly needed about her person. 'I'll just have a hot chocolate.'

'I'll ring down for Room Service.'

'Please don't.' Pulling open a cupboard Vaughan hadn't even known existed, she plugged in a tiny kettle, peeled open a sachet of powder and poured it into a mug, taking her time to make her brew before joining him outside.

'This is a terrible idea,' Amelia groaned, breaking the ice with her valid concerns. 'Despite what you say, I can hardly hope for objective advice. You don't even know what the problem is.'

'Don't tell me—let me guess.' Vaughan waited a moment till she'd sat down. 'The papers are asking for blood? "Forget the intimate portrayal, Amelia, we know you can deliver on that. You've got Vaughan Mason to yourself for a week and we want you to give us the dirt—give us a story that's going to grab the headlines".'

She didn't even feign surprise that he already knew, just nodded wearily.

'So why don't you? You know about the motor deal, you know about Noble and Bates—why don't you give the paper what they want and make a bigger name for yourself in the meantime? You said in my office that you desperately wanted to move into business reporting—well, here's your chance.'

For an age she thought, forming an answer she hadn't even properly run by herself.

'I don't know if it's what I really want to do any more, Vaughan.'

It sounded so straightforward, but as she tucked her legs under her, closing her eyes for a moment, he knew it was anything but.

'My father's a political reporter…'

'Grant Jacobs!' She watched as he made the connection. 'Now, that really is a hard act to follow—he's brilliant.'

'Brilliant,' Amelia sighed. 'My father is a *real* journalist—or so he keeps telling me. He dashes off at a moment's notice to some wartorn country, appears on horribly blotchy videophone news reports, talking about bombings and death and danger, and holds tiny faminestruck babies in his arms. For ages he hoped that I'd follow in his footsteps…'

'But it's not for you?'

'They haven't invented a waterproof mascara good enough yet,' Amelia admitted. 'Still, I've always liked journalism, I've always known that was what I wanted to do, and business was what always interested me. I was the nerdiest kid, Vaughan. I'd read my horoscope and then promptly turn to the business section to see what the US dollar was up to. Business has always fascinated me.'

'But?' he asked, because clearly there was one.

'When I took the job I'm doing now I saw it as a foot in the door with a major newsgroup—a step in the right direction, perhaps. Build up my portfolio a bit, make myself known.' She gave a wry smile. 'Pay off my car! But I never thought I'd end up loving it.'

'Which you do.' It was a statement not a question.

'Absolutely. My father winces every Saturday when he reads my pieces—says repeatedly that he can't believe that the daughter of a respected political correspondent could lower herself to write such trash.'

'I like it,' Vaughan ventured, and his small vote of praise was rewarded with a tired smile.

'So do I—and that's what's confusing me. I never intended for this to be permanent,' Amelia said, stirring her hot chocolate into a mini-whirlpool. 'When I was offered the weekly slot, naturally I was thrilled. But...'

'You had no intention of it lasting for ever?'

'None at all. It was only a maternity leave position. I actually wanted—'

'You don't have to justify your reasons to me,' Vaughan broke in, cutting to the chase in his usual analytical way. 'So what's changed in the last six months?'

'I like what I do.' For the first time since stepping onto the balcony she looked at him. 'In fact, I love what I do.'

'So where's the problem?'

She didn't answer—couldn't, really. But Vaughan did it for her.

'If you give them what they want now, then they'll

make your position more permanent—maybe even move you to the business side of things?'

Her silence was his affirmation.

'Well, why don't you do it, Amelia? You've got more than enough to grab the headlines—surely this will open a few doors for you?'

'That wasn't the deal. This was never supposed to be a business piece—that's the reason you brought me along. It's hardly fair for me to change my mind midway.'

'It wouldn't be the first time I've been stitched up by a newspaper. I'm sure I'd survive—and I'm sure Noble and Bates would too. As I said before, they probably want the story to come out.' His eyes narrowed, staring at her thoughtfully for a long moment. 'Let's not kid ourselves that you're worried about protecting my feelings, that it's some ingrained integrity holding you back. We all know journalists don't have any.' He didn't even soften it with a smile. 'If you really wanted to break into business, Amelia, you'd already have done it—the movement on the motor deal would have been announced and neither of us would be sitting here now. You chose not to break that story, Amelia.'

'I know.' Huddling further into her dressing gown, Amelia gave a tired nod. 'I know I did.'

'So now you have to ask yourself why.'

Shooting him a baleful look, she let out a long drawn-out sigh, almost annoyed with him for making her admit her truth. 'I don't want the doors of big-business reporting to open,' Amelia responded hesitantly. 'In fact now the bolts are off I'm actually realising just how happy I am doing what I do.'

'Why?' Navy eyes pushed her to delve deeper. 'What is it about your work that you love?'

'The depth,' Amelia responded. 'My father would shudder if he heard me say that, but even though they might appear throwaway pieces they sustain interest, whereas in the business world my stories will be old by lunchtime. I'm always going to be chasing the next story, always stabbing people in the back and reporting on other people's misery.'

'Sounds to me like you've already made up your mind,' Vaughan suggested.

'Which should make things simple. But given that I'm covering a maternity leave position, and that the job I love doing is going to be over anyway, now really isn't the time to be upsetting the boss.' She gave a pale smile. 'The baby's already got teeth.'

Taking a sip of her chocolate, Amelia peered down at the dispersing patrons below, at tired waiters replacing crisp white cotton tablecloths, setting up for the new day that would surely dawn. The piano was quiet now, allowing her to mull over her own thoughts. She was grateful that Vaughan didn't jump in with another flash of insight, that he didn't attempt an answer when there really wasn't one.

'You're wrong about one thing, though.' Dragging her eyes back, Amelia broke the companionable silence. She had something she wanted to say. 'Journalists do have integrity, Vaughan—at least this one does.'

She waited—waited for him to apologise, to retract his rather sweeping generalisation—but instead he inhaled the brandy fumes from his glass before taking a long, slow sip.

'I guess we'll just have to wait and see.'

Placing her mug back on the table, Amelia felt her dressing gown part a fraction. Her hand moved to close it, but even in that tiny second she felt the shift, could almost feel the scorch marks where his eyes had burned her exposed flesh, was aware all over again of her attire, trying to fathom how without a word, with just one tiny motion, the atmosphere could dip so easily into dangerous territory.

'I'd better go.' Flustered now, she stood up, and so too did he, holding the French door open and following her from the balcony back inside his room.

Even though she'd only been there a short while ago it was unfamiliar all over again—the massive bed, somehow bigger, the air thick not with his cologne now, but with the thrum of heightened awareness. Her fingers refused to obey as she struggled with the unfamiliar lock on the door, and his hand made contact with hers as he moved to help. It was almost more than she could bear and still be expected to breathe. Amelia had to get out—had to get away from this overwhelming presence that spun her into confusion. But even with the door unlocked, even with her escape route open, still she couldn't move, trapped in her own desire.

Finally she looked up at him, and the desire in his eyes was like a mirror image of her own. Even if she didn't fit the usual dress code of the sophisticated women he attracted and discarded so easily she knew he was aroused, and it both thrilled and terrified her. But what was more overwhelming, more terrifying, was how much she wanted him—how much she longed for him to take her in his arms, to hush her troubled mind with a kiss. How very easy it would be to take that step over the mental line she had drawn, to again let her heart rule her head and let passion override sensibility.

Again.

Like a mental slap to her cheek, Taylor's brutal betrayal forced her mind to reality, allowed her legs to regain their function, her hands to pull open the door. She knew she had to get out—that she needed distance, clarity and recall.

Needed to recall the pain she had suffered before to remind her not to go there ever again.

'Goodnight, Vaughan.'

She attempted formal, attempted distance, but he swept it away without effort, one hand coming up to her arm. And despite the thick robe she could feel the heat of his palm on her skin, the space between them alive with thick tension. Every pore of her body flamed into response as he moved a fraction forward, moved into her personal space uninvited but unhindered, so close she could feel his breath on her cheeks. The weight of a kiss that simply had to happen was only a whisper away, and if her mind screamed no, then her body screamed yes.

His face moved in, but his lips teasingly missed hers, moving instead slowly along her cheek, the scratchy feel of him dragging against her, the weight of his swollen lips so close—summoning her to reciprocate if she dared, to seal this union. And she couldn't not.

Her lips turned to his like petals to the sun, and the blissful weight of his mouth was on hers. The cool control of his tongue was parting her lips, meeting the tip of hers, and slowly, coiling, chasing, relishing, she tasted the faint flavour of him, tasted the tang of brandy, tasted the decadent wine of his expert kiss. Every move of his lips, his tongue, was slow and deliberate, stirring the need within her with each skilful stroke. Her whole body was pitted with lust, arching towards him in necessary reaction—because she needed to feel him. One hand was guiding her as she moved, firmly nestled in the small of her back, and she felt as if he were touching her deep inside.

The hand that had captured her hair blazed a heated slow trail along her neck, a finger stilling for a second on the beat of her pulse as still he kissed her, still he drew her in. It was working down, ever down, so slowly she could have halted him at any moment, so slowly there was plenty of time to pull away to end this liaison—but it would have been easier to die than to end it now. She needed this, *needed* it in a primitive, deep, inexplicable way.

Her whole body was his willing instrument, pre-empting what was coming with dizzy need, so that when his hand slipped inside her robe her nipples were so taut, so achingly ready, a groan of sheer lustful pleasure welled in her mouth. It was drowned by his kiss as he rolled the engorged buds between his fingers, then took the weight of her bosom in his palm. His other hand was on her back, more urgent now, pushing her further towards him, till she could feel him, feel the solid beat of his arousal against her stomach.

Captured between the heat of his hand and the promise of his manhood, she felt the chirrup of the pulse between her legs more insistent now. Great waves of lust were washing over her, and he could have taken her there— she wanted him to take her there. One kiss, one glimpse of his passion, one taste of his promise and she wanted more—so why, Amelia begged as she pulled her head back, was she ending this? Why, when her body screamed for its just rewards, was her head telling her to stop?

'We can't.' Utterly unable to meet his eyes, she attempted an explanation.

'We very nearly did,' Vaughan pointed out, his hand

still on the small of her back, his arousal still solid against her, her own body still live with desire in his arms. Wisps of passion still surged hopefully through her veins and she pulled away more forcefully now, snapping her robe together. But not quickly enough to miss the weight of his gaze on the creamy flesh of her breast. Her budding nipples were still jutting hopefully, and she knew he was taking it all in—the glittering eyes, the flush of arousal on her cheeks—knew how contrary her words sounded when her body clearly wanted him.

'You don't mix business with pleasure, remember?'

She needed help here—needed Vaughan to take some of the weight from her buckling shoulders, to offer a voice of reason that would stave off the onslaught of disaster. But Vaughan wasn't helping. Vaughan was only making it worse.

'I made the rule, Amelia. It's not yours to keep.' A finger traced her cheekbone, drew around the contours of her mouth, the pad of his thumb nudging the flesh still swollen from his kiss. She ached to relent, to part her lips on his command, to resume this delicious liaison—but she had to be strong, couldn't do this again and hope to come out intact.

'It's a good rule.' Snapping into business mode, she attempted a brittle smile. 'And one I intend to keep.'

'So what was that, then?'

'A goodnight kiss,' Amelia attempted. 'Vaughan, it was just a kiss.'

'Just a kiss?' The preposterousness of her statement was there in his voice. 'Tell me, Amelia, do you kiss all your subjects like that?'

'Of course not.' Amelia was flustered, unsure how to respond here, and lying was easier. Keeping her distance was safer than letting him glimpse her uncertainty, letting him see her naked truth.

How could she tell a man who could only break her heart that in a single kiss he had moved her beyond distraction? That it was taking every shred of strength she could summon to keep her hand on the door? That she had to physically force herself not to run to him?

'It's just safer, that's all…' Her mouth snapped closed as she instantly regretted her choice of words, wishing she could somehow retract them. But they were already out there, already being processed in that astute mind, already being hurled back at her. She braced herself for defence.

'Safer?'

'Yes—safer,' Amelia snapped back, more angry with herself than him, because with one single word she had allowed him to see her fears. 'Safer than doing something stupid in the heat of a moment when we'd both surely regret it in the morning.'

'Why do you assume we'd regret it?'

'Because…' a tiny nervous laugh, a silent plea with her eyes '…it's just not me, Vaughan. I can't be your lover for a night or a week—can't just give you a piece of myself, knowing it isn't going to last.'

'And you know that for sure, do you?'

He was moving in on her again, hands leaning against the wall on either side of her head—the master with the key, creating a prison she wasn't sure she wanted to escape from.

'I know that you want me, Vaughan, and I know that I want you. But…'

'Why does there have to be one?' His voice was so low, so raw she had to strain to catch it. 'How do you know that we won't still feel this way tomorrow?'

He was moving in to kiss her, moving in for the final delicious kill, and Amelia only knew she had to stop him—had to hit him with her final defence. 'Because you're Vaughan Mason.'

His hands dropped to his sides and she could have walked away. But she felt stronger now—strong enough to see this through.

'Because I've got a past you mean?'

'No, Vaughan, because *I've* got a past. I know your type…'

'My type?'

'Yes, your type, Vaughan. The type of man who attracts women, who likes women, who effortlessly attracts them and for a while adores them until just as effortlessly he moves on.'

'Now who's doing the sweeping generalisations?' Vaughan sneered. 'So what? You want commitment before you sleep with someone? Is that what you're saying?'

'No, I just know—'

'Know what?' Vaughan broke in. 'That I'm a bastard? That I'm setting you up for a fall?'

'Not deliberately, perhaps…' She shook her head in an attempt to clear it. 'Vaughan, this won't last—you surely know that. And I'm not going to allow myself to get involved with a man who can only hurt me in the end.'

'You think you've got me all worked out. You've read my bio and from that you know me. Well, I'm not some doped-up popstar with an ego that needs feeding.'

So brutal were his words that she felt as if she'd been hit—appalled that he knew, and that somehow he'd worked out so much from so very little.

'How—?' The word strangled in her throat. 'How could you know that?'

'I can read you, Amelia.' His low husky voice reached her ears. 'But don't worry, I'm not going to *make* you do what you *want* to. I'm not going to beg for something we both know you want. But think about this when you creep into that cold bed alone—just think about this as you lie there staring at the ceiling: any man you feel for could ultimately hurt you; any man who can make your body respond the way it just did could one day use it against you. So if you're looking for iron-clad guarantees, if you're looking to safeguard your heart against pain, you can kiss goodbye to passion.'

And even though he didn't move, not by a hair, he made love to her all over again. His eyes were almost black as he stared down at her body, the navy obscured by his dilated pupils, scorching through the robe she gripped tightly in her trembling hand. So bold was his stare she could almost feel his hand again on her breast, feel the champagne bubbles of arousal fizzing, and she ran a nervous tongue over her lips. Only it didn't help. The delicious taste of him was still there in her mouth. It was as if he held the remote control to her body—he pushed her buttons, turning her on at will and she only knew that she had to get out.

This time she meant it. Wrenching open the door and fleeing down the passage, she only breathed when her own door was safely closed behind her. Her body burned with dissatisfaction, her emotions utterly violated by his brutal words—and damn him, Amelia realised, he was right.

Creeping into bed, she lay there, supremely aware of him just as few metres away, on the other side of the flimsy hotel wall, her whole body burning with a desire she'd chosen to starve in the name of preservation, staring appalled at the life that lay before her.

A life without passion.

A life that was safe.

Chapter 5

'Good morning!' Her greeting rang out loudly as Vaughan made his way over to the breakfast table— one of the same tables they'd idly watched being laid up only hours ago.

The piano stood proud and silent now—no gentle background noise to fill this difficult moment as the restaurant area slowly filled up with bleary-eyed early risers and crisp businessmen and women grabbing a caffeine fix before they headed for the office. Melbourne was stirring into life after a long sultry night.

She said her greeting again when he sat down, and again Vaughan didn't respond—didn't even acknowledge the smile she'd firmly painted on this morning — instead sitting down and signalling to the waiter to fill his coffee cup.

She'd been determined to get in first and set the tone, put last night firmly behind them and resume normal services. But, Amelia realized as Vaughan sat down and scowled at his newspaper, not even bothering to thank the waiter who had promptly filled his cup, there had been no need to rush to greet him—Vaughan, it would appear, wasn't in a hurry to talk to anyone. Sulky and broody, he stared at his paper, his only movement an occasional hand reaching out for his coffee.

'Did you sleep well?' Amelia attempted, ready to rip the bloody paper from his hands if that was what it took, utterly determined to get this over with.

'No.' Navy eyes peered over the top of his paper. 'Are you going to try and tell me that you did?'

God, why did he have to be so direct? Why couldn't he act like any normal person and pretend that last night's events simply hadn't happened?

'I did, actually,' Amelia lied, spooning sugar into her tea and getting most of it on the table. She damn well wasn't going to tell him she'd spent the night pinned to the bed, simultaneously reeling at her boldness, her utter stupidity for going into his room so inappropriately dressed, for responding to his kisses with such blatant ease, yet all the while berating herself for terminating it.

His words had stung her to the core. All night she'd played them over in her mind—too terrified to flick on the kettle in case he heard her, reluctant to go out on the balcony in case he saw her. Knowing that with one crook of his manicured finger she'd run to him, that with one more taste of that decadent mouth she'd fall into his bed with nothing to save her.

'Vaughan—please!' Still she spoke to the sports page. 'If this is about last night…' She held her breath as the paper slowly dropped, his eyes frowning as he met hers. 'If this silent treatment—'

'Silent treatment?' He shook his head, a mirthless

smile almost evident on his taut lips, then to her utter fury lifted the paper again and proceeded to read.

'Look, if this is going to affect our working relationship…'

'Amelia, on reflection you made a very valid point last night.' Vaughan slowly folded up his paper and placed it on the table beside him as she sat squirming with embarrassment. He stretched out her discomfort for as long as possible before finally continuing. 'Perhaps people *should* get to know each other before they sleep together. Maybe people *should* know that just because someone chooses not to bounce across to the breakfast table squawking like a galah, it doesn't mean that they're ruing the fact they didn't get their rocks off last night, but that they are quite simply people who like at least a few micrograms of caffeine in their system before they enter into a deep and meaningful discussion.'

'Getting your rocks off?' Amelia sneered, embarrassed at her overreaction, yet sure, quite sure, that she had been right—that Vaughan 'in control' Mason was seriously rattled because, unlike most women, she hadn't succumbed to his undeniably skilful charms. 'I made more than one valid point last night, Vaughan. And a man who refers to it as "getting his rocks off" really isn't the type of guy I want to be sharing a bed with.'

'And a woman who refers to sex as "it" clearly doesn't know how to enjoy herself!'

'So I'm frigid, am I?'

She saw the tiny upward flicker of his eyebrow, knew that she had shocked him slightly, but years spent in journalism had taught Amelia not to shy away from embarrassing subjects, to face tough conversations head-on. This was tough, supremely difficult, but she was damn well going to see it through.

'Are you trying to say that because I—heaven forbid—chose not to sleep with you it means that deep down I can't really like sex very much? That it has nothing to do with the fact that I didn't want to be yet another notch on your well-worn bedpost? Does the fact I demand more of myself than to be another of your conquests mean, according to your fragile male ego, that I don't really like *it* very much at all? Oh, sorry,' Amelia snarled a correction, 'you don't like that word, do you? I meant to say—'

'I get the picture.' A hand shot up to stop her. He was clearly embarrassed at her boldness, for once looking anything other than cool. 'Look, let's just forget it, shall we?'

'That's what I was trying to do this morning,' Amelia pointed out. 'For your information, I'm not a morning person either.'

'Can we please start again?' Vaughan asked, and after a moment on her high horse Amelia relented.

'Good morning, Vaughan.'

'Good morning, Amelia. Did you sleep well?'

'Actually, no. How about you?'

'Terribly.' He slipped in one tiny cheat. 'I had, er, rather pressing things on my mind.' Seeing her cheeks darken he finally gave in with an apologetic smile. 'Would you think that I was avoiding you if I said I need to ditch you for the morning.'

'Of course not.' Amelia shrugged. 'Like I said, I was surprised how many meetings I got into yesterday. Anyway, I've got plenty of work I should be doing.'

'What if I also said that I need to speak with Mr Cheng alone this afternoon?'

Peeling open a croissant with slightly shaky hands and spooning jam onto it, she gave a pale smile. 'Then I'd be starting to think that maybe you are avoiding me after all. Not really.' She smiled when she saw his slightly worried frown. 'Vaughan, I always knew there would be things I couldn't come along to. I'm not a child you have to amuse for the day. I'll be completely fine.'

'We could meet for lunch—' He gave a small wince almost before the sentence was out.

'Except…?' Amelia said for him.

'I've just remembered that I've arranged to meet someone.' He hesitated for longer than usual, his frown deepening, then eyed her cautiously, as if weighing up whether or not to continue. 'I suppose you could come, but given your career revelations, how off the record is off the record?'

'It's completely non-negotiable,' Amelia replied, utterly without hesitation. 'Your secrets are safe with me. They just help.' Realising he didn't understand, she elaborated slightly. 'Help me to form a picture in my mind. But just because I know something it doesn't mean I have to reveal it.'

'You're quite sure about that?'

He'd really piqued her interest now. For the first time he was cagey and hesitant, and it only served to intrigue her more, but Amelia knew when to hold back, knew when to feign uninterest—at least when it was about work. 'Look, you do your lunch and I'll catch up with you later this evening—tomorrow, even. It really isn't a big deal.'

'I'm meeting with one of the directors of a children's hospital.' Vaughan grimaced slightly, as if he regretted even saying it. 'Every year I give a small donation.'

'So small that they take you out for lunch when you're in town?' Amelia said shrewdly.

'Okay, a *significant* donation,' Vaughan admitted reluctantly. 'The thing is, Sam, he's the director, is doing his best to persuade me to go public with my support.'

'Why don't you?' Amelia asked, her tone completely matter of fact. 'Almost every celebrity I've ever interviewed has done the rounds of the children's wards to soften their image.'

'Exactly,' Vaughan replied, his voice suddenly curt. 'But I'm hardly a celebrity.'

'But you are, Vaughan,' Amelia pointed out. 'You're good-looking, impossibly rich, reeking of scandal and still single! Take it from a woman who knows—you're a celebrity! Why don't you want me to use this? Heaven knows, a piece of good publicity couldn't hurt you right now.'

'So I should ask a couple of sick kids to pose with me?'

'You wouldn't be the first,' Amelia responded. 'And you would be doing some good—it might make a few other business magnates dig deeper.'

'So why not get the mileage?'

Now it was Amelia feeling shallow, all of a sudden uncomfortable with the conversation.

'Those children don't know me, Amelia. I'm not some popstar they adore, waltzing onto the ward for a photo shoot. I'm just a guy in a suit…'

'Who donates a lot of money.' She saw his lips tighten. 'Come on, Vaughan. A significant amount to you would be a fortune to most people. And maybe the children won't know you, but their parents will…'

'I'm sure if their child's sick enough to be there they'll have other things on their mind. Amelia, this is something I do because I want to—something just for me. That's what I'm going to explain to Sam today. He's hoping that if I go public it might trigger a few more in the business community to get involved.'

'Which can surely only be a good thing?' Amelia answered, still not entirely convinced.

She'd heard too many celebrities insisting this was something they wanted to do, been to too many contrived charity dos for a cynical edge not to have evolved. And if that sounded hard, she didn't care. At the end of the day the hospitals needed the money and Vaughan needed the positive publicity—it was win-win as far as Amelia was concerned.

'If you're so intent on it being kept private, then why are you asking me along? Why are you asking a *journalist* to an intensely private lunch.'

'You don't mince your words, do you?' Vaughan smiled almost reluctantly.

'I don't like being fed a line.' Amelia shrugged, happier now they were on safer ground. She was back—maybe not back at the driver's wheel, but at least up in the passenger seat, shoulder to shoulder with this complicated man.

For as long as it took for her second up of coffee to be poured!

'I listened to what you said about the bigger picture. I figure that an hour in Sam's company might bring you on board, and an up-and-coming journalist on side can only be a good thing for the hospital.'

'Oh.'

Placing a hand over his cup, he refused a refill, waiting till the waiter had walked away before standing up.

'Can I let the restaurant know to expect one more?'

* * *

An *extremely* significant donation might have been a better description, Amelia decided as she handed over her jacket and stepped into the restaurant. Wafts of herbs and garlic filled the air, along with the pop of corks, and there was the luxurious feel of deep carpet beneath her feet. Small donations surely didn't merit this five-star treatment.

A frown formed as Amelia glanced over to Vaughan's table and then at her watch. Vaughan had specifically told her one p.m. and she was five minutes early—yet already he and his companion were clearly at the coffee stage.

'Amelia.' The consummate host, Vaughan stood up and greeted her, introducing her to Sam and guiding her to a seat. 'I'm sorry about this, but something came up and we had to switch times.'

'My fault, I'm afraid,' Sam apologised, while not looking remotely sorry. 'I've got an afternoon appointment which means that I'm going to have to wrap this up.'

'Now that you've got what you wanted,' Vaughan said dryly, and Amelia frowned at the rather obvious irritation in his voice.

'You'll be great, Vaughan.' Sam grinned. 'It's for the kids, remember?' He smiled over to Amelia. 'It was a pleasure to meet you, Miss Jacobs. Hopefully we'll see you at the charity auction on Thursday.'

Glancing briefly over, she saw Vaughan shake his head, his eyes demanding her to say no. But in a curiously defiant gesture she smiled at the rather pushy Sam.

'Is that an invitation?'

'It certainly is.' Sam beamed. 'We can use all the

publicity we can get. Don't worry, Vaughan—' his wide
smile wasn't reciprocated '—you'll be just fine. Oh, and
before I forget—do you have those tickets you promised?'

Unclipping his briefcase, Vaughan pulled out a stiff
white envelope, handing it over to Sam before shaking
his hand and bidding him goodbye.

'Well, that was enlightening,' Amelia said with more
than a vague hint of sarcasm as Sam walked off. 'I'll
certainly get a lot of mileage out of that lunch.'

'Bloody salesmen,' Vaughan snapped at the depart-
ing back.

'I thought he was one of the directors from the hospital.'

'He's in the wrong job, then,' Vaughan clipped, but
he didn't elaborate further.

Amelia's curiosity was seriously piqued. She felt as
if she'd rushed in at the end of something and missed
the important part—like watching her favourite soap
without knowing what had happened last week.

'What was in the envelope?' Amelia asked, but
Vaughan didn't even attempt an explanation.

'Have something to eat.'

'I'm actually not that hungry, Vaughan. If you didn't
want me here, you should have just said.'

'Sam rescheduled at the last moment,' Vaughan argued.

Amelia fished in her bag, frowning as she pulled out
her mobile. 'I can't see your message here, Vaughan.'

'Because there isn't one,' Vaughan responded easily,
completely ignoring her sarcasm. 'There isn't one because I knew if I tried to reschedule then you'd assume
I was making excuses and wouldn't come.'

'You were right,' Amelia clipped. 'But only about

the fact I wouldn't have come. Vaughan, I do have an article to write. I've dragged myself through the city for a meal I don't really want to sit with a person I'll no doubt be seeing this evening.'

'I thought the entire purpose of this exercise was to get to know me better,' Vaughan retorted, flashing a triumphant smile.

'*Attempting* to get to know you better,' Amelia corrected. 'You don't exactly give much away. It's like pulling teeth without an anaesthetic, trying to extract information from you. Everything I manage to glean you counter with an "off the record" reminder.'

'Oh, come on, Amelia.' Vaughan gave her a look that showed her he was anything but moved. 'If you can't fashion a story after all the meetings you've been in, then you're not the journalist I thought you were. You don't have to name names all the time.'

'It's not them I'm interested in, though,' Amelia retorted. 'I meant what I said last night. It's a portrayal of you that I want to do, not a bloody business piece.' She took a deep breath, shook her head as the waiter handed her a menu.

The truth of the matter was she was struggling with contrary emotions. As much as she wanted to get to know him better, as much as she needed more information to write the piece she really wanted to write, she was terrified of being alone with him again—had been secretly relieved at the chance to spend a day licking her wounds and hopefully fashioning her brain into some sort of order before the next onslaught of emotional torture Vaughan so easily generated. She'd needed the space to get her head together, to ring a girlfriend and beg for sensibility before she surely caved in. A business lunch she could just about have dealt with, but an hour or two up close and personal with Vaughan Mason was way too much for her shredded emotions right now.

'Come on—have something,' Vaughan pushed, retrieving the menu and placing it in front of her. 'You can't come all this way and not eat.'

But the thought of chasing spaghetti around her plate in her present state, with Vaughan calmly watching on, wasn't particularly palatable.

'I'd far rather have a sandwich sent up to my hotel room,' Amelia resisted, hoisting her bag up onto her shoulder. 'I know you're busy, Vaughan, and, as I said this morning, you really don't have to babysit me—this was a business lunch that should have been rescheduled, not a date you've somehow managed to break and need to make up for. A phone call would have sufficed.'

'We could share a cheese platter,' Vaughan responded, completely dismissing her entire statement, obviously happy with *his* choice and clicking his fingers to summon the waiter, not even bothering to check if it was okay with Amelia.

'I could have a raving lactose intolerance,' Amelia bristled. 'I could blow up like a soccer ball at the mere sight of cheese!'

'Do you?'

'No, but that isn't the point.'

Despite his bland expression, she knew he was laughing at her.

'Would you care for some wine?' Vaughan checked. 'Or does that bring you out in hives?'

'Water will be fine.'

'So, what have you written about me so far?'

Amelia nearly knocked over her glass at his way too direct question.

'Am I allowed to look?'

'No!' Perish the thought.

Amelia gave a visible shudder. The thought of anyone reading her work at this stage filled her with horror, but it had nothing to do with what she'd written—was more the complete lack of it. Though she damn well wasn't going to tell anyone that she'd barely got past the first paragraph, that her mind was constantly wandering. This whole morning, when she should have been working, had been spent reluctantly recalling the sheer heady bliss of being held by him, and, as intimate as she wanted her piece to be, she certainly wasn't about to share *that* with her readers.

'That bad, huh?'

'Worse,' Amelia said with a teasing smile. 'Actually, I haven't touched on your appalling arrogance yet. I'm saving that for this afternoon's session.'

'Maybe you should have some wine after all. It might help soften the edges a bit.'

'Come on, Vaughan,' Amelia moaned. 'You have to give me something here. What's this about a charity auction on Thursday?'

'I'm the auctioneer,' Vaughan sighed, and Amelia finally started to laugh.

'This I have to see!'

Vaughan rolled his eyes. 'Please let's not talk about it. And even if I have to strap you to the bed, there's no way you're coming to watch.'

Ouch!

As innocent as it had been, in their present rather fragile state any mention of bed had them both inwardly cringing. And, though she couldn't be sure, Amelia could have sworn she saw the first hint of a blush darken his cheeks at the small *faux pas*.

'But I've been invited.' Amelia grinned, enjoying

his moment of discomfort. 'I wouldn't dream of missing it! So what's it in aid of? The children's hospital?'

'Actually, it's the cystic fibrosis unit holding it. Apparently they urgently need to purchase some piece of equipment, but the budget has already been allocated for this financial year, so rather than waiting they've decided to bite the bullet and raise the money themselves.'

'And what's your role in this? Apart from being the auctioneer?' Amelia grinned again. 'I assume that was a last-minute addition?'

'You assume correctly. I donated a holiday—that envelope contained the tickets—ten nights for two in Fiji at a luxury resort...' He smiled as Amelia let out a blissful sigh.

'With air tickets?' she checked, pouting with not so feigned jealousy as Vaughan nodded.

'You'd think that would have sufficed. But, not happy with that, Sam decided to bully me into standing with a microphone, making a complete idiot of myself.'

'I can't believe you'd ever be bullied into something you didn't want to do.'

Spreading creamy thick cheese onto a pepper cracker, she looked up to see him smiling again.

'What?'

'For a lactose intolerant person who's not particularly hungry you're doing a good job with that cheese. Don't stop,' he added when she put down her cracker. 'I'm just glad I'm forgiven, that's all.'

'You're not.' Amelia grinned.

'And you'll never be forgiven, young lady, if you even so much as smile at my efforts on Thursday night.'

'I can't believe you're so worked up about it.' Amelia laughed. 'Surely you're used to public speaking? I can't believe you'd get worked up about some tiny cocktail party for a children's ward.'

'I'm not getting worked up,' Vaughan snapped, then relented with a brief nod. 'I just can't really picture myself working an audience, telling them to dig deep for the kids. I'm not the world's most effusive person.'

Oh, but he was!

Staring across the table, glimpsing again that bland inscrutable face, it was hard to believe the passion that had smoldered last night—how the eyes that were guarded now had burned with fervour, how his demonstrative hands had expressed without words so many simmering feelings, how she had witnessed first hand the hidden depths of this extraordinary man.

'How did he do it?'

She was deep in thought and his question caught her off guard. Two vertical lines appeared on the bridge of her nose as she realised the conversation had shifted to strictly personal, and that once again the subject was her.

'How did Taylor Dean get that suspicious, cynical woman to relent?'

'I don't want to talk about it.'

'I do.' Vaughan leant over the table, the motion causing his knees to brush hers, and he held his legs there, trapped her at the table with a mere touch. 'I can't imagine you of all people falling for a popstar. You're not exactly...'

'Stunning?' Amelia offered, but immediately he shook his head.

'You have the self-esteem of an ant, Amelia. I was about to say you're not exactly groupie material. I just can't picture you falling for a line.'

'It wasn't a line.' Amelia blinked back at him and

he saw the pain in her eyes, saw the swirling confusion still there. The pain was obviously still new. 'At the risk of sounding like an even bigger fool, I actually think he did love me.' She took a gulp of her water. 'Hard to imagine, I guess.'

'No.' His voice was husky and thoughtful, the flip, slightly patronizing tone gone now, and he stared back at her—stared back and willed her to open up. 'No, it isn't actually that hard to imagine someone falling completely head over heels in love with you, Amelia. Can you tell me what happened between you and Taylor?'

He watched her face stiffen, the creamy shoulders tighten. But if it hurt to probe he didn't care. Insatiable curiosity was burning within, that this wary, suspicious woman could ever have succumbed to the negligible charms of a man like Taylor.

'Why?' Amelia begged. But she already knew the answer—knew that he needed to understand why she held back. And maybe by telling him, so might she.

'I was booked to do an interview. I had an hour slot with him. But there was a PA by his side—not a chance of digging deeper. Every time I asked something that wasn't on the list, every time I veered off course, his PA broke in—which was annoying, but expected. It happens all the time during interviews. Only suddenly it wasn't me getting annoyed. All of a sudden it was Taylor who was frowning at the interruptions. It was as if he really wanted to talk to me—really wanted to finally be honest. In the end he asked his PA to leave.'

Vaughan could see the tension burning in her eyes, the bat of her lids as she blinked in disbelief at her own recall.

'I thought at the time it was because he wanted to talk, wanted to open up some more and give some honest answers for the article. I never for a moment imagined he actually wanted to get to know me.'

'How long did you see him for?'

'A few months.' Amelia gave a tight shrug. 'Which, in the scheme of things, isn't long at all. But when I fall, I fall...'

'And you fell?' Vaughan checked gently.

'Hook, line and sinker. But...' She took a deep breath, the shame and humiliation that she'd been so naïve burning as she retold her story. 'But so did he. He was always asking me to come and watch him perform. But with work and everything more often than not I was too busy. One day I decided to surprise him. He was singing in Brisbane and I decided what the hell? So I jumped on a plane and headed over. His PA tried to stop me from going into his hotel room...but I went in anyway. I don't think I have to spell out what I saw...'

'I'm sorry.'

'So was Taylor.' Maybe she should have had some wine after all. Recalling this was too painful for a Tuesday afternoon. 'Devastated, actually. And I think it was genuine. He's just too used to having too much of a good thing and too weak to say no. He swore he'd never cheat on me again, and maybe he believed it—maybe he believed at the time he was speaking the truth. But by then it didn't matter.'

'No second chance?'

Amelia shook her head. 'Not for that. I think I must have been the first woman to ever dump him. He still rings, still sends flowers, still tries to convince me he's changed.'

'What if he has?'

'Too late.' Amelia shook her head firmly, but she saw the flicker of doubt in his eyes and it annoyed her. 'It's over, Vaughan. How could I ever trust him again? How could I ever forgive him? It has to be over.'

'But you still have feelings?'

Oh, she had feelings. Feelings so raw they hurt. But not for Taylor. She'd ripped him out of her mind as easily as a teenager tearing down a poster. Infidelity was the one sin she could never forgive. The hurt, pain and emotion were still there, yet she was learning to live with them. But, no, it wasn't her feelings for Taylor that terrified her now. It was her feelings for Vaughan—the one man who could do it to her all over again if she let him. The one man who could snake into her heart, into her bed. And quite simply she couldn't bear to let him in just to watch him leave, couldn't begin to imagine moving on from the devastation he would surely wreak, couldn't bear to build her world from ground zero all over again.

'I'm not a popstar, Amelia.'

His voice was as gentle as she'd ever heard it. She could still feel the weight of his knees against hers, feel his dry, hot hand coiling around her fingers, tempting her back to the forbidden garden where only last night she'd strayed.

'I'm just a guy in a suit…'

'You know that you're not.' Tears glittered in her eyes. She felt as if she'd been swimming against the tide for ever, swimming towards a bobbing life raft in the ocean only to find out it was a shark. 'We're from different worlds, Vaughan. You just want what you can't have, and I'm sorry if it sounds boring, but from a relationship I want more.'

'Such as?'

'Safety.' Taking a deep breath, she laid it on the line. The fact that she'd only known him a few days was irrelevant when she was staring down the barrel of a gun aimed at her heart. 'And if that sounds boring too then I make no apology. I've tried the fast lane and I didn't like it. Next time I give my heart away, Vaughan, I want the lot—marriage, kids, a partner to stand shoulder to shoulder with. A man I can trust, not someone always on the lookout for the next good thing, not someone whose ego needs constant massaging.'

'And is anything on that list negotiable?'

She could see a muscle flickering in his cheek, feel the tension in his body, his knees pressing into hers more urgently as he awaited her answer.

'I want the lot, Vaughan,' Amelia repeated, shaking her head.

It was as if a pin had been pushed into a balloon. The tension in the air dispersed, and the pressure on her knees was removed as Vaughan flashed her a very false smile.

'And you deserve it.' For the longest time his eyes sought hers, before finally they dragged away. His guard was back up, the shutters firmly down, and whatever she had said to make him keep his distance had worked a charm, because it was a stranger on the other side of the table now. Every shred of intimacy was suddenly gone. 'You deserve every bit of it, Amelia. Don't settle for anything less.'

'I won't…' Tears were pricking now, horrible hot tears she would never let him see.

Making her excuses, Amelia fled for the safety of the washroom, where she stared at her reflection in the mirror for an age, mentally scolding herself for daring to hope.

As if Vaughan wanted the same thing—as if allowing him to glimpse her dreams would mean for a moment that he wanted to share them.

Go for it, he'd basically told her. *Only not with me.*

Thank God for face powder, Amelia thought ruefully. And thank God for lipgloss to add sparkle to a rather strained smile. And as she made her way back to the table suddenly her mind was back on the job, her eyes narrowing in recognition as she watched a gentleman leaving the restaurant, eyes cast downwards, collar firmly up, clearly not wanting to be seen.

'Everything okay?'

Perhaps sensing her distraction, Vaughan eyed her with concern as she sat back down at the table, watching as she pushed a nod while nibbling nervously on her bottom lip. Those delicious eyes were distant as her hands reached out for a glass of water.

'You look as if you've just seen a ghost.'

Chapter 6

'What the hell was Carter doing at the restaurant?'

The one time she actually needed to speak to Paul he was completely unavailable. It had taken the best part of forty-eight hours to finally get him on the line.

'I have no idea.' Paul sighed. 'Perhaps he was hungry?'

'Don't play games with me, Paul.'

Two days of being put on hold and speaking into his message bank had taken its toll, coupled with the fact that, judging from the frenzied activities going on in the bar on the ground floor, her and Vaughan's idea of a cocktail party clearly differed.

The tiny informal gathering Amelia had foolishly predicted was clearly way off the mark. Every time she had graced the foyer today she had been greeted with the sight of a closed-off area and endless staff carrying fresh flowers and boxes into its dark depths. Even

Vaughan had swanned down to the hotel's health spa in his white toweling robe—no doubt to have a shave and a facial and manicure, Amelia thought. If only she'd been able to pack Shelly!

Paul giving her the runaround wasn't helping her already frazzled nerves, and now, throwing both caution and possibly her career to the wind, Amelia let rip along the phone line to Sydney.

'Paul, we both know Carter's barely human. Why would he need food when he survives solely on other people's misery? Why didn't he come over and introduce himself? I need to know what's going on. I need to know what it is you've got on Vaughan.'

'No, Amelia, you don't.' Paul's voice was non-negotiable. 'I know and that's enough. You just do your job and let me do mine. Keep right on buttering him up and get what you can out of him.'

'This isn't Chinese Torture I'm playing at here, Paul. I'm writing an article on the man, for heaven's sake, not preparing a case for the prosecution.'

'Carter said that you two were very cosy in the restaurant.' Completely unmoved by her vehement denial, Paul pushed harder. 'What were you talking about?'

'Nothing that would interest you, Paul.'

'Try me,' Paul insisted.

'As I said, it's nothing that would interest you, because we were actually talking about *me*.'

Replacing the receiver, Amelia saw that her hand was shaking. The horrible truth was starting to creep in. Her supposed big break hadn't just fallen into her lap. It had been calculated every step of the way. Carter hadn't hot-footed it to Canberra to follow the election trail. Thumbing through her pile of newspapers, Amelia confirmed what she already knew. Carter hadn't filed a single report. He had disappeared so that Amelia would interview Vaughan.

Dragging in air, Amelia tried to make sense of it all, tried to conjure an explanation. But nothing was forthcoming. Picking up the telephone immediately when it buzzed again, hoping against hope that it was Paul with some answers, she jumped out of her guilty skin when she realised it was Vaughan, in an unusually relaxed mode.

'The staff were wondering what time you're coming down. You didn't book a time.'

'Coming down?' Amelia frowned into the phone.

'To the health spa. If you want to have a massage and your make-up done, you really ought to step on it!'

'Oh!' Amelia chewed nervously on her bottom lip, almost whimpering at the delicious thought of a massage and facial before she braved the cool stares of Melbourne's most elite. But, given her rather shaky relationship with her credit card at the moment she could hardly justify it—and Paul certainly wasn't going to sign it off as a necessary claim. 'I was just going to have a bath up here.'

'Well, do you want them to come up to your room?' Vaughan asked, with all the arrogance of the truly rich.

'I can run my own bath, Vaughan,' Amelia answered testily. 'And I've had years of practice with a mascara wand.'

'Fine,' Vaughan clipped. 'It just seems a shame to waste it when it's included in the room. I'll let them know you won't be—'

'It's included in the room?' Amelia swallowed her squeal of delight, trying to sound as nonchalant as possible as she punched the air in joy. 'Oh, well, in that case it *would* be a shame to waste it. Tell them I'll be right down.'

Vaughan was just leaving as Amelia arrived, grinning from ear to ear in her towelling robe. Like a child let loose in a sweet shop, she ran her eye along the impressive list of treatments.

'Do you have any plans this afternoon?' Amelia checked. 'Anything I ought to…?'

'Nothing.' Vaughan smiled. 'Take your time. You deserve an afternoon off.'

Oh, she did, Amelia thought wickedly. She decided there and then to have everything on the list well, maybe not everything, Amelia mentally corrected, as the stragglers on her eyebrows were waxed away in seconds.

Brazilians must have a markedly high pain threshold!

Whoever had said that money didn't buy happiness certainly hadn't spent two hours in this hotel's health spa being wrapped in mud, massaged, pummelled and exfoliated to within an inch of their lives, hadn't felt the sheer bliss of a scalp massage, nor lain in a reclining chair as their fingers and toenails were simultaneously painted, hadn't known the sheer heady pleasure of staring down at two newly pretty feet that were finally actually fit for the jewelled impulse-bought sandals awaiting their mistress at the bottom of her suitcase in the top floor of the hotel! Absolute bliss!

Stepping out of the lift, padding along the floor towards her room, Amelia felt good enough about herself to smile at the stunning woman walking towards her, clouds of dark hair billowing over her shoulders, wafting a perfume that Amelia could never afford. She was more than happy to impart just a touch of her buoyant mood, and shrugged to herself when the smile wasn't reciprocated, when the rather haunted-looking beauty pointedly avoided her gaze and walked swiftly past.

Only as she reached her room did the smile fade from Amelia's face. The heady perfume that had filled the corridor was noticeably absent now, but Amelia knew, just knew, where the haunted beauty had come from.

Heart in her mouth, she retraced her steps, closing her newly made-up eyes in regret as she reached Vaughan's closed door, inhaling the heady fragrance.

Money did buy happiness.

The blissfully decadent two hours she'd just spent meant nothing now. The health spa *hadn't* been included in her room...

Vaughan had conveniently got rid of her.

She sat on her bed, huddled into her robe, staring unseeing into space, appalled at the jealousy that assailed her. A full hour had passed—a full hour watching the shadows on the wall lengthen, a full hour berating herself for even daring to dream that someone like Vaughan could ever really change and, more pathetically, that she, Amelia, might be the one to change him.

She should be getting ready!

Amelia winced as she glanced at her watch, and her expression blew into a full-face grimace as a pounding on the door forced her attention. She pulled off her robe and poured herself into her dress in record time, and headed to open the door.

'Can you sew?'

It wasn't the greeting Amelia was expecting when she opened the door to impatient knocking.

Her lilac strappy dress really deserved the garnish of a strapless bra and heels before it was seen—not, Amelia realised, that Vaughan would notice in his current state. She flattened herself against the wall as he strode impatiently in.

Wired to the max, he practically marched into her room, impossibly restless but still beautiful in a charcoal suit, his shirt impossibly white, a dark grey silk tie hanging around an unbuttoned shirt.

'Well, sewing's not something I pride myself on,' Amelia responded, deliberately missing the point. If he wanted her to sew for him then he could damn well ask her properly!

'I've lost my top button.' Vaughan attempted an explanation. 'Housekeeping said they'd send someone to mend it, but that's going to take for ever. I'm supposed to be down there in five minutes.'

'Here.' Smiling sweetly, she picked up the miniature sewing kit that hotels always provided, handing it to him and watching his frown deepen. 'You can use this.'

He didn't say it, but Amelia swore she could hear the irritated curse that was on the tip of his tongue. 'Amelia—' Taking a deep breath, attempting a pleasant smile, Vaughan tried again. 'Would you mind sewing my top button on for me?' He held up his arms to reveal two shiny silver cufflinks. 'I haven't got time to take my shirt off. Please,' he added, completely as an afterthought, as still she stood there.

'Seeing as you asked so nicely—' Amelia smiled '—then I'm sure I can manage a button.'

Or she should have been able to. It wasn't as if she had to rummage for a needle—one was provided, threaded, even, in the little kit the hotel provided—but he was too tall, too close, and way, way too near. She fumbled with the neck of his shirt, tried to keep her breathing even, tried to ignore the full mouth just a breath away.

'What did you do while I was gone?' Amelia asked lightly, way too lightly, holding her breath, mentally begging for an explanation—and dying a bit inside as she heard him lie.

'Slept.' Vaughan shrugged.

His skin was deliciously smooth, yet the blue-black suggestion of tomorrow lay just beneath the surface. Horribly clumsy, Amelia managed to push the needle through the stiff fabric without major incident, missing his jugular by mere centimetres. Her hand was shaking so much, and she knew that for the rest of her life, because of this moment, never again would she perform this minor task without remembering the scent, the feel, the sheer lusty presence of this man.

How easy it would be to just give in, to allow herself the luxury of even only once letting him in.

'Done.'

Slamming that door closed, Amelia stepped back.

He nodded his thanks, and a completely steady hand knotted his tie. Amelia vanished into the bathroom, her own hand not quite so steady as she touched up her lipstick and squeezed her feet into impossibly high shoes, before eyeing her reflection in the mirror. She was almost pleased with her appearance, almost pleased with the reflection that stared back at her. Except for the sight of two jiggling bosoms that really needed support.

If she'd had the courage to wander into the living room and rescue the offending article from her case she would have. But with Vaughan firmly *in situ* Amelia decided to risk going without. Rearranging her rather ample décolletage, and squirting another quick layer of perfume, she braced herself to face him in the bedroom.

'Shall we go down?'

She started speaking before she even left the bathroom, deliberately not looking at him as she set about packing her small evening bag, throwing in a lipstick and her room card. But she burned with awareness. It was the first time they'd been in a bedroom alone together since that one steamy kiss, and she knew he was remembering it too—could feel his eyes on hers as she fiddled with her hair in the mirror, finally daring to meet them with the safety of her back to him.

'You look—' A beat of a pause, and she watched as he walked a step nearer, close enough for her to witness a tiny swallow, the bob of his Adam's apple in his throat before he continued, 'You look beautiful.'

She always did, Vaughan thought, but tonight, despite the make-up, the glittering earrings and skilfully blow-dried hair, for the first time since they'd met she looked like the woman who had woken him so rudely— the woman who had spun into his office and into his life.

Her eyes were huge in her tiny face, tendrils of hair wisped around her face, and Vaughan tried to place just what it was that was different, what it was that reminded him so much of something. And then he got it. The smart business suits she'd worn since then had gone. Instead she was wearing clothing of her choice, and the sheer lilac was close to the shade of the top she had worn that first day he'd met her. That overtly feminine body was more visible now, without the harsh darts of her tailored suits, without the anonymous safety of muted greys. Her pearly shoulders were on display, and a teasing glimpse of her spinal cord, and his fingers bunched into a fist, fighting the urge to reach out and touch her.

He could see the swell of her bust in the mirror, the teasing movement of her unhindered bosom. The ruched top strained an erotic fraction with the rise and fall of her breathing—and if he'd wanted her before it didn't compare. He was hollow with lust now, could feel with total recall those full rosebud lips on his, the weight of her bosom in his hand. And he couldn't not touch her. Could no more just offer his arm to casually escort her than fly to the moon.

'We should go down.' Amelia's voice was slightly breathless. Her back was still to him, her eyes wide with apprehension in the mirror as only his head moved, bowing slowly.

He felt the shiver of reaction ripple through her as his lips met her shoulder, and he took a tiny slice of time, a fraction of what he couldn't have, inhaling her scent as his mouth parted over her soft skin before pulling away.

A touch, a tiny kiss on her shoulder, that was all it had been—yet Amelia knew it shouldn't have happened. She was angry at him for not playing by the rules, felt as if she'd been branded with a curious, erotic, almost possessive gesture she couldn't interpret. As if he'd sunk in his teeth, as if he'd left a mark, she could feel where he'd been, but she knew there was nothing visible to show for his touch. And as they headed downstairs, as they stood apart in the lift, made their way over to the cocktail lounge, still she could feel the weight of his lips where they'd made contact, spinning her into confusion all over again.

She wasn't sure which was worse—fighting the sexual tension, constantly being on high alert, or the safety of being with Vaughan when he was on his best behaviour. Since their lunch date, it was as if a light had been switched. Vaughan was polite, sometimes friendly, but always distant, treating her as he hadn't from the start.

As the journalist she was.

Until tonight.

Tonight she could feel the rules being rewritten. She felt like a pawn in one of Vaughan's games, moving at his will, her eyes constantly drawn to the master, acutely aware of him by her side,

'These are the auction items.' Clearly delighted by Vaughan's presence, Sam made his way over. 'And that fabulous holiday you donated is the cream of the crop. I hope you'll be pushing up the prices unashamedly for us.'

Vaughan didn't even deign to respond, just shrugged his tense shoulders, taking two glasses of champagne and giving one to Amelia. His face broke into the widest of smiles as a couple waved cheerfully at him, and only the tiny roll of his eyes told her it was false. That almost conspiratorial gesture had her glowing, made her feel for a teasing glimpse as if she was on his side, as if they really were a couple.

'How's your piece going?' Vaughan attempted, fingering his collar, clearly wishing he was anywhere else but here.

'Good,' Amelia responded, glad at least something in her life was straightforward. Because sexual frustration had done wonders for her writing skills. Had given her permission to dwell on what she'd spurned. To legitimately focus on what she'd chosen not to have.

And because it was Vaughan her work was beautiful.

The intimate portrayal she'd been trying to achieve was coming to life beneath her fingers now. Somehow she was injecting his flashes of dry humour that softened the cruellest blows, capturing the enigmatic force of the man as he entered a room and intermingling it with the occasional glimpse of a different side—the active brain that kept him awake—divulging to her audience the softer side he usually chose not to reveal. And, despite what Paul said, Vaughan alone was quite simply enough to fill the pages. Amelia didn't need to name names, to foster attention, didn't need to add drama to a subject as enigmatic as he—there was no need for salacious gossip that wouldn't see the weekend out, and she'd take it to the line with her boss if she had to.

Watching him in action now, watching him working the room, glass in hand, haughty face occasionally softened with laugher, Amelia knew in a proud moment of realisation that she had made the right choice.

His beauty was timeless, and in turn so too would be her article.

If her career was on the line then that was okay—if her paper didn't want it then someone else surely would.

Vaughan had done nothing wrong—it wasn't his fault that she loved him.

'God, I hate these things,' he said, ages later, when Amelia had air-kissed more women than she could ever hope to remember and shaken hands with more ruddy-faced businessmen than she'd ever wanted to.

But Vaughan hadn't looked as if he'd hated it. On the contrary, he'd been a social wizard, listening intently to the most boring of conversations, laughing loudly at the most appalling jokes, yet he had still been true to himself, Amelia realized. On his best behaviour Vaughan might be, but not once had he come across as gushing.

'I wish they'd just bloody get on with the auction so I can call it a night.'

'It's for charity,' Amelia chided. 'As Sam keeps saying, think of the kids. I really think you should let me use this.'

'Don't—' Vaughan started, but there was no stopping Amelia now. Two cocktails and this amazing man at her side and Amelia was sure she could put the entire world to rights.

'It really is a good cause, Vaughan. And with the best will in the world one auction isn't going to deliver the equipment the ward needs. Surely a bit of publicity can only do you both some good?'

'Leave it, Amelia,' Vaughan warned, but the bit was between her teeth now and she refused to relent.

'No heart and flowers, I promise. But surely a mention is deserved. Sam reckons two lines in a newspaper could triple tonight's efforts.'

'You've been speaking to him?' One hand gripped her arm, the other wrapped firmly around his glass.

'Of course I've been speaking to him. These kids really need all the support you can give.'

'Just a couple of lines?' Vaughan checked. 'Maybe a brief description of the type of equipment they need?'

'Done!' Amelia responded, mentally pencilling it in—the perfect touch to the perfect article. But Vaughan's hand was still on her arm, his fingers still tight around her bare flesh. Wriggling free, she turned to him. 'Relax, for heaven's sake.'

'I am relaxed,' Vaughan hissed.

Sam was warming up the audience, reminding them all of the importance of the charity they were bidding for, while simultaneously urging them all to drink and be merry, clearly hoping a few cocktails might loosen their wallets. Beside her Vaughan stood stock-still, his body rigid with tension, a muscle pounding like a jackhammer in his cheek. Amelia just smiled wider.

'Oh, come on, Vaughan. If you hold that glass any tighter it will shatter. You're going to be fine up there. Anyway, it's for a good cause, remember?'

'You really think that I'm worked up about this?' Incredulous eyes swung to hers, his head moving down to Amelia's slightly, ensuring only she could hear his words. 'You really think that I'm worried about taking the stage?'

Bewildered, she shrugged. 'Vaughan, if you don't want me to put this in the article you only have to say—'

'Amelia.' His tone was savage, and his hand was back in place on her arm, pulling her around to face him. 'Have you any idea how you look tonight?' He gave a mirthless laugh. 'I'm sure you do. Is that why you didn't wear a bra?'

Startled eyes met his, and she gave a tiny gasp in her throat as she stepped back, attempting to duck the onslaught. She was completely unprepared, and there was nowhere to go. The spotlight was beaming its way towards them, the trickle of applause building as Sam invited Vaughan Mason to take the floor.

But Vaughan wasn't going anywhere in a hurry. His features were severe in the white heat of the spotlight, his voice a threatening caress, his eyes dragging over her décolletage. She felt as if she were naked, her nipples sticking like thistles in her dress. So acute was his stare that she could almost feel the cool of his lips suckling them, feel the inappropriate stir of her own arousal as the room looked on—and surely they must know, surely they must see the pulse leaping between her legs, the twitching contractions of early arousal? If ever she had hated him it was at that moment, her angry, lust-loaded eyes glaring back at him, as she willed it to be over.

'Don't play with me, Amelia. Don't try and play games with the big boys, because as you know they don't always follow the rules.'

And he couldn't have cheapened her more, couldn't have made her feel more like a whore—as if she'd dressed deliberately provocatively to entice him, as if he hadn't come pounding on the door when she should have been getting ready. Worst of all, she had no choice but to take it, no choice but to force a smile as he took the microphone and with effortless ease worked the room, his clipped tones such a contrast to Sam's needy ones.

Yet it had the desired effect. Serious bidding was taking place, and she watched, burning with indignation yet dripping with lust, as bidding moved ever higher, as once again Vaughan succeeded where others would surely have failed.

Well, he wouldn't succeed with her.

The microphone was barely back in its stand, the small talk only just starting up again, as Amelia headed for the door, punching in the lift number, aching to get to her room, to scream into a pillow. But Vaughan was behind her, calling her back.

'It isn't finished yet.'

'Oh, but it is, Vaughan—for me, at least. You're so cocksure, so bloody arrogant, so certain all any woman wants is to sleep with you…' Her cheeks burnt with anger, but her lips were pale, so taut she could barely get the words out without hissing. 'I was right about you all along—you haven't changed a bit, you've just learnt to be more discreet.'

'What the hell are you going on about?'

'You think all you have to do is turn on the charm and I'll relent. You're so sure that everything is somehow engineered towards snaring the great Vaughan Mason! A woman doesn't wear a bra and you assume that it's for your benefit! My God, you really think the world revolves around you, don't you? Did it never enter your head that had you not needed help getting dressed then I might have had more time to get ready?'

'You've been flirting with me all night,' Vaughan insisted, but Amelia shook her head.

'*You* kissed *me*, Vaughan.' Her finger moved to the spot, the very spot, where his lips had scorched her flesh. 'You were the one who came uninvited into my room and stood and watched me getting ready. You were the one who kissed me. So don't you dare try and turn this onto me. Don't turn this around and make it so that it's me wanting you.'

She made to go, ready to run the last few steps back to her bedroom, painfully aware that another woman had had him today, had tasted him, adored him, determined not to relent. But his hand closed around her wrist like a vice, capturing her, swinging her around to face him in one fluid motion, confronting her with a fact they both knew to be true.

'But you do.'

His voice was thick with emotion, his hand looser now, and she could have left, could have walked away this very second. But instead she stood. 'You do,' he said for a second time, and she wished she had a solicitor present—someone to step in and call a halt to his line of questioning, to pull her out before she gave in, before she voiced a truth that could surely only sentence her. 'You've wanted me from the day you walked into my office. You've wanted me as much as I've wanted you. I know I've got a past, but...'

'Your past is a bit too recent for me to swallow!' Amelia retorted, and registered the tiny frown between his eyes. 'Who was she, Vaughan?' She choked the words out, hating herself for asking, but needing to know. 'Who was the woman who left your room this afternoon?'

She felt his hand tighten on her wrist, watched as he swallowed hard, a nervous dart in his eyes before finally they met hers.

'You have to trust me there...'

'Trust you!' An incredulous shrill laugh escaped her lips. 'Trust *you*?'

'Yes, me.' His voice was even, his eyes holding hers, imploring her. 'Trust me when I say that I cannot tell you now, Amelia, and believe me when I say that it's not what you're thinking.'

'I need to know who she is, Vaughan,' Amelia begged. 'You can't just ask me to trust you, to believe...'

'Because of what Taylor did?'

'Because I can't do this again, Vaughan.' She was sobbing now, consumed by her own arousal, terrified by her own weakness, knowing how close she was to relenting, to giving in, to backing him in the face of such appalling odds. 'I've been hurt before—believed someone when they said they'd mended their ways, that I was the only one...'

'But I have changed, Amelia,' he rasped. 'These past few months I've realised that I want more.'

'And what about this sudden change? What brought about this great epiphany?' Amelia asked furiously, but her anger was directed at herself, that she could even allow this discussion to continue, terrified of being dragged in a touch deeper, that she might believe his lies.

'A seven-year-old boy made me realise it was time to grow up!'

And something in his voice moved her. Something in the pain behind the hesitant words told her this was real.

'That's all I can tell you now, Amelia. All I can tell you without betraying a confidence I've sworn to keep.'

'It doesn't make sense...'

'It *can't* make sense while you're still a journalist contracted to do a piece on me,' Vaughan implored. 'I can't tell you any more than that.'

'And I can't just...'

He was kissing her cheeks, tiny butterfly kisses. His full lips soaked up her tears as they fell, and her words shuddered out of chattering lips.

'I can't...' Amelia gasped, her back against the wall, furious in denial. But she knew it was the flailing of a drowning woman. Skin on skin, his hands slid to her upper arms, and his lips mingled with tears as his words breezed past her cheeks, seared the tiny hairs in her ears, ripping apart her defences as he rasped his prosecution.

'You can.' One hand cupped her breast, the nub of his thumb grazing across her tender nipple. Her throat constricted, lust searing through her. 'You can.'

Yes!

She didn't say it, but her body was his affirmation, yielding towards him. As she dared to admit the truth mentally her mouth opened to speak—to say what, she didn't know. Beg a retraction, perhaps? Plead for mercy? But the tiny window of opportunity was open and he stormed right in, possessing her mouth with his, forcing her so hard against the hotel door she could feel the breath being squeezed out of her, mingling with his.

That first initial taste she'd craved like an addiction for days now was finally on her lips. Freeing her arms, she coiled them into his hair in a reflex action, fingers and nails burying into his thick jet-black hair. Pushing his full weight onto her, he confirmed her desire, catching her tongue with his, and if her own boldness surprised her, then Vaughan was already way ahead, his free hand slipping up the petticoat of her sequinned dress, moulding the soft flesh just above her stockings, capturing her groin for such a dizzy moment she could have come right there.

Shockingly unaware of their location, she let a tiny whimper of frustration escape as Vaughan's mouth paused. Somehow he opened the door. Wrapping her legs around his waist, he lifted her up and carried her inside to the bedroom. The soft mattress barely registered in her thoughts as he lowered her down onto the bed.

Allowing her not even a tiny second to acclimatize, he ripped the earth from beneath her, pushing up the sequinned hem of her dress, tearing at her panties, burying his face in her most intimate place. He danced her like a puppeteer, toying with the knot of tension deep inside her with each vivid stroke of his tongue. She could feel him everywhere, in her constricted throat, in her thighs, which convulsed as he stroked ever deeper, in her stomach, which contracted with the first twitches of her orgasm. A moan of pure lust and need ripped away from her as he leant back on his heels, leaving her moaning and twitching with unfulfilled desire—until she saw him.

Saw the sheer naked sex of him slowly undressing. She hated him for her exposure as she lay breathless on the bed, watching his teasing disrobing. Cufflinks that took for ever to remove, an impatient rip at the button she'd so nervously sewn, a pull at the tie that, if scissors had been handy, she'd have cut. She glimpsed the silver of his zipper, the beauty of his package as his boxers were lowered. His jutting arousal did it to her all over again. But need took over then, knees inside knees, his thighs deftly parting her thighs, the scratch of his legs against her skin, the delicious thrill of anticipation.

'This is what you want?'

Beyond the point of no return, still he gave her the option, still he offered her an out. But she didn't want it—couldn't even begin to fathom the consequences of saying no to such a basic need. Amelia just knew that she had to, wanted to, needed to see this through to its delicious end, board this rollercoaster ride of passion. Yes, it was terrifying, exhilarating and dangerous, and yet it was something she simply had to do.

Her thighs dragged him in as his impatient hands pushed her dress up around her waist. Cupping her buttocks with his hands, eyes closing, he stabbed an entrance, thrusting deep inside her warmth. And she revelled in the delicious friction of him gliding inside her, came alive in his arms, dancing to his tune with a beat of her own now. Ecstasy was a mere breath away, a rush of heat galloping along her spine, flooding her neck, and her whole body aligned as he spilled inside her, the needy gasp escaping hushed by the salty warmth of his shoulder in her mouth. She sucked the flesh beneath her lips, capturing his manhood deep within, holding him tight, capturing the final throes of his orgasm with the intensity of her own. As her grip on his shoulder softened, the sheer force of emotion that had catapulted her imploded within, tears that had always been there but never been shed springing forth as still he held her.

'No regrets?'

Minutes, perhaps hours, later, the room came into focus, and she touched her bruised heart, waited for the appalling sting of reality, for the fingers of regret to start creeping in. But Vaughan's navy eyes were still adoring her, his body next to hers. The most exhilarating, breathtaking ride of her life had come slowly to a halt, and all Amelia knew was that she didn't ever want to get off, wanted to keep going, over and over again.

'None.' Amelia smiled back at Vaughan. 'Except for the fact I didn't take my make-up off.' Shifting herself onto her back she smiled into the darkness. 'That's a mortal sin, by the way.'

'So is falling asleep fully clothed.' His hand was toying with her zip, parting the flimsy fabric that ran along the curve of her side and dragging it down in a move that could only be translated as provocative. Kissing the hollow of her waist, he took his time at the curve of her buttocks, wriggling the sheer fabric down around her ankles before focusing on her shoes. 'And falling asleep in your shoes, young lady, is positively indecent.'

She knew he was waiting for her to laugh, knew as he looked up that he was expecting a smile. She could see the tiny frown on his brow as he sensed her distraction. 'What's wrong, Amelia?'

'Nothing.' Rolling into a pillow, she stared at the curtain. 'Nothing,' she said again, hoping for more conviction this time. But Vaughan wasn't to be fooled, and the concern in his voice matched hers as he spoke into the darkness.

'You're not on the Pill, are you?'

'No.'

A hundred questions shrilled in her brain. How could they have been so stupid? for one. It was the twenty-first century, for heaven's sake. There were condoms by the bed, courtesy of the hotel. It was beyond stupid not to be careful, but nothing, *nothing* prepared her for the tension that filled the body beside her, the slow hiss of air as he breathed slowly out.

'We have to do something. You have to take something. You *cannot* get pregnant.'

'Vaughan?' Questioning eyes turned to his. She was angry enough with herself at her own stupidity, but Vaughan's reaction wasn't exactly helping matters.

'There's a pill—the seventy-two-hour pill,' Vaughan said urgently. 'I can ring down for a doctor. Now.'

'We've still got seventy-one hours left!' It wasn't a joke exactly, merely an attempt to defuse the situation. She was scarcely able to believe what she was witnessing now—Vaughan Mason, completely perturbed, hands raking through his hair, wrestling with demons of his own that Amelia couldn't cope with right now. 'Vaughan, we made a mistake—a stupid mistake...'

'You're telling me...'

And suddenly she was angry. Angry and humiliated. He was acting as if she had a shotgun wedged under the pillow, as if she'd forced the night's events upon them, had somehow planned all this. But, seeing his anguished face, sensing something deeper was happening here, Amelia realised now probably wasn't the time to point out that it took two to tango, that the mistake had been as much his as hers.

'You're overreacting—' she started, but that only inflamed him more.

'Amelia, you don't understand. Trust me on this— you just cannot be pregnant...'

'Oh, but I think I do understand.' The air-conditioning must be up too high, because suddenly she was shivering, the intimacy they had shared slipping away like sand through her fingers. 'Trust you?' She shook her head angrily. 'I'm getting a little bit tired of being asked to trust you, Vaughan. In fact I'm starting to think you're treating me as some sort of—'

'Amelia,' Vaughan broke in icily. 'You're not the only one being asked to trust here. Might I remind you that you're a journalist? That's the entire bloody reason we're together, after all. You could be sleeping with me just to get a better slant on your story for all I know…'

And it was just too close to the mark, just too appallingly reminiscent of the innuendoes that had tarnished her reputation six months ago. Levering herself off the bed, Amelia searched for her dress, pulled it over her trembling body with her back firmly to him, attempted dignity in the face of utter humiliation. 'I'm not pregnant, Vaughan, so you don't have to worry. My period is due tomorrow, which means the chances of me getting pregnant are slim. Does that make you happy? What just took place wasn't about making babies but about making love—at least it was for me.'

'Don't go.'

Her hand was on the door; her instinct was to leave. The vileness of his accusation, the horror in his voice at the possible consequences of their actions had sounded a church's worth of alarm bells for Amelia, but almost instantly he quelled them, reverting in a second back to the man she was starting to know. He followed her to the door and pulled her tense body beside him, working her taut shoulders as he buried his face in her hair and whispered a heartfelt apology in her ear, leading her back to the bed.

'I'm sorry, Amelia.' His voice was pure anguish. 'I'm overreacting. It's just…' His voice petered out, but Amelia wanted more, still reeling from the abrupt change in him.

'Just what, Vaughan?' Amelia asked. 'You're talking as if I set out to trap you, as if—'

'No.' Instantly he refuted her accusation and pulled her back down to lie beside him. 'I'm angry with myself, not you. Angry with myself that I didn't stop and think.'

'It's called emotion, Vaughan. People don't always stop and think before they act. As you've said, this is the bedroom, not the boardroom. You don't always go in prepared.' He nodded at her explanation, pulled her in just a little bit tighter, yet she sensed his distraction, could almost feel his mind whirring as they lay staring into the darkness.

'Have you sent your article?'

Frowning into his chest, she waited for him to elaborate, pulling away when he didn't and propping herself up on her elbow, staring down at him. 'What's that got to do with anything?'

'I just want to know, that's all.'

'No, it hasn't gone.' Her words whistled through tight lips. 'Vaughan, what am I missing here? Are you worried I'm going to say something? That what took place tonight might change what I write?'

'Of course not.' And like the wind he changed again—the pensive mood gone, the dynamic man back in her arms again. 'But if you do, remember to write just how damn good I am.'

She did all the right things—laughed at his joke, even got fully undressed again and climbed right in beside him, curving herself as he spooned in behind her, relishing the delicious feel of his hand cupping her stomach, the rhythmic rise and fall of his breathing. Yet still Amelia frowned into the darkness, still she didn't feel entirely comforted.

Something had happened a moment ago that she didn't understand. She had witnessed a side to him she truly couldn't fathom.

There was something big that Vaughan was holding back.

Chapter 7

'You can break the news of the motor deal.'

Blinking as she opened her eyes, Amelia attempted to focus. Sun streamed in through open curtains, accentuating the chaos of the rumpled bed, her shoes on the floor, her dress as crumpled as a dishrag. But it didn't matter a jot, because sitting on the bed beside her, immaculate in a sharp suit and smiling down at her, was the one thing that made waking up a sheer, indisputable pleasure.

'What happened to good morning?' Stretching like a cat, she caught the first delicious aroma of morning coffee, the absolute perfect touch to the perfect awakening. Scarcely able to fathom that not only had she made love to him, but also she didn't for a second regret it, she said, 'Is that for me?' Reaching over, she took a grateful sip, aware all the while of his eyes smiling down at her, not remotely self-conscious, feeling as beautiful as the eyes that adored her. 'How long have you been up?'

'An hour. I've been in the lounge suite, chatting to Mr Cheng.'

'Do you always put on a suit to talk on the phone?' Amelia teased, but of course Vaughan always had an answer.

'It was a video conference. I didn't think he'd appreciate the sight of me in my bathrobe.'

'More fool him, then.' Amelia smiled, her forehead puckering as she recalled the news she had woken to. 'I can break it?'

'Yep.' Vaughan smiled as the penny dropped. 'Write that you have it on reliable authority that the deal is going to be formally announced on Monday.'

'But—'

'No buts,' Vaughan interrupted. 'I've spoken to Mr Cheng and he's more than happy to let some details out before the announcement. We both agree we'd rather it came from someone we know.'

'Trust, even?'

'Yeah.' Vaughan smiled as if he'd just discovered the word. 'That too.'

'You don't need to do this,' Amelia said, her voice suddenly serious. 'I've already told Paul that I'm going with the original article. I'm more than happy to stand by my decision and weather the consequences.'

'Well, you don't have to.' Vaughan squeezed her thigh through the sheet. 'This way you both win. You get to write what you want, and Paul gets the first sniff at the story—which will buy you some time to properly make up your mind.'

'I really can have it all.' Her hand reached up to his face, capturing that delicious sculptured cheek in her palm, feeling the soft scratch of his chin. Gently she guided his face in towards hers, enjoying the feel of a more leisurely kiss this time. The urgency had gone but the passion was deeper now, the giddy, insatiable lust that had spun them into the bedroom replaced with something just as exhilarating—a cavernous journey of emotion patiently awaiting their exploration, the thrill of peeling back the layers together, the silent promise of all tomorrow might hold.

'I have to go.'

Grumbling as he pulled away, Amelia lay back on the pillow.

'Where?' Seeing the dart in his eyes, Amelia held her breath. A single word had spilled from her lips, and her question had been entirely innocent, but something in Vaughan's stance told her she'd hit a nerve. 'You don't have to answer that,' she said quickly, swallowing back the hurt. But Vaughan saw through her defences.

'I want to tell you, Amelia, believe me. But I can't just yet.'

'Because you don't trust me?'

'No,' Vaughan responded immediately. 'Because this particular secret is not mine to reveal. You're the one who's going to have to trust me—for a little while longer anyway. I need to sort a few things out today. I need to run something by…' He paused for a beat. 'I need to speak to someone who matters, Amelia, and I can't do it with you there. Can you try and understand?'

She gave a brave nod, completely none the wiser but determined to trust him.

'And you, young lady—' Vaughan smiled '—have to write your article. What time's it due in?'

'Two—I thought I'd nearly finished and could spend the morning shopping, but, given what you've just told me about the motor deal I'd better drink this coffee and get writing. Paul was very clear that he wouldn't give me an extension.'

'How about a drink at the bar around three, then?' Vaughan suggested. 'Like I said, I've got a few things that need taking care of, but I should be finished by then and I promise then we can talk. Really talk,' he added, with feeling.

'Vaughan...' He was making to go, but her hand pulled him back, capturing the arm of his suit, and as his questioning gaze tried to meet her eyes she stared instead at her fingers, shy at what she was about to say, yet knowing she had to. 'What you said last night about...' A tiny nervous swallow halted her words and Vaughan took that moment to move in.

'The morning-after pill?' Vaughan checked.

'If I don't get my period...'

'Amelia...' His voice was soft, the uptight man she had witnessed last night gone, seemingly a momentary lapse, as he took her hand and finally said the right thing. 'I was out of line last night. But please believe me when I say it was with good reason.' He glanced reluctantly at his watch. 'We'll talk this afternoon properly, but in the meantime, please, no doctors, no pills. Just hear what I have to say first.'

Even the clock ticking by at a rate of knots didn't darken the delicious day. Fashioning the piece Paul so desperately wanted was easy now, with Vaughan's consent. Yet she refused to let her feelings mar her objectivity, and she carefully outlined the potential pitfalls as well as celebrating the deal. The left side of her brain enjoyed the intellectual challenge as she rediscovered the passion that had initially brought her into journalism.

And maybe, just maybe, Vaughan was right. Why

couldn't she keep her feet in both camps? Why did concentrating on one mean that she had to give up the other?

Maybe she really could have it all.

There was no stress headache as she filled up her bath this Friday. No anxious pangs, no superstitious routines firmly in place. Just a reckless feeling of exhilaration as she e-mailed her article. Slipping into the bath, she had no desire for retrieval, no surge of anxiety about commas to add or exclamation marks she might have missed—her work was good and Amelia knew it. Knew that the hard slog was over, that finally she'd made it, and could just lie back in the soapy water and allow that nagging right side of her brain to finally let rip, to concentrate on the one thing in her life that right now demanded her sole attention—the man who very soon would be waiting for her downstairs.

Chapter 8

'Miss Jacobs?'

The smiling face was familiar, but Amelia took a moment to place it. Already onto her second glass of champagne, she had long since grown tired of staring expectantly towards the foyer, tired of the slightly curious stares of the hotel staff as she waited for Vaughan to join her, his empty glass on the table beside the bottle she'd ordered.

'Katy Vale!' Placing the face, Amelia gestured to the empty seat in front of her, but from the dismissive way she shook her head, clearly Vaughan's PA had other places she needed to be. 'What can I do for you?'

'I've got a message from Vaughan—something came up; he's not going to be able to meet you.'

Amelia waited for further explanation—the offer of an apology, even—but apparently Katy had said all she was going to. Already she was making to go, clearly satisfied that her message was delivered. But an hour and a half of sitting alone in the hotel bar nursing a lonely glass of champagne had Amelia's patience hanging by a thread.

'Did he say anything else?' Watching as the woman slowly turned, her eyes taking in the champagne bottle, the empty chair and glass, Amelia felt her cheeks darken. She cleared her throat to ensure her next sentence would be delivered in slightly less needy tones.

'Something came up.' Katy raised her palms to the ceiling. 'You know what Vaughan's like.'

Only she didn't.

The Vaughan who had sat on her bed this morning would no more have stood her up so coldly than fly to the moon—and yet, Amelia reminded herself, the Vaughan she'd glimpsed last night, the Vaughan she'd read about over the years, was more than capable of sending his PA to terminate things.

'Is there anything I can help you with?' Katy offered, her voice bordering on sympathetic as Amelia attempted a dignified shake of her head. 'Frankly, I'm surprised you're still here. I got the impression from Vaughan that your article was already in. Was there something you wanted to double check? I'm pretty well versed on everything...'

But Amelia wasn't listening. Her attention had been drawn to the foyer and, perhaps realising she'd lost her audience, Katy turned around too, following Amelia's gaze, watching in knowing silence as Vaughan entered the lobby.

As Amelia's world literally fell apart.

His hair for once was tousled, his tie loosened, white cotton shirtsleeves casually rolled up. But worse, far worse, was the fact he wasn't wearing his jacket. Instead it was draped around the shoulders of the beautiful woman Amelia had seen in the corridor yesterday. Her dark exotic features mocked Amelia a thousand times over, her tiny fragile body, her legs surely too thin to hold her up. But what did it matter when Vaughan was practically carrying her, one arm possessively draped around her shoulders, guiding her towards the lift?

Amelia's mind flailed for a reasonable explanation, begged, despite the blatant evidence, that perhaps she'd got it wrong. But as they reached the lift doors and Vaughan dragged his feminine parcel towards him, buried his face in her hair and held her tight, not even Amelia could attempt an excuse in the face of such overwhelming odds.

'Your article is in.' Katy's voice had a slightly bitchy ring, and eyes way too knowing for such a pretty face flashed in triumph or malice as Amelia slowly nodded. 'Then it would seem, Miss Jacobs, that your allotted time slot is over.'

A luxurious five-star hotel might have appeared the best place in the world to lick her wounds, but lying on the counterpane, too mentally and physically exhausted to climb into bed, Amelia stared at the screensaver on her computer, agonisingly aware of what was surely going on next door, but too raw, too ashamed and utterly too humiliated to interrupt—to barge her way in and demand an explanation when she already had one.

Her allocated time slot was over—Vaughan Mason had already moved on.

Why had she expected anything more? Vaughan had promised her precisely nothing, save a drink in the bar and a chance to talk.

What a fool to think she could have held him for

more than a moment. What reckless thoughts had possessed her to believe for a moment that she alone could be enough to tame him?

Reliable, dependable—boring, perhaps. Even her period came on time. The low heavy thud hit her, just as she'd told Vaughan it would, and the dull, aching feeling in the pit of her stomach was painfully familiar. She felt the sting of nausea as she dragged her tired body out of the bathroom in response to the knocking on the door, even managing a wan smile at the cheerful face of the housekeeper as she bustled into the room.

Amelia wandered into the corridor, agony etched on agony as she heard low murmurs behind Vaughan's closed door, and the green 'Do Not Disturb' sign he'd hung blurred through tear-filled eyes.

She'd rather die than let him see her tears, Amelia decided; would rather walk away a bitch than a loser.

An idea was forming in her mind, growing in momentum as she strode down the corridor, took the lift to the lobby and walked out into the balmy evening sun. Call it determination, or self-preservation perhaps, but she'd been here before, just six months ago, had stood weeping at a hotel door for the first and very last time, and there was no way she was going to go there again.

Ever.

Chapter 9

'Vaughan!'

As he opened the door she got her greeting in first, smiled an efficient smile at his scowling frown.

Prepared for the worst speech of her life.

'I'm sorry to disturb you.' She gestured to the sign on his door, prayed that the foundation she'd plastered on was really as good as it said in the adverts, that her burning cheeks and reddened nose weren't somehow peeping through. 'It's just that I need a quick word.'

'Amelia.' She could see his distraction, sense his obvious discomfort. He had one hand firmly on the door, careful not to allow it to open further, but even a mahogany door between them wasn't quite enough to drown out the unmistakable noise of a shower running in the background. 'I'm sorry about before. Did you get my message?' His voice was deliberately low, presumably so not to alert his companion to this annoying distraction, and at that moment Amelia hated him with a violence that shocked even herself. Loathed him for the degradation that suffused her.

She'd trusted him.

Trusted him with the most painful part of her life. And he'd chewed it up whole and spat it in her face, prostituted her with a pay-off—an article she hadn't, in the end, even particularly wanted.

For a small moment she was tempted to drag out the torture, to barge into his room and confront the woman she knew was in there, to force him to admit what Amelia already knew. But she couldn't bring herself to suffer the indignity of being proved right, to choke back tears as he humiliated her all over again.

If she were even to attempt a retreat with her dignity apparently intact, somehow she had to do this—somehow she had to look him in the eye and deliver the biggest lie of her life.

'This isn't a great time for me, Amelia. Something unexpected came up...' His voice was low and urgent, and again he briefly checked over his shoulder. 'Can we maybe catch up later?'

'Later is no good for me, Vaughan,' Amelia responded firmly, registering the dart of confusion in his eyes at her clipped, assured voice. 'The office just called. They need me to head back to Sydney—something big just came up.'

'And you have to go right now?'

'Right now,' Amelia confirmed, a brittle smile flashing on her face as Vaughan briefly eyed the bulging suitcase on the floor beside her before turning his gaze back to her. 'I just stopped by to say goodbye.'

'Then call me when you get back to your home—'

Vaughan started, and a frown formed between his eyes as Amelia shook her head.

'Look, Vaughan, like I said, something big just came up. I could be stuck in the office for hours. I might even have to go on assignment. So I've no idea when I'm going to get back.' Glancing down at her watch, she gave what she hoped was a convincing wince. 'I'd better rush if I'm going to get my flight.'

Vaughan's frown deepened as Amelia shook her head and somehow managed a kind but slightly patronising smile.

'Let's not go making promises we can't keep. Let's not pretend that last night was anything more than…' She allowed him a tiny pause, a brief moment to let it sink in, because it wouldn't be easy for a man like Vaughan to fathom that a woman was actually rejecting him, Amelia realised. Like Taylor, he was completely used to getting his own way—flashing a winning smile and instantly being forgiven. But, as much as Taylor's infidelity had hurt, Vaughan's abuse of her trust had cut her to the core, shredded every fibre of her faith; yet somehow from agony came strength; somehow the torture of his betrayal allowed her to draw on an inner reserve, to look him in the eye and lie outright.

'It was business, Vaughan.'

He shook his head in vehement denial, the colour draining out of his already ashen face. His face quilted with raw emotion and, forgetting the door he held, he instinctively reached out for her, grabbing her upper arm, shaking her, his eyes imploring her to take back what she had just said.

'That was never business. What we had last night was way more than that, and you know it, Amelia.' His voice was rising now. A housekeeper passing with her trolley looked over in concern, and Amelia watched as Vaughan struggled to hold it together, dropping her arm from his vice-like grip, swallowing down hard to rid his voice of coarse emotion. 'That wasn't just business.'

'No, Vaughan, you're right.' She gave a small shrug and, bending over, picked up her case. 'It was pleasurable too. Unlike yourself, I can actually manage to mix the two.'

'So that's it?' Bewildered, he shook his head, and Amelia knew she'd thrown him into confusion, could see the utter abhorrence in his eyes that a woman could so easily turn the tables on him. 'You were using me?'

'We were using each other, Vaughan,' Amelia explained, apparently patiently, though her heart was hammering in her chest, bile rising in her throat as she cheapened herself to his level. But not for a second did she reveal it, standing not very tall, but somehow proud as Vaughan received a small taste of the medicine that over the years he'd so regularly given out. 'I've got the story I wanted and you've got the press on your side—for now, at least.'

It gave her the first stab of pleasure she'd felt since seeing him in the foyer, a tiny hint of bitter joy in reprisal, and it stirred her on to twist the knife in its final turn.

'It's been *nice*, Vaughan.'

Offering her hand, she wondered if he'd take it, wondered if he'd recover his ego quickly enough to attempt the upper hand. But Vaughan was clearly struggling, raking his hand through his hair, his breath coming loud and harsh as he turned to the door that had slammed behind him. For a tiny instant Amelia actually felt sorry for him, watching this dignified, proud man rummaging in his pockets for the swipe card, then standing back as the housekeeper who had been hovering moved to let him in, then stepped back again as the door opened of its own accord.

'What's going on?'

Dark hair still wet from the shower spilled down over olive shoulders, and the face devoid of make-up was nothing short of exquisite. Somehow Amelia processed these facts. Somehow she managed to stand as gravity lost its pull. Those exotic eyes she had viewed from a distance in the foyer were even more beautiful close up, with flecks of gold in their feline depths as she slowly took in the scene, then looked up to Vaughan, demanding an explanation.

'Is there a problem?'

If this woman couldn't work it out for herself then Amelia wasn't going to enlighten her—which maybe went against the grain of sisterhood, but frankly, at that moment in time, Amelia didn't care.

'There's no problem, Liza.' Vaughan offered a reassuring smile. 'Amelia's just a journalist, sniffing around for a story.' Navy eyes that had once adored her stared at her now with disgust. 'Isn't that right?'

'But what does she want?' Liza demanded, wary eyes slanting more suspiciously now—only not at Vaughan, but directly at Amelia. 'Don't you lot have any respect for other people's privacy? There's a "Do Not Disturb" sign on the door—how dare you just intrude...?'

'It's okay, Liza.' His voice was supremely gentle as he guided her back inside—an utter contrast to the black look of hatred he was shooting at Amelia. 'It's nothing for you to worry about; nothing at all.'

Slamming the door in her face, he left her standing. And despite what he'd done, despite the pain he'd caused, somehow he'd still managed to win. Somehow he'd managed to turn the tables on her. His rejection, his outright abhorrence towards her, was such a far cry from anything she could have imagined. The pain in his eyes, the lack of dignity in his defeat…

In one fell swoop he'd soured her tiny taste of victory—and worst of all, Amelia realised as she stood there, shocked and reeling, had been the softness in his voice when he'd spoken to Liza. The protectiveness of his gestures had cut her to the core.

It was jealousy that was choking her as she gathered up her case and stumbled to the lift, jealousy seeping from every pore, every fibre in her body, as she hobbled like a wounded animal along the long, lonely corridor.

Vaughan Mason was a bare-faced liar, a cruel, vindictive bastard, and yet…

Punching the lift button, leaning back against the cool glass mirrors, finally she gave in to the tears that would surely choke her…

She wanted it to be her.

Wanted Vaughan to be wrapping his arms around her. Wanted Vaughan shooing away the world for her when it all got too close.

Vaughan Mason was the man she truly loved.

Chapter 10

'Sorry, there's absolutely nothing.' The ground stewardess tapped away at her computer one more time for luck. 'I'm afraid Friday night out of Melbourne is possibly the worst time to get a cancellation. There's nothing till the red-eye tomorrow at six a.m.'

'That's fine.' Amelia ran a tired hand through her hair. 'If you can book me on that, it would be great.'

Perhaps the stewardess had expected a wail of protest, a demand to see her supervisor, because when Amelia meekly accepted she offered her first smile. 'You can check your luggage in now, if you like.' As she snapped a label around Amelia's case, her smile moved to sympathetic. 'Do you want me to call the airport hotel? See if I can get you a room?'

Amelia shook her head. 'I'll just wait in the terminal.'

And she would. Because time seemed to have taken

on no meaning now. There was no point paying for a bed she surely wouldn't use, and—bizarrely—she didn't want today to be over. Didn't want to close her eyes on a day that had started so perfectly and ended in disaster. Didn't want to go to sleep tonight because that would mean she'd have to wake up tomorrow, wake up and move on to the next phase of her life. And right now she wasn't ready to face her grief alone.

But sitting at a café, drinking coffee after coffee, listening to the piped music, Amelia decided that Melbourne Airport was perhaps the loneliest place she'd ever been.

Hordes of people milled around, with trolleys clipping ankles, children dodging parents, reunited couples embracing, tearful lovers parting, and she watched it all. Occasionally she headed outside to stand in the warm night air, staring at the illuminated glass tunnel that led towards the terminals, remembering walking along it with Vaughan at the start of their adventure, remembering how good her life had been the last time she'd been there—the broad set of his shoulders as she'd clipped along behind, laughing at some throwaway comment Vaughan had made. She was scarcely able to comprehend that it had been just a few short days he had been in her world; that a man she had known for such a short space of time could be etched on her heart for ever.

Thought she had known, Amelia corrected, shaking her head as an anxious flyer attempted to cadge a light for his final cigarette before boarding.

Her pensive mood shifted slightly then, the inner reserve that had seen her through her degree, helped her forge her way in the cut-throat world of journalism, revealing just a tiny glimpse of the silver lining around the blackest cloud to enter her life.

She'd be okay. Amelia knew that deep down—knew that she deserved better than Vaughan Mason was prepared to give. She'd been right in what she'd said to Vaughan at the restaurant—she wanted it all, and she wouldn't settle for less.

The bundles of early editions outside the closed newsagent's had Amelia stopping in her tracks, and it would have taken a will of iron to move on and not take one. This was her work, after all. It was her name beside the headline.

What Price a Heart?

Frowning, Amelia glanced up at the newsagent, shutters firmly down, but that was the least of her problems. The headline didn't make sense. Okay, she hadn't sat typing wearing the rose-coloured glasses of first love, but she certainly hadn't portrayed Vaughan as ruthless.

Nothing in her article had portrayed him as heartless.

She could see the curious looks of a cleaner as, intending to pay in the morning, she ripped open the plastic bundle and pulled out a newspaper, intending to take it over to a table and sit down and read.

She didn't even make it one step.

The fragile beauty of Liza was captured in a photo as she unfolded the paper. Vaughan's arm was protectively around her, just as she had witnessed back at the hotel, but the caption beneath screamed words she had never even thought of, shaming her to the very core as somehow she read on.

Mason comforts his sister-in-law Liza.

Horrified, her eyes widened as she read the article, trying to drag in a lungful of air as her breathing came shallow and fast, her pulse pounded rapidly in her temples. Though Amelia had never had a panic attack this was as close to one as she ever wanted to come—she was drenched, literally drenched in revulsion as she read tomorrow's news, and the only thing that stopped her from collapsing, stopped her knees literally buckling beneath her, was the knowledge that she had to forewarn Vaughan—somehow tell him how appallingly he'd been treated, try and get him to understand that even though her name was on the article she'd played no part in this.

She just made it to the washroom in time.

She retched over and over at the mere thought of the damage that had been done. Everything made sense now, but she knew—*knew*—that never in a million years would Vaughan understand that she hadn't wittingly played a part in this.

The taxi ride was hell. Every light to the city was red as the yellow cab bumped through the empty streets. The taxi driver, oblivious to her despair, attempted idle chit-chat, but she couldn't even feign politeness, just stared out of the window as the city closed in. The beauty of Collins Street in the early hours of morning had zero impact, the fairy lights adorning the trees that lined the streets, the impressive entrance to the hotel barely registered in her mind—just the knowledge that in a few short minutes she had to face him.

Only as she reached his door did it strike her that he mightn't even be there, or, worse still, that perhaps Liza might be with him. The thought of facing her, of facing them both together, of watching their reaction as they read the paper she held in her trembling hands assassinated Amelia as she summoned the courage to knock on the door.

'What the hell—' Dressed in dark boxers, his hair tousled from sleep, his eyes squinting to focus, never had he looked more desirable—or more completely unreachable.

'I need to talk to you,' Amelia choked, but Vaughan was already closing the door.

'Well, I don't want to listen.' Dismissing her, Vaughan shook his head, but as she held up the paper the closing door stilled, his eyes catching the headline just as Amelia's had.

He ripped the paper from her and headed inside, leaving her to walk in uninvited and watch as he sat on the edge of the bed, shoulders slumping as he read on. She let him do it in silence, knew that the time for excuses could only come when Vaughan was fully armed with the facts.

'Bitch.' He whistled the word out through taut pale lips, his eyes damning her to hell as he hit her with the full weight of his blistering stare. And even though it was agony to receive it, Amelia knew that from where Vaughan sat she deserved every last crumb of his contempt.

'I didn't know.' Her voice was a pale whisper, her teeth chattering so violently she could barely get the words out.

'That's not what it says here.' His voice was like ice. 'In fact,' he sneered, 'it says in black and white "What Price a Heart", by Carter Jenkins and Amelia Jacobs.'

'I didn't know about your nephew.' Tears were coursing down her cheeks but she didn't even notice, didn't even attempt to wipe them away. 'I didn't know anything, Vaughan, I swear.'

'Bull!' he cracked. 'You're asking me to believe that you had no idea the paper was planning this?'

'No!' She screamed her denial. 'I knew they had a story but I had no idea they were planning this! Vaughan, I thought Liza was your girlfriend. I was so jealous when I saw you with her that I decided to beat you to it—decided to pretend that our night had all just been about business. I didn't know your nephew had cystic fibrosis. God, I didn't even know you had a nephew, let alone that he was waiting for a heart-lung transplant...'

'Everybody knows now.' The despair in his eyes, the chasm of his pain, was palpable. 'They're insinuating that I'm trying to *buy* him treatment.' His voice was a raw whisper, but it did nothing to veil the hatred behind it. 'They're insinuating that I'm waving money so that he can jump the queue!'

'They're not going to deny him care on the strength of this,' Amelia begged, but Vaughan just shook his head.

'They're going to have to dot every "i" and cross every "t" now—to ensure they're seen to do the right thing—instead of going with their gut instinct. And that is that he needs it—soon. That's why Liza was here, Amelia, to tell me that Jamie's nearing the end, that without a transplant he's going to die...'

And far worse than his rage and anger was watching this proud, commanding man literally crumple before her, head in hands, every muscle in his shoulders strung with tension, fists balling into his temples as he processed the full horror of what he had just learnt.

His animosity was gone as he spoke on, but Amelia wasn't blind enough to believe it was over. He was merely voicing his fears. The fact that she was there was almost immaterial now.

'I've bent over backwards to ensure this didn't get out—knew that if the papers got hold of it somehow they'd twist it.' He gave a low, mirthless laugh. 'And the saddest part of it all is that I couldn't buy him a heart and lungs if I tried. Believe me, I've wanted to—I'd lose it all without even a hint of regret if I could give Jamie this chance. But even all my money, all my power, counts for nothing against the doctors. They deal with it every day, make choices no one else can, and not for a moment does money come into it. You didn't write that did you?' His anger was coming back now, disgust sneering on his face as he looked up to her. 'Just layered innuendo on innuendo, half truths combined with fact.'

'That wasn't me.'

'Well, that's not what it says here, Amelia.' Punching the paper away with his hand, he hurled it across the room, his naked anger confronting her. 'I quote: "handing a white envelope over to one of the hospital's directors in a secluded Melbourne restaurant…" It was a prize, for God's sake. A holiday prize I didn't even want my name put to, Amelia. You've made it sound like a bribe.'

'Carter was there…' Amelia gulped. Things were making more sense with hindsight.

'You saw him?'

Amelia nodded, her eyes riddled with guilt by association, and knew that she was going down for the third time—knew that nothing she could say would convince him she hadn't known what the paper was planning.

Knew that she'd lost him.

Vaughan was right. The article had her name on it. Fact and innuendo was a dangerous blend indeed, and

Paul had been careful, because from Amelia's one look through the newspaper there wasn't a single lie. Her carefully crafted words were interlaced with Carter's insinuations. Overtones of corruption sounded in every paragraph, paling everything else into insignificance. Even the motor deal announcement barely merited a mention.

If ever she'd been ashamed of her profession it was then.

'I trusted you.' She noticed the past tense of his words and it lacerated her. 'I even thought I loved you, Amelia. I went to the hospital today to speak to Liza, to ask her if I could tell you about Jamie. To tell her that I'd met this amazing woman who just happened to be a journalist, that for once I was sure I'd got it right. What a fool!'

Ignoring his last line, Amelia probed gently, filled with regret for all she had done, the love she had thrown away, but needing to hear how close she had come to realising her dream. 'What did she say?'

'I didn't get to tell her.' Vaughan's face hardened, yet she could see the pain behind it, see his knuckles whitening as he clenched his fists together in an effort to hold things back. 'Jamie's condition had deteriorated overnight—nothing definable, of course, nothing the doctors can put their fingers on or qualify to the press as reasons for moving him to the top of the transplant list. So I doubt it will happen now.' He stared at her paling face, rammed in the knife just a touch further, shaming her all over again. 'I brought Liza back here for a break, so she could have a shower and bawl her eyes out away from her son, to give her a chance to admit her terror. It didn't seem the right time to talk about my love-life.'

His head was in his hands again, and he was speaking more to himself than to her. 'Or appalling lack of it.'

'I'll go.'

Her voice was a mere croak and Vaughan looked up briefly, pulling his head out of his hands just long enough to loathe her.

'Why not? After all, you got what you came for.'

Chapter 11

It felt as if she were coming home after a funeral, mourning the loss of what she'd so recently had. And her apartment seemed steeped in a life that was divided into two—before and after Vaughan.

Before, when things like bath oils had mattered, when horoscopes had held promises, when she'd thought she had it tough, had been so naïve as to think that Taylor's infidelity was as low as life went.

How naïve, how pathetically naïve to think then that she had known pain. The loss she had felt at the end of her relationship with Taylor didn't even compare to the raw grief that held her in its vice-like grip now.

The waxy pink petals of the orchids Vaughan had sent her were the first thing to catch her eye, and she couldn't help but realise that they had lasted longer than them, and there wasn't a single thing she could do.

'I guess I just fell in love,' Amelia whispered,

scarcely able to comprehend that something so beautiful could hurt so much.

And was it worth the pain?

She could almost hear Vaughan asking the question and remembered that first night at the hotel, standing on tired, aching feet at the threshold of the love affair of a lifetime, thought of her bruised, raw, shredded heart. Without hesitation she nodded into the lonely room.

'Absolutely.'

She knew he'd never forgive her, knew her time with Vaughan was over, yet she ached to put things right, to somehow repair some of the damage she'd unwittingly inflicted. But at every turn she was thwarted. Her angry demands for a retraction were met with an incredulous laugh from Paul, who was completely unable to comprehend why she wasn't wallowing in the glory of it all.

Hours dragged into days, her anger giving way to lethargy, and it was a supreme effort just to lever herself off the couch to answer the door. Flowers were being delivered, even a bottle of champagne, and her telephone was constantly ringing with messages of congratulations. Even her father, for the first time, was proud of his daughter's work.

But the one person she wanted to see, the one person she wanted to hear from, kept a dignified silence.

No outburst of temper on the six o'clock news, just the stern fix of his jaw as he left the hospital with his sister-in-law and nephew to wait for a call that might now come too late. The navy eyes were hidden behind dark glasses, yet nothing could shield from Amelia the depth of his despair, the pain behind the 'no comments', the agony of her apparent betrayal.

And Amelia was as guilty as the rest of the general

public—greedy for insight, surfing news bulletins, listening avidly as reporters explained the disease that afflicted his nephew, that Vaughan Mason himself might carry the gene. She learnt that even in his apparent anger, his seeming withdrawal after their lovemaking, Vaughan had been concerned for *her*—had somehow been trying to protect her.

He *had* loved her. With torturous hindsight she knew that now—knew that in his own unique, special way Vaughan Mason had truly adored her.

The loud ringing of her doorbell only made Amelia jump. The prospect of another visitor did nothing to raise her spirits, and she didn't want another bouquet or congratulations she didn't deserve. And anyway her apartment already looked like a funeral parlor—felt like a funeral parlor.

Amelia didn't want to see anyone.

Unless it was Vaughan, standing grey and washed-out in her doorway, looking as awful as she felt, yet the most beautiful thing she could ever hope to see.

'You look awful.' Perhaps not the most romantic of greetings, but it was all her quivering lips could manage. She braced herself for the crash landing of his temper, another hit to her bruised and battered heart.

'Turbulence.'

She blinked as he managed a wan smile, still scarcely able to believe he was here, unable to comprehend that he didn't appear angry. Surely after the hell he'd been through these past days he should be raging? But instead he was talking almost normally—completely unable to meet her eyes, of course, but fairly normally all the same.

'Bloody turbulence all the way from Melbourne.'

'Turbulence?'

'Did I forget to tell you that I'm terrified of flying?' He didn't even soften it with a dry smile, and Amelia closed her eyes in another second of regret. The ritual trip to the newsagent made sense now, and the white-knuckled silence in helicopters. She was glimpsing again the softer side of the wonderful man that she could have had.

'How's Jamie?' Still holding the door for support, Amelia asked one of the many questions that had been plaguing her. 'How's he dealing with all the publicity? And Liza…?'

'They're fine,' Vaughan said slowly. 'They're dealing with it. In fact it's almost a relief that it's out in the open now. Almost,' he added, and Amelia knew it still must hurt.

But suddenly the conversation shifted, suddenly they were talking about them—or at least Vaughan was.

'Amelia, I don't care.' Dragging her into his arms, he held her fiercely, breathing in the scent of her hair, holding her as if for support, and all she could do was hold him back, words strangling in her throat as he loved her for all the wrong reasons. 'I don't care just as long as we can move on—I can see why you did it, why you had to go for the story. It's your job, Amelia,'

'You don't understand…'

'No, but I'm trying to.'

Pulling his head back, he held her cheeks, kissed her parted lips, drinking from them as if they were the life force he needed, as if her kiss, her embrace, was the one thing that could make him go on. But she pulled back, his touch desperately wanted but the truth needed more.

'Vaughan, I need you to see something.' Letting him go even for a second was a feat in itself, but somehow she managed, somehow she made it to her desk. She rummaged through the appalling mess and for the second time in their short relationship held her breath as he read a piece of work with her name upon it—only this time it was the truth. Each word was laced with the esteem in which she held him, each carefully crafted sentence a pure deliverance of the truth.

'This is what I filed, Vaughan. This is the piece I wrote.'

'I guess I should have had more faith.'

'Yes, Vaughan, you should.' Something in her voice made him look up. 'Vaughan, how you can say that you love me when you think I did that to you defies explanation. It wasn't me. It never was me. Apparently one of the other mothers in Jamie's ward tipped off the press— that's why Carter was following you; that's why they jumped so high at the chance of my spending a week with you. They thought they were on to a big story. This woman thought that her son was sicker than Jamie, that Jamie was somehow getting preferential treatment because of who his uncle was, so she—'

'Poor woman!'

His reaction confused her. She'd expected some of the venom he'd directed at her when he'd thought she'd betrayed him to somehow appear again. But not for the first time she marvelled at his insight, at the hidden depths behind this amazing man.

'When you're desperate you'll do anything. I'd probably have done the same.'

'I've tried to get the paper to print a retraction.' Amelia shrugged her shoulders helplessly. 'Perhaps if we both lean on Paul...'

'There's no need.' Vaughan shook his head. 'Jamie's still where he should be on the transplant list, despite the news coverage. Those doctors have stood firm. It takes more than a newspaper article to scare those guys, Amelia. They face death every day.' His eyes found hers. 'I'm sorry, Amelia, more sorry than you know for doubting you. I've just been so used to being let down, so used to being misquoted just to grab a headline. But when I thought it was you I lost my head for a while. I was so angry I couldn't think straight…'

'Touché,' Amelia blushed, thinking of her bitch-on-heels act at his hotel door.

'Yet even with the hell of these last few days, Amelia, all I could think about was you—the real you I was sure I'd seen. Despite the agony, despite the accusations, all I could think was that if I never got to see you again you were the only thing in this world I'd truly miss.'

'Apart from your family,' Amelia said softly. Though it was the one thing with Vaughan that didn't need saying. She had seen the love that lay burning behind the 'no comment'.

'Apart from my family,' Vaughan confirmed. 'I just wanted to protect Jamie. I didn't want the papers to get hold of it. I'd promised my brother and Liza I'd keep Jamie out of the public eye. But I knew if we were ever going to move forward then I'd have to tell you. When I heard you say that babies were firmly entrenched on your list…' The frown on his forehead deepened. 'I carry the gene, Amelia…'

'I'd already worked that out. That's why you overreacted when you found out I wasn't on the pill, wasn't it?' Amelia took his hand in hers. 'I should have known, Vaughan. It was beyond irresponsible…'

'I'm sorry.' He swallowed hard. 'I'm always careful—*always*,' he emphasized. 'I was more angry with myself than you—couldn't believe I'd let myself get so carried away. And after you said at lunch that nothing on your list was negligible I figured that was it—that there wasn't any point. I never thought it would go any further until…' The beginnings of a smile ghosted on his lips. 'You have a very good knack for making me lose my head, Amelia.'

'I know,' Amelia replied—because she did. She knew for the first time in her life the reckless abandonment that came hand in hand with love.

'If you carry the gene too…'

'Let's not worry about that now.'

'We have to. Because if you feel even a tenth of what I do then it's something we're going to have to face. Nothing on your list's negotiable, Amelia. You want the lot. And if I can't give you everything…'

'It's the top of the list that matters most…' His eyes were holding hers, days of pain slowly drifting away as she spoke from the bottom of her heart. 'Safety,' she said softly. 'The safety of always being loved, knowing that no matter what I do, no matter how bad it seems, I've always got you to lean on.'

'You do,' Vaughan said simply, kissing her on her waiting lips, affirming the desire that blazed in his eyes. 'So what happens now?' A smile inched over his face. 'Does this mean I'm finally ready to settle down?'

'No way,' Amelia answered, enjoying the tiny moment of confusion in his loving eyes. 'I have it from an extremely reliable source that you don't believe in settling down! I don't have my notes, of course, so you'll forgive me if I misquote…'

'I already did,' Vaughan drawled, raining tiny kisses on her face.

His hand toying with the hem of her skirt was making it terribly hard to concentrate.

'But I believe "hotting up" was your appalling choice

of phrase. In fact, I'm sure you said something about hardly being able to keep your hands off the very lucky woman.'

'No.' Vaughan grinned. 'I think you're taking it out of context.'

'I can always get my notes,' Amelia gasped, as the hand that had been toying grew rather more insistent.

Making to stand up, she heard his moan of frustration as he pulled her back down.

'Damned journalists,' Vaughan whispered in her ear. 'Well, I suppose if you've got it in writing then I'm just going to have to stand by it. I guess I'm going to have to spend the rest of my life living up to my lousy, oversexed, completely insatiable reputation.'

'Yes,' Amelia gasped again. A witty response was on the tip of her tongue, but so too was Vaughan, and coherence flew out of the window. 'Yes, please.'

Epilogue

Safe.

Peering out of the window as Vaughan's car pulled into the driveway, as he climbed out and retrieved his computer and briefcase, she knew that this time there was no sliver of detriment behind the word, no question of settling for second best as there had been when she had first voiced it.

He made her feel safe.

Safe enough to shoot for the stars, safe enough to go too far, safe enough to be herself, knowing he was always beside her, was always there, proudly ready to catch her if ever she fell.

'Hey!' That delicious smile greeted her, but his eyes didn't hold hers, searching instead for the baby she held in her arms—his reward to come home to after a long day in the office. And she watched her resident tycoon, supposed playboy, scoop the precious bundle into strong arms, shower a giggling gummy face with kisses, before planting a slower more deliberate one on Amelia. 'God, I've missed you two.'

And she knew that he had.

Knew with complete conviction that wherever his work took him, whoever he met along the way, his heart was always with his family.

'How's Rory been?'

'Grizzly,' Amelia replied, rolling her eyes. She put her son down, his fat legs circling the air, and he gave out tiny unprovoked giggles, looking anything but.

'His mother too?' Vaughan grinned and Amelia pursed her lips, knowing what was coming next and deciding to get in first.

'I'm not bored,' Amelia insisted. 'I love being a stay-at-home mum.'

'He's got teeth, Amelia,' Vaughan pointed out. 'And if I remember rightly that was about the time Maria decided to come back to work and put you out of a job.'

'She didn't put me out of a job,' Amelia retorted. 'I'd already handed in my notice. After the way they treated you it was the last place I wanted to be.'

'But you miss it, though,' Vaughan said perceptively. 'Miss using that crazy brain of yours.'

'I like being with Rory.'

'Of course you do, and that's the beauty of your work—you can do it from home, set the world alight right here from our lounge.' He watched two spots of colour burn on her cheeks and completely misconstrued them. 'Amelia, you can write the pieces you really want to now. It's not as if we need the money. If nobody buys them it won't matter a scrap.'

'It will matter to me.' She watched as his eyes narrowed, flushed some more under his scrutiny.

'I don't need to persuade you to work again, do I?'

Amelia shook her head, pulling a few rather well-thumbed pieces of paper from under a sofa cushion and nibbling on the skin around her thumb as Vaughan read through them.

'This is great, Amelia.' Hearing the admiration in his voice, Amelia remembered to breathe, knowing Vaughan's appraisal would be honest. 'Why didn't you tell me you were interviewing Mr Hassan?'

'I wanted to be sure I could still do it,' Amelia admitted honestly. 'I wanted to be sure I could do his work justice.'

'And you have,' Vaughan said simply, and she could hear the emotion in his voice, see the flash of what could possibly be tears in those navy eyes. 'I know sometimes I get a bit pumped up with my own self-importance, but what that guy does for a living—well, it kind of puts things into perspective...'

His voice trailed off and Amelia knew he was struggling, knew he was recalling the agonising days before, during and after Jamie's transplant—the miracle they had all been granted under the skilful hands of Mr Hassan.

'It's brilliant—your article's perfect. This is going to really help awareness. The only trouble is now you're going to have to top it. You're going to have to think of something just as interesting to write about...' A knowing smile inched across his lips as Amelia for once remained silent, those two spots of colour spreading across her face and down her neck.

'Amelia? Are you going to tell me what you're up to?'

Back under the sofa cushion, she pulled out some more papers—only this time photos were attached, dark almond eyes were staring back at him, and she watched his curious frown, his mouth opening to speak and closing again.

Amelia tentatively tried to explain. Tried to explain to this wonderful, difficult man how she was feeling, tried to capture with halting words that the more love she received the more she had to give, that love really was the cup that runneth over.

'You remember when I stalled on taking the blood test? Remember how terrified I was that I might carry the gene as well?'

'Of course,' Vaughan said warily.

'And you remember how we decided that if we weren't going to have children then we'd consider overseas adoption, and you got all the information, showed me how many children there were in need of loving parents?'

'Mmm.'

'Well, I was thinking of doing a piece on that— thinking of following a couple on their journey.'

'Good idea!' Vaughan grinned, relief evident on his face. 'So who did you have in mind?'

His relief was short-lived, his eyes widening when Amelia didn't answer, just stared at the photo he was holding in his hands—a two-year-old boy who, according to the bio, quite simply couldn't be placed. Newborn babes were the order of the day for most young couples. Two-year-olds with attitude were far harder to find a home for.

'If we'd ended up adopting we'd have loved him.' Amelia swallowed hard. 'We'd have loved him just as much as we love Rory. He wouldn't have been second best.'

'No.' Vaughan raked a hand through his hair. 'But, Amelia, he might already have a family by now.'

'And he might not.'

For the longest time he was silent, staring at the photo for an age before turning to her. 'Are you unhappy, Amelia? Is there…?'

'I've never been more happy, Vaughan. Never been more fulfilled. Over and over I pinch myself—can't believe how lucky I am, how lucky we all are to have found each other.'

She knew he was listening, but his eyes had left hers now, were staring instead at the sad, bewildered eyes in the picture he held. A soft smile formed on his lips. 'He is kind of cute,' Vaughan said very slowly, very cautiously, and Amelia knew she had to hold back a touch, couldn't let her mounting excitement sway him for even a moment. This decision was way too important to be rushed into. It was a child they were talking about, not some crazy impulse buy they could take back and exchange if things didn't work out.

But already she loved him.

And from the look in Vaughan's eyes, the way his thumb was stroking the pale cheeks on the photo, he was starting to feel that way too.

'I'm supposed to be a bastard.' Putting down the papers, he dragged her into his arms and she went unrelenting. 'I'm supposed to be a complete cad, making a mere token effort to settle down.'

'I know.' Amelia smiled, closing her eyes in bliss as he held her ever closer to his chest. 'I read all about it last week.'

'You know,' Vaughan whispered, pulling her in, safe in the warm glow of love, 'this is going to completely ruin my reputation.'

* * * * *

We hope you enjoyed reading

THE BRIDE

by *New York Times* bestselling author

MAYA BANKS and

IN THE RICH MAN'S WORLD

by reader-favorite author

Carol Marinelli

For more glamorous, passionate romances look for
the Harlequin Presents series!

Experience glamorous settings, powerful men and
passionate romances with Harlequin Presents®!

Look for eight new romances every month from
Harlequin Presents!

Available wherever books are sold.

Find us at

www.Harlequin.com

NYTHP1213

SPECIAL EXCERPT FROM

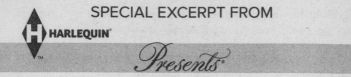
HARLEQUIN®

Presents®

Read on for an exclusive extract from
THE DIMITRAKOS PROPOSITION, the sensational
new story from Lynne Graham!

* * *

TABBY looked up at him and froze, literally not daring to breathe. That close his eyes were no longer dark but a downright amazing and glorious swirl of honey, gold and caramel tones, enhanced by the spiky black lashes she envied.

His fingers were feathering over hers with a gentleness she had not expected from so big and powerful a man, and little tremors of response were filtering through her, undermining her self-control. She knew she wanted those expert hands on her body, exploring much more secret places, and color rose in her cheeks, because she also knew she was out of her depth and drowning. In an abrupt movement, she wrenched her hands free and turned away, momentarily shutting her eyes in a gesture of angry self-loathing.

"Try on the rest of the clothes," Acheron instructed coolly, not a flicker of lingering awareness in his dark deep voice.

Tension seethed through Acheron. What the hell was the matter with him? He had been on the edge of crushing that soft, luscious mouth beneath his, close to wrecking the non-sexual relationship he envisaged between them. Impersonal would work the best and it shouldn't be that difficult, he reasoned impatiently, for they had nothing in common. She cleaned up incredibly well, he acknowledged grudgingly, gritting his teeth together as his gaze instinctively dropped to the sweet pouting swell of her small breasts beneath the clingy top.

He had done what he had to do, he reminded himself grimly. She was perfect for his purposes, for she had as much riding on the success of their arrangement as he had. Thankfully nothing in his life was going to change in the slightest: he had found the perfect wife, a nonwife….

Two hours later, Acheron opened the safe in his bedroom wall to remove a ring case he hadn't touched in years. The fabled emerald, which had reputedly once adorned a maharajah's crown, had belonged to his late mother and would do duty as an engagement ring. The very thought of putting the priceless jewel on Tabby's finger chilled Acheron's anticommitment gene to the marrow, and he squared his broad shoulders, grateful that the engagement and the marriage that would follow would be 100 percent fake.

* * *

Will sharp-tongued, independent firestorm Tabby Glover accept Greek billionaire Acheron Dimitrakos's outrageous marriage proposal?

Find out in January 2014!

HARLEQUIN® Presents®

Save $1.00 on the purchase of

THE DIMITRAKOS PROPOSITION

by Lynne Graham

available December 17, 2013,
or on any other Harlequin® Presents® book.

Available wherever books are sold, including most bookstores,
supermarkets, drugstores and discount stores.

Save $1.00

on the purchase of
THE DIMITRAKOS PROPOSITION
by Lynne Graham
available December 17, 2013,
or on any other Harlequin® Presents® book.

Coupon valid until February 19, 2014. Redeemable at participating retail outlets
in the U.S. and Canada only. Limit one coupon per customer.

52611201

Canadian Retailers: Harlequin Enterprises Limited will pay the face value of this coupon plus 10.25¢ if submitted by customer for this product only. Any other use constitutes fraud. Coupon is nonassignable. Void if taxed, prohibited or restricted by law. Consumer must pay any government taxes. Void if copied. Nielsen Clearing House ("NCH") customers submit coupons and proof of sales to Harlequin Enterprises Limited, P.O. Box 3000, Saint John, NB E2L 4L3, Canada. Non-NCH retailer—for reimbursement submit coupons and proof of sales directly to Harlequin Enterprises Limited, Retail Marketing Department, 225 Duncan Mill Rd., Don Mills, ON M3B 3K9, Canada.

U.S. Retailers: Harlequin Enterprises Limited will pay the face value of this coupon plus 8¢ if submitted by customer for this product only. Any other use constitutes fraud. Coupon is nonassignable. Void if taxed, prohibited or restricted by law. Consumer must pay any government taxes. Void if copied. For reimbursement submit coupons and proof of sales directly to Harlequin Enterprises Limited, P.O. Box 880478, El Paso, TX 88588-0478, U.S.A. Cash value 1/100 cents.

5 65373 00076 2   (8100)0 11890

® and TM are trademarks owned and used by the trademark owner and/or its licensee.
© 2013 Harlequin Enterprises Limited

REQUEST YOUR FREE BOOKS!

2 FREE NOVELS
FROM THE ROMANCE COLLECTION
PLUS 2 FREE GIFTS!

YES! Please send me 2 FREE novels from the Romance Collection and my 2 FREE gifts (gifts are worth about $10). After receiving them, if I don't wish to receive any more books, I can return the shipping statement marked "cancel." If I don't cancel, I will receive 4 brand-new novels every month and be billed just $6.24 per book in the U.S. or $6.74 per book in Canada. That's a savings of at least 22% off the cover price. It's quite a bargain! Shipping and handling is just 50¢ per book in the U.S. and 75¢ per book in Canada.* I understand that accepting the 2 free books and gifts places me under no obligation to buy anything. I can always return a shipment and cancel at any time. Even if I never buy another book, the two free books and gifts are mine to keep forever.

194/394 MDN F4XY

Name	(PLEASE PRINT)

Address	Apt. #

City	State/Prov.	Zip/Postal Code

Signature (if under 18, a parent or guardian must sign)

Mail to the Harlequin® Reader Service:
IN U.S.A.: P.O. Box 1867, Buffalo, NY 14240-1867
IN CANADA: P.O. Box 609, Fort Erie, Ontario L2A 5X3

Want to try two free books from another line?
Call 1-800-873-8635 or visit www.ReaderService.com.

* Terms and prices subject to change without notice. Prices do not include applicable taxes. Sales tax applicable in N.Y. Canadian residents will be charged applicable taxes. Offer not valid in Quebec. This offer is limited to one order per household. Not valid for current subscribers to the Romance Collection or the Romance/Suspense Collection. All orders subject to credit approval. Credit or debit balances in a customer's account(s) may be offset by any other outstanding balance owed by or to the customer. Please allow 4 to 6 weeks for delivery. Offer available while quantities last.

Your Privacy—The Harlequin® Reader Service is committed to protecting your privacy. Our Privacy Policy is available online at www.ReaderService.com or upon request from the Harlequin Reader Service.

We make a portion of our mailing list available to reputable third parties that offer products we believe may interest you. If you prefer that we not exchange your name with third parties, or if you wish to clarify or modify your communication preferences, please visit us at www.ReaderService.com/consumerschoice or write to us at Harlequin Reader Service Preference Service, P.O. Box 9062, Buffalo, NY 14269. Include your complete name and address.

ROM13R

HARLEQUIN®

A *Romance* FOR EVERY MOOD™

Love the Harlequin book you just read?

Your opinion matters.

Review this book on your favorite book site, review site, blog or your own social media properties and share your opinion with other readers!

HREVIEWS